THE SPLIT

Names: Nally, Gigi, 1996– author.
Title: The Split / Gigi Nally

ISBN 979-8-9940920-1-9 (paperback)
ISBN 979-8-9940920-0-2 (ebook)

Cover Design by: Enchanted Ink Publishing
Map by: Mattia Saba
Editing by: Casey Lewis, Lilly Frederick, Enchanted Ink Publishing
Proofreading by: Beth Attwood
Author Photo by: Matt Lewis
Book Design and Typesetting: Enchanted Ink Publishing

To my husband, Andre.

You are the foundation beneath my feet.

THE SPLIT
S
Macoby
Egal

THE SPLIT

GIGI NALLY

CHAPTER ONE

Waiting is the worst part, but fig newtons are precious cargo. And I'd wait all afternoon if I knew the boys found the strawberry ones. I'd sit my ass in this dank truck the whole damn day—

No. I wouldn't. Not when I'm up against the clock.

I roll up the truck's back door, cold metal rattling as I heave it open. On the ledge, I lean against one hundred and thirty-two cans of chickpeas—not enough to feed everyone for even a day, but at least we'll go home with something.

My belly rumbles.

I blow hot air into my hands and grab a can from the stack, picking at the frayed label. What's one less? Will anyone miss *this* can of chickpeas?

I loosen my grip and let the can hit the truck floor with a metallic *clang*. If a can drops in a truck and nobody's around to hear it, does it make a sound?

Shit. I don't know. But a belly full of beans beats a belly full of brains. And if I die of starvation, I'll join the leagues of zombies with brains on the menu for the end of time.

Order up, Kota—your serving of juicy pink noggin is hot 'n' ready!

But, no. Chandler has a plan. Chandler knows how to divvy up the food. I'll get my proper share, and my hunger pangs will go away. I just have to get through the next few hours.

Gritting my teeth, I pick up the dented can and stack it back on top of the mound.

You're beautiful, I tell it. *It's what's inside that counts.*

My stomach roars, the angry sound echoing through the truck. I close my eyes and, just for a moment, let myself daydream about the real good stuff—Chef Boyardee Ravioli and Green Giant Peas, Frosted Flakes and Dinosaur Egg Oatmeal. We scavenged those luxuries a year ago. If we want more than the basics, we'll have to venture further from the Split.

Problem is, we can't risk entering the city. Berea's fine and dandy, but Greenville's crawling with zombies. The old church on Main Street: ridden with zombie Baptists. The now-broken Liberty Bridge: weighed down by hundreds of tourists-turned-zombies. Swamp Rabbit Café: full of stale, never-to-be-eaten, moldy biscuits, plus zombies.

The factory across from me is in good enough shape, given the state of the parking lot. Jagged concrete blocks and busted metal beams, splintered light poles, overturned cars, and bits of rubber litter the ground.

And bones. There are always bones.

We never got the chance to bury my brother's.

The factory shudders. Perhaps, like me, it feels the effects of the unpredictable weather. November in South Carolina's a toss-up, especially after Z Day, when virus-tinged water seeped into the atmosphere to wreak havoc on weather patterns.

Grandma said that when she grew up, there were four seasons. Throughout my twenty-one years, however, there's never once been a summer day without snow, or a winter without a spike of heat. Yesterday, it was ninety. Today? The truck's thermostat read fifteen.

Another rumble from the factory. This time, a big *C* tumbles off the side and hits the ground with a *thud*. The official death of PepsiCo. Though we parked far from the building, the impact rattles our truck.

Did something happen inside the factory? Are the boys okay?

My worries are futile; there's nothing I can do but wait. I opt for self-torture. With cold, numb fingers, I pick up a yellowed product catalog—one we found from last week's failed supply run to this factory—and scan the soft paper in search of the three-letter word: *fig*.

100% Real Fruit!

As a kid, Grandma would send me to school with two strawberry bars for snack time—one for me, and one for my friend Anika. RIP, Anika.

Assuming, of course, since practically everyone else in the grand US of A is dead.

I wonder if she knew Fig Newtons were made with real fruit. I wonder if *she* turned into an *it* and eventually burst at the seams with brains.

I miss fruit sometimes more than I miss my friend.

When we tried hitting up this factory last week, one of our tires blew out and attracted a horde of shamblers—zombies who've seen better days. Still deadly, but slower than they were three years ago when they sprang to life.

Back to life, I suppose.

So as not to go home empty-handed, we bounced and circled back to the Walmart closer to the Split, cleared out the last of the Saltines. Crackers are great and all, but less so when you're granted only three ounces of water to wash them down.

Not an ideal cracker-to-water ratio. I had crumbs stuck in my throat for two days.

I twiddle a knob on my watch, waiting for the minute to change. 4:49 p.m.

Ticktock, ticktock, ticktock.

I pull my tangled, dark blond hair into a faded blue scrunchie. When Anika first gave it to me, the fabric was dotted with little stars, but the pattern is barely visible anymore. The rubber band inside still holds.

4:50 p.m. The boys have exactly ten minutes to get back—starting now. I shouldn't look forward to the adrenaline rush that inevitably comes with the countdown, but here we are. It's intoxicating, the thrill of not knowing if the boys will come back with food or with shamblers riding their asses. Sitting inside a groaning truck with nothing but a shitty flashlight, stacks of canned food, and a lackluster view of a decrepit parking lot has grown dull.

I check my watch. 4:52.

Ticktock, ticktock, ticktock.

My knuckles turn white as I clutch the balisong at my hip. Chandler won't give us guns. The focused blare of gunshots attracts zombies, and would draw them toward the Split. While zombies aren't smart by any means, they seem to associate the sound of bullets with fresh bodies—food. My theory's that part of them refuses to forget.

Anything other than a perfect shot is a waste of bullets, anyway.

Dying has never been glamorous. Far from it. Listening to Mom's gurgling breath as her lungs finally gave out? Wouldn't make my list of Top Ten Favorite Experiences. And that was before Z Day—before death meant rebirth.

These days, when a person kicks the bucket, they transform into a zombie. Death by brain injury is the sole way to prevent it. Sharp stab in the skull, hammer to the temple, well-aimed bullet, the likes. That's how to kill zombies, too, and since we aren't allowed guns, the boys and I got good with our hands. I found this knife in my brother's pocket after Grandma killed him—the zombie version of him. It hasn't left my side since.

I tighten my grip.

Wind whips through the lot, shaking the truck. Burnt rubber fills my nose, the ash-laden air forming a thick layer on my tongue. Gray clouds roll through the sky, casting haunting shadows behind twisted pole lights and yawning potholes. The full moon peeks out beside the sun, gloating. Laughing at me about how easy it was for it to stay intact while everything down here on earth got fucked.

I pull my jacket closer, wrapping myself in the soft but sullied fabric.

Soon. The boys will be back soon.

The truck creaks as I scoot forward, bracing for action. I bite a grimy fingernail and watch the cloud of warm breath dissolve in the twilight.

A scream pierces through the air.

A deep, distinctively British voice hollers, "Help!"

Indy.

I sweep my gaze to the left. My lanky friend storms out of the warehouse and collides with a zombie—not a shambler. No, this one's *hungry.* And fast. Indy wrestles the zombie, pushing against its rotting, concave chest to get out from under its grip. My heart stops as a hiss escapes its gaping jaw.

Indy wails when the zombie's sharp fingernails pierce his skin, blood splashing on the asphalt. Steam rises from the ground, a crimson haze. His legs flail as the zombie nearly overpowers him, then he scrambles for the knife he dropped somewhere along the way.

In the back of my head, I hear him. Peter. "Stay inside the truck, Kota. Try to help, and you'll get yourself killed."

And maybe Peter's right. Indy has an entire foot on me, and even *he* is barely putting up a fight. Maybe I don't stand a chance against this zombie. But I'll be damned if I just sit here and watch my friend get ripped to shreds. I won't lose him like I lost West.

I wipe my sweaty palms on my pants, whip open my knife, and jump out of the truck.

"Kota!" Indy yells, breaking free from under the zombie—but its spindly hands cling to Indy's leg like a child to their mother in a shopping mall. Only, less adorable.

The zombie rises to a hunch and lunges at Indy. His foot kicks Indy's knife, and it goes skidding out of his reach.

I sprint. My thighs shake, my knees could buckle at any moment, and my heart pounds faster than my feet. I don't stop—I can't. Indy yelps, and I resist the urge to tell him to shut the hell up. I settle for a hissed "*Quiet.*"

C'mon, Indy. That's rule number one: Keep your mouth shut, or else the zombies will come.

"Please," Indy whimpers, his wide eyes pleading with me as the zombie's unhinged jaw snaps at him. "Help."

I mouth, *I'm trying!*

Indy holds the zombie at arm's length, his back turned to me. I need to get around him, but they're dancing across the parking lot, Indy leading the zombie in an apocalyptic tango. As they spin, the zombie's temple comes into view.

Aim for the brain.

I drive my arm forward, but the zombie turns its contorted head at the last minute, and my knife plunges into its soft cheekbone.

It shrieks.

Oh no. I've made it angry.

The zombie's entire body pivots toward me as it chomps. A yellow molar flies out of its mouth and hits me square in the forehead. It almost looks human—*almost*. Its eyes are green but unseeing, and its lips are intact, though crusty and split. Black blotches and blood speckle its face, and its scalp is torn in half. A growl rips through its throat as it turns its clawed hands on me.

I bring up my knife and strike the soft spot in the zombie's head. It writhes, black blood gushing out of its head—but the zombie doesn't fall. Oh, *god*, did I miss? I did. I've missed the brain. I haven't killed the zombie; I've fueled its appetite.

My stomach lurches.

I try to yank the knife out of the zombie's skull, but it won't give.

No, no, no.

The zombie hurls itself at me. I brace for the end. This is it. My twenty-one years have led up to this. Eaten by a zombie. Just like—

Blood splatters my face. Warm, wet, salty. Black.

Not my blood.

The sharp sound of metal slices through the air as Peter stabs the thing in the brain. The zombie crumples to the ground and withers like a dying snake, like it has no bones. Like its insides are soft, rotten, poisoned. The zombie is dead. *Dead* dead.

I gaze at Peter through blood-covered eyelashes, his lips drawn into a thin line as he wipes the knife on his pants.

"It's a good thing I was here," he says.

Indy collapses like a house of cards, all six feet of him. Alive, but in shock. He huddles on the ground, shaking, next to the zombie.

"Get up," Peter tells Indy, kicking him with his boot, unsympathetic.

"Peter," I say. "Jeez. Give him a moment."

Sometimes Peter forgets *we* are more than just warm bodies. I understand, to an extent. We all lost family to the virus, but Peter lost a twin. His same DNA. I have to remind him often that we're human, that we'll all die—and probably soon—but it's okay to care.

Peter clenches his jaw. "Get. Up," he repeats, directing his words toward Indy, but his venomous stare toward me. He nods toward the truck. "And you, get back to the truck—*now.*"

"I—" I stop.

Peter balls his fists.

Obediently, I step over the zombie's body and reach for his hand, but he turns his cheek and aims his glare at Indy, who's lying curled up and shaking like a child.

"I said, get *up.*" Peter bends down and hoists Indy up by the collar. He shoves him back before releasing him and getting in his face. "See what happens when you disobey my command, when you go where I tell you not to? You fuck us all. And you put her at risk."

Peter points at me, his finger a territory marker. Indy meets my eyes, apologetic.

It's all right, I try to convey with a soft smile.

Can Indy see through my lie?

"Tell Chandler nothing about this," Peter says to Indy. "Do you understand?"

Indy nods. "I understand," he whimpers.

Peter grabs Indy's left hand and, before he has a chance to react, takes his blood-soaked knife and slices through his ring finger.

"Bloody fucking hell!" Indy shrieks. My thoughts exactly. "*Why—*"

I slap a hand over his mouth and only remove it when I'm sure he understands.

Quiet.

Indy bites hard onto his wobbling lower lip. His face turns bright red as he holds in his breath and his pain. Peter lowers his face and looks into Indy's tear-filled eyes.

"You tell no one about this. Your finger got caught inside a vending machine in the factory, and I cut it off to free you."

"Wh-what snack was I reaching for?"

"Fucking Fritos. I don't care." Peter rips off a piece of his T-shirt and throws it at Indy. "Wipe the blood off your chin." He turns toward me. "Get Indy back to the truck and see that he's bandaged."

"Okay," I say, even though it's not, and because it's the only word my lips can form.

What the hell did I just witness?

I grab Indy's arm, and we stumble back toward the truck at half speed. His face pales as I throw open the passenger-side door and help him lumber into the seat. My head turns at a shuffling in the distance. Milo emerges from inside the factory, balancing three stacked boxes in his arms.

"First aid kit's in the glove compartment," I tell Indy. "Can you bandage your finger? Need to help in the back."

"Yeah," he says, exhaling a shaky breath. "I can."

"Great." I pat him on the back. "You'll be fine."

His pale face tells me otherwise.

Why Peter cut off his finger, I have no idea. The zombie didn't bite him—I saw that clear as day. Did he realize Indy would be without a ring finger for the rest of his life? Indy clutches his cleaved-off finger in his fist, but by the time we return to the Split, it'll be too late to stitch it back on. Even if we made it back in time to sew him up, we don't have the personnel *or* the antiseptic. The Macs have taken everything good from us. Even our people.

I meet Milo at the back of the truck and jump on the lip.

"What did you get?" I ask, hauling a box into the truck. I lurch forward as Milo passes up a particularly heavy box. I struggle to set it quietly on the truck floor, then I turn and ruffle his early-onset gray hair, coated in dirt and muck. His young face is at war with his salt-and-pepper hairdo, but it suits him.

"Flour."

"Anything else?"

"Fred's got some snack bars."

My ears perk up. "Figgy Newts?"

"Kota"—he shakes his head solemnly—"I have bad news . . ."

"Break it to me gently," I say, laying a hand on his shoulder.

"Pepsi didn't make Fig Newtons."

"Goddammit!" I throw my hands up.

"We found Quaker Granola Bars, though? S'mores. Fred's got them."

My heart leaps. "That'll do." Milo shuts the lid and slides the box into the back of the truck. "Where is Fred, by the way?" I look down at my watch.

"Slow-ass boy's always down to the wire. You know that, Kota."

One minute. Fred's got one minute until Chandler's rules say we need to lock up the truck and leave. Why's he always pushing it? We almost leave him behind, stranded, nine times out of ten.

With forty-five seconds left on the clock, I spot him.

Fred, a constantly sweating nineteen-year-old who is just as clumsy as he is skinny, balances two boxes atop each other and struggles his way over to us.

Milo runs to Fred and grabs a box.

I don't know why Chandler won't reassign Fred. I don't think I've ever seen someone so sluggish. But who am I to judge? Only reason I got the job as driver was because Peter vouched for me.

Last driver died because he wasn't able to make a split-second decision, he said to Chandler. *Kota's willing to leave a doughboy behind if it comes down to it. She killed her brother the minute he turned.*

Peter knows the truth. It wasn't me who shoved a knife into West's skull. The lie doesn't bother me, though. It lets me spend more time with Peter, which is what he wanted, and means I don't have a boring job. Like stitching. Or building. Or scrubbing the piss smell out of the latrine.

I jump out of the truck and look down at my watch. At this point, we're past the ten-minute loading window, but we only have one more box to load up . . . and Peter hasn't said anything about breaking code, so we'll keep the truck door open until he says otherwise.

Just as I'm wondering where the hell Peter went, he walks up beside me and throws a hand on my hip. He watches the boys work with a concentration that tells me his mind is elsewhere. And I know better than to ask what he's thinking about.

Milo makes it back and loads up his box. Fred's not far behind him, but stumbles as he reaches the truck—trips over a damn shoelace. Not rubble, not a piece of tire or a pole or broken asphalt, nope. One of his own shoelaces.

Oh, Fred.

The bottom of the cardboard box flies out of his hands and rips open. Hundreds of Quaker bars spill out. Peter's grip on my hip tightens.

"Pick them up," Peter tells the boys. "All of them."

"We should just go," I whisper in his ear.

We're losing sunlight.

Peter looks at me, his eyes narrowing.

No, I think. *I'm not the asshole. You are.*

But I can't tell him that. Peter must be treated like Grandma's fragile china.

I lean into him and say, "C'mon, babe."

"We can't afford to leave them. We're behind quota." He turns back to Milo. "Go help him. Pick up every single one."

Milo nods, grabs an empty box, and jogs over to where Fred kneels by a rusted, overturned sedan. He hastily picks up bars, one by one, and throws them in.

As Milo reaches Fred, someone emerges from a loading bay.

My eyes widen. It's not a zombie. Worse: It's a human. One that I don't recognize . . . which means he came from the other side of the Split. He's a Mac.

Too busy tossing bars back into the box, Milo and Fred don't notice him. The man doesn't seem to notice them either, though, as he strides toward our truck. He walks with a power inherent in every tall, muscular man I know. Though the shadows of dusk mask his face, his energy is tangible, buzzing in the air like a warning.

What I would give for that confidence. What I would give for the strength of a man, for the assurance that I could protect myself against anyone.

There's only so much training I can do, only so much strength I can build as a five-foot-one woman. I can work all day and night, but a man will overtake me in hand-to-hand combat every time. This new world has made our differences all too pronounced.

That's why Grandma taught me to get scrappy with this balisong.

"Peter," I whisper, tugging his sleeve. "Do you recognize him?"

"No," he says, dropping his hand from my hip. His warm breath tickles as his lips brush my ear. "Close the truck. And get in the front with Indy. Lock the doors."

I reach for the door handle but pause. "What's your plan?" *Assuming you have one.*

Peter doesn't answer.

Across the lot, Fred and Milo finally spot the guy. Fred hoists up the box and won't let up when Milo tries to take it from him. The two play the stupidest game of tug-of-war I've ever seen before the contents fly out. The morons leave all those sweet, crunchy Quaker bars behind in their attempt to make it back to the truck before the mystery Mac man.

"Kota," Peter says. "Truck."

And it's these two words, this simple command, that renew my determination.

I am *not* a doormat. Not anymore.

I pounce across the parking lot, hurling myself over totaled cars and disembodied wheels.

I won't survive another day without a taste of pre-packaged garbage.

Give me snack bars or give me death.

I crouch down and stuff bars into the kangaroo pocket of my sweatshirt. I've crammed maybe a dozen into the space when two faded work boots step onto the edge of a wrapper, careful not to crush the oat bar.

I look up. It's the Mac. In his hands, he holds the one weapon that we're banned from using: a gun. With a gravelly voice, he says, "Craving something sweet?"

The polished metal glistens in the last bits of sun as he aims it at my head. For the second time today, I prepare to die.

CHAPTER TWO

I'M NOT GOING TO SHOOT YOU," SAYS THE MAN HOLDING A GUN TO MY HEAD. He nods to the balisong in my hand. "Are you going to try anything with that?"

I shake my head and whisper "No," as if the idea is outrageous.

Like, okay, I *may* have hurled myself across a parking lot for Quaker bars, but I had a chance to make it back to the truck unseen. Or so I thought. Right now, I'm in no position to fight.

"Smart," he says.

He keeps the gun aimed between my eyes as he bends down, picks up the wrapper from under his boot, and tears it open with his teeth.

I'd guess he's in his mid-twenties, but his handsome face is weathered, with the shadow of a beard dusting his jaw.

A smile curls across his lips as he takes a bite, chocolate wafting off his breath. His face is mere inches from mine.

If I had the upper hand, I'd shove my hand into his mouth and yank the bar out. Just to piss him off.

"My name's Jasper, by the way. What's yours?"

I say nothing. Eye him up and down.

You look more like a Jackass than a Jasper.

"Well then," Jasper says, brushing himself off as he stands. "Why don't we go see what's in the truck?"

When I neglect to answer again, he stuffs the crumpled wrapper in his pocket and offers me a hand.

Big shocker here: I don't take it.

I push myself to a stand and cross my arms. A small act of defiance. The Egals (us) and Macs (*him*) have a treaty. We live in the Split, a protected community inside the now-empty Lake Jocassee, divided by a concrete interior wall. It's modeled after the Berlin Wall, but they never taught us about that in high school, and Mom was a yogi. So I think of our situation more like a yin-and-yang symbol—except the Macs don't come into our territory, and we don't go into theirs.

The same is true outside the Split. We have a treaty, and Jasper's in violation of it. Cherokee Foothills Highway is our dividing line: Egals get to search for supplies east of the road, and the Macs go west. They've been blurring those lines lately as we run lower and lower on supplies. Three years into the apocalypse, and that's bound to happen, I suppose, even when there's barely anybody left.

Jasper walks behind me with the gun's nozzle against my back, a sweet little kiss between my shoulder blades. Peter, Milo, and Fred stand next to the truck, wearing expressions like *Kota, what the fuck?* But as soon as we reach the truck, the boys surround me like a shield.

"Get inside the truck," Peter orders. He steps to the front of the brigade, facing Jasper head-on. Mano a mano.

A smirk creeps onto Jasper's face. "What else have you got hiding in there, bud?"

Peter's nostrils flare.

Oh, god. Did he just *bud* Peter? This isn't going to end well.

"Kota," Peter warns.

"Won't let your girl choose for herself?"

No, Peter likes to choose for me.

My fingers curl around the passenger-side door's handle, but I don't pull it open. Not yet.

I peer through the window. Indy's head rests on the dashboard, like he can't handle watching this scene play out. Well, I can't *not* watch.

"Back off," Peter grunts at Jasper.

"Fine," Jasper says, his surrender surprising me. "Wouldn't want to waste bullets on a group who's going to get themselves killed." Milo glances at Fred, who still hasn't retied his shoelaces. "And I don't particularly feel like attracting the attention of more zombies. This pistol could wake the dead down in Georgia."

Jasper steps toward me, checking out my kangaroo pouch. "Hand over those bars, and I'll be on my way."

This time, Milo speaks. "Dude, there's like a hundred on the ground over there." He points to the spot across the lot where the box tore open.

"Right," Jasper says, "but I want those. What would your people do with only two dozen bars, anyway? I know how you Egals ration supplies. *'Equally.'*" He puts air quotes around the word. "So, what, everyone gets one bite each? Where's the fun in that?"

Peter's had enough. He brings his knife, still steeped in Indy's blood, to Jasper's throat. "Get out of here."

Though Jasper has lowered his gun, it's still cocked, and his finger twitches on the trigger. "I don't want to call the zombies, man, but I'll do what I have to."

"So will I," Peter counters. "For my people."

Jasper scoffs. If this situation weren't so dire, I might, too.

The next few seconds are filled with tense silence as the two men stand off. Wind murmurs through the air, its whispers weighing heavy on my shoulders.

If Peter died, you'd be free. If Jasper died, you'd remain safe. What is it you want, Kota?

Milo, Fred, and I spectate as we await the outcome. This must be how it felt to watch dueling cowboys back in the day. Stand, stare, still, *draw*!

But before either one of the idiots makes a move, squealing tires rip through the lot. I whip my head to the left. A Jeep zooms in from around the back corner of the building, charging through dangling power lines and chunks of concrete. The car goes airborne as the driver surges over a pothole.

"My ride," Jasper says, smiling wide. There's a squelching *crunch* as the Jeep crushes the freshly dead zombie's body. "I'll take those Quaker bars now."

"You sure as shit will not," Peter says, regaining his resolve. He reaches around, yanks open the car door, and shoves me inside.

What the hell? I think as I land in a heap on top of Indy, his body crushing the bars in my sweatshirt. My legs, still jutting outside the car, keep the door propped open.

I may be small, but Indy is most certainly *not*. There's no room for two in this passenger seat.

"Sorry," I whisper to Indy, pushing off him. I stand up and glare at Peter.

Jasper finds great amusement in this display. A laugh erupts from his lips as the Jeep comes to a screeching halt before us. The driver flashes the headlights twice before rolling down the windows and popping her head out. The woman appears a few years older than me, with a sharp bob brushing her chin. She looks like a dipped ice cream cone, with jet black roots melting into platinum blond.

She honks. Once, twice, three times. The sound echoes throughout the parking lot.

"Sorry about that," Jasper says. "My friend here has a tendency to be loud."

Honk.

The zombies will be here in no time.

"Let him have the damn bars," I say to Peter, unloading my sweatshirt and kicking them over to our enemy. The defeat on the boys' faces is palpable. Sure, we're losing food. But more than that, we're letting the Macs win.

"There's an empty box in the back," the woman calls from the car.

Jasper tips an imaginary hat at us, then pulls a box out of the Jeep and loads up. "Pleasure doing business with you."

Milo, Fred, Peter, and I watch in silence as Jasper sweeps the bars into his box.

"Get in, loser!" the impatient woman says, revving her engine.

Jasper hops into the Jeep's passenger side seat, and the two speed off toward the rest of the bars. They quickly load up and drive off, leaving us in a cloud of fumes.

Indy unrolls the window and peeks his head out of the truck's front door. His pale face, still covered in blood and bruises, now wears a smile. "Well," he says, sucking in a breath. "That could've gone worse."

"Shut up," Peter says, unlatching the truck's back door for the second time. "Everyone in. We're leaving."

The boys do as they're told, and I head to the driver's seat, the only place I have power.

CHAPTER THREE

S WE SPEED AWAY FROM THE PEPSI PARKING LOT OF HELL, WE HIT a snag in the road.

The truck jangles, and the five of us jolt off the front seat we're crammed into. The boys yell at me to slow down, but I don't, not even when swerving around a dark bend. I need to get us back to Egal safely. What if the Macs double back for us? We're in no position to fight, but we can't give anything up. We need this food. It's ours.

Indy shouts, "Kota, stop the truck!"

But no. I don't want to hear his complaints about being squished against the door. I told him the pressure would make his finger throb. *He* chose the spot. *He* wanted fresh air.

"Stop!" Indy says again. "We lost a crate!"

I slam on the brakes.

I didn't latch the door.

I peer into the rearview mirror. A dozen cans of chickpeas topple into the middle of the road, right in front of a couple of shamblers, probably drawn to us from all the racket we're causing.

Milo reaches over Indy and shoves open the door. He rolls over him and runs to the back, latching the truck as the shamblers meander down the winding road. Even if he could take out the two shamblers, the cans have rolled down the street. They're out of sight. They're gone.

The blood drains from my face as I turn to Peter. His expression is blank, unreadable. "Peter," I whisper. "I'm sorry . . ."

His nostrils flare.

It strikes me at once: I could lose my job. I could get kicked out of Egal. All because I broke protocol. The Macs have won again.

THE RUSTING IRON GATES CREAK OPEN AT THE SPEED OF A SLUG, RAKING THE ground and leaving brittle blades of grass in their wake. The sun dips below the barbed wire spikes atop the gate, casting a warm glow over our gated valley below.

Ah, shelter. Refuge.

I've never wanted to turn around so badly.

Slapped together with concrete scraps and bits of brick—pieces of the blown-apart dam and ruined buildings from local towns— the thick wall exists to keep out the undead. While we share *this* particular barrier with our enemies, a second roughly constructed wall—split smack down the middle of the Jocassee Valley—keeps them at arm's length. In theory, whatever they do on their side of the valley isn't our problem, and vice versa. Same with our invisible borders outside the Split. Yet those Macs keep hopping over Cherokee Foothills Highway to steal our shit, like our treaty means nothing. Fucking up *my* life, like it means nothing!

We're three years into this whole apocalypse thing, and there's little food to be found. We haven't necessarily been successful at securing it, either. Clearly.

Terrance, a guard of Egal's entrance, waves our truck by. I offer a smile, but he doesn't return it. He never does. Maybe Terrance is jealous that the doughboys and I get to leave while he's stuck on the post. I would be. All the excitement happens outside Egal.

I shouldn't want to leave.

I accelerate slowly and, for a moment, let the rural expanse beyond deceive me. I pretend the short yellow grass that blankets the valley is healthy; I pretend the bluebirds singing in the dim evening are happy. But here, zomweeds creep along the grounds, threatening to engulf the grass; the birds sing haunting songs of terror, in an endless flight to escape zombirds.

This is no longer our world. This world belongs to zombies and the zombirds and the two zombees buzzing by my window. They're easy to spot: The zombee's body is an unstriped, awful yellow, and it usually flies around with a bee lodged into its stinger. When it lands on a surface to feast on its prey, *like my driver's-side window*, it leaves a fat splotch of booger-colored pus.

I roll down the window and swat the zombee away. The virus can't be transmitted cross-species, but these fuckers are the bane of my existence. Nearly impossible to kill. How does one stab the brain of a bee? I don't know. None of us do. But it's about time we figured it out.

That's why I can't understand why the Macs keep provoking us. We're the last South Carolinians, maybe Americans, and we can't even come together as one. We're literally *it*. We should be remedying the virus together, not stealing each other's goods.

And yet antagonism between us rages on. It's pathetic—*I'm* pathetic, because I despise them, too. I despise that *they've made me* despise them.

I park the truck in front of the storehouse. It operated as a rectory up until three years ago, when the local government flooded this valley town to increase water supply. Z Day happened just two weeks later. The bombs dropped smack down on the lake's dam, et voila. The town of Jocassee was made new again. The buildings here are waterlogged and moldy, but at least we have roofs over our heads.

The old one-story brick rectory stands proudly before me with a whole lot of character. A willow-less willow tree weeps in front of the building's entrance. A small arch curves around a door that looks like it was hand-plucked from the Georgian era. The entire exterior is wrapped in dead ivy—none of us can muster up the courage to peel it off. There's a cross in each window pane, though Mrs. Patty is the only one who still prays. And pray, she does. Three times a day in front of the church. Kneeling. With holy water. And a rosary.

There she is, right now, screaming at my sister and Grandma walking hand-in-hand to the church. *"THIS IS ALL YOUR FAULT, YOU PAGANS! Look at what you've done!"*

If it were anyone but them, I'd roll down my window and give it right back to her.

It's not us that you should be hollering at, Mrs. Patty. It's whatever higher power that abandoned us to *this*.

But Grandma can handle her own. I can't hear what she says, but her words cause Mrs. Patty to keel over, hand to heart, and then fall backward on her ass.

Hell yeah, Grandma.

Next door, the rectory doesn't hold a mere ounce of holiness, but it *does* hold all of our goods. Food, medical supplies, weapons, and gear. The other citizens and I take our meals at the church next door.

The stench of rotting flesh burns my nose as I tug my hoodie up and over my head. I forgot it's Burn Day. My favorite time of the month.

I wrap the hoodie around my waist and take Peter's hand as we enter the storehouse, passing by the medical supply room.

If only I could get my hands on some extra meds for Grandma and Bunny . . .

My stomach flops as we reach Chandler's office. A plaque is nailed to the door, the words *Executive Officer* hand-chiseled into the wood. As our leader, I understand her need to be ostentatious. Without a flair for the dramatics, the citizens may not respect her as much. At least, that's what she told me.

Peter gives my hand a squeeze before releasing it to ease the door open. It's just a squeeze, but I'll think about it all night. What does he mean by it? Is it a warning or a caress?

Chandler's office smells faintly of evergreens, of Christmas, of a time far gone. She keeps a fat stack of worn car fresheners on her desk, next to wrinkled papers and maps. I'm flooded with childhood memories of decorating the Christmas tree with Bunny and West.

I suck in the evergreen scent with greed.

The office is dark, the only light emitting from a single window looking out over Egal: brick row houses, dry, yellowing fields, and in the distance, the wall.

Chandler stands behind her desk, her back taut and fingers gripped on the metal seat tucked beneath. She's in her early thir-ties, but she's got the presence of an old, pissed-off politician.

I press my thumb into the soft part of my palm, a nervous habit. Watch the rough edge of my nail form a dimple in my flesh. Press and release. Wait, *one, two, three*, as the white spot fades away.

I've just got to keep myself, and my family, alive. I've just got to remember that good things did once exist. And that maybe they will again.

"You made it back." Chandler's firm voice snaps me out of my haze. Her foxlike eyes find me first, her red hair twisted into a sleek bun so tight that her eyebrows nearly meet her hairline.

I glance down at the long, ratty ponytail draped over my chest and flip it over my shoulder, then scratch the back of my head.

How does Chandler not have a headache?

"Sure did," I say, my fists balled in my lap. I press down harder with my middle finger.

Find your center, Mom would say. *Breathe.*

Phony sentiment from a chain-smoking yogi.

A ball of blood beads on my palm.

"Productive run?" Chandler says, flipping her eyes to Peter and crossing her bony arms.

"We got what we needed," he answers.

"Show me." Chandler clears her throat and walks past us, the smell of evergreens trailing her shadow.

With shaky legs, I follow Peter out of the office into the food supply room.

Chandler holds out a hand, and I pull my written log out of my pocket. I'm in deep shit. The log says 132. She'll notice the missing 12. What story will Peter weave about the error? Will he throw me under the bus?

Zara leans over the long rectangular table in the center of the room, her doll-like mouth pinched like the time Bunny gulped down Grandma's not-yet-sweetened lemonade. She didn't drink lemonade again for months.

Blond curls bouncing around her chin like an old Hollywood movie star, Zara smacks her red-painted lips and offers me a sour smile.

I don't think I miss lemons all that much.

And where'd she find lipstick?

"Zara. Pleasure," Chandler says, the only acknowledgment Zara will get. Chandler's eyes are busy scanning the details of the room, gauging the success of our job.

Stacked cardboard boxes, filled with our new deliveries, are crammed in the corner. Floor-to-ceiling cabinets take up most of the wall, stocked with flour, oil, instant mashed potatoes, canned vegetables, pickles, instant mac 'n' cheese—the works. Any non-perishable food we've scrounged from stores, warehouses, and factories lives here.

Though it's all expired and boxed up, I salivate at the mere thought of a home-cooked meal. Of creamy pasta, roasted carrots, and a twice-baked potato.

Zara tucks a runaway blond curl behind her ear. "Literally *always* a pleasure being in your presence, Chandler." She picks up a clipboard and clicks her pen. Suck-up. "All ready to unload?"

"I'll give the final word," Chandler says, her hands interlaced behind her back. She tips her head down into the opening of a particularly mangled box. "What happened here?"

Peter balls his fists. "Fred."

"Unsurprising."

Zara leaps forward. "Shut *up*, is that Pepsi?"

"Sure is," Peter says.

She pulls out a bottle and squeezes. "They don't even feel flat. How many bottles did you find?"

"Only eight." Peter smiles and puffs out his chest. "Found them in a break room fridge." Ever the proud scavenger.

"Mmm, I'm dying for some bubbly."

"Zara. Peter. Enough." The two exchange a look that would've probably kept me up tonight, repeating in an endless loop, if I wasn't so goddamn tired from today's run. "We can't do anything with eight bottles of soda. Need I remind you that rations need to be split equally among *148* citizens? That would mean a drop of Pepsi per person. How do you think that will reflect on us? Do you think it will fill them with hope for the future of our great community?" Chandler turns her back to us. "Store them in the basement until you've secured an appropriate amount."

With a pouty lip, Zara says, "Maybe the bakers can use the bottles to make soda cake for everyone? I *love* soda cake."

Ignoring Zara's comment, Chandler inspects the boxes along the wall. "I hope we've also secured real food that will provide our people with adequate nutrition."

Peter rolls his shoulders back and steeples his hands. "In fact, we secured a solid amount of nutrition today, Chandler. Fifty-pound bag of flour, twenty-five-pound bag of sugar, and—how many cans of chickpeas, Kota?"

"Er—"

Do I lie? What will get me in the least amount of trouble? Fuck.

"We did secure 132 cans," I say. A half-truth.

"I'll verify that," Zara says, clicks her pen—twice—and scribbles on her clipboard. "Last time, your count was off by one."

No, no, no, no.

Chandler turns her unsatisfied eyes to me. "A small discrepancy, Kota, but numbers do add up. Our people rely on us to provide them with equality. If we can't distribute food equitably, we aren't doing our jobs."

A rock settles into the depths of my belly. I'm in deep shit now. "Yes, Chandler." I bow my head. "You're right."

"One," Zara counts out loud, tapping the cans with her pen. "Two." *Clink.* "Three—"

I bite my lip and think back to the *Judge Judy* reruns that played in an endless loop at our old home. Grandma got a kick out of civil court shenanigans. From what I remember, the defendants who pleaded guilty received lesser sentences. Will the same happen here?

Fact is, I don't know jack shit about Egal's justice system—Chandler shares information on a need-to-know basis, and this is the first time I've transgressed. What I *do* know is I can't risk getting the boot, and *Judge Judy* is my only benchmark.

Judy would want me to confess.

"Four."

"My count is off by twelve!" I shout. "The truck door was unlocked. I latched it, but forgot to lock it because . . . because . . ." I hope Peter chimes in because I'm not sure how much story I can share, but he's tight-lipped. I'm on my own. "It doesn't matter. I turned too fast, and some cans fell out the back. They rolled off before we could get them back."

"Why wasn't the door locked, Kota?" Chandler prompts.

Peter steps forward. "We had a run-in with the Macs. In our haste to get away, Kota neglected to lock the door. But it won't happen again, will it, Kota?"

"No," I say, breathless. "It won't."

Chandler is silent for a moment. The longest moment of my life. I don't realize I'm holding my breath until she opens her mouth. "One more failure, and I will find another driver. You will lose your position. You do understand what that means, don't you, Kota?"

"Yes, ma'am," I say.

Wow, my shoes are filthy. Also, *Shit. I can't lose my job. I can't get kicked out.*

I owe it to my brother to live.

I turn to Peter, but his eyes are fixed on our leader.

Chandler says, "We'll discuss the Mac situation later." She turns to Zara. "And you. I don't recall you reporting this earlier discrepancy to me. Why not?"

"I, um, I was . . ."

"Waiting to use the information against me?" I ask, surprising myself.

Zara's cherry-colored mouth drops open. I bite my tongue as other intrusive thoughts threaten to spill out.

"Enough. You're all dismissed. Zara, ensure the bakers have the flour and supplies they need for a week of production. Then all of you get to dinner—or don't, and lose your rations. I don't care." Chandler spins on her heel but turns back around before she makes her grand exit. "And you two—if you can't work together, I'll have to reassign both of you."

"Yes, Chandler," Zara and I say in unison.

As soon as Chandler's gone, Zara sticks her tongue out at me. Being petty for the sake of it. Bunny says she's not a girl's girl. I thought I was different, but I want to pull her tongue real thin like Silly Putty and wrap it around her neck.

Instead, I smile. "Enjoy your counting."

CHAPTER FOUR

OFFER PETER MY HAND AS WE ENTER THE CHURCH, BUT HE DISMISSES IT with a scoff. He slings his arm over my shoulders instead, says something about it being his duty to keep me warm. Duty, not love.

We'll never go back to the way we were two years ago, when he found me, Bunny, and Grandma in a dilapidated Walgreens, huddled behind the pharmacy counter. When he smiled, offered his hand, and brought us back to the Split. When he got me the driver job, when he first kissed me and told me he loved me. A strong, handsome man loved *me*.

Maybe he still does, but maybe it doesn't matter. I need his protection, his influence, more than I need his love. If I have to give and receive affection on his terms, then so be it. I'll comply with his version of love if it means keeping my family safe.

And . . . there's a chance that, one day, he'll look at me the way Dad did Mom. I have to believe that.

I jolt backward as water splashes my face, and I lick my lips. *Salty.* Droplets swim down my forehead, and despite my best efforts to contain myself, I wipe them away and suck the wet beads off my fingers.

I blink my eyes open. The wide, clear blue eyes of Mrs. Patty stare at me, mere inches from my face. "Pagan," she hisses. "Repent!"

"Mrs. Patty, did you use your water rations to make holy water?" Peter shakes beside me, a big smile plastered on his face. Laughing.

Mrs. Patty steps forward, a sour, smoky scent wafting off her pudgy frame. She's been using bark from cedar zomtrees as incense again.

"I'm saving your soul. You'll thank me later." Her eyes snap frantically around the church. "You all will." She pushes through Peter and me, dipping plump fingers into the cup and setting her eyes on her next target: Fred.

Watch out, bud.

I turn to Peter. "She doesn't think you need salvation, then?"

"More like the old crone knows what would happen if she came near me with that shit."

"What, Peter?" I say. "What would you do to her?"

He leans toward me and whispers in my ear. "A transfer to the crematory team would be good for her, don't you think? Burning the bodies of the ones she claims to have saved. Spreading their ashes." He pulls back and smiles. "C'mon, let's eat."

Despite the grim images Peter's words bring to mind, my mouth waters as we walk toward the front of the church. Large steaming pots and wicker baskets are spread atop the altar. Scabs of ceiling flake down onto a Gatorade tub of water next to the food. Peter pulls a piece out of my hair.

"Not dandruff," I say. "Promise."

Sconces filled with candles line the walls, illuminating the scavenged tables where Egals dine. 148 people, all crammed inside the church, dining together as one.

I look around the open space for Grandma and Bunny, but instead find Milo, his gray bangs damp and plastered to his forehead.

I say, "She got you, too?"

He nods, balancing a plate of food in each hand. "Called me the worst kind of sinner, taking two plates for myself. This one's for Indy, though." Milo leans toward Peter and elbows his side. Winks. "Told him not to lift a finger."

Peter grunts and pushes past him toward the altar. Milo teeters, but manages not to drop the plates.

"Sorry," I say to Milo, once Peter's out of earshot. "Best not to joke about food when he's hangry." I peer down at his measly plate. Bread and beans. Again. "Today was a lot for him, I think."

He steps toward me, leans in close. "Bigger day for Indy, though, huh?"

Ouch.

"Yeah, well . . ." I grit my teeth and step back, forcing myself to look into his eyes. "Rules are meant to be followed." The words taste like mulch in my mouth.

Milo gives me a challenging stare, but I can't give him the response he wants. We both know Peter only follows the rules when it serves him, but neither of us can risk calling him out. For one year, I lived outside these walls with Grandma, Bunny, and West. For one year, we hid, helpless, *waiting* for one of us to turn into a zombie. It was inevitable. I'm not going back.

I clear my throat. "Table's clear behind you," I tell Milo, hoping he'll take the hint to move on from the touchy subject.

Smiling, he sets the plates down behind him, picks his slice of bread off a plate, and spins back around.

Milo says, "Your grandma outdid herself today. I'm glad they reassigned her." He holds the bread up and stares at it like the crust is shimmering with gold. "I mean, just *look* at this slice. It's a fluffy, fragrant, divine masterpiece. It makes me feel like . . . like . . . like I'm in a *real* church." Milo looks around with wide eyes. "Wait a second!"

I breathe a sigh of relief and let out a laugh. He winks and bites off a hunk of bread, bits of crust getting stuck in his stubble.

"Oi!" Indy calls from across the room, always distinguished by his thick British accent. "Milo! Where's my plate, lad?"

Milo shoves the rest of the bread in his mouth and grabs the plates. "Gotta run," he tells me. "Come join us after you've made your plate."

Oh, right. *Food.* Milo's words remind me just how hungry I am, not that I can ever really forget. It's always there, in the pit of my belly, clawing.

As I walk toward the altar, my stomach lets out a roaring growl.

A delicate hand squeezes my shoulder. Grandma says, "Pretty sure the entire church heard that monster inside your belly. Soon, you'll have the Egals thinking a zombie's roaming around. Don't want that, now, do we? Go on, take my slice of bread."

"*Grandma*," I say, giving her a hug.

Her body's getting slighter by the day. The smell of rose perfume clings to her skin, mingling with the flour and burns that tatter her blouse. She's had the perfume since Z Day. Tucked it into her fanny pack as we ran from our splintered home to find shelter. And when Chandler proclaimed we could each bring one belonging into the Split, Grandma chose that damn perfume without hesitation.

"Tell you what," Grandma says, her soft voice a sweet song in my ear. "If we ever figure out how to rebuild humanity, I'll bake you a whole loaf myself."

I pull back. Her brown eyes, so much like my own, soften and crinkle at the corners. "Think we might be waiting a while for that, Gran."

"Hope, dear." She places a palm on my cheek. "Have a little hope."

Grandma snaps her hand back and wraps it around her wrist. Her arthritis, it's flaring up again. And she's already used up her quota of medication for the month.

"I'll figure something out," I say, although I'm not sure what I'm going to figure out. Can't ask Chandler for a handout. Can't go out on my own to scavenge. *Can't, can't, can't—*

No. There is one thing I can do.

"Oof!" A breathy noise escapes my mouth as little arms wrap themselves around my waist, squeezing the air out of me. Bunny giggles and pokes my belly button.

"What're you up to, kiddo?" I ask.

"I'm not a kid," she says, and she's right. She's gone through more than any ten-year-old ever should, though many have.

Growing up, I read my sister stories filled with princesses locked inside castles to keep the monsters away. I never thought those stories would spring out of the pages and into our lives. But they did—and they didn't bring ballgowns and tiaras.

"Your pigtails tell me otherwise," I say, tugging on a blond curl.

She sticks her tongue out. "Kota, your *stomach* . . ." Bunny sticks her ear to my belly. "I think it's trying to say something. I think it's saying . . . *huuuuuuungry.*"

I want to put Bunny in a jar like a firefly and keep her in my pocket. Instead, I place a finger under her chin, lift her gaze to mine, and ask, "Have you eaten yet?"

"Nope!" She takes my hand in hers and pulls me toward a large pot of beans.

"Girlfriend, are you trying to pull my arm out of its socket?" I ask in exasperation.

Grandma trails behind us and lets out an amused laugh.

We each load up our plates: one cup of baked beans, one gleaming hunk of bread.

"Can we sit with Peter?" Bunny's honey-like voice breaks me out of my thoughts. The church buzzes with Egals eating and talking, and Bunny smiles at every table we pass.

"Of course we can."

We find Peter with the boys. Milo smiles wide, his stubble seeming to have eaten more beans than his mouth. Indy's face is still blanched, but at least the blood's washed off. He hides his hand under the table. Sandwiched between Milo and Peter, Indy's not wearing boots, but if he were, he'd be shaking in them.

"Hey, guys," I say, setting my plate down. "Mind if we join?"

"We're in the middle of something, Kota," Peter says, his voice low and face closed off.

"Right." I bite my tongue. *You're doing it for them. To get the extra rations. Be cool.* "No problem." I pick my plate up, and Peter turns back to the boys. I'm dismissed.

I point to the corner next to the stained window and turn to my little sister, saying, "We'll sit over there, just the three of us. Okay, Bunny?"

She nods, her round cheeks rosy like cherry gumdrops. We secure the best spot in the house: a table beneath the stained glass window. The mosaic that survived it all. Red glass twists into a delicate rose, its long green stem curling around the arched window. Filtered light streams through, highlighting the delicate blues and yellows that swirl and surround the flower. Beautiful things do, in fact, still exist.

I spoon a heap of beans into my mouth. "What'd you do today, Bunny?"

"You're not going to believe what happened," she starts. "I pricked my finger when getting a vial of Joyce's blood. We were low on O. Anyway, look!"

Working in the Sick Room is certainly not the childhood I imagined for my baby sister. Bunny, a diabetic, giving shots to the ill. The job's supposed to give her prime access to insulin. God forbid Bunny gets hyperglycemic when the workday's over, when it's 2:00 a.m., and we have to spring to the Sick Room to get her insulin because Chandler won't allow us to keep extra doses in the house. Bunny's diabetes isn't "dire enough" to break protocol. According to Chandler, no situation is. Could be worse—at least shelf-stable insulin hit the shelves before the country went to shit. Otherwise . . .

I shudder.

Otherwise, Bunny would be dead.

"Earth to Kota," Bunny says, wiggling her pointer finger in front of my face.

I peer at the tiny dot on her skin. "Should I kiss it to make it better?"

"*No*, I told you, I'm not a—"

I kiss it. It's better.

"So . . ." I shift my attention to Grandma. Her hair falls in silver strands around her pointed chin. "Hands doing all right, Gran?"

Grandma presses her lips into a thin line. Delicate wrinkles wrap around her mouth like a map. Three years ago, her hair was long and thick, her face fresh, cheeks plump like mine and Bunny's. She hasn't lost her spirit or strength, but the deep wrinkles on her face have been etched with the toll of the new world.

"I'm fine, dear. Nothing to talk about." She sips her water like she used to sip a martini, swishing it around in her mouth before swallowing.

"Not talking about it isn't going to make it go away," I say.

When Gran turns her cheek, I kick myself for letting the words spill out.

Grandma sets down her fork and places her hands in her lap. "All finished, then? Shall we head home?" she asks.

I look at Bunny's plate, speckless like it never had any food on it to begin with.

"You're officially inducted into the Clean Plate Club," I say, shoving the entirety of my bread portion into my mouth. "Good girl."

"Grandma, I can't believe you're sitting there, watching her speak with her mouth full!"

Grandma giggles. For the next few minutes, it's like we're back at home, sitting at Grandma's dining room table, enjoying supper. I'm even able to ignore the growing pit in my stomach, the one warning me that my favors from Peter are almost up.

CHAPTER FIVE

THE MOON CASTS PEARLY SHADOWS ON THE GRAVEL SIDEWALK AS I knock on Peter's door, the hand-carved *P* above the rusty knocker being the only thing that differentiates his brick home from the others in Egal. The sixty-some homes are attached, forming one giant row house. The compound was part of the original town of Jocassee, and held up well enough. Besides the plumbing—hence, our glorious latrine. The row houses are identical, just the way Chandler likes it. Equality, baby. That's the name of the game around here. We eat, sleep, and shit as one.

"Hey." Peter opens the door, shirtless and wearing tight boxers.

Lucky for Peter, his well-muscled exterior counteracts his asshole interior. My attraction to him has become purely carnal. I don't know if you can consider sex a redeeming quality, but . . . it gives us both what we need. Sex gets him on my good side, and frankly, I so rarely experience physical pleasure that I take what I can get. Sometimes, when I close my eyes, I pretend he's still the man who offered me a hand in Walgreens after I shot insulin in my dying sister's abdomen.

As for Peter, well, he gets what he wanted all along: power. Dominance. His ego stroked.

"Wow," I say. Peter leans a muscular arm against the open door, a black snake tattoo weaving around his forearm and up his bicep. "Gun Show McGee."

"Who?" He balls his fist, and his bicep pumps as he flexes.

I duck under his arm and step into the foyer. "It's an expression. Forget it."

The inside, lit by haphazardly placed candles, is sparsely decorated. Considering he's out on runs half the time, and personal belongings are to be approved by Chandler because *uniformity fosters unity*, Peter hasn't made his house homey.

His house consists of three rooms: a small kitchen with rusty appliances that don't work, a living room with a futon he found in the wreckage somewhere in Chick Springs, and the bedroom. With a bed. Where we spend most of our alone time together.

"Kota." Peter approaches me from behind. His arms wrap around my waist like the snake slithering across his arm. "I've missed you."

"You could have talked to me at dinner," I say, my voice wavering. "Just . . . putting that out there."

"I had to talk with the boys."

Right. But not me. I'm never involved. I'm his delicate doll.

I stare at the dark doorframe to the left. "I want to know why you said what you did to Chandler, especially after *you* broke protocol by cutting off Indy's—"

Peter cuts me off with a kiss on my ear. Lips grazing my jaw, he whispers, "You look so beautiful tonight, Kota. My Kota."

A shiver runs down my spine, though it's not from pleasure. I spin around, then Peter cups my head in his hand and pulls my lips to his. His breath is warm and smoky as he slides his tongue into my mouth. I push against his chest.

"Peter," I say, pushing again as he comes in for a second kiss. "We need to have a conversation. A real one. About Indy. About *me*."

Peter cocks his head sideways, narrows his eyes like he's ready to bite. I fold my arms across my chest. *Stand down.* I worry he won't, but then he drops his hands from my face and balls them into fists.

"You won't lose your job."

My stomach sinks. Can he see through me?

Maybe I should shove my thumbs into his eye sockets and press until they pop.

"I—that's not what I . . . You could've told Chandler the whole story earlier. I didn't forget to lock the truck door because of a simple run-in with the Macs. I was distracted trying to *save* my friend. You know, the one who was about to get mauled by a zombie?"

"Oh, so you wanted me to tell Chandler that not only did your stupid decision lose us food, but you also left the truck? That you broke protocol?"

"No, I want you to have a bit of empathy! To care! To care about Indy, and about *me*."

"*I* took care of the zombie, need I remind you. *I* saved Indy." Peter's shoulders tense up, and the snake pulls back, preparing to attack.

He marches toward the living room, leaving hot red steam in his wake. Knuckles white, Peter grips the doorframe so hard I fear the wood might split. I fear *I* might split.

The wood creaks under his pressure, and the smell of mold thickens the air.

I huff. "Yeah, well, you took care of Indy, too, didn't you? Like a pathetic asshole."

Peter whips around, his eyes wide in surprise. Never, I realize, have I spoken my mind in front of him . . . but it feels so good. So good that I don't think I can stop. I don't want to stop.

I stand up taller, square my shoulders.

"Why'd you really do it?" I ask defiantly. "Why'd you hurt him?"

"Nine out of ten fingers is pretty good," he says, the corner of his lips ticking up. "Don't you think?"

"When you're talking about Powerball odds, sure, but not fingers!"

Peter's smile falters. "You don't understand. The world isn't rainbows and butterflies. People need to learn the hard way—you, Indy, everyone. Otherwise, you'll all continue to repeat your mistakes." He spits the words at me like I'm some child. "And then we'll all be back where we started—outside these walls, fending for ourselves." He takes a deep breath and releases his knuckles. Muscles at ease, the snake settles into his skin. He bridges the gap between us and places a soft palm on my cheek. "Just stop being stupid; that's all I'm asking."

I want to bite his goddamn finger off. I want to show him how it feels. But no. I need him.

I close my eyes and lean into his touch. Refocus my energy.

My next words come out soft as velvet, so as not to enrage him again. "I'll do better, I promise."

But I want to do so, so much worse.

"Kota, you should know I'd do anything to protect you." Then he leans in and kisses me again, hard, before pulling back. His mouth is swollen from our kisses, and his green eyes crinkle at the sides.

"I know," I say.

Liar, liar, liar.

Peter grabs my hand to guide me toward the bedroom.

I tug on his hand to stop his movement. "Not tonight."

"Fine," Peter says, miffed. "Go hang out with your fucking sister and Grandma. *That* sounds like a grand old time."

"Jesus, a guy gets blue-balled *one* time . . ."

"Go home."

Without a word, he strides into the bathroom and closes the door. I look around the entryway, aghast. No, I'm not being dismissed like that. Not tonight.

I pound down the hallway.

I swear to God I'll—

The door opens in my face. Peter grips a bottle in his left hand. When he reaches me, he extends his arm. Naproxen.

"Saw your grandma's hands," he says.

I extend a hand to accept the gesture, but Peter rears his arm back and hurls the bottle at the door behind me. I gasp as it breaks open when it hits the door. Pills scatter across the floor. I stare at him, wide-eyed and open-mouthed. Rage is apparent on every inch of his red face.

He bares his teeth and says, "Fix your own fucking problems."

With that, Peter turns around, struts into his bedroom, and shuts the door behind him.

CHAPTER SIX

DRIFT TOWARD THE SEA, TENDER WAVES CARESSING THE SHORE WITH gentle kisses. I'm soft, I'm weightless, I'm a feather. Pastel pink and buttercream birds fly above, their wings soft and legs hurried. There's Mom and Grandma, Bunny and West. Dad, a raven, closely behind. I flutter in beat with the family of birds, my wings working at double speed to keep up. But I don't mind. I relish the salt air that dampens my tongue, let the vanilla-colored clouds sweeten my skin. Tranquil, I fly above the sea.

Crack!

White clouds turn gray, then ooze into black. Neon lights flash as thunder rips through the air, threatening to deafen me with its boom.

The birds break formation, then scatter. East, west, north, and south. They leave me behind.

I'm falling. Five-hundred-pound weights are tied to my ankles, and they're pulling me down, down, *down*. I hurl toward the ground, gravity berating me. Three more seconds, and I'll go splat. Three more seconds, and I'm a bug on a windshield.

The ocean approaches like a brick.

Three more seconds, and—

"Aagh!" I tumble off the couch onto the dusty living room floor. Two small yellow tennis shoes step next to my face.

Bunny crouches and covers her mouth, giggles threatening to escape. "Kota, you rolled off the couch again."

I rub at my eyes and yawn. "Sure did, didn't I?"

Oof. And there's my hip.

My head pulses as though I got *maybe* three hours of sleep, but the hazy sunlight streaming through the living room window tells me otherwise. I slept soundly through the night, and yet I still feel like shit. *Wonder why.*

I tuck Bunny's hair behind her ears, and she immediately undoes it. "I can't see your face like that."

"Liar. You totally can," she says, sticking her face all up in mine.

"*Whoa.* Morning breath. We ran out of toothpaste?"

"Yep. Grandma says it smells like a dragon." She breathes fire into my face.

I plug my nose. "Grandma's right. Why don't you go rub your teeth with a towel, and we'll head out to breakfast?" Bunny nods and hops off to the kitchen. "And don't forget your tongue!"

Breakfast around here is at 7:00 a.m. sharp. Like all of our meals, if you miss a meal call, you're shit out of luck. Your portions get thrown into the pool for the next meal.

That never happens. We're all malnourished. Nobody misses meal times.

"Tongue scrubbed!" Bunny smiles. "Do you think they'll have pancakes?"

She never stops asking for pancakes.

I throw my long hair into a ponytail and sigh. "One can always dream, Bun."

"I'm so hungry," Bunny says. Her hands start to shake. Her face pales. "I think I'm going to—"

She collapses.

Fuck.

Her breath should have signaled to me that her blood sugar was low.

I lunge toward my sister and shout, *"Grandma!* I'm running Bunny to the Sick Room!"

Though I try to keep the worry out of my voice for Grandma's sake, it's clear as day.

I heave my sister into my arms, and her unconscious body flops around as I bust ass out of the house and through the streets.

This is happening too often.

Three minutes later, the Sick Room is in sight—a small brick building with a wooden plus symbol nailed to the front. Two nurses attending to patients on rickety futons look up as I burst through the door. "Sugar! *NOW!"*

If only I could get her a Pepsi.

Mariana, a female nurse, jumps into action, hurrying to the cabinet along the wall. I set my sister down on an empty futon as the second nurse says, "Candies." Norman, I think his name is. Bunny's other coworker. "We've got caramels in the cabinet, next to the suppositories."

Mariana finds the caramels, wrenches open Bunny's mouth, and shoves two in. After what feels like an eternity, Bunny's eyes flutter open.

"These aren't pancakes," she says.

I place a palm on her cheek. "No, sweet girl. No pancakes today."

Norman says, "Oat bran's on the menu. Nothing to write home about, but exactly the healthy carbs you need."

"Yuck," Bunny says. "It's always so watery."

I can't help but smile.

"She'll need to rest through breakfast hour," Mariana tells me. "Monitor her blood sugar. Do you mind running to the church to grab her portion? I'll write you a doctor's note."

"Of course," I say. "I'll go now. See you soon, Bun?"

Bunny nods. "But don't you *dare* skip breakfast. I know you'll want to hurry back here, but you need to eat, too, Kotie." She narrows her eyes. "I'll do a breath check on you when you're back—I swear I will!"

"Okay, little dragon. I'll eat." I push away from the futon. "I'll be back soon. Promise."

BY THE TIME I'VE SCARFED DOWN MY OWN BREAKFAST—LEST I FAIL THE BREATH test—and brought Bunny's hers, it's eight o'clock. And I have a cramp. I'm going to be late for the download.

On Thursdays, Chandler gives us the details of our next supply run. The boys and I go on runs twice a week—not for safety, but because we can't afford to use more gas than that. We also don't have the space in the rectory to stock up, if that ever were to happen.

"Gotta go, Bun," I say with one last forehead kiss. "I'll be late for work."

I push up from the futon and run from the Sick Room to the rectory.

I find the boys inside, hovering around Chandler's desk. Milo and Indy debate the superiority of the now-meaningless US and UK flags. Milo swears the US flag gives off "better vibes," but Indy won't hear it. Not when there's a chance that *his* home country is still standing. Fred stares off into space, scratching his butt.

Jesus. I get itches, too, but you don't see me with my fingers wedged up my ass crack.

"Where are Peter and Chandler?" I ask. While I'm grateful they're not here yet, it's unusual for them to show up late.

"Maybe they're together. Canoodling," Fred says, sniffing his finger.

I send him a glare, but he doesn't seem to notice.

"The hell kind of remark is that, Fred? His girlfriend's standing right here." Indy nudges me with his elbow and leans in close. "I highly doubt they're canoodling."

"Yeah, sure," I say.

Oh my god, if Fred scratch-and-sniffs *one more time*—

"Welcome, doughboys," Chandler says, stepping into her office. Her hair is pulled into a tight, fiery bun, and her hands are tightly clasped behind her back. Same shit, different day. Until she winks at me, which makes me feel weird. Chandler doesn't wink. "And of course, welcome to our driver."

Not a personal greeting. A warning.

Chandler pulls a large piece of paper out of her back pocket and unfolds it. Sprawling green areas, faded patches of blue, and zigzagging lines cover the crinkled paper, with handwritten notes scratched in the corners. "I've prepared the details for your next mission."

"Shouldn't we wait for Peter to go over the details?" Indy asks.

Where is he? If I had my way, he'd be on his knees, picking up the pills he lobbed at the door yesterday. But no, he's probably sulking somewhere, pissed off he didn't get laid.

"I've debriefed him already," Chandler says. Her tone has a finality to quell any additional questions. She must see that we're not satisfied because she adds, "He's filling up the truck."

"Where are we going?" Fred asks. The bozo steps forward onto his shoelace and tumbles over. He falls to the ground with a laugh, then brushes himself off. "Classic me. Classic Fred."

Chandler pinches the space between her brows. "If you all could keep still for *five seconds*, I could have a chance to explain. Jesus Christ, you all are unbearable this morning."

Silence.

Chandler spreads the map on her desk, which charts the route from one side of South Carolina to the other. She extends a slim finger, dragging it through inky roads and highways to a red circle inside Greenville. *Greenville.* Outside the safe zone.

"Tomorrow, you will leave for Costco."

The warmth seeps from my face, and my buzzing bones go still.

Indy unconsciously clutches his bandaged hand before shifting his eyes to hers. "You're . . . you're sending us on a suicide mission?"

"Don't be ridiculous."

Milo steps toward Chandler and peers down at the desk. "No disrespect, Chandler, but Costco is only fifteen minutes from downtown." He drags a finger along the map. "And it's right next to a Bass Pro Shop. There'll be hordes of shamblers crawling around there."

"Thank you, Milo, for pointing out the obvious." Chandler pushes up from the desk and paces around the room. "We're running out of options. You all will have to get used to this. Going inside the city. Facing the undead. Our people need the supplies."

"But Chandler—" Fred starts.

She whips around. "But Chandler *what*?"

Fred's face pales. I think he just shit his pants.

"Your mission is Costco," she reiterates. "You take everything, *everything*, you can fit into the truck. Do you understand?"

Indy clears his throat. "Can . . . can we get guns?"

Chandler looks like she wants to snap Indy's neck. "No guns. *Never* guns." Her face pales as she squeezes her eyes shut. "I won't risk awakening them. I won't risk losing you."

Ha! Risk losing *us*? Or the truck, the gas, the supplies?

"Listen," Chandler says, twisting her face into a grimace that I *think* is meant to be a smile. "I wouldn't send you all to die. I believe in you. You can pull this off. You *will* pull this off."

A chill runs down my spine as Chandler peels her mouth into a toothy smile. She's never smiled in the two years I've called her leader. She could've been toothless, for all I knew.

Milo leans over to me. "Does she need to be exorcized?" Chandler glares at Milo and snaps her mouth shut, dropping the act. "Oops, I think she heard me."

Motioning toward the door, Chandler says, "Get out of here." She folds up the map and shoves it into a desk drawer. "I have work to do."

Fred stares at her, open-mouthed. Indy taps his shoulders twice, but he's as frozen as a statue. Exchanging a glance, Indy and Milo grab his shoulders and urge Fred toward the door, practically dragging him. I linger behind, waiting until their footsteps fade and the rectory's creaky front door slams shut.

"What do you want, Ariti?" Chandler asks, her eyes focused on the papers on her desk. Being addressed by my last name sends a jolt through me. I jump straight to the point. Or at least try to.

"I was wondering if—"

"Spit it out."

"When we go to Costco—only if we find it—could I take one extra vial of insulin for my sister? There was an incident this morning, again, and I think her diabetes is—"

"No."

"She *needs* it. Please."

Chandler pushes up from her desk and comes to stand on my left. As she places a cold hand on my shoulder, my spine straightens, and a rock settles in my gut. "Hate to break it to you, Kota, but we all need something."

"I just want to help her. I don't know what else to do."

"You can do your job." I shiver as Chandler pulls her spindly hand away. "Start there."

She walks back to her desk and shuffles her papers. "Now please leave."

"Yes, ma'am."

I leave without a backward glance.

She doesn't know it, but Chandler's no has inspired me. Challenged me.

One way or another, I'll get my family what they need.

CHAPTER SEVEN

MILO, INDY, FRED, AND I SPEND THE DAY PREPARING FOR tomorrow's mission—sharpening knives, patching the truck's tires, resetting locks, folding boxes. I still haven't seen Peter. His absence pisses me off. I doubt he's away doing something important for Chandler. No, he's being petty. He's ignoring me.

Fuming, I slam the truck's back door shut, letting the violent metal clang amp me up. I have to apologize to him, don't I? Because I still need his help, now more than ever. Peter has no problem sneaking me drugs when I'm his sweet, submissive plaything. When I offer something in return. Like sex.

I sigh. I really don't want to offer up my body to him. Not today. Maybe not ever. But it's my only choice. It's not like I can sneak into Costco during our supply run and steal the insulin myself.

Uniformity fosters unity.

No. This is fucking unfair.

I storm from the rectory's small parking lot toward Peter's home, energy buzzing through my veins. The world is cloaked in darkness. My warm breath penetrates the black night, casting swirling, smoking shadows through the cold evening. The workday's over, so most people are in their homes. It's probably not smart of me to roam in the dark—unarmed, no less—but my foul mood has inspired some recklessness, so I walk along the edge of the Split instead of the safer, more direct path to Peter's house.

Walking along the Spilt is permitted, but hardly anyone gets this close to the wall unless they have to. To be this close to the enemy, to know they're separated from us by only a foot of concrete, is chilling. There's always the chance one of the Macs will scale the wall and ambush our supplies. Or worse, they somehow figure out how to chuck over a zombie and put us all in more serious danger than starvation. It wouldn't be easy, but if anyone could do it, it'd be them.

These fears are irrational, of course. The wall is twenty feet tall. But that's what happens when you live in a zombie-filled world. Even the irrational feels rational, sometimes.

When I get to Peter's house, I knock on the door. *Tap, tap, tap.*

No answer.

I try again.

Nothing.

I'm going inside. There are no keys in Egal, and since all supplies are distributed equally—since we each get but one personal belonging—there's technically no need to steal. I push open the front door, and the house is quiet, the pills from last night's events cleaned up. Did he sweep them back into the bottle, or toss them?

I walk past the small living room toward the bathroom, noticing the door to his room is shut. Maybe he's in there, asleep. I hope so. There's a chance the pill bottle's back in the bathroom. He'd never notice if I snuck a few pills. There were hundreds in the bottle. I can definitely suck up and apologize to Peter if I can bring Grandma some peace tonight.

A small *thud* sends a wave of suspicion down my spine. I tiptoe toward the closed door, moving slowly so as not to make any noises. Another thud—and then a grunt.

So, not asleep. What the hell is he doing in there?

The grunts are joined by a female moan, one that I recognize all too well.

I pat my sweaty palms on my pants and reach for the door. My knees wobble. Sparks of violent red and icy white fill my vision. My ears burn like the Sixth Circle of Hell.

I push open the door.

His bedroom is dark, but not dark enough to hide what's happening right in front of me. Peter and Zara. Half naked. Rolling around in the bed.

"*Peter?*" I bellow. "Peter, what the actual fuck?"

They spring apart.

"Kota, you weren't supposed to see this," Peter says, pulling up his pants.

Zara lifts the sheets to cover her breasts, a satisfied smile painted on her messy lips. Her bright red lipstick is smeared across Peter's face.

"No shit!" I grip my knife in my hand, tempted, oh so tempted, to do something terrible with it.

Oh, god, I can't breathe.

I can't breathe.

"Just go home," Peter says. "We'll talk about this later."

"Do *not* tell me what to do."

Zara quirks her head and wipes her swollen bottom lip with her thumb. A greasy smile spreads across her cherub face. *Goddamn angel of hell.*

"Kota, sweetie," she says, voice saccharine, "I'm so sorry for stirring up drama."

"No, you're not," I say, clenching my fists. "You're not sorry at all."

"You're right," she giggles. "I was having fun."

"Shut up, Zara," Peter snaps.

Zara makes a puppy face and huffs. First dog I've ever wanted to kick across the room.

"I'm leaving," I say. "Of my own volition."

"Kota—"

"Shut up, Peter."

I storm off, slamming the bedroom door behind me, then the front door, and fight the urge to fall to my knees and ram my face into the ground.

Last night, Peter was the angriest I've seen him. That much is true. But I didn't expect this blatant betrayal. I can't apologize to him now. Not when he's ruined everything. Letting go of our fucked-up relationship is one thing, but now I've got *nobody* to help me. I'm on my own. And I can't do it on my own.

The ground crunches under my feet as I stomp away from Peter's home. Red blurs my vision. I keep my eyes down as I trudge forward aimlessly. Zombie cicadas chirp in my ears, their songs an octave too low, off-key.

"Shut up," I say through gritted teeth, channeling my anger in any way I can.

Footsteps rustle behind me. A loud, gruff grunt slices through the haunting cicada melodies.

"Kota, wait."

The fucking nerve.

Every bone in my body wants to turn around, to hear what Peter has to say, but I can't give him that satisfaction. I deserve more than that.

I charge forward, only just realizing how close I am to the gate. I have to turn back around to get home. Dammit. I dare to look over my shoulder. Peter's towering figure muscles toward me, boots smashing against the craggy earth.

"Kota," he says, breathless, "we need to talk."

I flip him off and turn around—mentally planning a way to circle around him and get back home, far away from him. He's stronger than me, but not faster. Not as good with a knife.

I'm about to break left when the gate opens. I stop dead in my tracks.

A silver SUV rolls through the gates—the medboys. Home after sunset, far later than is considered safe. Did they run into trouble? What did they come home with?

Peter's hand grabs my bicep, yanks me back.

"Let me go, you're hurting me." I struggle against him.

"Turn around. We need to talk."

"Will you let me go if I—ow, fine." I whip around and yank my arm free. "Let's talk. Talk about how you cheated on me. With *Zara*. Right under my nose, huh? She doesn't mind getting my sloppy seconds, does she—"

"Enough, Kota." Peter purses his lips and wraps his hand around mine. He drags me toward the gate like I'm some puppet he can toy with. "We're going somewhere private."

"So you *do* make all the rules now?"

Peter ignores me and drags me toward the gate. Terrance draws the gate closed with a slapped-together cable pulley system, but before Egal is secured, Peter waves a hand. "Terry! Do me a favor? Kota and I need to get outside for a minute. Doughboy orders."

Liar.

"You have a written slip from Chandler?"

"Yeah, 'cause paper and pens are so easy to come by. Sky's raining with office supplies."

"All right," Terrance says. "You have five minutes."

"That's all we need."

Peter pulls me through the small opening, toward a patch of trees a few yards from the gate.

"No, no, no," I say, trying to wrestle out of Peter's firm grip.

Terrance doesn't hear me, and I can't scream. I can't draw the shamblers toward the Split. My stomach is sick. Flashbacks of trekking through ravaged neighborhoods with Grandma and Bunny spring to mind. No weapons besides our knives. No preparedness since West did all the scavenging for us. No idea what kind of world we were walking into. What kind of hell.

"What are we doing out here? Why can't we talk inside the Split? Aren't you afraid of zombies?"

"Relax. Terrance is keeping watch. You have nothing to worry about."

Except for you.

Seeing my expression, Peter says, "I need to explain myself—somewhere I know you won't run from me."

"So, you're putting us both in danger?"

"You're never in danger when you're with me, Kota. How many times do I have to tell you that?" He cups my cheek, but I swat him away.

"You're a liar," I say, pushing my hands against his chest. "And a cheat, and a—"

Leaves crunch behind me. Instinctively, I twirl around and take two steps back toward Peter, and hate myself for it. That I need his protection even when I don't want it.

"Please," a deep voice says. "Don't stop on my behalf. Sounds like you were just getting started."

"Who's there?" I say. I search in all directions but see no one.

A branch snaps nearby.

Peter steps forward and wraps his arms around me. "You're safe," he murmurs. As if his promises mean anything to me. "I'll take care of it."

"What a prick," the voice says. My ears quirk. The dark, velvety quality is . . . oddly familiar.

"Me? I'm not the one who's hiding. Come on out, buddy, I'll show you who's—"

Peter goes limp. His arms release me as his body crumples to the ground. Before I have the chance to yelp, a hand claps over my mouth. It smells like chocolate.

It's the Mac—Jasper.

"Be quiet," he says, breath tickling my ears. An entire army of spiders crawls down my spine. "He's not dead. I hit him with a blow dart, look."

Hand still firmly over my mouth, I dare to look down. A thin, long dart sticks out the side of Peter's neck. I breathe a sigh of relief. I despise him, but I don't want him dead.

I try to bite Jasper's fingers, but he pulls his hand away a second too soon. I spin around to a familiar pair of brown eyes.

"What are you doing here?" I spit. "What do you want?"

He sighs. "You can make this easy on yourself and come with me, or you can follow the path of your boyfriend."

"I'm not going anywhere with you."

I look around, ready to make a break for it. Where are the guards?

Jasper says, "Blow dart took care of them, too."

"*What the fuck is wrong with you?*"

He twiddles the weapon between his index finger and thumb. "I've got one left, but I really don't want to use it."

My balisong. It's in my back pocket. And this time, I'm not afraid to use it. There's no gun on his person.

I reach into my back pocket and grab the knife when a *whomp* slices through the air. A sharp sting pierces the soft flesh of my neck.

"Didn't want to do that, Kota, but you left me no choice."

Jasper's dark silhouette looming over me is the last thing I see before the world fades to black.

CHAPTER EIGHT

THE GROUND RUMBLES BENEATH ME, MY BRAIN FOGGY AND EARS clogged with the whir of an engine. The night is as black as ink. I can't see anything besides my immediate surroundings: my tied hands, the holey knees of my jeans, and the blacked-out windows of a—

Shit!

The car jolts me up and down and around and back up again, and *oh my god, my ass*. The sharp middle seat rips into my tailbone as we speed over bump after bump, the seat belt digging into my belly, right above my uterus. I'm going to be ripped in half if they don't slow down.

My wrists are bound. With the back of my hand, I wipe the string of drool that drips down the corner of my lip, then bite the rope in a futile attempt to loosen the knot. I'm struck with a sensation like rubbing a dry paper towel on an unpolished wood surface.

A chill runs the length of my spine. What were those knot tricks West learned from Boy Scouts? Fuck, it was years ago, and my head's too fuzzy to focus.

I finally have the strength to lift my bobbing head. Out of the darkness, I make out two heads—the backs of them, at least. One male, one female. Their attention is focused on the long road ahead.

A scratchy piece of rope fiber catches in my throat. I sputter out a cough, covering my chin in more wet spittle. I give up on untying my hands. What am I going to do—attack whoever's driving this car and kill us all?

The male turns around at the racket I'm causing.

"Shit," Jasper says. "She's up."

"Then do something about it, Jasper," the female says.

"*Do something about it, Jasper*," he mimics.

She pulls a hand off the wheel and flicks his forehead.

I sit up straighter.

The moonlight glints off her hair—black roots, white-blond ends. Dipped Ice Cream Cone Woman.

The car speeds up.

I squirm in my seat. I know I shouldn't—I'm doing nothing except exhausting myself, and I need the energy for whatever they're about to do to me. Jasper turns around to fully face me, staring blankly as he watches me flounder around.

"Please don't," I say. "Please."

The woman says, "Please don't *what*?"

"Knock me out? Kill me? Use me as zombie bait?"

"Zombait!" she says, hitting her hands on the wheel. "Now, that's a good one. Think we oughta add that to the Dictionary of Z." She slaps Jasper's thigh. "Write it down, will you, Jas?"

"Ignore her," Jasper whispers before flipping back around. She snaps her head toward him, jolting the car to the right. My neck aches from the whiplash.

"Now hurry up and do something about her," Dipped Cone spits, the humor drained from her voice. "We're almost there."

"I'm aware of our estimated time of arrival, thank you very much."

My heart stammers. Where are we going, and how long have

I been out? The clock on the dashboard reads 2:23 p.m. Unless we've entered an alternate dimension—which, I wouldn't be all that surprised if we had—the clock's not accurate.

"Fine, I'll do it." She slams on the brakes.

My body jerks forward, and my head smacks into the center console. I feebly lift my head up, watch in pain as the woman pulls a dagger out of her side door.

A flurry of stars floods my vision.

I'm going to die. She's going to kill me.

"No, please, *no*," I murmur. Bile rises in my throat as I writhe back and forth. The rope chews my skin, forming bloody welts. "I—I'll do whatever you want. I can't see anything—I don't know where we are—but I'll close my eyes. Look, see? They're closed. *Super* closed. As closed as can be." I squeeze my eyes shut so hard that colors swirl together behind my lids. Splotches of lime and orange and violet.

I won't let the last thing I see before I perish in a Jeep be colors. I picture Bunny. Grandma. West. Mom, Dad, Peter—

Not him.

"Sorry, girlfriend," Dipped Cone interrupts my thoughts. "Can't trust anybody around here, and certainly not you."

I peel open my eyes, flashes of color still sparking at the edge of my vision.

Jasper lets out a frustrated sigh. "Greeley—"

"Jasper."

"She's scared."

"*Oooh*, she's scared? Please, tell me more." Greeley juts out her lower lip. Her voice is whiny, baby-like. "She's a scared, whittle girl captured by two big, *scary* people."

"Yeah," I say, my voice shaking. "I am. I am scared."

Greeley laughs.

" 'Least you're honest." She leans toward me and twists her lips into a big, open-mouthed, vicious smile. Then she lifts her dagger. "Say please."

"Please," I breathe, the word barely a whisper. "Please don't."

She does.

Greeley slams the back of her knife into my head, right in the space between my eyebrows.

The spots in my vision fade, and the last thing I see before I pass out is red.

Just red.

CHAPTER NINE

AWAKE IN A METAL CHAIR. MY HANDS ARE TIED. ONLY NOW, THEY'RE pulled together behind my back. I give them a hard yank. The effort's in vain, but trying means not giving up. And I refuse to give up. I will not die of apathy. So I pull—hard.

Fuck.

The rough rope grinds against my wrists. Jagged fibers scrape my skin and mingle with my blood. I can smell it. The salt, the metal. I feel the pain.

I register my surroundings. Four concrete walls, covered in soot and oozing brown liquid. One flickering candle. One closed door. One metal chair that holds me captive.

One ass that hurts like hell.

I peer down at my lap. My jeans are covered in dirt, ripped at the knees and ankles. My shoelaces are tied together, bringing to mind the first summer after Z Day. Tennis shoes tied together and slung over inoperative traffic lights. *Caution: zombies ahead.*

I suck in a deep breath—my first mistake. A sharp pain stabs the spaces between my ribs. I'm a slaughtered pig growing cold on a metal table. Body cut open and filleted.

No.

I am Kota, and I am alive. My body is intact. I am fine.

I repeat this mantra another three times, holding my breath, before taking an inhale. This time, I let the air slowly climb from my belly button, through my sore ribs, up into my throat, and out my nose.

Control your breath, Mom would say, cigarette between her lips.

I breathe, my chest expanding with air, then gag. This place smells like rotting garbage. But there's nothing in the room that would cause . . . *Oh.* I curl my head down to my shoulder and sniff. It's me. *I* am the garbage.

I am the pig.

What if Jasper and Greeley cut me open and feed me to the zombies? What if Bunny has another episode tonight, and I'm not there because I'm human meat chunks? What if Grandma's arthritis flares up and she drops a hot bread pan—and loses her job? With no value to Egal, she has no worth. She'll be kicked out, and Bunny will have nobody. Grandma's tough, but she won't survive outside the Split on her own. Nobody can.

Breathe. Focus.

Be the dam, Kota. Shut off your thoughts and be the dam.

But the dam didn't hold. It broke and flooded the city.

Dakota, your mother has bleeding in her lungs.

What's going to happen to her, Dad? Will she be okay?

No, sweetheart, he said, tucking my hair behind my ear. *She won't be okay.*

She—she won't? What can we do?

Hold her hand. Love her.

I do love her.

That's enough, sweetheart. That's all you need to do.

Then Mom died.

Dakota, Bunny, I'm going to Florida.

Can we come?

No, darling, you two are going to stay with your grandma.

What about West?

Don't worry about him. Your brother will stay in his dorm at school.

Oh. Okay. You told him where you're going, right?

No need to trouble him, Dad said, smiling and smoothing down my hair. *Now, I ought to get going. Your grandmother will be home soon. Ask her to whip up some of that lemonade for you and Bunny, why don't you? Go on, get inside. There should be a spare key under the mat here somewhere . . .*

Dad, when are you coming back? You are coming back. Aren't you?

Yes, sweetheart. I won't be gone for long.

Dad never came back.

West, what are you doing home? Don't you have exams?

The state closed down all public schools. Everyone at USC was sent home. Said the situation in California's getting serious, that we should all hunker down.

Don't listen to the news, Grandma said, chuckling. *I've been on this earth for seventy-one years, and have not once listened to those fearmongers. We'll all be fine.*

We weren't fine.

Sunday, June 25th, 2017: The bombs were dropped on the Jocassee Dam, and thousands more across the country. The water-borne virus spread. Far enough from the city, our neighborhood stood, and only a foot of water flooded our house. The next day, fights broke out. Neighbors became strangers. For one year, Grandma, Bunny, and I hid at home while West went on supply runs for us.

It's bad out there, he said, *I don't want you to see it. But if it ever comes down to it, I want you to be prepared.*

West gave me his old balisong and, in the shadows of our home, taught me all his tricks. The problem? I never put them into practice. I never learned to hunt, to fend off zombie animals, to kill. My inability, my inaction, haunt me to this day.

The last day I saw my brother, he returned from a supply run with a backpack full of those little mini cereal boxes. It was like Christmas. Frosted Flakes, Corn Pops, Cheerios. We feasted, the four of us, sitting cross-legged on our living room floor.

There was a moaning outside, and West went to take care of it before the zombie attracted others. We waited, anxiously, but West didn't come back. When Grandma and I finally went out front, he launched himself at Grandma and me. Grandma saw the bite mark on West's forearm, and she killed him. No hesitation, no second thoughts. But me? I stood there, knife in hand, shaking like a child. I failed him.

We barely survived the next week. I thought that we would die, trapped in that Walgreens. Until a kind man, Peter, saved us.

Peter.

The weight of it is all too much. Emotions build in my chest— loss, betrayal, despair—until they have no choice but to erupt.

I cry.

I cry big, fat, wet tears. Let them roll down my face and onto my pants and in the holes between the fabric, wetting my filthy skin. Let the tears choke me, drown me, leave me to puddle on the dirty floor.

Who's going to save you now, Kota?

My shoulders shake and my stomach heaves as I cry and cry and—

The door groans, and Greeley steps through. "There she is. There's our girl."

She wears a big smile as she strides toward me. Each step she takes in those black combat boots echoes through the room, masking my pathetic whimpers. Her bob accentuates her sharp jaw. She licks her lips, cracks her knuckles.

Does she want to eat me? I've heard rumors of the Macs being cannibals, but I assumed they were baseless. There's no way we'd share the Split with *cannibals*. Now I'm not so sure.

I writhe around as Greeley pushes up the black sleeves of her shirt, then kneels down before me, one knee in the pathetic puddle I've spilled on the floor.

"Miss me?" she says, her lips curling into a venomous smile. She pulls a dagger out of her pocket and scrapes the tip on the metal chair I'm bound to. The sound screeches in my ears. I squirm around and inadvertently tip myself over, toppling sideways onto the ground. "Ouch. That's gonna leave a bruise like an overripe peach."

Fuck.

"Gree, stop messing with her."

Jasper emerges through the door, though I can't see his face, only those scuffed work boots. I can only imagine the satisfied sneer on his lips, seeing me pathetically worm around on the floor. A second pair of boots follows closely behind. These boots are bigger, polished.

Please don't be my executioner.

"Just having a little fun," Greeley says, putting her face in mine and snapping her teeth. She hoists up my chair, and my vision swirls as I settle back into my upright position. "It gets so dull around here."

Jasper, Greeley, and a massive man—at least six foot four—stand before me. Every bone in my body rattles. My captors stare and *stare*. Moments pass, then eons. Finally, I can't take it anymore. The words erupt from my mouth before I have a chance to register what I'm saying. "Say something. One of you, please, just say something."

"Happy Friday the 13th!" *November 13th*. I've been captured for less than twenty-four hours. That's a start.

"Apologies for our friend here," the tall man says, his voice so deep it vibrates under my feet. His skin is dark like mahogany, his eyes the same color. They crinkle at the sides, unlike his glistening bald head, which is the smoothest head I've ever seen. I could slip and slide down it. "She gets excited when we have guests."

I twist my neck around, glancing toward my tied hands. "Is that what I am? A guest?"

"More like our next meal," Greeley says. Tall Man glares down at her. She bows her head, but I catch her rolling her eyes.

"That's enough, Greeley," he says. "Why don't you go home? Get some rest."

She crosses her arms, the dagger in her right hand pointed dangerously close to her chest. "Rest is for the weak."

"Go home," the man says, his words final.

She sighs, sheathes the dagger at her side, and offers an exaggerated bow. "Yes, Chief." As a final gesture of asshole-ness, Greeley salutes me. "Girl," she says. Her lips curl into a smirk. "It's been a pleasure."

"Kota," I whisper. "If you all are going to kill me, at least call me by my name."

"Kota," she repeats. "See you on the other side." Then she spins on her heel and slams the door shut behind her. Could she be any more cryptic?

Two big, scary men stare down at me.

I close my eyes and ready myself for execution.

CHAPTER TEN

JASPER AND CHIEF ARE SMILING. SMILING. NOT SMIRKING, NOT grinning, *smiling.* Like two schoolboys who've just ridden their bicycles to the ice cream shop and saw a big fat sign that said "*FREE!* Free cones for anyone who can pull a wheelie!" But no, standing before me are two grown-ass men smiling at a tied-up, shaken, and snotting twenty-one-year-old woman.

Jasper's curious eyes take me in. His smile, surrounded by a gruff layer of stubble, makes my spine curl. I shift my gaze to his accomplice, who clears his throat. He is tall and broad, and his white teeth gleam like pearls against his dark skin. While Jasper appears to be in his mid-twenties, I'd guess Chief is in his forties. Both men hold power in their stances, with shoulders drawn back and feet firmly planted. Jasper stands behind Chief, a small gesture that tells me who's in charge. Chief will make the calls today.

Guns are strapped into holsters at the sides of both their hips. I can't say what kind, as my experience with guns is zilch, but I *do* know that guns mean business. I also know that guns could introduce me to my maker in two seconds flat.

A single tear rolls down my cheek as I tell my family goodbye.

And still, they stare. They smile. They say nothing.

Brownish goo drips from the ceiling.

Plink.

My heart beats in my chest.

Thump.

The chair groans beneath me.

Creak.

I close my eyes and, though the movement strains my bound wrists, press my middle fingers into my palms.

Plink, thump, creak.

Breathe.

Fuck this. I can't take it anymore. Listening to Mrs. Patty hoot and holler about Jesus was more bearable than this.

"Are you going to chop me up into tiny pieces and store me in a freezer somewhere?" I suck in a quick breath, regretting the words as they spill off my tongue.

Maybe I do need Jesus.

The two men exchange a brief look, sniggers slipping from their mouths.

Chief takes a small step toward me, saying, "No freezers around here, young lady."

"My name," I repeat, my voice shaking. "Call me by my name."

"Kota." He clasps his hands together. "Lovely name. You can call me Chief."

"Name or title?"

"Both," he says. "I understand you're scared, Kota, and that you've been taught to despise us." He shrugs. "That's just fine. If snark and slander ease your mind, you're welcome to send insults my way. As long as you refrain from reaching for this gun at my hip, you have nothing to be afraid of. You are safe."

I haven't been safe in three years.

"I've never held a gun," I say. "Today's certainly not the day I try to change that."

"Very good." The nod he gives to Jasper is so small that, if I had anything else to pay attention to in this gray room, I would have missed it.

I gulp.

I don't trust this guy as far as I could throw him. And I couldn't—throw him.

Jasper's footsteps echo throughout the room. As he walks around behind me, the skin on the back of my neck prickles. The fresh smell of lavender washes over me. Bar soap.

The audacity.

I haven't bathed in a week.

Jasper places his hands on the back of my chair, far too close for comfort. I lean forward to get as far away from him as possible, but the action is pointless. Jasper has full control over what happens next. A fact I'm sure he is all too aware of.

I've always had a slow heart rate—the doctors told me that was why I was such a good swimmer. I liked to think I won swim races because of my hard work, but maybe it all came down to genetics. Maybe everything comes down to luck of the draw. In any case, if the doctor checked my pulse right now, I think he'd be shocked at how fast my heart is racing.

A bead of sweat drips down my neck. I whimper. My rational mind believes Jasper will untie me, but a small voice in the back of my head—one that sounds a lot like Zara—says he's going to shoot me. That tinny voice grows louder and louder until it's all I hear.

"Don't shoot me," I beg. "Please. Please let me go."

Jasper's closeness tickles the back of my neck. As I prepare to reverse headbutt him, the sharp sound of metal on rope makes me pause.

"Didn't shoot you the first time we met," Jasper says. "And I'm not going to shoot you now." My wrists pulse as blood rushes back into them. I wring them out and massage the red abrasions. "But you're also not going anywhere." Jasper walks in front of me and sheathes his knife. "Eyes up here, Kota."

I'm alive. I'm alive.

Chief takes another step toward me. I curl my toes in my shoes and try to keep my spine straight.

I will not cower before my enemy.

My family, my home, my friends, they're all gone. But I will not let him take my strength.

Thighs shaking, I stand up.

Chief cocks his head and takes a deep breath. "You're probably wondering why you're here."

"Spot on."

"Let me start by saying this: You're not here by mistake. Your boyfriend unwittingly helped us out—tremendously, I might add—but that was purely serendipitous."

"He's not my boyfriend," I say, as if that's what matters right now.

Jasper looks at Chief. "Guy's a total asshat," he says. "I'd venture to guess she's no longer loyal to him."

I glare at Jasper. Who is he to make assumptions about me? And why is he right?

Chief says, "Ah. An unexpected turn of events, but highly beneficial."

A laugh bubbles in my chest. "If you think that Peter's behavior will make me more agreeable to whatever it is you're up to, you're wrong."

"Perhaps," Chief says. "But what if I told you that your people have broken our treaty?"

"My people? There's no way."

"How well do you know Chandler, your leader?"

"Well enough to know she wouldn't do whatever it is you're accusing her of." Chandler doesn't live by the book. She is the book.

Chief's eyes bore into my own. "Chandler has taken two of our men."

"Proof?"

"We have it."

"Then show me."

"I understand your hesitations." I don't react to Chief's placating words. They won't work on me. "Loyalty runs deep. Chandler, unfortunately, is not the person you think she is. Give me two days, and you will understand everything."

"What happens in two days?"

"A trade."

A weighty pause fills the air as I absorb what he's saying. "You kidnapped me for collateral. Is that what you're getting at?" Chief nods. "Even if your insane theory is true—which I doubt it is—you'd only get one of your men back. Chandler believes in equality."

Uniformity fosters unity.

Chief scoffs. "Nonsense. No, Miss Kota, I think you're more important to Chandler than you think."

"How do you even know who I am, let alone how important I am?" Have they been watching me? Have they infiltrated Egal? "And you're wrong—I'm highly replaceable. Not that it even matters. In Egal, equality trumps all else."

Chief *tsks* his tongue. "Who else in Egal knows the supply routes like the back of their hand? Who else knows the codes to get in and out of the Split? Who else knows where the food is stored, and exactly how much of it there is?"

I still don't believe him. How Chief received this information about Egal's operations, I may never know, but anyone could have my job as driver. I'm not important. Period.

I ask, "What's going to happen to me when Chandler doesn't want me back? I have a family."

Chief smiles. "Fear not, Kota, you will be reunited with your family. Think of this as a little vacation."

I look around the room, waving my arms a bit for dramatic effect. "Hold up. Is this . . . Are we . . . are we in Fiji?"

Jasper laughs.

"Welcome to Macoby," Chief says, interlacing his fingers. "Is this everything you imagined?"

"And so much more," I say dryly. "You said two days. You're not leaving me in this room until then, are you?"

Chief offers me his hand, but I don't take it. I don't need his hand to stand on my own two feet.

Stars crowd my vision. My knees buckle, my lower back aches, and my tailbone throbs. But I stand tall, chest proud, and look Chief in the eye. Little sparkles dance in his pupils. He's beaming.

Chief says, "The horrors beyond the Split are enough to keep you inside our territory, I imagine."

I nod. No reason to argue there.

Chief turns to his right-hand man. "No, we will not keep you prisoner here. Rest assured, you will be closely watched. Greeley will house you."

"On second thought," I say, walking backward. "I'll stay here. I don't mind sleeping on the floor."

"Told you she'd react this way," Jasper mutters.

"Then why didn't you offer to house her?"

"You promised Greeley knives," Jasper says. "I've got plenty. So does Greeley, admittedly, but—"

This square gray room is looking nicer by the minute.

"Really," I say. "Happy to stay here. This metal chair will do wonders for my posture."

"You're not staying here," Chief says. "But I will leave the choice in your hands, Kota. Would you prefer to stay with Greeley or Jasper?"

Oh, so you're giving me a "choice" to make me feel like I have autonomy. I see what you're doing here, Chief.

Since I can't say what I really want, which is *neither*, I pick the lesser of two evils.

"Jasper," I say. He may be dangerous, but at least he's not psychotic.

"No," Jasper responds, his voice steely.

Chief keeps his gaze on me. He says, "Peanut butter," then turns toward his subordinate. Jasper's body stills completely. "Would you do it for peanut butter?"

Jasper bites his lower lip and flicks his eyes to me. I stare back.

"How much?" he asks.

"A sixteen-ounce jar. Sealed."

"Does it happen to be—"

"Chunky? Indeed."

Jasper groans, closes his eyes, and pinches the bridge of his nose. "Fine. You have a deal. She can stay with me for two days— but not a second more." Jasper's eyes find mine again, and he points a finger at the space between us. "You."

"Me."

"Come with me. And *you.*" Jasper points at Chief. "I want that sixteen-ounce jar delivered to me by five o'clock."

"It will be waiting on your doorstep." Chief's gaze sends a chill down my spine. "And that, Miss Kota, is what we in Macoby call a successful trade."

CHAPTER ELEVEN

AS I FOLLOW JASPER AND CHIEF OUTSIDE, FAT WHITE SPLOTCHES of sunlight crowd my vision, awakening the dull throb between my brows that threatens to pop like an overripe zit. The bright sky is a stark contrast to the squat, windowless building behind us. I press two fingers into my temples, rubbing off a layer of Hershey bar-colored sweat when I pull them away. I'm delusional, yes, yet I must repeat to myself three times not to lick my fingers.

It isn't chocolate. It's the mud beneath your feet. It's the dust woven into a Jeep's seat cushion. It's whatever the hell was dripping from the ceiling in that godforsaken room. It isn't chocolate.

Last thing I need is to give myself a stomach bug. Not when I'm being held hostage in enemy territory and have no means of getting medicine.

I look around on the off chance I recognize the area, but those damn white flurries still dance in my vision.

Wish I still had the Ray-Bans my brother gave me for my seventeenth birthday. The sunglasses were the most expensive thing I owned. West was making good money at his college bartending gig and felt bad about Dad abandoning us—not that it was West's fault, but still. He couldn't be there to be the "man of the house," so he replaced my Dollar Store shades with some UV-protected ones. Those sunglasses were a luxury I'll never have again.

While UV rays are now the least of my concerns, I wish I had those damn Ray-Bans. I wish I had West.

Chief tips an imaginary hat to Jasper and me, pulling me back to the present. "Safe journey home," he says. "I'm off to inform Greeley she will not be getting those knives."

"Good luck, Chief," Jasper says.

Chief waves and walks to a motorcycle parked on gravel a few feet away. He revs his engine and takes off, his wheels kicking up a puff of brown dust behind him. Bits of dirt catch in my throat, and I sputter out a cough.

Water.

I need water.

A zombird caws overhead, its shrill, unearthly sounds somewhere between a strangled tweedle and a cat who just got its tail stepped on. It's a red cardinal, the kind that used to perch on the front porch as Dad sipped his morning coffee. One of its mutated wings is broken as it speeds toward a bluebird, only for the zombie cardinal to pelt itself into a warped, waterlogged tree. The bluebird flutters away. I watch it, entranced, until it is out of sight. I hope it's flying home to its family.

Doubtful.

I smack my lips and swallow, my tongue sticking to the back of my throat until the little saliva I have lubricates it. Before me is a long gravel road. A wall of healthy yellow trees lines the left side. On the right, bare, sagging trees sprout out of the ground like ingrown hairs. The oozing black splotches that pucker their bark tell me that these trees are undead. Beneath my feet, they reach snarling tendrils toward the living trees. Eventually, these roots will twist around the base of the healthy tree and wind up the trunk. The two morph into one horrifying zomtree. This pattern will repeat until all of the healthy trees are devoured.

I shiver, and not just from the cold wind whistling through the warped branches. With a frustrated sigh, I wrap my arms around myself and stare down at my feet. *Think.* I've got two days to concoct a plan to convince Chandler I'm important. That won't be easy. Especially considering how mushy my brain feels.

I gulp.

"Need some water?"

Behind me, Jasper leans against a rusty bike rack. A backpack is slung over one of his shoulders, and a look of nonchalance is plastered across his scruffy face.

I narrow my eyes. "Keen ears. Can you hear my thoughts, too?"

"Sure can."

He unlocks the matte black cruiser on the rack and struts over to me. It looks like the bike's spray-painted, since there are no visible logos on the body. This must be how Jasper got to Egal's gates unnoticed.

Once he's in fist-throwing distance, Jasper reaches down and pulls a water bottle out of the holder. As he twists the cap open, he says, "You can hardly wait to ride on the pegs of this sweet, sweet bike for seven miles. That's all you can think about. Did I nail it?"

Jasper takes a sip of the water before holding it out to me.

I cross my arms. "Pegs. Those bike pegs. For seven miles?"

He smirks.

"What's my alternative?"

"You could stay here—"

"Okay."

"*But* the coyotes around here have been slowly starving for the past three years, and—"

"You're not serious," I counter. "I've never seen a zombie coyote in Egal."

"You're on the other side of the Split now, Kota. World's different over here."

How different could it possibly be? Granted, the Great Zombird Chase of 2020 *did* just go down.

I weigh my options. I could stay out here, alone, with the threat of lurking zombie animals, or I could go with Jasper, the kidnapper.

A distant howl echoes through the wind, and I make my decision. "Fine. Pegs. Whatever. Tell me about this water—what's the catch?"

"Come again?"

"You're sharing your water rations. Why?"

Jasper laughs. "That's not how it works in Macoby. There are no rations. Why do you think the wall was built in the first place?"

I realize I don't know, not really. I've heard that the Macs are thieves, rapists, *cannibals* who we need to wall off. I assumed they operated under the same system as us: working set hours for set rations. Equality in effort, equality in reward.

I say, "So you don't bother us."

Jasper lowers his arm. "So as not to ruin the fragile system Chandler forces you to live under?"

"I'm not *forced* to do anything."

"That so? You're not forced to turn in, say, a bottle of water *you* found? Not forced to split ounces of water among hundreds of people?"

"148 people."

"In Macoby, if you want something, you either take it or trade something for it. Supplies aren't regulated. *People* aren't regulated." Jasper re-extends his hand. "If I offer you water because you're clearly parched, it's my right to do so. Now, do you want the water or not?"

God, that water would taste so good.

I stare down at my feet. "But I don't have anything to trade."

"First round's on me."

I look up.

While I'm certain there *is* a catch, I'm so thirsty. I'm so goddamn thirsty.

With a sigh, I snatch the water from him, tip the bottle to my lips, and chug greedily. Tepid water has never tasted so glorious. My empty stomach gurgles as the water washes down my body. I'm human again.

Jasper smiles at me.

I hand the bottle back to him. "You playing the nice guy now?"

"I've always been the nice guy," he says. I want to smack the smugness off his face. Whatever he's playing at, I won't fall for it. "Ready to go home?"

"If by 'home' you mean back to where you so kindly kidnapped me from, then yes."

"That's not at all what I meant."

"Didn't think so, nice guy."

Jasper pulls his backpack over both shoulders, tightens the straps, and throws a leg over the bike seat. His gaze slips to my tattered sneakers, and he raises an eyebrow.

I flex my foot and show him the faded, worn red sole. "They're Prada."

"Think they'll hold up for the journey? Can't have you splayed on the side of the road like roadkill."

"But then you won't have to worry about finding dinner."

Jasper looks at me like I just kicked a toddler. "We don't eat people over here, Kota."

"Whatever you say. Now . . ." I pat the threadbare seat. "If you're the nice guy you say you are, you'd let me sit right here while you ride the pegs." I pout my lips and flutter my eyelashes. "Promise I'll drive safe."

"Not happening."

"What about that girl's Jeep—"

"The Jeep belongs to Greeley. The bike is mine." He cocks his head to the side. "Now hop on."

I tighten my scrunchie and take one last swig of water before grabbing Jasper's backpack to balance on the pegs. My knuckles turn white. "Pull any tricks, and I'll take you down with me."

Jasper wraps his hands around the handlebars. "Hold on tight, Pegs."

CHAPTER TWELVE

COLD AIR WHIPS THROUGH MY HAIR AS JASPER AND I RIDE HIS bike over dirt roads flanked by decrepit houses. Most, if not all, of these houses are occupied. A man peers at us out of his window. Two men sit on a rooftop. An elderly couple perches on the stoop of a rickety wooden house. Their figures meld with the wood like they've been there for their entire lives. But it's the little girl on the sidewalk that makes my gut twist. One hand grasps her mother's while the other holds a paper sign. A half-empty carton of Minute Maid and four Dixie Cups rest on the ground beside her feet. *"Lemonade for trade."*

I wonder what she wants for it.

I always pictured Macoby as some kind of black hole—a place where bad people did bad things. Not a place where eighty-year-olds hang out on stoops holding hands. Not a place where little girls smile.

The sheer number of homes surprises me. In Egal, any standing house was torn down, the scraps used to build the row house.

I bring my mouth close to Jasper's ear and ask, "Did most of these homes survive the flood? Or were they rebuilt after Z Day?"

Jasper shouts back, his voice muffled by the wind. "We're scrappy around here."

"That doesn't answer my question," I say, but my words fall on deaf ears.

Jasper picks up speed. My fingers, clinging on to his backpack for dear life, have grown numb. Grandma was right—nothing's as strong as L.L.Bean stitching. If only my quads held such strength.

I'm in good enough shape—slinging box after box into the truck has kept me fit—but my body is tired. Worn. Hungry. My wrists are sore from where the rope dug into them, and my muscles are on fire. Fire. Burning like Dante's Seventh Circle of Hell.

Mr. Martinez, are you proud?

What I would do to sit, bored, only half listening, in a literature class right now.

Jasper is taking our long journey in stride. His back is tense, strong, and his traps pop out of his T-shirt. He maintains speed as he climbs the rough, hilly streets, bearing my extra weight with ease.

He slows down as we approach a long dirt driveway bordered by a haunting blend of tall, warped trees and stumps—used for firewood, I'd imagine. The sun is high in the sky, casting shadows that dance like ghosts on the ground. Jasper comes to a halt right before we run over the most phallic-looking rock I've ever laid eyes on.

"Hop off real quick," Jasper says.

"You don't have to tell me twice," I say, stretching out my legs. Jasper picks up the rock and lobs it into the eerie forest to our right. "Was that rock shaped like a penis?"

"I don't want to talk about it."

"Did you mold it yourself? Is that what you do in your spare time—carve rocks into penises?"

"Kota." Jasper fixes me with a stern look.

I shrug. "Just getting to know the man I'll be spending the next forty-eight hours with. Don't worry, I won't write home about it. *Though*, if I did, I'd say something like, 'Dear Grandma, my kidnapper has a thing for sexy stones. He saved face and threw it into the woods, but my gut tells me he'll sneak out late tonight to find it, and then maybe curl up with it in bed. Anyway, what've you been up to, Gran?' "

"Please stop."

"Everyone has their quirks, Jasper."

"I regret offering to house you."

"You didn't offer. You were bribed."

He narrows his eyes at me. "Same difference."

Jasper wheels the bike down the driveway, and I limp by his side. My thighs won't stop shaking, which makes me worry how they'll feel tomorrow. Mom always said soreness kicks into high gear on the second day. Though memories of Mom are sparse and hazy, she was rarely wrong. I wish she were here to carry me and my trembling limbs home.

I jolt backward as a one-story stone cottage comes into view. It's like something out of a fairy tale. Gray-brown stone hugs the curved front door, and square windows on either side make it look like a smile. A stone chimney juts out of the roof. The door is an unpolished, muted brown. To my naked eye, the cottage shows no signs of damage or deterioration.

I grab Jasper's arm, stopping him in his tracks. He looks at me with wide eyes, like an orchid just sprouted from the top of my head. In fairness, I'm probably giving him the same look. "How'd you manage this?"

"Plenty of spare time when you're not working toward the communal good."

I ignore the jab. I'm not certain he's wrong. "You mean, while you're not shaping stones into sex objects, you're building houses out of them? I'll have to update my letter to Grandma. Where'd you even get the materials?"

"Plenty of spare parts around Greenville if you know where to look," Jasper says, wheeling the bike forward. "But no, I didn't build the cottage—the stone held up great in the flood. I just put on the roof. And now I'm going to picture dicks every time I hear the word *stone*."

"And the roof . . . it won't collapse on us?"

"That's the hope."

A gust of wind sweeps through the air. The house creaks as we walk onto the front porch. Jasper twists a key into a padlock lodged in the rusty door handle. Does everyone have locks here? The idea of personal property has already become foreign to me.

Jasper's body fills the frame when he opens the door. He makes a sweeping gesture. "After you."

The bright interior takes my breath away. Not only because the living room is three times the size of the apartment I share, but also because it's *clean*. The stone floors, a mishmash of rustic colors and sizes, bear little dirt. The walls, too. Cobbled together with worn wood planks, the ceiling appears sturdy. With a mixture of materials and trimmings, the cottage feels warm and cold, all at once.

Our home—the one I lived in with Mom, Dad, Bunny, and West—was a simple bungalow. When Mom died, Dad sold the house and took everything—except for us, of course. He bid us adieu on Grandma's front porch with little else beyond the clothes on our backs. Grandma let Bunny and me paint our room, to give us a fresh start. Bunny chose pink. To match Grandma's rose scent, she said. We even ripped out the carpet to reveal the hardwood underneath. Grandma's eyes were ablaze with astonishment when the first slat peeked through.

These haven't seen the light of day since when I was a kid, and cartoons were still played on Saturday mornings! she exclaimed.

Later, I'd set swim team trophies on the dresser and stick glow-in-the-dark stars on the ceiling for Bunny. The room became ours, and Grandma's house became home.

Jasper gestures to the small hallway. "I'll show you to your room."

"Don't you mean cell?"

He frowns. "Kota, I'm not your enemy."

"What are you, then?"

"I'm your . . ." He trails off, shaking his head. "Forget it. Your room awaits."

My body groans as I trek through the house. I walk slowly, dragging my hand along the walls, thinking of the stories this texture tells. The eyes of three portraits follow me through the living room: a toddler with two missing front teeth, a child with bright blond pigtails, and a teenage boy who looks like he'd rather be anywhere else. I lean left, right, left again. Still, the portraits stare. I've never seen the *Mona Lisa*, but I imagine it feels something like this.

"Who are these people?"

Jasper shrugs. "No idea," he says, pushing open a curved wooden door.

Then why does he keep them? Maybe they make him feel less alone. I can't imagine having a whole house to myself.

"Shoot," I say, looking down at my feet. I've left dusty brown footprints on the stone floor. "Is this a no-shoe household? Or should I call for the maid?"

"Your relentless sarcasm is astounding."

I curtsey. "Thank you."

Truth is, the big mouth I've sprouted astounds me, too. Why can I speak freely with this stranger when I never could with Chandler and Peter? Is it because he doesn't hold anything over me? Because he can't threaten my family?

Jasper motions for me to get a move on. "Keep it up, and you'll turn into Greeley." He narrows his eyes. "And are you? Planning on keeping it up?"

"As long as I'm a prisoner here."

"Kota, the moment you realize that what's on the other side of the wall is ten times scarier than what's in here . . . you'll see this place as a palace."

"You mean Egal, don't you? Not the world outside the Split." Jasper nods. "We're doing just fine back home, thank you. We're *peaceful*. Happy. And we don't steal."

"So we're the big bad guys because we steal? To survive?"

I pause, at a loss for words. "Yes," I finally answer. "You stole *me*. From my family. That makes you a bad person."

"You don't really believe that."

"I—" I don't know what I believe.

I bite my tongue and shove past Jasper, marching into my room. *No*, my cell. That's what it is: a cell.

Right?

CHAPTER THIRTEEN

WAS WRONG—THIS ROOM IS NOT A PRISON. NO CELL BARS, NO STONE floors, no exposed toilet in the corner of the room. I have a *bed*. A real bed. I pinch the skin on my hand to remind myself that my wildest dreams have not come true. Though I slept on a shoddy sofa back in Egal, I'd rather be there.

I'd rather be there. I'd rather be there.

Back aching, feet wedged between the cushions to stay warm. I'd rather be there.

Grandma's crinkly voice barges into my head. *Don't be a martyr, Dakota,* she says. *Be grateful for the damn bed. Tuck in and sleep.*

Grandma, as always, is correct.

I flop on the bed and sink into the plush mattress. Plush by my standards. Clouds of dust swirl into the air and sprinkle down on me like snow. It gets cold in the South, certainly, but never cold enough to snow—not anymore. Is it easier to outrun zombies in northern states, where thick snow and black ice coat the ground? Or has the frost completely screwed them, killing off any remaining plants and trees?

I close my eyes and imagine myself floating down a river. Light as a feather, as the current carries me gently downstream.

I have to pee.

I sit up and glance around the room, absolving the bed of my undivided attention. I register my surroundings: one window, a ticking clock, a framed collage, and a large mirror perched atop the dresser. A single crack slithers across the mirror's unpolished surface. I sit up taller. And look at myself. And gasp.

My long hair is tangled and twisted in ways I didn't know possible. Half of my ponytail is a greasy, matted wad. Birds could lay eggs in the nest atop my head. Deep circles are painted below my eyes, my cheeks are sunken and white, and my lips are chapped.

I lower my pants and spin around to inspect my butt. There it is. A purple splotch right above my coin slot. I yank up my pants and smooth out my hair.

I wish I looked pretty. I wish I could feather my lashes with mascara and rosy my cheeks with blush and smear on Zara's bright red lipstick.

And though I imagine Jasper's reaction to my cleaned-up face, I refuse to admit my newfound desire is because of him. He may be a self-proclaimed Nice Guy and about my age and attractive, but he is my captor. No, certainly my desire to look pretty stems from *Peter's* actions. My subconscious must want to prove to Peter that I *am* beautiful, that I *was* enough for him.

Even the thought feels wrong. I don't care how pretty Peter thinks I am.

I meander to the window. Hazy light streams in through an opaque cream curtain, leaving pale yellow shadows on the floor. I peel back the curtain and gasp. A small creek babbles just yards from the house, and behind it, the sun slowly sinks behind a line of leafless, bent trees. I've never wanted anything as much as I want to wash off in that creek. And pee, assuming Jasper's plumbing doesn't work.

I wrench open the window and smile despite myself. I can do anything I want. After all, Jasper said I'm not a prisoner.

Jasper jogs down an overgrown path to the creek. He musses his brown hair and bends down to touch the water. Satisfied with the temperature, he rips off his boots, shirt, and—I should look away, but I don't—his pants.

That is the tightest, most muscular ass I've ever seen.

Jasper wades into the creek. I catch sight of the faintest smile when he glances up at the emerging moon. I should stop spying on him. I should be the bigger person. But he shot a *blow dart* in my neck, so who am I to be the morality police? I don't feel bad about invading his privacy.

He interlaces his fingers and stretches toward the sky, revealing his entire front side.

Okay, maybe I feel a little bad.

When Jasper is up to his calves in water, he lowers himself and sinks under the surface. I bring my nose to my armpit and sniff.

Me next.

For the next ten minutes, I pace around the room, close and open the curtain, and then pace some more. A bath sounds better than when Peter snuck me a stale pack of M&Ms from a battered Walmart. I accepted what he gave me without question. I lapped up his attention, not knowing when he'd decide to look at me again. What prompted Peter to give me candy that day? Did he make love to Zara and then make it up to me with illicit M&Ms?

I peek out the window. Jasper's on the opposite side of the creek, shaking out his hair. Shirtless—but thankfully wearing shorts—he strides into the woods. Don't know where he's going, don't know what he's doing, but I do know one thing: *It's my turn.*

I wrench open the door and pop down the hallway. My footsteps echo in the barely furnished space. I shiver and make for the front door. The corroded knob jangles. Locked in from the inside.

Hmm, thought this place wasn't a prison?

I dart back down the hall, ignoring the shadows that creep along the stone walls like the undead.

Back in my room, I unlatch the window and shove it up until there's enough space to climb through. I hurl myself up, wincing as my lower belly presses into the hard window frame. My head hits the bottom of the window, and a flurry of stars splotches my vision.

"Pull it together, Kota," I mutter.

As I slip through the window, a cold breeze tickles my nose. I hit the ground with an "Ah-choo!" The sneeze lurches through my core. I clamp my hand over my mouth, suddenly dry heaving. Nothing comes out. My stomach is empty, hollow.

John Mayer's "Your Body Is a Wonderland" suddenly plays in my head, louder than the creek twisting through the scabbed earth.

Goddammit, John, nobody invited you.

I close my eyes and focus on the soft stream babbling over rocks. We have one creek on our side of the Split, and everyone can access it once a week.

Jasper has an entire creek all to himself. Perpetually. Now, so do I.

A fleeting thought races through my mind: I could escape. *Technically*, I could. Jasper's off in the woods doing who-knows-what, and I could slip away unseen. But then what? I have zero idea where Macoby's gates are in relation to Jasper's cottage. And I'd be running on an empty stomach with trembling quads. On the off chance I navigated to the gates, I'd be weaponless outside the Split. Out in the open. In the dark. Vulnerable to zombies and shamblers and Mac's trigger-happy guards.

No, I think I'll just enjoy the creek.

Wrenching off my sneakers, I glance around to see if the coast is clear. Jasper's still nowhere in sight, and I'm starting to attract flies, so I pull off my shirt and pants. Fuck it, I pull off my bra and undies, too.

I tiptoe into the water and flinch as the cold bites my ankles. The water washes over my bare skin as I kneel on the soft, weathered pebbles. I dunk my head under and let the soundless world below drown me for a moment. My lungs still hold up years after swim team, and thank *god,* because I don't want to come up for air.

For only a moment, I pretend the world is as it was in high school. Sure, tensions between California and the rest of the country were rising; sure, talks of war made the daily news; sure, my father made no attempt to contact his three children despite incessant calling and calling and *the number you have reached is no longer in service.*

The world wasn't so weighty back then. Survival was a given. Not a day went by that I didn't brush my hair or gloss my lips or apply deodorant. Not a day went by without Bunny or Grandma or a phone call with West. Not a day went by alone.

Alone.

Bathing in a creek behind a kidnapper's house.

The moment the sun tucks itself in for the night, my bath becomes a freezing embrace. Goose bumps prickling my arms and legs. My chattering teeth echo in my ears. Shivering, I pull myself out of the creek and study the moon. The glowing orb sits fat and happy above the trees. Full enough to bring out the werewolves. Full enough to bring out—

Jasper.

Jasper jogs out from the woods and stops in his tracks when he sees me. His jaw drops open.

"Close your eyes!" I scream and yank my clothes off the ground.

Jasper whips his hands over his face, then realizes he can just turn around.

"What are you doing out here?" he yells at the wall of trees. *"Naked?"*

"I saw *you* naked," I say. I probably shouldn't admit that. "And I smelled like a trash can." I probably shouldn't admit that, either.

Jasper turns around.

I scream, "Hey! No peeking, perv!"

"Hurry up and get dressed, then!"

"Working on it!"

I pull my clothes off the ground and huff before sliding dry jeans over my wet legs. I hoist my shirt up and over, but my head gets caught in the opening.

"You've got to be kidding me," I mutter.

"What was that? Did you say you're done?"

"Didn't your mother teach you patience is a virtue?"

"No, she didn't."

"Why's that?" I finally get the shirt over my head. "I'm dressed."

Jasper turns around. "She died before she had the chance."

"Oh," I say.

If telling me that was an attempt to get me to feel bad for him, well . . . shit. I fear it may have worked.

Jasper stares at me from across the creek and runs a hand through his damp hair. The unkempt look suits him.

Shaking away my thoughts, I say, "It's just a creek. Go on, cross it. I don't bite. I'm not convinced *you* don't bite, but . . ."

Even as I say the words, I know the dialogue's outlived its shelf life. If he were going to eat me, he'd have me on a spit by now.

Jasper crosses the creek, his boots sloshing in the water. He steps up onto the bed, towering over me. There's at least a foot difference between our heights.

I square my shoulders. "Fine. You're not a cannibal, but that doesn't mean you're a *nice guy.* You kidnapped me. You shot me with a blow dart, for fuck's sake!"

"I can show you how to use one sometime."

"What? A blow dart? Seems pretty simple to me." I step toward him and blow air in his face.

His lip curve up in a half smile. "Good, you've got that one down. But a blow dart will only get you so far. How would you hold a gun?"

I cross my arms. "I didn't sign up for a weapons lesson."

"Want to?"

What is he getting at?

Jasper lowers his voice to a whisper and says, "With a gun, you could defend yourself against nice guys—and not-so-nice guys." He glances up at the moon. "I'll let you think about it. I'm going inside, and you should, too. It's not safe out here at night."

"Is there a curfew?"

Jasper almost laughs. "No, we're free to do as we please. That also means it can get dangerous in the dark."

"Coyotes?"

Jasper leans down and whispers in my ear, "Raiders."

A chill runs down my spine.

With a wave, Jasper says, "Later, Pegs," then disappears into the dark house.

I should follow him inside. I *will* go inside. But I need a minute. A minute completely to myself. When was the last time I was truly alone? When I wasn't under someone's orders?

The day Mom died, six years ago, is the last I can remember. I swam laps in our neighborhood pool until my lungs nearly gave out, just like hers. Then Dad shoved us off to Grandma's, and the weight of the world landed on my shoulders. My life was no longer my own.

For a moment, right now, it's simply me and the wind.

I close my eyes and listen.

Cicadas chirp in the chattering trees, and water trickles gently down the creek. There are a lot of things I miss about electricity: the yellow glow of my bedside lamp before bed, the mystic theme song of that Viking video game West played, a freezer for grape popsicles. What I don't miss? Electricity's incessant hum.

As I stand outside Jasper's home, every sound is loud enough to be heard.

A strong breeze twists through the air, plastering wet strands of hair to my right cheek. I peel the hair off. Over my shoulder, pebbles skitter along the winding path that leads to the cottage. Shadows dance in the woods. The shapes and sounds turn eerie, and my peace dissolves in the chilled air. I'm the first line of defense if the raiders barge down that path—and I'm defenseless.

I should go inside.

I scurry back to the cottage and twist the front door's cold knob, only to find it's still locked. Fine. Back in the way I left, then. I shove myself through my room's open window and manage to not bang my head this time. It's a small win, but I'll take it. I high-five myself.

I slam the window down and latch the lock. As I turn around, I catch my reflection in the mirror. I certainly wouldn't win any beauty pageants, but at least the grime's washed off my face and—wait. It's not pitch black in here.

Two lit candles sit on the threadbare dresser. Their feathery flames cast a soft orange light throughout the room. My eyes fall to the bedstand, where a third candle burns next to a scrap of paper, my balisong, and a Quaker granola bar.

Oh my god.

I shove the balisong into my pocket, then cram the granola bar into my mouth and chew. Chocolate. Oats. Cinnamon. It's the most magical taste in the world, and it's gone much too soon.

I lick the sugary remnants off my lips and pick up the paper. Mom would've chastised me for not having done so before eating the bar. *Before you open a present, sweetie, read the card first.* Manners be damned.

As I pick up the note, my stomach cramps. And not because I ate too quickly.

All I ask in return is that you trust me.

Oh, that's *all* Jasper asks? As if. As if he can buy my trust, just like . . . just like Peter did.

Jasper can't have my trust, though. He hasn't earned it.

I blow out all three candles and flop backward on the bed.

Why is he doing this? Giving me water, a room, sharing food that he stole from me? Jasper's actions have seemed genuine, but I admit I don't have the best track record for seeing through people.

No, Jasper's hiding something. He must be. He and Chief can't possibly believe I'm important enough to act as a political pawn.

I have to find another way back home. Bunny's and Grandma's lives depend on it.

I consider my options.

Option one: I do what they want. I wait it out and meet with Chandler in two days, knowing full well I'll be stuck here anyway. Chandler wouldn't have taken two Macs—she has no reason to. But if Chandler says as much, why should Chief believe her? He went so far as to kidnap me. In Chief's mind, Chandler's guilty. He'll keep me in Macoby until he has proof otherwise.

Option two: I make a run for it. Right now. Hungry, tired, and defenseless. I bolt and hope for the best.

Option three: I manipulate. I trick Jasper into leaving the Split tomorrow and go to Costco. I escape when the doughboys arrive.

I chuck option two out the window. I may be reckless, but I'm not stupid. I've got to go with option three. It's the quickest route home, and if luck's on my side, I can scavenge and smuggle some insulin for Bunny. The boys would be none the wiser.

Then, it'll be smooth sailing back home. I can win back Chandler's favor by divulging what Chief and Jasper think she's done, in case they retaliate.

Soon, it will be like this adventure never happened. Soon, I will mourn this plush bed like I mourned my mother, my father, West.

Soon, I will return to my rations and routine, and memories of Macoby will float away in the wind.

CHAPTER FOURTEEN

A GROWL RIPS THROUGH THE AIR.

I jolt awake and search for the source of the sound as bright light streams into the room. Nothing is awry: the window is locked, door shut, and wrapper where I left it on the nightstand—right next to Jasper's note. *All I ask in return is that you trust me.*

Nope!

My stomach growls.

Ah, so I was the monster all along.

See, Jasper? Your gesture was worthless. If you were really *being kind, you would've given up six of your precious granola bars. You would've known I needed hella calories to put a dent in my ravenous belly.*

I flop over in bed and yawn, curling my toes under the sheets. Crusty sleep dangles in the corner of my eyes. I crumble it between my fingers and yawn. Hunger aside, I'm more rejuvenated than I've felt since those bombs dropped in the dams. No nightmares. No birds leaving me behind. Jasper left me alone. *And* I don't smell.

What will today hold for me?

A second later, I have my answer. From somewhere inside the cottage, Jasper shouts, *"Fuck!"*

My heart rate accelerates. Is he in danger? Am I?

Thunk. A dull, heavy sound reverberates in my ears, snapping me to attention.

Zombie. There's a zombie in the house.

I bolt out of bed, cursing Jasper for leaving me weaponless. And then I remember—*he returned my balisong last night.* I bite my tongue and pull the butterfly knife out of my pocket. Sunlight glints off the sharp blade as I flick it open.

Jasper didn't have to return my balisong. He didn't have to feed me.

He didn't have to kidnap me, either.

"Fuck!" Jasper shouts again, louder this time.

Dammit. This is my chance to escape, to bust open the window and haul ass out of here.

And yet, a big part of me wants to stay and help Jasper.

I think of his brown eyes. Of his kind, dimpled smile. The world can't lose that smile.

I can do this.

Shoulders back, I bound out of my room. I run into the living room and scan for danger. I whip my head left, right, then left again. Something's wrong. Not a thing is out of place.

It's only when I reach the kitchen, tucked in the far corner of the cottage, that I find Jasper. Alone. Eyes rolled back. Shoveling a fat spoon of peanut butter into his mouth.

"What the hell are you doing?" I yell, pointing my glass shard in his face. "Why did you scream? I thought there was a zombie attack!"

Jasper raises his eyebrows and pulls the silver spoon out of his mouth. "There are no zombies in the house, Kota," he says, his words sticking to the roof of his mouth. A glob of peanut butter cements his jaw together.

"Then why—"

"This peanut butter's really fucking good," he says, smiling.

Jasper takes one look at my face before bursting out laughing.

"Don't laugh," I say. He laughs some more. "You have chunks in your teeth."

I do not want to enjoy this moment.

Shoulders sagging, I close my eyes and search for a seed of anger, but I come up empty. Because behind my eyes, there is light. The cottage is full of it. Streams of golden sunlight pour through the many windows, warming the stone floor beneath my feet. Sandwiched between two row houses, our home in Egal is dark. Small. Cramped. Here, the space is endless. I could eat in private. It's not that I dislike dining in the church with a hundredish people, but I miss supper with my family. For the first fourteen years of my life, we had Sunday dinner with Mom and Dad, Bunny and West, and Grandma. Never missed a week. Even when Mom died and Dad left, Grandma insisted that we continue our tradition. Sometimes, West would drive down from college to dine with us.

Jasper sets his spoon on the worn butcher countertop. Grandma's silverware looked similar to this spoon, actually, embellished with a delicate rose on the tip.

He moves to twist the blue top on the Jif jar when a waft of peanut butter reaches my nose. I launch forward to snatch the jar out of his hands, but Jasper deftly pivots away and darts to the living room. He plops down in front of the couch, cross-legged, and holds the jar close to his heart. I walk around opposite him and narrow my eyes.

I nod to the peanut butter and say, "So Chief was true to his word, then?"

"Of course," he says, fishing a nut out of his teeth. "That's how it works in Macoby."

"Do you trust Chief?" I sit down and rest my elbows on the coffee table.

"Pardon?"

"Chief. He's your leader, right? So you trust him?" Jasper nods slowly. "Then you understand what it means to put your faith in a leader."

"Chandler's really brainwashed you, hasn't she?"

"Chandler has kept me safe. She's kept me with my family." *And you're jeopardizing that.*

"Two days," Jasper says. "And then you're free." He slides the jar of peanut butter toward me. "I'm not trying to keep you from your family. But I need you for two days. Then you can run back home to your family and fucked-up system." When I say nothing, Jasper continues. His voice softens. "I understand how you feel. My family was torn apart after Z Day, just like yours."

"You know nothing about my family," I bite back.

"No," he says. "I don't. But I do know that you love them."

"Then why are you keeping me here? Why are you doing this to me?"

"This thing with Chandler, it's bigger than you." He uncrosses his legs and pushes himself to his feet.

I look up at him, clenching my fists. "Bigger how? Who are these missing men, and what do you think Chandler has done with them?"

"That's not for me to say," he says, walking back toward the kitchen.

"Fuck you." I stand and glare at his back.

He turns around when he reaches the counter. "How long have you been in Egal?"

"Two years."

"So you haven't been in the Split since the beginning. You weren't here to make a choice—it was made for you."

"I would never live here," I say, the unspoken words lingering on my lips. *Not without my family.*

"Don't let these past two years strip you of your future."

Jasper reaches into a cabinet and slides out a backpack. He pulls a lighter and a knife out of his pocket, throws them in, then slings the backpack over his shoulder. His arm brushes against mine as he walks to the front door, a scent of lavender bar soap trailing behind.

"Wait!" I say, hating myself for sounding so desperate. "Where are you going?"

"On a supply run. That's the way it goes around here. If I need something, I go get it myself, or I trade with someone who has it."

"You're allowed to just leave? Anyone? At any time?"

"Yep," he says. My stomach growls. I make goo-goo eyes at the jar of peanut butter. "Are you coming?"

I blink, shocked at the invitation. But I hesitate only for a second before nodding. This turn of events could bode awfully well for me. I don't have to trick Jasper into leaving the Split—he already has plans to do so. *And he's inviting me.*

"Sure am," I say, trying not to sound too eager.

Then, before he can do anything about it, and because *nothing can stop me now!*, I snatch the peanut butter off the table. I've never moved so fast in my life, twisting off the lid and digging my pointer finger deep into the jar. I shove the sweet, salty wad into my mouth.

Jasper says nothing, so I shovel another glob into my mouth. I'm a chipmunk as I say, *"Fuck!"* My voice pierces through the quiet house. That's some good peanut butter.

Jasper smiles, wider than I've ever seen before. Just like that, any agitation either of us felt fizzles away. He opens the door, and I follow him out of the house, licking my salty lips.

CHAPTER FIFTEEN

SHOULD HAVE PLANNED BETTER.

Not that I had the luxury of time. My plan to escape via Costco only became real an hour ago. And how am I supposed to work out the details with Jasper and Greeley bickering in the front seat of Greeley's turbulent Jeep?

"Watch this," Greeley says.

We're taking a side route through an old school zone, and Greeley accelerates as we approach a speed bump. *Please slow: kids crossing.* My head smashes into the roof of the Jeep.

"*Ow!*" I screech, clutching the top of my head, now a bruised cantaloupe.

As I steady myself, I catch Greeley's satisfied stare in the rear-view mirror. "Toughen up," she tells me. Greeley turns to Jasper and says, "Bunch of softies, those Egals. Too reliant on each other. Bet you this one won't survive the supply run."

"She *needs* to survive," Jasper says. He swivels around and faces me. "You won't die."

"Gee, thanks," I mutter.

"Tell you what, if you survive this, I'll retract my statement. Probably." As we exit the school zone, Greeley races over another speed bump, but this time I'm prepared. I clutch on to Jasper's headrest as she adds, "But if you die, my beliefs remain unchanged. You Egals are a bunch of communist losers following a psychotic leader who's brainwashing you into thinking '*Guns Bad, Weakness Good.*'"

Fine. If she wants to hate me because I'm *me*—an Egal—then I can play.

I tear off a yellowing hangnail and let the blood spurt from my finger like a fire hose. Instead of sucking my finger to stop the flow, I squeeze the wound so big, fat drops tatter the back seat of Greeley's Jeep.

Let it stain, I think, swirling the blood around on the fabric like the post-apocalyptic van Gogh I am. *Let my blood leave its mark, even when I'm gone.*

Today, I *will* escape with the doughboys. I will go back home. Back to Bunny and Grandma.

Greeley's hatred of me isn't even *about me*, and that's what pisses me off the most. We're barely three years post-America, and we've already fallen back into the divisiveness that ruined our country.

I was too young, maybe, or too ignorant to realize what was happening. It was easier to believe Grandma when she said nothing was wrong. It was easier to zone out and idly pick at the threads of her pastel floral couch while President Burns addressed the public on Grandma's staticky box TV.

From Burns: *The country is taking proactive measures to eradicate thirst.*

From Grandma: Proactive? *The Colorado River's been drying up for fifteen years! No, no, not to fear, though, sweetheart. Plenty of other rivers to drink from. Those kids in California will be just fine. Now, dear, how about some lemonade?*

But with a population boom, the government couldn't provide enough water for everyone. When Jenkins, California's governor, got elected as president in 2016, shit went downhill fast. The moment he started blaming Burns was the beginning of the end. President Burns was Native American, and Jenkins's party took that thread and ran with it.

Kill them, his followers said, *and there will be enough water for us.*

Jenkins was enigmatic. Governors loved him. Soon, states began to strip Native Americans of their land, turning reservations into reservoirs.

Stolen. Sunk. Salvaged.

But that wasn't enough. Still, there were too many mouths to wet.

Native Americans were moved to urban developments near their old homes, forced into lives so close yet so far from what they knew. Jenkins's most extremist followers—his Californian state cabinet—took matters into their own hands.

It's those damn Natives! Drinking all our water, taking all our resources! If we can't have water, they can't either!

In 2017, extremists bombed dams across the United States, flooding areas with the largest populations of Native Americans.

Did they know their bombs would release a toxin that would turn the dead into zombies? Was their intention to destroy humanity, or were they blinded by unfounded hatred?

It was easier to believe Grandma when she said everything would be okay, that the news would simmer down. Grandma forgot to put simple syrup in her lemonade the day Jenkins was elected. I think she was afraid the sugar water would boil over.

I glance up at the rising sun, hoping it'll give me answers and also maybe photosynthesis.

Give me energy, please! Give me life!

"Pit stop for seeds at the Home Depot?" Jasper asks, pointing to a large building with a bright orange roof.

"So you can waste more time planting shit that won't grow because uh, hello, pollinators are now zombinators?"

"*Greeley.*"

"What?" She slams her hands on the wheel, jerking the Jeep to the right. "Better off drinking water than gambling it away on seeds."

"You of all people know that's not true."

Greeley gives Jasper a scathing look. She chomps her teeth at Jasper, her molars clinking together like a champagne toast. I can't help but wonder who Greeley really is. She's been nothing but a total shit, so there must be a reason Chief and Jasper keep her around.

I blurt out the question. "Why?"

Greeley spins around, jerking us onto a cracked sidewalk. Jasper adeptly grabs the steering wheel with his left hand and brings us back onto the main road. She says, "Nothing you need to know, Blondie."

I narrow my eyes, but let it go because I don't want her to throw me out of the car. I've never been this close to the city before.

I drag my attention to the I-85 on-ramp, the Greenville city skyline coming into view. The once-tall buildings are now in ruins, nothing but crumbling heaps on the ground. The roads are over-run with totaled vehicles. Motorcycles, cars, army tanks, trucks, vans . . . even the sky looks different here. Thick, dark gray clouds roll in, and heavy, polluted air slithers into the Jeep—a gentle re-minder that the atmosphere is also totally fucked.

As we hop off the highway and onto Woodruff Road, a few shamblers roam the streets, but not as many as I expected. Since practically everyone in the state is dead, there's nothing left for the zombies to feed on, so they've gone dormant. With no stimuli, zombies go into a trance. They don't die; they hi-bernate. But to them, loud noise brings with it the promise of food . . . Those that remain are slow and meander through the streets without a purpose.

Before Z Day, I think that's how I felt. But now I have a purpose: to survive. I don't know which is better or worse.

Anxiety erupts in my stomach as Costco comes into view. The parking lot is littered with broken cars, loose wires, and burnt hunks of concrete. A chill rattles my bones as it dawns on me that this lot may be so full of trash and destruction that we won't be able to pull in.

Greeley slowly brings the Jeep to a halt. "We'll go on foot from here."

"Oh, *god*," I splutter. I clamp a hand over my mouth, angry I've let the words escape. I can't let Greeley see me as weak.

I crane my head around to the back window of the Jeep, squinting into the distance at the road. Exactly how far back were those shamblers we passed? Would we make it from here to the doors of Costco before the sound of our breath and footsteps attract their attention?

Greeley and Jasper turn around in their seats, watching *me* watch the outside. I turn back to them in time to catch the glance they share with each other. They're regretting bringing me along.

This is a test to see if I can actually survive on my own.

As I look across the tattered lot, I don't know who I'm going to prove wrong: Greeley or Jasper.

Greeley pushes open her door, and the cold air slaps me in the face like a whip. She slings a black backpack over her shoulders and tosses Jasper the car keys. "Better not waste anyone's last words with chitchat. On we go, folks."

She tugs a tattered baseball cap onto her head, shielding her blue eyes from the bright morning sun. Her half-blond hair glints in the light like a sun ray, which is deceiving, because Greeley is what I'd describe as the opposite of a ray of sunshine.

Greeley slams her door, tells Jasper to lock up, and strides forward without a backward glance. Jasper roots around the glove compartment, and once he's found what he's looking for, he turns to hand me—no. There's no way.

Jasper is handing me a gun.

CHAPTER SIXTEEN

YOU'LL WANT THIS," JASPER SAYS WHEN I JUST STARE AT THE METAL monster in his hand.

"You're giving me a gun?"

"Lending it," he says, impatience an undercurrent to his words.

I leave the gun in his outstretched hand. "They make too much noise. Chandler never—I don't know how to even—"

"You won't care how much noise a gun makes if a hungry zombie attacks you in there."

We're in a stare down for only a moment before Jasper realizes that I won't be taking the gun from his hand. Or he realizes that it'd be stupid to give a gun to someone who doesn't know how to use one.

He tucks it into the waistband of his jeans.

"Get out," he says, picking up the backpack at his feet and hauling himself out of the Jeep.

Shit. A backpack. Why didn't I think of that? I've been letting people do the thinking for me for far too long.

I look around in the back seat and yelp when Jasper raps a knuckle on my window. "There's one in the trunk," he says, then walks to the back of the Jeep.

I check my surroundings before easing open the door. Lots of rubble, yes, but no zombies—at least in the near distance.

It's wild. Grandma used to load up her Lincoln with cardboard boxes and take Bunny and me to Costco once a month. We'd drive around the massive parking lot searching for an open spot before finally settling on one way in the back. And then it'd take Grandma fifteen minutes to squeeze into the space. We'd get inside and fill the cart with way too many paper towels, juice boxes, gigantic apples . . .

We'll be lucky if we find anything of use today.

The parking lot is as full as it used to be, only it looks so much different. Stop signs lie bent on the ground, cars sink into massive holes in the asphalt, and red-lipped carts are flipped over, their wheels having been blown off. Bones scatter the sidewalks, gray-brown dust floating up from the broken earth.

Jasper offers me the gun. I blink.

"Take it."

"No."

"Yes," he insists.

I squeeze my eyes shut and weigh the pros and cons of accepting this gleaming hunk of metal. Pro: Self-defense. Con: Self-harm. *I may very well shoot myself in the foot.* Pro: Greeley and Jasper see me as strong. Con: I prove them wrong. By shooting myself in the foot.

I blink my eyes open and stare at the goddamn fortress that is Costco. Sure, the building stands, but it *has* changed—no longer do families push oversized carts around its aisles. No longer do workers serve up samples of on-sale snacks. No longer do hot rotisserie chickens sweat in the meat case or flat-screen TVs light up the entrance. This place will never be the same.

If Costco can change, I can, too.

I hold my hand out, and as Jasper gently places the gun in my palm, the weight of it settles in. Physically and emotionally.

"Cock it," Jasper says.

I do as he says. I think. "How'd I do?"

It's slight, but his mouth lifts into a smile. His eyes crinkle at the sides. "Five gold stars. Your grip, on the other hand . . ." Jasper grabs the gun by the muzzle, flips it around, and clenches it on either side. He narrows his eyes and aims the gun at a silver Mercedes—that certainly didn't used to be a convertible—across the lot. "Hold the gun like this. Firm. Confident."

I blow out a breath. "Easier said than done."

"Just try," he says, handing me the gun again.

It weighs heavier in my palms than even a second ago.

This thing has too much power. I don't *want* this much power.

I look up at Jasper, surprised to find him nodding encouragingly at me.

"You believe in me," I say, pointing the gun at a defunct shopping cart. "Why?"

"One of us has to." He maneuvers behind me and places his hands over mine. Squeezes them so tight my palms dig into the rough grip of the gun. "Like this," he says, adjusting my aim.

"Are you going to stand behind me when the zombies attack?"

His warm breath tickles my ear, sending a shiver down my spine. "No, but I'll have your back. Greeley might not, but . . ."

I lower the gun and flip around to look at Jasper. "She won't try to kill me, though, right?"

"Maybe with insults." He shrugs. "But that's all you have to worry about."

"That, and zombies," I say, turning back around. I close my left eye and narrow my right, staring at the spot where the sun glints off the metal of the shopping cart like a fish scale.

"So I just . . . pull the trigger."

"Let's hope we don't have to find out."

"That's encouraging."

"Maybe not, but it's honest," he says. "Yes, Kota, you pull the trigger. And then you run."

CHAPTER SEVENTEEN

LOWLY, METHODICALLY, THE TWO OF US MANEUVER THROUGH THE Costco parking lot. We weave between the litter and carnage, careful to step only on asphalt, careful not to make too much noise. Which is only one of the many reasons I'm scared to shoot the gun in my backpack—sounds bring zombies.

Jasper's a few paces ahead, but he doesn't to stray too far. He glances back every couple of steps and points to obstructions to watch out for, like melted orange cones, bits of jagged concrete, and large shards of glass. Femurs, elbows, kneecaps, the like.

A gust of wind blows tangled hair into my face, sending greasy strands into my mouth. I gag and pull my hood over my head. The temperature is dropping, but the adrenaline coursing through my veins keeps me warm.

Before I know it, I make it to the entrance of Costco.

Zombies: 0. Kota: 1.

Let's do this thing.

Jasper waits for me at the double doors, which are either wide open or blown off. Greeley is still nowhere to be seen.

"Get a move on, Kota," he urges, waving me forward.

My stomach plummets and my heart jumps into my chest. This is my chance, isn't it? My chance to change. *To shoot.*

I spin around and aim my gun at—

Nothing.

There's not a zombie in sight. I breathe a sigh of relief as I turn to Jasper, confused.

"I think there are only a few boxes of those big blueberry muffins left."

"Very funny," I say, my voice shaking.

We tiptoe inside and—

To my left, a zombie lies splat on the ground, black blood oozing from its temples. Its mutilated face is contorted into an open-mouthed scowl. Gnarled teeth protrude from its unhinged jaw, ichor dripping off its ashen tongue. Bones jut out from every angle of its body. Brittle ribs, sharp and splintered elbows, dented knees. But what's more horrifying is the smell— like a hot, rotten flounder that's been soaking in bodybuilder sweat and toe jam. Flies circle its misshapen head, feeding off the zombie's rancid meat.

"Jesus Christ!"

I jump backward and fall into Jasper, knocking us both a step back. He wraps his hands around my arms and stills me, squeezing once before releasing me. My racing heart slows as I realize we aren't in immediate danger. We're going to be okay. The zombie is dead.

Greeley steps out from the shadows, a knife gripped in her palm. "Clean up on aisle one!"

I drop my gun, and it hits the ground with a *clang*.

"Yeah, so don't do that again," Jasper says to me.

"Sorry."

Greeley tucks her knife in her side and strides forward. She scrunches her nose as she kneels down next to the zombie, the grotesque smell of its pus-oozing sores penetrating the air.

She lifts the zombie's withered, spindly hand and waves it, only to pull it right out of the socket like taffy. Black blood pours from the wrist. "Oops." She throws the hand back to the ground.

Jasper, for some ungodly reason, offers Greeley his hand. She refuses. "Did you find anything yet?"

"Nada," she says, looking around the warehouse. "This place has been sifted through."

I follow her gaze. Costco is more intact than I expected. But it's also bare. Discarded boxes are strewn everywhere, the shelves completely picked over. I expect this was one of the first places surviving populations came after Z Day. They probably stocked their shelves with whatever they could, hoping to hunker down at home and wait it out. Only, there *was* no waiting it out.

Because the zombies came in droves.

We hid in Grandma's attic, peeping through the small window at our neighbors shooting and screaming at one another. Just the day before, Bunny delivered Thin Mints to the bungalow in the cul-de-sac, and Tagalongs to the house with the white picket fence. Their kindness dried up in minutes.

Our neighbors turned on each other, and then they turned into zombies. The zombie population outgrew the human population in a matter of days.

Which is why I cannot comprehend the lack of zombies around here. Other than the one Greeley slashed at the entrance, there are none. No zombies. Anywhere. Zero, zip, zilch.

"I'll take the back," Greeley says, thumbing toward the meat and seafood area. Her eyes glitter with excitement. "Here's hoping I find a few more!"

"I'll take electronics. Jasper points to one of the only areas in the warehouse that's still stocked.

Greeley says, "To take yourself home a defunct iPad, or guard the entrance like the upstanding gentleman you are?"

"Give it a rest, Gree."

"In your dreams, pansy."

"I'll see what's left in the health section." I nod my head to the left.

"You're not going anywhere on your own," Greeley says. A grin spreads across her sharp face as she tells Jasper, "Don't let her slip from your sight."

Jasper nods as Greeley skips toward her destination.

"Is this like a treasure hunt for her?" I turn to Jasper. "Only zombies instead of gold?"

"Afraid so," Jasper says. He glances at the gun in my hand. "Don't hesitate to use this. And don't drop it again."

"You're letting me wander around by myself?"

"Only a fool would try to escape," he says. "And Kota, you're not a fool."

⁕—⁕—⁕—⁕—⁕—⁕

I MAKE MY WAY TO THE MEDICINE SECTION AND SIFT THROUGH THE SHELVES. Since I'm currently *not* under Chandler's jurisdiction, I can technically take back medicine for Bunny. And Grandma. *Technically.* But I'm not seeing a huge selection here—laxatives are basically all that's left. Dieting isn't a priority in a post-apocalyptic world, I reckon.

Ah! And there it is: Kirkland Signature aspirin. I whisper a thank-you to the Costco gods above and pocket the bottle.

If only I could find insulin . . .

I slide over the pharmacy counter and search, gasping when I spot it just waiting for me. The tiniest, dustiest, most beautiful box of shelf-stable insulin I've ever seen.

Is this my lucky day, or what?

Because here come the doughboys. Oh, does it feel good to see them. Well, everyone besides Peter.

Peter, Milo, Fred, and Indy stride into the store like they own the place. And they're noisy. If these idiots are always this loud on supply runs, then no wonder they attracted a raging zombie on the last run.

"Shit!" Milo shouts at the zombie Greeley offed. At once, the four boys unsheathe their knives. The initial joy of seeing my friends *(not Peter!)* wears off as a weird, uncomfortable feeling squirms into my belly. It feels a lot like disappointment.

Peter bends down and inspects the splat zombie. He pinches the skin on its face and pulls off a section like a black banana peel. "Someone's been here." He tosses the rotting skin to the ground. "Today."

Fred whips his head back and forth like a kid who just learned he should look both ways before crossing the street. "What do we do? Should we leave?" He takes three quick steps backward, right into a wall.

"No." Peter's voice echoes through the warehouse. "We stand our ground. We get what we came for."

The boys have their knives at the ready as they move deeper into the warehouse. Their heavy shoes clomp on the ground as they mutter to one another. Really, boys. Can't be quiet even in the presence of imminent danger?

"I think I'm going to puke," Fred says, covering his bulbous nose with his shirt.

I crouch down behind a shelf as the boys move further away from me. It's time to make a choice: Do I move toward the boys or away from them? Should I give them some sort of clue that I'm here? To save me?

Toward. Definitely. Right?

I duck behind the tattered shelves, the worn soles of my shoes allowing me to move quietly but quickly through the shelves. The boys walk toward what used to be the seafood section, full of empty display coolers and wall-to-wall, banged-up glass windows. It also stinks like spoiled seaweed, reeking through the warehouse. Three years weren't enough to get the worst of it out.

The air is full of a frightening excitement, the tension buzzing through my veins. The boys are occupied with the empty seafood display, fixated on what's right in front of them. I have to warn them about Greeley. She'll open fire. And it will be the end for all of us.

I reach an aisle with the tall orange shelves that once stored boxes of excess supplies. I could hoist myself up, get a bird's-eye view of the warehouse. But no. I have to get to the boys and get the hell out of here.

I pull the gun out of my waistband as Fred trips over Peter, who shoves him off. If it comes down to it, can I *shoot* Greeley? Was Jasper's thirty-second shooting lesson enough? And where the hell is Jasper?

I spring forward as Greeley steps out of the shadows, behind the glass, and points her gun at my friends.

This is certainly not going to end well.

CHAPTER EIGHTEEN

REELEY, STOP!" I YELL, JUMPING OUT OF THE SHADOWS. MILO AND Indy run toward me, their eyes bugging out at the sight of the gun in my hand.

"Kota," Milo says, pulling me into a hug. "Are you okay?"

"For now," I answer, pushing him off. Peter stands still, facing off with Greeley through the glass barrier. "We've gotta get out of here."

Greeley cocks her head to the side, a sly smile playing on her lips. She lowers her gun, seemingly interested in letting the scene play out. " 'Bout time you showed up, Blondie. Ready to roll out?"

I move to Peter's side and aim the gun at Greeley. My hand shakes as I say, "Let us go."

Greeley huffs. "You really want to go back with that fuckwad?"

No. I don't. Staying with Peter is the last thing I want. But I have to leave with him to protect Bunny and Grandma.

"We're leaving," I say.

Greeley raises her eyebrows as if to say, *Good luck with that.*

Peter steps forward. "I'm not leaving without getting what we came for: food. Supplies. Medicine."

"Already searched the place," Greeley says. "There's nothing left. You've wasted your time coming here."

Milo says, "Well then, so have you!"

"Nah," Greeley answers. "I live for the drama." She ducks behind the fish-filleting table and disappears from sight.

Indy gasps. "Bloody hell, where's she going? She's armed!"

"So am I!" I bite back. I turn to Peter. He grits his teeth, his body tense and unyielding. "We need to go. Jasper will find us and—"

"Do *not* tell me what to do," he says. "Ever."

Peter pulls a gun out from under his hoodie.

The boys gasp.

No guns, Peter said to me when he brought me home to Egal. Chandler's rule, but for good reason. They're loud and attract zombies. And they're a crutch. What happens when you run out of ammo and don't know how to use a knife? No guns. Learn how to use a knife. Or leave.

Gaslighter. Cheater. *Liar.*

"C'mon, lover boy, show me what you've got," Greeley says, stepping out from the shadows. She points her gun at Indy. "And you—show me what you can do with those fingers! All nine of them!"

"You," Peter says to Greeley. "*You* stole our bars from the factory. *You* stole our driver. *You* looted this warehouse when you knew it was Egal's territory. And now we've got an unguarded vehicle and a hundred-something people whose rations are about to get severely cut. And it's *your* fault."

I step forward. "Rations are getting cut?"

"Shut up," Peter says. He wraps a hand around my arm, keeping the other trained on Greeley.

Bunny and Grandma—they won't survive on cut rations. *I'd* be fine, but . . . I can't bear this domineering grip any longer. I won't be forced to watch my family suffer. I can't go back.

Peter says, "I'm going to sleep very well tonight after sending this bullet through your skull."

"Lad," Indy says. "Think about what you're doing before you—"

"No!" I scream, just as Peter lifts his gun.

But I'm too late.

He pulls the trigger.

Greeley dodges the bullet as a sharp blast sounds through the warehouse. With Peter's fingers still wrapped like a snake around my arm, I throw my hands over my ears, the noise reverberating in my head.

A deafening silence fills the warehouse. Nobody moves as we wait. I press my middle fingers into my palms. Goose bumps prick my arms. Indy and Milo stare at each other, and Fred turns blue. Peter's grip on his gun wavers.

And finally, it happens: A single gravelly growl breaks the quiet.

We've awakened the zombies.

Inhuman roars, rattling bones, haunting bellows. Too many sounds to count—and they're inside Costco.

Indy shouts, "They're coming from the break room! Run!"

"Let me go," I say as Peter drags me through the warehouse. I won't leave with him. "Peter! I'll shoot!"

"Don't make me laugh," Peter says.

He thinks I'm a joke, and maybe I am. I can't shoot while I'm running. I'll end up blasting myself in the foot.

Peter's grip on my arm tightens and burns my flesh. My loose skin pinches the hair on my arm. Before I know it, he lifts me up in the air and slings me over his muscled back. I can see nothing but his feet and the dirty ground as I flop against him.

No. I'm not his helpless doll.

I slam my curled fists against his back and shout, "Put me *down!*"

"You're making a scene, Kota."

I hit his back with the butt of my gun, but he doesn't release his hold on me. He holds me tight to his body as he moves through the warehouse at a jog. I imagine this is what Zara felt like when Peter was slamming into her again and again and *again*—

Blood rushes to my head. White flecks speckle my vision. A high-pitched hum buzzes in my ears. The peanut butter's coming back up.

As my stomach heaves into my throat, something yanks Peter, and he tumbles backward toward the ground. I throw my hands in front of me to protect my skull from cracking on the hard earth. The wind gets knocked out of my lungs as I hit the ground, and Peter's body slams into mine. I land with a *thud*, my upper body taking the brunt of the impact. I feel around my head. I'm okay. I'm whole.

I gasp for air, Peter's bony tailbone cutting into my back like a knife. I slide out from under him. Jasper points a gun at his face. "Run, or I shoot."

Peter rolls over and looks at me. "I'm not leaving without—"

"You have two seconds."

Without another word, Peter pushes himself up and bolts.

"Come on," Jasper says, outstretching a hand to me.

Zombies roar from inside Costco's break room.

"Thanks," I say. The word hurts to get out, but I'm free. I place my hand in his and feel a wetness between our palms. I look down and see red—blood. "Jasper, you're bleeding."

He shakes his head. "I'm not," he says, hoisting me up. "*You* are."

Jasper urges me forward and pulls me toward the exit. At least two dozen zombies have come out of hiding and meander toward us. They're slow, but only because they're hungry. The moment they get a bite of flesh, they get *fast*.

Their grotesque bodies are covered in sores: sickly mustard-colored spots of dried pus and blood. They wander toward us with rattling jaws and broken teeth. Their bones jut out at odd angles, gray-black skin peeling off in big flakes. Monstrous sounds erupt from their throats. A smell like rotten fish knocks me backward.

"*Move*, Kota!" Jasper's tone has lost its tenderness. He squeezes my arm, and I force my feet to move.

I spin around and wave the boys forward. Indy takes off, knocking over a bin of Tide Pods, but Milo stays by a dry-heaving Fred's side. After a few gentle pats on the back, Milo gives him a good whack, and finally, Fred pukes. Milo takes one look at the lumpy vomit splattered on the ground and blows chunks of his own. I flip back around as the horde of zombies progresses toward them. More zombies make it out of the freezer section and into the center, where sweatpants and socks were once sold. Still, no sign of Greeley.

I'm not sure if it's the commotion, or if they can sense fear and smell sickness, but the zombies pick up speed.

When the outbreak first happened, the zombies were fast. They feasted on any human body available, but as more people died—mostly from bombs or zombie attacks—the number of warm bodies dwindled, and the zombies proliferated. The same thing happened to the animals. That's why we're here, in Costco, risking our lives for non-perishables.

Together, Jasper and I weave between registers, careful not to stumble over cardboard boxes or sideways carts. Adrenaline courses through my veins. I check back over my shoulder.

"Stop turning around," Jasper says, tugging me forward.

I'm relieved to see all the boys are on their feet now, hurtling toward the exit. Milo catches my gaze, and his eyes widen with confusion. *Why aren't you leaving with us?* they seem to ask.

Why *aren't* I leaving with them? Why don't I want to?

Panting, heart racing, we reach the entrance. Somewhere in the parking lot, a horn honks. Greeley. I stop dead in my tracks.

"Keep moving." Jasper takes my hand and urges me forward.

I shake my head. "We have to help them."

A wall of zombies reaches the boys.

Bang.

Peter shoots off a round.

A zombie crumples to the ground, but springs back up half a second later.

Milo screams, "Don't shoot! More of them are coming from the back!"

I raise my gun, ready to launch into battle. "Kota," Jasper says, stepping around in front of me. "Save the ammo."

"But—"

Honk.

"Kota, we have to move. *Now.*"

I ignore Jasper and raise my gun as a zombie gains on Fred and nearly grabs on to the nape of his shirt. My heart beats in slow motion.

"Kota."

Thump . . . Thump . . . Thump . . .

Fuck it.

I close my left eye, aim, and shoot, just as Fred stumbles forward—onto Milo. As the entire weight of his body clashes with Milo's, a zombie T-bones him from the left. Milo lets out a shriek that sends goose bumps down my arms. I've never heard anything like it. Animalistic, savage, heartbreaking. *Helpless.* Chills shimmer down my spine like a thousand poison darts. At the same time, my bullet hits the zombie—but in the cheek. Its body contorts as the bullet slices through, the monster writhing like a vampire in sunlight, but relentless in its hunger. Refusing to stop. Refusing to give up its fresh meal.

The zombie bites a chunk out of Milo's neck. A filet of uncleaned fish.

The horn honks.

"Kota," Jasper is pleading now.

I turn. His eyes are wide and scared. But it's too late now. I have to finish this. I lift my arms, readying to shoot, to put Milo out of his misery. He's no longer Milo. He's a feast. And soon, he'll come back as one of them. Milo deserves more than that. We *all* do.

Shoot, Kota, just shoot. Do it for Milo. One, two, thr—

A bullet. But not mine. Not my bullet that pierces through Milo's skull. I never pulled the trigger.

Blood splatters onto the pouncing zombies. I draw my arm back, my stomach turning as the zombies form a dome over Milo's body. They feast. And feast.

A single tear falls down my cheek.

Jasper grabs my arm, but my feet are already moving. Together, we run to the Jeep.

And then man became flesh.

CHAPTER NINETEEN

"WHAT THE HELL WAS THAT?" JASPER SLAMS THE JEEP DOOR shut, chest heaving.

I fly into the back of his seat as Greeley rips us out of the parking lot, my entire body shaking. I scrub tears out of my eyes as if doing so will wipe out the memory of Milo, too.

Jasper's voice stiffens. "I asked you a question."

"Sorry," I mutter, barely able to get the word out.

Milo is dead.

"Not you, Kota," Jasper says, the edge gone. His gaze finds mine in the rearview mirror and I hate that it's full of pity. I rip my eyes away before more sobs can bubble out of my aching throat. Jasper turns to Greeley and points. "*You.*"

Greeley's hands grip the steering wheel so tight her knuckles pop out like pearly stones. She's tight-lipped, but Jasper persists. "Well, Greeley? Do you feel better now?"

She steps on the gas. "No, *Jasper*, I don't feel better." The odometer reads sixty as we veer onto a jagged side road. I snap on my seat belt. "We're going hunting."

We whip through a tunnel of trees, and I can see Milo wincing.

Fifty-two. That's fifty-two zombie trees I've counted since the beginning.

You're keeping count?

Someone has to. The trees signal the countdown to our demise. Wanna know how many actual trees I've counted?

Not really.

Twenty-five. Oh shit, I turn twenty-five next month. Think we could convince your Grandma to bake me a cake?

Twenty-five years old. Milo died the same age as West.

The zombie trees have begun to eat their neighbors. Their roots crawl beneath the earth, their bark speckled with black welts and gray mold. Their rotting tendrils wrap around any breathing limb they can, taking all the nutrients for themselves. *Take.* That is all this new world does. It takes the people I love from me. It chews them up and spits them out in my face.

We exit the dark, haunting passage and the few remaining living trees plead. *Don't leave us*, they whisper. *Save us.*

"We are *not* going hunting," Jasper says. He whacks the dashboard, and I flinch at the impact.

Greeley smiles.

Seventy miles per hour.

I'm sorry, Milo. I'm sorry for being too scared to pull the trigger. I'm sorry I let the world take you.

I catch my eyes in the rearview mirror.

Weak.

Weak eyes that watched their friend die. Eyes that may never meet Bunny's bright gaze again because of a choice *I* made. Eyes that may never form crow's feet wrinkles like Grandma's because I'll never grow old. Eyes that will die without saying goodbye.

The engine roars.

Seventy-five.

"We don't have a choice," Greeley spits back. "I don't have anything to trade." Her voice is like knives to my ears. *She* put us in this situation. *She* wanted violence. *She* taunted the boys.

When I look at Greeley, a thick, wet haze of red clouds my vision. I don't see the strong, brazen woman she so desperately wants to be. I see a woman who let this world win. I see raw, grisly skin stuck in rotten teeth, blood smeared across decaying chins. Flesh crammed into fingernails. Guts splayed on the ground.

Milo.

She caused Milo's death.

"Kota needs a breather," Jasper says, pointing at me with his thumb. "Let's go hunting tomorrow."

"What about *my* needs? My stomach is going to eat itself."

She can have mine.

"I just killed her friend, Gree!" Jasper yells.

"Don't 'Gree' me," she says. "I don't give two shits about Blondie's feelings."

That's enough.

I sit up taller in my seat, heat blossoming on my cheeks. "Think you could stop being a fucking psycho for five minutes?"

"Delicate as a flower, this one is." Greeley releases a hand from the wheel and squeezes Jasper's shoulder. Winks. "Great shot, by the way."

"Look at her," Jasper says. "She's turning *blue*."

"My car, my rules," Greeley twists around and sizes me up. "Damn, she looks like a Smurf."

Greeley swerves onto I-85—at the last possible second—and hops into the left lane. The right two lanes are piled up with broken cars, motorcycles, and trucks. People thought they could outrun it, but they had no chance of escape. None of us do. The virus is inside all of us. We are all doomed.

"*She* is right here," I say. My voice wavers, but I'm more determined than ever to assert myself—because I can't escape this car.

Because I'm stuck here with Mr. Nice Guy and a complete bitch who believes me less than. And maybe I am weak, but that doesn't mean I don't deserve respect. "She is a human, and she can speak."

"We know you can speak, Kota," Jasper says, his tone gentle. And that's what pisses me off. Why does he—my kidnapper—get to be sweet? "We're just trying to—"

"I don't care!" Violent noises swirl through my head.

If Jasper and Greeley can't take a single second to think about what just happened, what kind of monsters are they? Not the kind I want to be in leagues with. I chose to run away with them, and at what cost? Will I lose my humanity and turn into a monster, too?

I'm seething as I say, "I know that I'm nothing more than a pawn in this stupid game you're playing with Chandler. I get it. But I'm not your puppet. You don't control me."

"Say the decision was up to you, Kota," Jasper says, his brown eyes filled with pride at my words. He stares at me for a long moment, sizing me up. My heart pounds. "Where would you go?"

I exhale. Close my eyes. Say, "To the forest to get some fucking food."

Greeley pulls her shoulders back and pumps her fist in the air. "She doth locate her spine!"

Jasper shakes his head. "Enough with the theatrics, Greeley."

"In another life, I was a Broadway star." She gestures wide with her arms.

The Jeep lurches to the left.

"Ten and two, Shakespeare." Jasper grabs the wheel and pulls us back into the lane. "Just because there isn't traffic doesn't mean we won't end up in a ditch."

"Your use of double negatives confuses me." Greeley spins around and grabs the headrest, forcing Jasper to take full control of the wheel. "Jasper got his kill," she says, winking at me. "It's time to get ours."

I peer at the gun at my feet.

Greeley's hunting for food, but she may be my first kill.

CHAPTER TWENTY

WO HOURS OF DRIVING DRAG ON.

"Oh my god, I love this song," Greeley says, playing an old CD on the stereo.

"No shocker there," Jasper says.

Greeley turns up the music, and for the next stretch of highway, Nirvana drowns in my ears. Greeley plays "Smells Like Teen Spirit" three times in a row, and I stare blankly out the window, trying not to cry.

"Almost there," she says as we circle up a mountain. "You ready to hunt?"

"Ready as I'll ever be," I say, even though I'm not. Nausea builds as around and around and around we go. I can't help but picture Milo's bloody face at every curve of the mountain. Why do I expect to see him standing on the other side of the bend? Why can't I have a moment to mourn my friend?

I hear Mom's strained whispers in my ear. *I won't be here much longer, sweet girl, but don't stop living. No matter what hardships you face, you must move forward. Breathe for me. Live for me. Keep going.*

I inhale, swelling with resolve.

Okay, Mom. I'll keep going. For you, for West, for Milo.

When we near the top of the mountain, my ears pop. Greeley turns into a gravel parking lot. *Skytop Orchard* is hand-drawn on an old wooden plank piked into cold mud. Brittle yellow leaves float down from tall trees, but the trees themselves bear no fruit.

A tinge of foolish disappointment settles in my belly.

I pull my gaze from the window and catch Jasper's wary eyes in the side-view mirror. He says, "Ever thought you'd see an apple-less apple orchard?"

"It's as beautiful as I imagined," I say flatly.

And while this sad excuse for an orchard is less surprising than, say, zombies, it's another sour reminder of something we'll never get back. An experience I'll never share with my sister, or my dead brother.

"Snap out of it, Blondie." Greeley waves a hand in my face. "Whatever it is you're thinking, move on."

"I'm thinking that you keep calling me Blondie, but *you're* blond, too."

"Only half," she reminds me, flipping down the car visor to check out her jet black roots. "And less every day." Greeley huffs and cranes her neck forward, peering scornfully at the bright sky over the dashboard. "You happy, Pops? You never understood why I hid my heritage, but do you get it now, old man? *Do you get it?*"

"Brakes, Greeley, *brakes*!" Jasper braces himself as we nearly plow into a twenty-foot-tall zombie tree. Its limbs jut out in every direction, reaching for the brittle branches of its neighbors. The Jeep screeches as Greeley hits the brakes, and a slim branch skims over the hood.

"Close one," Greeley says. "Anyone want to do it again?"

"This is our only vehicle. Wreck it, and we have no means to hunt or trade."

Greeley finds my eyes again. "Blondie, have you ever met such a buzzkill?"

"I think I'm going to be sick," I say, unlatching the door and rolling out of the car.

I land on my back, let my head sink into the soft dirt. Cold air bites my cheeks, the sun hiding behind looming gray clouds. The sky will not fall. Humans, animals, plants . . . we will change and we will die. But the sky will linger. The sun and the moon. We are different, but the sky is the same.

A fleshy, bloodstained palm obstructs my view. "Up you go, then," Jasper says, offering his hand. I take it. "Your other one, too."

And then he pulls me up.

I shake mulch out of my hair and look around. We're at the border of the snarled orchard and an open field that leads to an old podunk store. *Apple cider donuts, pastries, and more!*

We're too high up for the bombs and floods to have battered this land, but time and weather weigh on the small storefront. Coppery rust tinges the metal awning, and two cedar pillars sag under its weight. Wind-bruised wood siding peels off in thick olive-green strips. The invisible virus spread to the mountains, though. Water connects us all.

But are there any survivors up here? If so, I can't imagine there are many. The mountains hold their own dangers.

Zombie animals are the darndest things.

It was Milo, actually, who told me why we stay clear of the wild. Three years ago, when Chandler first formed the group that we now refer to as the doughboys, she'd selected the strongest in the community. Young, brazen men with strong muscles and good cardio. They went out on their first supply run into nearby woods, thinking it the perfect place to find meat—the lean, dense protein that our people so desperately needed. Only our community didn't then realize that animals were also affected by the virus. So while the men planned to hunt wild boars, deer, and foxes, they didn't expect to be hunted *by* the zombie versions of those species. They certainly didn't expect to be hunted by a zombie black bear.

Egal lost three men that day.

The last two men—Peter and Milo—wrangled the bear, killed it, and brought it home. Only when they got there, the stench was so great they couldn't bring it inside. Chandler ordered them to skin it, but when they did, they discovered meat so gray it was practically black. They couldn't eat it. Who knows what would happen if they did?

After that, Chandler brought on Indy and Fred—and later me—and banned the doughboys from hunting animals. Zombie animals pose too big a threat.

As for the living, breathing animals, just like humans, if death is a result of a direct impact to the brain, then the zombie virus isn't activated. It's death, plain and simple. But if you miss the animal's temple, you risk a newly born zombie animal attacking you. And you end up with spoiled zombie meat. Yet here I am, at the edge of the woods, hours after watching my friend get killed, hunting.

"I'm thinking deer's on the menu tonight, ladies and gents," Greeley says, rubbing her palms together.

"I'll stick to the edge of the woods," I mutter. "Look for a squirrel . . ."

Greeley rolls her eyes. "Where'd your balls go?"

"Are you serious?"

"It's how she shows she cares," Jasper says, moving to place a hand on my back before thinking better of it. Only, I wish he didn't. I've never needed human touch more than I do right now.

"False," Greeley says. She twirls her knife around, then tromps into the forest without a backward glance.

I turn to Jasper. "If I had an ounce of her confidence . . ."

"You'd be as deadly as a bomb." The corner of his mouth ticks up, and his brown eyes widen. They have threads of amber, like a warm pot of honey. "Come on. I'll show you how it's done."

"What, detonating?"

"I think we've witnessed enough bombs to last us a lifetime. You ready to hunt, or not?"

"Not ready."

He sighs. "You'll be fine. I've got your back." He looks at my hip. "And you've got a gun. Load it."

CHAPTER TWENTY-ONE

THE GOLDEN SUN DIPS BEHIND THE WALL OF TANGLED TREES AHEAD. Dark shadows pepper the earth. As I step into the dense woods, a lithe vine wraps around my ankle like it has a mind of its own. My heart stops. I suck in a breath. What if it *does* have a mind of its own? What if it's the hand of a zombie hiding under a brush, lying flat on its stomach, waiting for prey?

I squeeze my eyes shut as the quick, metallic slice of a knife rings in my ears.

"Open your eyes," Jasper says, kneeling on the ground by my ankles. He holds a limp vine in his hands. "Could've been a lot worse. You're lucky this wasn't a zombie snake."

"Have . . . have you ever come face-to-face with a zombie snake?"

Jasper nods and sheathes his knife. "There's worse in those woods."

"How comforting," I say, the grip on my gun getting sweaty. "I'm completely and utterly at ease." I wipe a palm on my pants and tighten my grip. "So just to confirm—you *do* expect me to trek further into the woods with you?"

"Gotta eat."

"Plenty of peanut butter back home . . ."

"Your choice," he says, then strides ahead.

My choice. Right.

I sigh, square my shoulders, and follow.

As we move deeper into the thicket, wild branches blot out the sun and force the day into night. Dirt crunches beneath our feet. The sound is masked by scuttering birds and chirping crickets, whistling wind and rustling leaves.

A shudder runs down the length of my spine.

Where are all the animals?

The lack of danger makes me clench my gun even tighter.

Jasper's a step in front of me, his muscled shoulders tense. He moves more intentionally than I do, careful to make as little sound as possible. His body ripples with an intensity that tells me he was born to do this. Born to hunt.

I step on something squishy and gasp. Squeeze my eyes shut.

Don't look down, don't look down, don't look down.

I look down.

It's a dead squirrel. Not zombie dead. *Dead* dead. And rotting.

"It's squishy," I groan. "Like Jell-O."

Jasper spins around to face me. His eyes catch mine and send a silent warning. *Quiet*, he mouths.

"Doing my best over here," I snap back.

He bends down, his lips brushing my ear. "Do better."

"Appreciate the support," I say, hoping he doesn't notice the stupid blush that spreads from my ears to my neck.

Really, Kota, feeling butterflies at a time like this? Bottle it up.

Jasper's words are hushed as he says, "You'll appreciate not being eaten."

As he pulls away, I quickly kneel, keeping my head bent, and rub the sole of my shoe on a rock. "Oops—did you want to keep the squirrel goop? Save it as a snack for later? We could still scrape it in a Ziplock and freeze it to make popsicles—"

Jasper puts his pointer finger against my lips, shushing me. "Quiet."

"You're right," I whisper against the fleshy pad of his finger. He pulls back, leaving behind the tastes of copper and dirt on my lips. "We don't have freezers anymore. Dammit."

"Kota."

I open my mouth to send another quip his way, but from the look he's giving me, I think he's about ready to smear *me* against a rock. There's no hint of humor on his face. So I glue my jaw shut.

Stop sabotaging yourself. Do you want to die? Focus.

Just last week, I was chiding Indy for making too much noise in the face of danger. I should follow my own advice.

I take a deep breath, open my eyes, and mouth *Sorry* before zipping up my lips and tossing the key.

We creep deeper into the dark, trembling woods. The temperature drops, and cold air numbs the tips of my fingers. Monstrous trees blanket the sun completely. Goose bumps prick my arms. Something white zips between two boulders—a fluffy tail, like a puffball.

A bunny.

Bunny.

In front of me, Jasper pauses. He holds out an arm, motioning for me to stay still. I squeeze the knife in my right hand and shift to grab the gun with my left. Jasper shakes his head.

A nearby bramble shakes. My heart rate spikes. My ears hum. Jasper nods, signaling me to move forward. This is real. He is giving me the opportunity to make the kill.

I'm going to kill a bunny.

My palm sweats as I squeeze the life out of my balisong. I take a small step toward the prickly, overgrown, *moving* bush. I'm going to end up with a stick up my ass.

I drop to my knees and crawl. The bush rustles.

One.

I extend an arm.

Two.

I breathe in deep.

Three.

I jam my arm into the bush and wrench out my hand—and with it, a white, breathing, bouncing ball of fur.

The bunny squeals as I pull it into my chest. "Shhh," I prompt, petting its head. It tries to break free, but I hold it tight.

"We're not adopting it, Kota," Jasper says. "Make the kill."

I look at the bunny in its big black eyes and see my sister. Innocent, joyful, alive. I look into its eyes and see Milo. Humorous, caring, determined.

I pet the bunny's soft ears.

Why does my life outweigh that of this sweet creature? Why can't we bring it home and keep it as a pet? Why can't we stick to scavenging?

Because, Kota, there's barely anything left. Not even at Costco. What are you willing to do to survive?

Jasper sighs. "You're making this harder on yourself. Get it done."

"I—" I can't. Salt-tinged tears wet the dirt on my skin and drip down my face. *I wish I were more like you,* is what I want to say.

A deep, monstrous squeal jolts me out of my thoughts. Jasper's eyes widen. This is the first time he's actually looked afraid.

"*Fuck,*" he whispers, then pulls the bunny out of my hands. I stand frozen as he shoves his blade into its brain. Blood spurts on my face. I can't bring myself to wipe it off. He unzips his backpack and places the bunny's limp body inside.

Another raw, blood-curdling squeal rumbles through the woods. Birds scatter. The ground shakes.

"Run," he whispers.

Jasper takes my hand and pulls me through the woods. Deafening squawks rip through the trees, growing louder and louder.

What is that thing?

I've never moved so fast in my life. Whatever beast is chasing us is on our tail. And it's coming for us.

We're the prey.

Adrenaline pumps through my veins. My thighs burn with every step. I keep my eyes on my feet as I step over loose rocks, gnarled roots, and sharp twigs jutting out of the ground.

Don't trip, Kota. Don't you dare trip.

"Shit," Jasper murmurs.

The beast grows louder.

"What," I say through shallow breaths, "is," I press through my feet, launch myself forward with all the strength I can muster, "it?" *And can we grow wings and fly away?*

Jasper's grip on my hand tightens. I know he can run faster than me, but he isn't leaving. He isn't leaving. "Wild boar."

The woods become so dense that there's no path forward. The trees have melded into one giant, menacing wall. Jasper stops dead in his tracks.

"Climb," he says, pointing to a divot in a zombie tree.

He helps hoist me up. I find a sturdy branch and pull myself onto it, crawling up the rough bark. I sit in the crook of the mottled tree and make room for Jasper. Only he's not climbing. *He's not climbing.*

Instead, he stands in front of the mammoth tree trunk, pointing his gun straight ahead, his shoulders braced. I gasp. The boar emerges from behind a patch of trees. It's easily the most disgusting thing I've ever seen.

Massive yellowed incisors line the bottom of its detached jaw. Its mouth is twice the size of my head, and it sputters and drools like a rabid dog. It splatters nearby trees with spit as it sings a horrible anthem of destruction. It wants violence. It wants Jasper. It wants me.

The undead animal surges forward, its claws tearing into the earth, pulling out loose roots and flinging rocks every which way. Dark pink bruised skin peeks through patches of gruff, wiry hair. Like a man balding in patches across his head. Or a lawn that's been seeded but is struggling to grow.

Or my brain trying to focus on the danger at hand.

Focus.

The boar lunges, leaping off the ground like a goddamn acrobat.

"Jasper!" I scream, right as he pulls the trigger.

The shot is clean. The bullet goes right through the beast's skull, and its warped, bloated body falls forward onto him. The two pitch backward and land with a *thud* that shakes the earth. The boar's body pins Jasper down. The two lie there, unmoving, as leaves settle around them. Is he . . . ?

I block the thought out before it can fully form.

No one else. Not today.

I jump off the tree and drop to my knees. Rocks and sticks leave angry red marks on my palms as I scramble toward them on all fours. I dust my hands on my thighs before placing them on the boar. One, two, three, *shove*. It doesn't move. Not an inch.

Jasper's head pokes out from beneath the boar, and I breathe a sigh of relief.

"Are you all right?" I ask.

He offers the slightest of nods.

"Let me try this." I shove my arm under the boar's bloated stomach in search of Jasper's hand. I try not to gag as the boar's stench wafts off its body. The odor is a putrid combination of sewage, unwashed hair, and expired Brussels sprouts.

I find Jasper's arm and pull.

"You're gonna rip it out of the socket," he says.

"What else am I supposed to do?"

"Use your legs."

"My legs?"

"Trust me."

"Last time I trusted you, I—"

"What? Got eaten by a zombie boar? No, wait, you didn't because I saved us."

"You want out from under this thing or what?" I challenge him with my eyes.

"Please," Jasper says. "Help."

I smirk and lower myself to my back. My hair snags on some twigs as I shuffle toward the boar, convincing myself I can do this. Jasper nods encouragingly. *He* seems to think I can do this. I crack my knuckles, square my shoulders, and push. My thighs burn with the exertion. I heave like I'm giving birth to this zombie pig.

I reckon three contractions pass until the boar lifts just enough for Jasper to wriggle out. Every muscle in my body loosens as I flop backward next to Jasper. We lie there together looking up at the blanket of trees.

"Can check that one off the bucket list," I say.

Jasper turns his head toward me. It makes me uncomfortable, this look he's giving me. Like he can see that a tangle of emotions lies behind my quips: pain and shock and horror and hope.

"Have you ever had a close call?" he asks.

"You mean with death? Yeah," I say, the words coming out breathless. "Trying to get insulin for my sister at a Walgreens. That's how I ended up in Egal. Peter found us." His name tastes like vinegar on my tongue.

"For what it's worth," Jasper says, rolling his head back up toward the canopy of trees. "I wish someone else had found you."

I stiffen, questions tumbling through my mind. If Jasper found us and brought us back to Macoby, would things be different? Would Bunny and Grandma have better care? Would we be not just surviving, but *living*?

I open my mouth to respond—to agree, I think—but the sound of leaves crunching stops me short.

If there's another zomboar in these woods . . .

"Sup, losers!" Greeley emerges from the woods, a white-tailed deer slung over her shoulders. She walks as if the limp body weighs one pound, not a hundred. "What's all the commotion about?" She looks down and gives the boar a little kick. "Big boy you got there. Who's up for bacon?"

"We need to go." Jasper stands, leaning his weight on his left leg. "There are probably more where it came from."

"Y'all get anything edible?"

Jasper nods. "A bunny."

Greeley scoffs. "Hope you like the taste of hunger." She turns toward me. Her eyes widen when I push myself to a stand, and my knees crack. "What about you, Miss Balls of Steel? Got milk?"

"No," I say, disappointment filling my belly. "I got nothing."

"Pity," she says, striding up to me. She drops the deer, bends down, and gives my knees a tap. "No utters to suck from around here. Have to fend for yourself if you want these bones to grow big and strong."

I want to kick her. I should kick her.

Jasper leans toward me and whispers, "Don't kick her. You'll be sorry."

"Thanks," I mutter. Greeley hauls up the deer and swings around. The antlers bump my head. "*I'm going to—*"

Jasper places a gentle hand on my shoulder. "Don't."

We stand there, still, watching Greeley go back the way we came.

I sort of wish I were the deer right now. At least I'd be at peace. At least I'd have a purpose. At least I'd be carried.

CHAPTER TWENTY-TWO

N THE WAY HOME, MY STOMACH GROWLS MORE THAN ONCE. Worse than the hunger, though, is the settling stone of disappointment. If I can't kill even to feed myself, what hope is there for me? Would I be able to kill for Grandma, for Bunny? What if it's not that I *can't* kill, but that I don't *want* to? Would I doom us all to starve?

I let my head sag against the headrest and close my eyes. I place my hands in my pockets to keep them warm. My fingertips brush against a plastic bottle.

How could I forget?

I have something to trade. And getting it didn't require killing.

ROP ME HERE," JASPER SAYS.

By now, I know to brace myself for Greeley's driving, so I dig my fingernails into the seat's fabric at his words. For the first time, I don't slam into her headrest as we come to a screeching halt. Instead, I'm elated. Victorious. Triumphant. And then she hits the gas again and veers to the right. Accelerates down a side street.

"Brakes!" Jasper yells.

Greeley sticks her tongue out and blows a raspberry, but she stops the car.

A cardboard sign is staked into the ground with *Robbins Lane* scribbled in faded Sharpie on the surface. At the end of the street is a single house, the years of blight hidden in the dark night. Jasper grabs his backpack and steps out of the Jeep.

"Where are you going?" I ask.

Greeley turns around, one hand on the headset. "You ever seen a Snickers commercial?"

"I'm not sure I want to answer that question."

" 'You're not you when you're hungry,' " she mimics, jabbing a thumb at Jasper. He glides down the street like a ballerina on speed. "That one turns into a silent diva when he's hungry."

"You're one to talk," I mutter.

She cocks her head to the side. A slight smile takes shape on her lips. "Come again?"

"Thanks for the ride," I say, hopping out of the car.

I slam the door behind me and jog to catch up to Jasper, my chest burning with every step. Nausea rolls through my empty stomach, and I throw my hands on my thighs before I puke. Only, nothing comes out. I spit out a mucusy wad of saliva and close my eyes. Breathe. Wait for my heart rate to come back down.

Ahead of me, Jasper says, "You made your choice. I'm not sharing."

I hock out another spit. "I wasn't asking." Hand shaking, I pull the pill bottle out of my pocket and give it a shake.

His eyes widen. "What's that?"

"Aspirin. Want some?"

Jasper shakes his head and turns around. "You can't come." Though he walks toward the house, his pace is much slower than before—and still, he keeps all the weight on the right.

"I know you need it," I call, giving the bottle another shake. The pills rattle. "Your leg hurts. Doesn't it? It's sprained."

Jasper turns around, takes three steps toward me, and pauses. "What do you want for a pill, Kota? Spit it out."

I stand and point at the white farmhouse illuminated in the dark. "What's in that house?"

"A hot meal."

"That's what I want."

"Fine," Jasper says.

"Fine what?" I ask.

"You've got a deal."

I tuck the pills into my pocket and extend a hand. "Shake on it, I insist."

As he extends a hand, I spit into mine.

"I'm not doing a spit shake," Jasper says.

"Blood oath?"

"Just—give me your other hand."

"No," I say, wiping my spit-covered hand on my pants. I grab his hand and shake it so hard that my whole body moves, then give him three pills. "Shall we do this thing?"

He sighs and pops the pills into his mouth. "I guess so."

JASPER KNOCKS ON THE BATTERED DOOR THREE TIMES. WHEN NO ONE answers, he sticks an ear to it and turns the knob. I follow him inside and shut the door, taking in the modest entryway. It's dark but warm in here, the light like golden honey. A single tea candle glows between a photo of a family smiling in front of the Eiffel Tower and a framed ink stamp of an infant's footprints.

The space opens into a much brighter living room, set alight with candles of every shape and size. The excess sends a wave of shock through me. In Egal, each household is allowed one candle per week. Where have the owners of this home found these candles? Or what have they traded to get them?

On a threadbare teal sofa sit two salt-and-pepper heads: one long and curly, the other short and wiry. They twist around at our entrance, then pop off the sofa like Whac-A-Moles.

"Nobody panic," Jasper says. "It's just me."

"And me," I whisper to myself.

"And her," Jasper says louder as the couple bustles over to us.

I lean up toward his face. "You've got ears of a bat, you know that?" His mouth ticks up. "What're you smirking about?"

"My sister used to say the same thing."

"Your sister." I nearly forgot Jasper doesn't exist in a silo. He's a real human, with a family and relationships and thoughts and feelings. He has a history, and it's brought him here, to *this* side of the Split, to this home. For better or worse, my history has brought me here, too. We're in this together. We all are.

My train of thought comes to a halt when the man and woman squish Jasper in a bear hug.

"Careful, Sling, you'll scratch Jasper to death with that beard of yours," the woman says. The man's beard, black as night, reaches his collarbone and looks to be made of steel wool.

The man—Sling—chuckles deep from his belly and pulls back, keeping his hands wrapped around Jasper's upper arms. He gives them a squeeze.

"A bit of style adds light to an otherwise bleak world, don't ya think, son?"

As if reading my mind, Jasper turns toward me and says, "Sling's not my dad."

"Ah, but Jas here *is* part of the Robbins family, no doubt!" Sling looks at me expectantly. I force a pathetic excuse for a laugh out of my mouth. Sling doesn't catch the facade, though, smiling wide as he gestures us forward. "Into the kitchen, kiddos."

I follow him to the left into the small L-shaped kitchen. Open cabinets line the walls, and well-loved pots and pans hang from the ceiling. My boots leave muddy marks on the tile floor, and a stitch of guilt rolls through my body. Though chipped, the tiles are bright and clean, and I'm a grimy, uninvited mooch. But as soon as I see it—the crème de la crème—the uncomfortable feeling washes away. Anticipation kicks in.

They have a gas stove. And a tank of propane.

"Clara!" I jump backward as the woman shouts through the house. "Oops! Didn't mean to frighten you, dear." She gives my arm a squeeze, which only makes me more skittish. "*Clara!* Young lady, get *in* here. Jasper is here! And he's brought a guest—a *lady* guest!" Deep dimples pucker her cheeks as she smiles, her eyes as frantic as her tapping foot. Mom always said to watch out for people with blue eyes like hers. "Your name, sweetheart?"

"Kota," I say, overcome with the desire to dig a hole and hide in it. This woman gives off more energy than the Jocassee hydraulic system.

Jasper clears his throat, and all attention shifts toward him. He plops his backpack down on the counter and pulls out the dead bunny by the ears. It hangs limply in the air like a half-stuffed animal. "We brought dinner."

The woman tucks a stray gunpowder curl behind her ears. She claps her wrinkled hands together. "Fabulous! Just *fabulous*! My dear, it's so wonderful to meet you. Jasper's never brought home a guest, never mind one so effervescent—you must be quite important to him." She winks.

My stomach drops. Effervescent? That's a new one. And untrue. I'm probably the dullest, most drained version of myself I've ever been.

She pulls a hand from my side and shakes. Holy shit. If she keeps this up, I'll lose circulation. "Nice to meet you," I say, struggling to think about anything other than this woman squeezing my hand like Grandma making lemonade.

"Oh! How rude—I haven't even introduced myself." She drops my hand—*thank god*—and slaps a palm against her forehead. "I'm Bama, like the state. Roll, tide, roll! And this is my husband, Sling."

Sling smiles widely and waves a butcher knife.

Jasper offers him the bunny, and he cuts off both ears with one fell swoop.

Clonk.

"No meat in those," he says. "All cartilage. Much too chewy."

Bama nods. "Save the fur, though, honey. Clara needs mittens for the winter." She bustles past me and pulls open a stocked pantry. "We've got canned carrots and dried mashed potatoes—Hungry Jack. Have you ever had Hungry Jack, dear?"

"No." Bama's wide eyes linger on mine like she's waiting for a better response. Okay, then. "That sounds wonderful, thank you. Your house is beautiful."

"*This* mess? You're too kind, dear, too kind!"

How long has it been since this woman has interacted with strangers? Is she always like this? Her frantic behavior sets me on edge.

As I try to think of what to say to Bama next—how to get her bug eyes off me—a small child, maybe seven years old, emerges from the back door. Bama pivots her attention to her. *Saved by the bell.* "Clara, my sweet child, meet our guest. She's brought a rabbit!"

A jagged scar runs down the left side of her face, from her cheek to her chin, but it only makes her cuter. I briefly wonder where she got it, but push the thought aside. We all have scars.

She extends a tiny palm up to me, hands covered in charcoal, and says, "Hi, I'm Clara."

"Hi, Clara, I'm Kota. I like your pigtails," I tell her, and I do. They're lopsided and slapdash, pieces of black hair strewn in every which way.

"Thanks. Can you help me up?" she asks bluntly.

I find Bama's gaze, and she winks, so I pull her up onto a stool, right in front of the now-decapitated bunny. Clara watches as her parents hastily prepare the kitchen for cooking. Sling lights the gas stove with a match while Bama hoists herself onto the counter and unhooks a pot from the ceiling rack. They weave between one another with chaos and urgency, but somehow don't stumble or knock into each other once. The couple is helter-skelter, certainly, but they're a well-oiled machine.

If their food is as good as their coordination, they'd have been great on *Chopped*.

"Clara, elbows *OFF* the counter!"

"What can we do to help?" Jasper asks, coming to stand beside me.

We.

If all I am is a hostage to him, why does he treat me as an equal—as someone he actually cares about?

More importantly, why do *I* care how he sees me?

"Oh, nothing, nothing," Bama says. "You've already done too much—bringing us meat and an effervescent date!" *Did she learn that word today?* "Why don't you two go wash up in the creek out back? There's a bar of soap on the big rock next to the dog statue."

I follow Jasper out the door Clara burst through, and whoa, she wasn't kidding about the dog statue. Sitting three feet tall is a near-perfect-condition stone statue of a Great Dane.

"That's Darcy," Jasper says, grabbing a half-dissolved bar of soap off the rock. "Well, Darcy's buried underneath." I jump back. Jasper laughs. "Don't worry. She's *dead* dead."

"How'd they build this statue?"

"They didn't build it, that's how. Sling comes out sometimes with me and Greeley. Found it in a vintage store. We were looking for building materials. He convinced us it was imperative to bring it home for Bama. For her birthday."

"That's . . . sweet, I guess."

"And a stupid waste of resources. Could've fit a whole deer in its place."

"Love makes people do crazy things."

Jasper shakes his head. "I don't think it was an act of love. He needed some semblance of normalcy. Needed to feel he had control over his surroundings."

"Or maybe he just wanted to make this house a home."

Jasper shrugs, and I follow him to the small babbling creek behind the house. Two of the two homes I've been to have a creek? How did the Egal side of the Split get so unlucky? We only get fresh water once a week, and the Macs get to go apeshit with it?

My thoughts dissipate as I dip my hand into the cold water. Chills run through my body. I suck in a breath through my teeth, determined not to miss this opportunity to get clean. The smell of the wild boar clings to my skin and lingers in my nostrils. An image of the bloated beast's inert body sticks in the space behind my eyes. I blink as Jasper jumps into the shallow depths, spraying me with icy water.

"Seriously?" But he can't hear me below the surface. For a while, he doesn't come up for air. Damn, his lung capacity is impressive.

My toes curl as I submerge my feet in the creek. I use an exposed root to scrape off crusty dirt, and when I move to scrub the dried blood off my hands, I get a twisted satisfaction from picking it out from under my fingernails. The apocalypse broke my nail-biting habit. Before, I'd nip Grandma's rose-colored nail polish from the third shelf in her bathroom cabinet to paint my nails. *Lovely*, she'd say. *Now don't ruin them with that nasty mouth of yours.* And then, I'd ruin them, mere hours later. Every. Single. Time.

Nowadays, my nails are painted with blood; they're chipped and jagged without the involvement of my hungry mouth. I'll always be hungry, won't I? Nails, food, water, or brains, I'll never be satisfied.

Jasper comes up for air, shaking the water out of his hair like a wet dog.

"Dude. Can you not?"

"Dude. You're sitting at the edge of the creek. What do you expect?" He hoists himself up and sits down next to me. Then he throws his work boots into the creek and watches as they fill with water before sinking to the bottom. When he pulls his sopping boots out and slings them on the ground, the water washes onto my legs.

"Seriously, enough with the water!"

"Just helping you clean up. You've got some guts there." He points to my shoe. "And some blood there." His finger shifts to my shoulder. "And a spot of dirt there."

He boops my nose, and I swat his hand away, glaring. Jasper's growing casualness toward me is clear as day, but I refuse to give in.

You are not my friend.

I dip my hand in water and rub the apparent dirt off my nose. The water doesn't feel cold anymore, but my fingers have turned a shade of purple. "So, who are Sling and Bama? How'd you meet?"

"You don't know Sling?"

"Should I?"

"He was a big-time newscaster back in the day. On WYFF4—the Greenville Daily Report."

I look down at my knees. "I only ever watched national broadcasts," I admit. "Grandma never watched the news before Jenkins was elected president. She preferred *Wheel of Fortune.*"

"Well," Jasper says, "I interned for WYFF4 in college. Not that I wanted to be a producer, but Mom and Dad banned me from art school, and making shit graphics for the broadcasts seemed easy. That's to say, I knew Sling before Z Day. We stumbled into one another a couple weeks after finding the Split and sort of stuck together once the community divided into Egal and Macoby. Sling's a kick-ass butcher, so I share meat in exchange for his services."

"You don't ever bring him human meat, do you?"

"Kota, we're not cannibals."

Right. Not cannibals. I can trust these people, can't I? Why is giving in so hard?

Another thought comes to mind. "If Sling was a newscaster, does he know what happened to Jenkins? You know, after he and his psychotic followers blew everything up?"

"Whoa, slow down," Jasper says. "Just before everything went dark, Sling got word that Jenkins is hiding out in California—that there's a safe haven in Los Angeles."

"Seriously?" This is huge. This information could change everything. I could take Bunny and Grandma and we could—

"Before you get too excited," Jasper says, reading my mind, "I've already considered it. There's no way to get to California alive. You think downtown's bad? Now imagine traveling through cities four times the size of Greenville. Imagine the zombies. Imagine traveling through the wilderness—coming face-to-face with zombie lions and tigers and bears."

"Oh my."

Jasper smirks. "Fell into that one, didn't I?" He rakes a hand down his stubbled jaw. "In all seriousness, think about the zoos that were destroyed on Z Day and the thousands of animals that escaped as a result. They're roaming across the country in zombie form now."

I never considered that. "What do you think is worse—zombie chimpanzees or zombie crocodiles? Wait, no. Zombie Komodo dragons. *Zomodo* dragons. Dear lord."

Jasper ignores my comment. Doesn't even entertain me for one second. The nerve. "There are actual cannibals out there, Kota. Now imagine traveling across the country with your sister and grandmother."

I imagine it. It's not a pretty sight.

"So, then." I sigh. "There really is no hope, is there? We're stuck here, in the Split, forever."

Jasper sticks his hand in the stream, swirling the dirty water like paint. We sit there for a minute, lingering in the silence.

After a beat, Jasper opens his mouth to speak. "I know what I said, but . . . I will never lose hope. A better world exists for us; we just have to find it. If we're patient and resourceful—and if we refuse to give up—we will find it."

"Or maybe," I whisper, "we'll create this better world for ourselves."

Jasper turns to me. His soft brown eyes find mine. I study his face: his strong brows, thick lashes, Roman nose. If Z Day never happened, would Jasper still be at the news station? Or would he have eventually defied his parents to pursue his dream? I like to think that Jasper would have taken his life into his own hands. That if things were different, he'd be painting right now.

"Jasper." I stick my own hand into the cold water and squeeze his. *Thank you.* Thank you for sharing your story with me. Thank you for helping me see our limited existence differently. Thank you for opening my eyes. "I'm really glad you're not a cannibal."

Jasper smiles. By the way his hand squeezes mine back, he seems to understand what my words actually mean.

CHAPTER TWENTY-THREE

BAMA EMERGES FROM THE HOUSE AND WHISTLES LIKE A BIRD. "Dinner!" she calls, her Southern accent sweet and thick like honey. "Dinner is ready!"

"Heard you the first time, Bam," Jasper responds.

I catch his arm.

"Wait," I say. "I just realized—you traded the rabbit, but I didn't give them anything."

"Your company is what they want," Jasper says. "That's more important to them than a couple tabs of aspirin."

"Really?"

"Really."

I'm not certain I believe Jasper until we walk inside. Five hot, steaming plates sit on the dining table. An actual, real-life, three-dimensional dining table. In a dining room! It's even dressed with a plaid red tablecloth. In the center of the table, a warm candle melts in an antique candle holder. I'm suddenly six years old again at Grandma's house for supper on a summer afternoon, clothed in my Sunday best, holding a tray of ready-to-bake Pillsbury sugar cookies.

This display might be the most beautiful thing I've ever seen. Each plate is set properly with a fabric napkin and utensils. And on the plates themselves, there are equal servings. Each has a hunk of fire-roasted meat, sliced carrots, and fluffy mashed potatoes.

If only there were room for two more seats at this table. How can I enjoy this meal knowing Grandma and Bunny had shriveled rations tonight? I wonder if they sat beneath the stained glass window, hunger pangs hushed as they ate bread made by an arthritic old woman and a couple of spoons of expired fucking chickpeas. Did they look out the window and think of me? Did they believe they're the lucky ones, that it's *me* who's starving in Macoby?

"Ah," Sling says, placing a fabric napkin over his lap. He sinks into his seat with a grin. As he takes a deep breath, the tension in his shoulders visibly releases. I try it for myself, but can't say I'm successful. I'm still wearing my shoulders like earrings. "What a nice meal. Thank you, my Banana Bama." He extends an arm and squeezes Bama's shoulder, who takes a seat to his left.

Clara stacks three books atop her seat—Yellow Pages, *Harry Potter*, and the Bible—and perches herself on top. She scrunches her face as her parents make kissy faces at one another.

"*Moooom. Daaaad. Stooooop.*"

"Clara!" Bama says, pulling away from Sling. "What did I say about elbows on the table? And—*are you sitting on the Bible?* Off you go, young lady!" I quickly pull my own elbows off the table as Clara tugs the Bible from beneath her butt and drops it on the table. "Be gentle, dear, that's Jesus you're holding in your hands. Now, shall we say Grace?"

I look down at the hunk of bunny meat on my plate. *Bunny is alive and well. Bunny is alive and well. Bunny is alive and—*

I jerk backward as everyone clasps their hands together, then bows their heads. Bama, Sling, Clara, and Jasper close their eyes in unison like robots. I stare in silence. Under the floor-length tablecloth, Jasper nudges me with his foot. I look to my left. Jasper cracks open an eye and winks at me. I groan silently but bow my head anyway. Anything for a bite of food.

"Dear Lord," Bama begins, "we thank you for this meal, for this shelter, for this company. Clara, would you care to finish the offering?"

"Bless us, O Lord, and These Thy gifts—"

Hard work, not gifts.

"Which we are about to receive, Through Thy bounty—"

Through Jasper's bounty.

"Through Christ our Lord, we pray. Amen."

Bama claps, the sound like a gunshot. "Amen!" she practically sings. "Let us eat!"

As I stare down at my plate, I realize I haven't had meat in three years. The smell is undoubtedly mouthwatering, but I'm scared of what it might do to my stomach. And I'd be dishonest if I said I wasn't scared it would poison me.

I'll start with the sides, let the others go first.

The table is silent except for the scraping of metal on ceramic plates, which I'm thankful for, because the last thing I want to do is talk. I want to gorge myself. To taste every bite. To—

OhmygoddidIjustorgasm?

I let out a moan as warm, fluffy potatoes slide down my throat. They're almost . . . buttery? But there's no way. There are no cows around here for milking. It's been so long since I've had anything so good, so fresh. The closest I've come is Grandma's bread. While that bread *is* divine, the portions are always so small. Never enough. Bama and Sling have given us so much. They may be Jesus lovers, but they're good people. Nothing like Mrs. Patty back home. *Repent or perish! Repent or perish!*

I try the carrots next. Sweet, soft, full of earthy flavor. A slight twinge of aluminum, the result of having sat in the can for several years. It's easy to ignore.

"You're not a vegetarian, are you, dear?" Bama asks, staring at my plate. In the span of a few minutes, I've achieved a squeaky clean plate—besides the portion of rabbit. Bama tilts her head to the side, her gray curls spilling over her shoulders like a veil.

"No, it's just . . . been a while."

Bama simply stares at me, her hands resting gently on the table. Right. It's my turn then. I slowly bring a forkful to my mouth and chew. The rabbit is tender and gamey, and the meat melts onto my tongue. My belly expands with food. The last meal that left me satiated like this was Zaxby's sandwich in between races at a swim meet.

Bama swallows a mouthful of potato and sets her fork down. "Clara, how was school today?"

"Max is so bad at the multiplication table, Mom." She raises her black eyebrows and bites into a carrot. "It only took *me* forty-five seconds to complete."

Sling says, "Way to go!" at the same time Bama goes, "It's not kind to put others down, Clara," and I blurt out, "You go to school?"

Clara looks around the table as if unsure who to respond to. Sling takes the mic. "Of course," he says. "A child's education is very important." Bama nods her head in agreement.

"Where do you go to school?"

"Just down the road," Clara says. "On Sycamore Street."

"And there are other kids that go?"

"You live here, don't you, dear?" Bama says, cocking her head to the side. "You don't know about school?"

I look at Jasper, who warns me with his eyes to play cool. "Actually, I'm from E—"

Jasper interrupts me, saying, "Kota doesn't watch the news."

Sling and Bama burst into giggles. Clara glances between the adults like she doesn't understand.

"That's not funny," I say. Their laughter dims. "Know what else isn't funny? Kidnapping. As I was saying before I was interrupted, I'm from Egal. And I was kidnapped by *him*."

Thick silence envelops the table as our Southern hosts absorb the new information. No forks move to mouths; no knives clank on plates. Bama doesn't even blink when Clara's elbows find the table once again.

"Did you all hear me?" I say. "He kidnapped m—"

Bama picks up her fork and takes a dainty bite of bunny. "Better off here, though, isn't that right, dear? Sweet Jasper here did you a favor."

"I'm a hostage."

"Well," Bama continues, "one could consider Clara here a hostage if you want to go that route."

"Mom." Clara scrunches her nose. "What does *hostage* mean?"

Bama waves her off. "She is 'forced' to sleep under our roof, certainly, but we clothe her, we feed her, we take her to school. We're her *guardians.* Now, that's a fresh perspective, isn't it?"

Sling starts, "Bama—"

Through gritted teeth, I say, "What if you were taken into Egal, and Clara here was left to fend for herself? And you had no power to get back to her? You had no way of knowing she was safe? How would you feel about that 'guardian'?"

"That's all theoretical—"

"Mom! Tell her I can take care of myself, for fuck's sake!"

"CLARA!"

I can't think beyond the anger seeping into my bones. Anger for Bunny. Because she could be here, learning, eating. Grandma could be here instead of this wacky woman. I clench my fists, jagged fingernails biting into the palm of my hand.

I direct my next words at Bama, but keep my eyes trained on Jasper. He looks down blankly at his empty plate. "You'd do anything to protect Clara, wouldn't you?"

Silence fills the room. Nobody knows what to say. That's fine; they don't need to say anything. They understand.

The legs of my chair scrape against the wood floor as I thrust backward in my seat. I stand and hurl my napkin at my empty plate. "If you'll excuse me."

This place. This place is not what I expected. And I hate it.

Because it's better.

And Bunny, Grandma, and I . . . we can't have it.

CHAPTER TWENTY-FOUR

WHERE'S YOUR RESTROOM?" I DON'T EVEN KNOW WHY I ASK. Muscle memory, maybe? I've pissed in a latrine for the past two years, our bathrooms having been converted into storage. Sling and Bama have probably done the same. Whatever. I need privacy.

"Just by Clara's room," Sling says, interrupting my thoughts. "Rigged the plumbing system myself." His chest fills like a balloon with pride, and I don't want to pop it. He should be as proud as he sounds. Shitting on a toilet is a luxury.

When Sling turns to point me in the direction of the bathroom, he hits Bama's plate with his elbow, and it lands upside down onto her lap. She's finished everything but her hunk of meat, but she recovers quickly, flipping the rabbit back onto the plate.

Bama says, "No worries, dear, five-second rule!"

There's bits of dust and lint on the meat, but that doesn't stop Bama from shoving the last of it into her mouth.

"I'll get going, then," I say, heading down the hallway.

Tea lights line the floor, casting dim shadows along the peeling walls. I stop before reaching the restroom. The door on the right, painted white, has a crooked *C* etched into it.

I tune into the conversation happening in the dining room. Sling's going on about Tide To Go Pens. Wasteful, he says, when you could use a tub of bleach and a bag.

We got too reliant on conveniences. Too fond of consumerism. There! You see? Bit of bleach got that meat stain right out of your skirt, Bammy.

While I'm undeniably curious to hear his full opinion on the matter, I'm more interested in what's behind this door.

I grasp the handle, the metal cold to the touch. With one last look over my shoulder, I quietly turn the knob to Clara's room and tiptoe inside. I shut the door behind me and rest my head against the wood. Just to breathe. Just to soak it in for a second—soak in everything that Bunny could have had. Everything that she still could.

I walk to the windowsill and pick up the large scented candle lighting the room. It smells like warm cinnamon and sweet pumpkin, and reminds me of Thanksgiving. We don't celebrate anymore. For obvious reasons.

A fluffy, albeit dingy, white rug spans the length of the room, and a peach blanket covers the small twin bed. In the center of the room is a small table strewn with crinkled paper and colored pencils. I pick up a random sheet and bring the paper close to my face to read the words scrawled at the top of the page—in handwriting that's impressive for Clara's age. *When I grow up, I want to be . . .* Below the words, Clara has drawn an astronaut in green and blue.

You're not the only one who wants to depart from this galaxy, girlfriend.

I set the paper down and decide to inspect the contents of her dresser next. I shouldn't. I know I shouldn't. I'm invading her privacy. But . . . I want to see her clothes. I want to know what she has.

I pull open the top drawer. A soft pink camisole is folded atop jean shorts, and to the right, little socks with cats printed on them are bunched up. And—*is that what I think it is?*

There, underneath a pair of flower-patterned leggings, is a gun. A child has a gun. Does she know it's in here? Should I tell her parents and—

"What are you doing with my pistol?"

I spin around. Clara stands behind me, in front of the closed door, her arms crossed over her chest and eyebrows raised.

"This is yours?"

"Sure is. And it's loaded, so I'd be careful if I was you." I put the gun back into the drawer, feeling Clara's eyes glaring at my backside. "You shouldn't go through people's things. Mommy and Daddy say it's an invasion of privacy."

"You're right. I'm sorry. It's just—I have a sister. She's a few years older than you, but—"

"You were going to steal my stuff for her."

"No! No, of course not."

Clara shrugs. "Wouldn't be surprised. That's how things work around here. People steal shit, and Mommy and Daddy say there ain't nothing we can do about it." Clara narrows her eyes and takes a step toward me. "And you don't look too trustworthy to me. What's in your pockets?"

"My pockets?"

She nods.

"Um . . ." I flip them inside out. Clara inspects the bottle of aspirin and vial of insulin clutched in my hands.

"Can I have the pills?"

"No."

She huffs, walks over to the table, and sinks into the little wooden seat. After pondering the array of crayons spread before her, Clara picks purple. She scribbles eagerly on a piece of paper.

I say, "Do you mind if I ask—why *do* you have a gun?"

"To protect myself from thieves, of course."

"But the treaty says no gun use inside the Split . . . and there's no way your parents let you outside the gates . . ."

"Mommy and Daddy say better safe than sorry." She picks up a light pink crayon and gets back to scribbling. Her message is crystal clear: This conversation is over.

"Well," I say, opening the door. "It was nice meeting you."

She looks up and hands me the paper. "Here," she says. "I know we ate it, but Mommy says we should always remember where our food comes from, because a lot of people don't have any."

I choke out a thank-you and leave. Closing the door behind me, I clutch the drawing of the bunny close to my heart. The door shuts with a soft *click*.

CHAPTER TWENTY-FIVE

VIVID DREAMS OF SLING'S TOILET SWIRL THROUGH MY subconscious. I sit tall on a throne of porcelain, flushing again and again simply because I can. It never ceases to satisfy me, watching the clear water get sucked down the drain. The toilet makes a whirring noise, and I giggle with giddiness. Only, my laughs soon turn to screams.

The toilet opens its wide mouth and drags me under. I spin around, my shoulders submerged beneath the surface. The water is warm as it inches up my neck, reaches my chin, then wets my lips.

No. This can't be happening.

I take one final breath before my head plunges into the water and—

I awake with a scream, my body soaked in sweat. Sheets swaddle me like a cocoon, warm from the sunlight streaming through the window. I twist and turn until I'm free, then use the small dresser next to the bed to hoist myself up. My palm slides on a thin sheet of paper. Clara's drawing. Clara. A child armed with crayons and a gun.

A wave of curiosity overwhelms me. What if there's a gun in the dresser?

I yank it open.

There's no gun. What was I thinking? Of *course* there's no gun. Jasper wouldn't be so careless.

But the drawer isn't empty. A stack of elongated, curled papers rests on the bottom, covered in dust. Unlike Clara's scratch sheet, these papers are worn but smooth, like they were glossy once upon a time.

7 Deadly Zins. My father's favorite wine. These are wine labels.

I squint at the collage next to the mirror, and it dawns on me that the art was made with these labels. Jasper may not have gone to art school, but he's been practicing his craft.

My bedroom door flings open. Jasper stands in the doorframe, his head brushing the top. He doesn't look at me as he says, "Time to go."

I narrow my eyes. "Go where, exactly?"

"The warehouse. We're meeting with Chief and Chandler."

My chest pounds. Has he asked Chief to push up the meeting to spite me for speaking out yesterday? If anything, I should be angry at him. Not for hiding me, but for confusing me. I'm not ready to go home, and I'm not sure I ever will be. But I have to—for them.

Everything you do is for your family, Kota. They are all you have left. Food and freedom mean nothing without them.

Either way, I need more time. More time to figure out my next move. When I return to Egal, I need a solid plan to get Bunny and Grandma the meds they'll need routinely. If Peter's words yesterday are to be trusted, there's no way they'll survive on cut rations.

I spring out of bed. "I've only been here a day. I thought the meeting was in two days."

Jasper pulls his gaze toward me, his brown eyes soft.

Fuck. And I need more time with Jasper.

"That was before yesterday's Costco fiasco." With disappointment clear in his voice, he adds, "The meeting got pushed up." I press my fingers into my temples and close my eyes. "Don't worry. It'll all work out in the end."

A day ago, I wouldn't have asked, but after being ripped from my life and having my beliefs thrown into a fucking Vitamix, I use my voice. "Work out in the end? In whose favor—yours or mine?"

"Depends on what you want," Jasper says, stepping toward me. "What is it that you want, Kota?"

A long silence stretches between us. I turn away, my eyes catching on the Quaker bar wrapper still crumpled on the bedside table. Finally, I say, "To go home."

The words taste fishy on my tongue.

"Well," Jasper says, his face unreadable. Does he believe me? Do *I* believe me? "If all goes to plan, then you'll go home." Jasper pauses as he turns to leave, hand gripping the doorframe. "But you probably know by now that, inside the Split, plans tend to blow up."

He leaves without waiting for my response.

EITHER LAST NIGHT'S RABBIT MADE MY THIGHS STRONGER, OR I'VE JUST grown numb to the pain that is riding on bike pegs. Probably the latter. Definitely the latter.

We reach the same squat gray building that housed my first conscious arrival on this side of the Split. A blast of cold wind twists through the air and shocks me into the moment. *We've arrived.* I hop off Jasper's bike, and I hug my hoodie tighter around me.

A pang of nervousness rips through my core, but I shove it down with the other myriad of emotions I'm feeling. Loss. Confusion. Anger. No, not anger. *Rage.* Because, as emboldened as I've become, I'll enter this building as nothing more than the chess piece Chandler and Chief see me as. If the powers that be decide to keep me in Macoby, I'll lose my family. But if I'm tossed back into Egal, I'll once again be Chandler's bitch.

Where's the equality in that?

My spine crawls as I walk into the windowless building. *This* building, this shadowed, dingy warehouse where I was drugged and held captive, holds the keys to my future. Going back in is the only way out.

The hallways are musty, windowless, the darkness all-consuming. My best guess is that, once upon a time, this building functioned as a storage unit, given the endless rows of metal roll-up doors. Now, with the lack of anything besides burnt-out lights and mold to focus on, my thoughts spiral.

I wonder how Grandma's latest loaf turned out. Was it golden and flaky? I wonder if Bunny's pricked her finger again with a syringe. Is she angry with me, thinking I've left of my own volition? Will she hug me or hate me when I go home?

If. If I go home.

This hallway is endless. I wouldn't even be in this devilish, transient space if it weren't for Peter. He probably fucked Zara yesterday, in some pathetic attempt to gain power after the failed mission. To pretend he's a man, though he's nothing more than a boy. Is her lipstick smeared across his cheek? Does he prefer her kisses to mine?

Fine. My lips aren't meant for him any longer.

"Through here," Jasper says, ducking under a small doorway at the end of the hall.

I enter behind him, thankful for the room's dim lighting. A flame lantern hangs precariously from the ceiling, slapped up with duct tape that peels at the corners. It's so cold my breath leaves warm, white clouds in the air. A musty smell showers me in memories of Bunny hiding in the back of Grandma's old closet.

Come out, come out wherever you are!

And there they are. In the center of the room, Chief and Chandler sit facing each other, divided only by the metal table between them. Chandler's back is to me, and she doesn't turn when we enter. Red hair is pulled into a tight bun on the top of her head. Maybe that's why she concocted ridiculous rules—because the strain on her brain was pulling out her rational thoughts. I smile despite myself, and Chief returns it. He gestures for me to sit in one of two empty seats, next to Chandler, and I'd rather smash my head into a rock.

As I take a step forward, I trip over my shoelaces and plummet face-first. I nearly slam into the cold, hard floor when Jasper grips my arms and pulls me upright.

Thank you, I mouth to him.

Chandler spins around in her seat.

My stomach curls.

"Kota," Chandler says, her voice lacking any warmth. "Pleasure."

Pleasantries be damned. I offer a curt nod and take the seat next to her. She smells like evergreens, as usual, but there's a disinfectant-like tinge to it I hadn't noticed before. Jasper sits opposite me, his presence more soothing than I care to admit.

"Let's cut to the chase." Chief lays his fists on the table. "We're here to trade. Chandler, you have our men. We have her."

Her.

"Kota," Jasper and I say at the same time.

Chandler rolls her eyes so far back that her pupils disappear. For a second, I fear I'll be staring at her bloodshot, yellowish whites forever.

Then her soulless gaze snaps back into place.

"I do not have your men."

Chief leans forward. "Yes, you do. Eagan and Garrett went missing on the 20th of September—about two months ago."

"And? Lots of men go missing outside the Split—both Egals and Macs. Where's your proof I had anything to do with it?"

Chief pulls a device out of his pocket. He sets it on the table and presses a red button. *Beep.* My ears fill with static and crackles and pops. Two voices, in conversation, project from the speaker.

A male voice with a Southern drawl says, "We don't have what you want."

Even in the poor recording, the distress in his voice is clear as day.

"You are what I want," says the woman, her voice straight-laced.

"We have nothing to offer you."

"You're not listening. You *are* the offering."

"Why me? Why us?"

Chandler clears her throat and reaches for the recording device, but Chief snatches it away and holds it out of arm's reach. She says, "There's no way of telling who's speaking. It could be anyone."

The woman's voice on the recording continues. "You know things about the virus—things I don't. I've made progress, but I need more information. More science."

"Chandler," the man pleads, "we don't have any idea how to stop it. We can't help you. Please let us go."

"Young man, there are more ways you can be of use to me than you think."

The recording stops, and Chief places the device back on the table.

Jasper leans back in his seat and crosses his hands behind his head. "I only know one Chandler in the Split. How about you, Chief?"

Chandler shifts in her chair and turns to me. Her red brows knit together like fiery snakes. "Kota," she says, "you remember this day, don't you? I took you and the boys too close to the city— T.J. Maxx, I think. You were up in arms about the trip. Eventually, I listened to your pleas and we returned. The two young men speaking are Milo and Peter, not Eagan and Garrett, like these two imbeciles think. You do remember, don't you?"

The desperation on Chandler's face tugs at my stomach. If I tell her I remember, maybe I'll go home. But what will happen to those two men? To Eagan and Garrett? Why is my life more valuable than theirs? Are Bunny's and Grandma's lives more valuable than theirs?

And Milo. Including my dead friend in a lie would dishonor him.

No. I won't lie for her.

I square my shoulders. "You've never gone with us on a supply run, Chandler. Ever."

Ignoring me, Chandler spins around to face Chief. "You planted this device." She grabs the recorder and slams it on the table. "How? Why?"

"You were following Eagan and Garrett for weeks. Weren't you? We had to protect ourselves somehow, Chandler." He picks up the device. "Jasper here found this in Garrett's deserted Sedan on SC-11. A bright red Camry—quite easy to spot."

Jasper speaks up. "A Camry that Garrett loves dearly. One he would never abandon. Full tank of gas, too." He looks Chandler square in the eyes. "You have our men. Return them to us."

Chandler turns to Chief and pushes herself up from the table. "Fine. You want to play this game? Let's play. I'd never trade two men for one woman—especially one so dispensable. Bring me something I want, and we can talk about a trade. In the meantime . . . keep her. She's yours to babysit."

Jasper springs from the table. "So you admit it. You broke the treaty."

"Sit down, Jasper," Chief says, motioning with his hand.

Jasper pauses, but eventually concedes.

"I admit nothing," Chandler answers.

Aaand Jasper's back up again. He jabs a finger at her. "You're a liar, you're a thief, and you're a—"

Chief balls his hands into fists. "Jasper."

The door bangs open, and Peter storms through, hunched to keep his disheveled head from brushing the ceiling. His biceps bulge beneath a torn, bleach-stained T-shirt, his snake tattoo peeking out. He's a cross between the Hunchback of Notre Dame and the lead singer of an emo boy band, and I want to punch him in his fucking throat. What's he doing here?

Before I get the chance to throat-jab him, Greeley bursts into the room. Her chest heaves as she slams her hands into Peter's back, knocking him a foot forward. "He was hiding in the truck—behind a pyramid of fucking Wheaties."

Ah, so it's not dried spittle gracing the corners of his mouth. It's crumbs.

All he ever gave me was crumbs, and now he's keeping even those for himself.

Greeley comes to stand behind Chief, gluing her hands to the back of his chair. Her knuckles whiten as he whispers something to her. I imagine it's something like *He's a major douchecanoe, but you can't kill him*, because Greeley swears under her breath.

Chief directs his next words to Chandler, who sits opposite him with a blank face. *So we're playing poker now, are we?* He says, "You're better than this, Chandler."

"You don't know me."

"No," Chief says, finding her eyes. "But I used to."

Chandler's eyebrow twitches just before her entire mask slips. She bears her teeth, bucking toward Chief and slamming her hands on the table. *Bang.*

"Enough," she spits. "You're on thin ice." Chandler's presence fills the room like a crimson storm cloud. "I know you found our supply routes—and you know our schedule. But my people *need* supplies to live. They need *order* and *routine* to function in our society. You understand that, don't you? You call yourself the leader, the chief, of this place," she scoffs. "But why should that come at the expense of my people? Why can't you control your goddamn thieves? *You're taking everything that's left.*" She fixes her eyes on me. "Even things you don't need."

"Cool it," Jasper says.

Chandler spits at his feet. "What good is a treaty if you can't respect our side of the Split?"

"Bold of you to talk about respect," Chief says.

Every muscle in Chandler's body tenses. Her fists tighten. Her jaw clenches. The whispering strands of her red hair grow still. Chandler's going to wring Chief's neck. I'm sure of it. I reach for her wrist to calm her before she inevitably detonates when—

Boom.

The ground vibrates. Dust falls from the ceiling. The lantern flickers.

The room falls silent. We share a dazed moment, all of us.

What just happened?

Jasper is the first to sprint out of the room. Greeley is on his tail, shoving past Peter. Chief and Chandler push up at the same time, narrow their eyes at one another, and run. I'm trapped; Peter guards the door. His entire hand wraps around my bicep. Squeezes. He smells like whiskey and burnt rubber.

"Let me go." I pull against him, but his grip tightens. I turn my chin up to face him. He's an ugly person with a pretty face. A small man in a big man's body. A narcissist disguised as a leader.

He says, "I did it for Milo."

I'm not sure what *it* is, but it doesn't matter. He's wrong.

"No, Peter." This time, he lets me go. There will be a bruise on my arm tomorrow. "You've only ever done anything for yourself."

174

CHAPTER TWENTY-SIX

THE WORST POSSIBLE SCENARIO COMES TO MIND: THE SPLIT WAS bombed. Mass casualties. Zombies inside the gates. Grandma blown to bits. Bunny bitten.

What else could that deafening boom have been besides a bomb?

I will my legs to move, but my thighs tremble, and my feet are stuck in sludge. Everyone's outside; their dampened shouts leech through the cement walls.

Put on your big girl pants and join the conversation, Kota.

With a deep breath, I shove open the metal door to the outside.

Greeley's Jeep is engulfed in flames.

"You *bitch*!" Greeley screams at Chandler. They stand mere feet apart in front of the blistering Jeep. Behind it—*too* close to it—is a line of trees. This fire needs dousing. And soon. "I knew you weren't over me!"

Chandler's mask is back on, but Greeley wears her rage on her sleeve. She sprints toward Chandler, but as she lunges forward, Jasper grabs her arms. Greeley flails desperately against his chest.

"This isn't about you," Chandler says. "When will you learn? The world does not revolve around you. *My* world doesn't revolve around you."

Greeley pulls against Jasper's taut embrace. "Like hell! *I'm* the one you wanted—before Z Day as a lover and now as a scientist. But you couldn't get your hands on *my* big brains, so you took the next best thing. Joke's on you, because Eagan and Garrett are just my assistants. And I'd aim to guess they're not nearly as good in bed."

"Keep quiet," Jasper says as she yanks herself free.

She springs toward Chandler.

Jasper tries to catch her, but I'm faster. I beeline toward the two women and land between them, holding them apart. The heat from the fire swelters this close to the Jeep, and both of their collarbones are slick with sweat. Their hearts pound in their chests, their rhythm in tandem.

Greeley presses her chest against my hand. "Move aside, Blondie." She could easily overtake me, but I hope she recognizes that hurting Chandler wouldn't benefit either Egal or Mac.

I wince at the sight of the burning Jeep. "There's a bigger fire to put out right now."

Chandler slaps my hand away and walks toward Chief. He drags his hand down his face like a disappointed father. "Why have you done this?"

She sneers at his reaction. "You play with fire, you get burned," Chandler says, her voice erupting over the roaring flames.

"Leave," Chief orders. "You were welcomed to Macoby today under special circumstances, but you are no longer welcome here. Ever again."

Then Chief turns to me, his eyes grim.

My stomach drops. Is he going to send me back with them? What will Chandler do to me?

"Kota," he says. "There's a fire extinguisher inside, hanging by the door. Do you mind?"

I nod and hurry off.

I've heard enough, anyway. I storm into the windowless building, searching for the extinguisher in the dark. Another set of footsteps trails behind me. Like a whimpering child, Peter says, "I'm sorry."

"You did this," I breathe. "You torched Nancy."

"The Jeep? Yeah," he says, reaching for me. "But that's not why I'm sorry."

I keep my back to him. "For what, Peter?"

"For letting things go on with Zara for as long as they did." *As long as they did.* My gut seizes, and the walls around me shrink. No matter how little Peter means to me now, the thought still stings. "I've ended it with her. When you come back home, I'll be yours. Only yours."

"You were never mine," I say. Peter has only ever made choices to benefit himself. I was never considered; I was convenient. I let out a deep breath. "I see that now." The air feels like it's been trapped in my chest for days. "Your lies built walls between us. I thought I could be the one person to get through, but you never made a door for me. You let me bang my head into the wall, over and over again. You watched me bleed, Peter, and you never lifted a finger to help."

"I don't understand what you're saying," Peter says. I trace my hand along the cold, smooth wall until I feel a hard metal tube. "Can't we go back to the way things were? I miss you. I miss your touch."

I ought to knock him out with this fire extinguisher. Right here, right now.

But I'm the bigger person.

I pull the insulin and aspirin out of my pocket, where they've stayed safely since Costco. I shove the medicine into Peter's hand. "If you meant what you said, you'll give this to Bunny and Grandma."

"You have my word."

His word doesn't mean shit, but I can't tell him that, not when he's the only thing that could keep my sister breathing and my grandma from suffering. Because we both know I'm not going back. He said he loves me, but Peter won't fight for me. He's loyal to Chandler, but he was never loyal to me.

I mutter a thanks and run past my stupid ex, shrouded in darkness.

I wrench open the door and propel forward under the blazing sun. In one swoop, I extinguish the flames on Nancy, clouds of white foam coating the newly decimated vehicle. For good measure, I run around the Jeep and blow foam on the trees behind.

My chest heaves as I drop the extinguisher. It clanks on the concrete as it lands, and I kick it into the line of trees. Not my smartest move. The bone in my foot hurts like hell from the impact.

Fuck this. It was *me* who got the extinguisher. It was *me* who doused the flames. It was *me* who saved the day. And I won't get rewarded for it. No, I'll just keep getting hurt.

I turn around. Jasper holds Greeley by the bicep, and Chandler stands by her own truck, a satisfied smirk on her gaunt face. Chief is wide-eyed, looking like a psychic who predicted a calamity but hoped desperately it wouldn't come true.

Sorry to burst your bubble, Chief.

"Always a pleasure," Chandler says once Peter's back outside. He keeps his eyes fixed on the ground as he walks toward the passenger-side door and opens it for Chandler. Before she slides in, Chandler turns her venomous eyes toward me. "See you when you have something of value to trade."

And with that, they leave.

Greeley lets out a scream that sends the zombirds flying away.

CHAPTER TWENTY-SEVEN

WE LIVE INSIDE A FISHBOWL, A DRAINED LAKE THREE HUNDRED and fifty feet below the rest of the undead world—and Chief lives in a house built into one of the bowl's curved sides. His hobbit-like house is a skin transplant, a patch that doesn't belong in the sloping hill. But it blends in enough, with grass and kudzu taking over the stone.

"I need the story behind this," I say to Jasper as we stand outside the entrance. Even the door is round, the wood polished to an outlandish degree. "Tolkien fan?"

Jasper looks away. Sunlight casts gold streaks in his brown hair. I wonder what color his hair was as a child. "He was a builder before Z Day. Did you know he was the first one here, in the Split?"

"How would I know that? It's not like I've got a lot of friends around here."

He shrugs.

After this morning's disastrous hostage negotiation, Jasper insisted I return to his place while he and Greeley go to Chief's house to discuss Macoby's next move. I said, respectfully, *I think the fuck not.* No longer will others call the shots for me. I will be an active participant in my life, whether the Mac Dream Team likes it or not.

Jasper looks off into the distance, his attention focused on a wispy white cloud.

I say, "Looks like a chicken foot," and my words don't even get a smile out of him. "There's more you're not telling me."

"Chief's son *was* a Tolkien fan."

I grab his arm, force him to look me in the eye. "His son? What happened to him? And don't you dare say you'll tell me later."

"Took the words right out of my mouth."

"So find some new ones." He looks down at my hand. I let go of his arm. "Please."

"Fine, but not here. Come with me."

This time, it's Jasper who tugs me. He gently guides me by the elbow toward a tree looming over its anemic neighbor. Its veined roots wrap like tentacles around the base of the smaller, limp tree. Sucking out the nutrients. Feeding on its sap organs. Soon, zom-trees will take over. Soon, we'll all suffocate.

"Chief should cut that down," I say. Even the grass around the tree is brittle and dry.

"We're running an experiment."

"Take it that's another thing you'll tell me about later?"

"Chief's son was named Macoby. He was six years old, and he died on Z Day—got stuck in crossfire. There, are you happy?"

"Oh," I say, taken aback.

So that's where the name came from . . .

"And Chief couldn't save his son, but he can still save Eagan and Garrett. That's part of the reason he wants them back so desperately. He sees it as his life's mission to protect the people of Macoby, and he needs them back to prove he can. The moment people lose faith in Chief is when this all blows up in our face."

"Hate to break it to you," I say, "but something *did* blow up today."

Jasper shakes his head. "There's never been trust between Macoby and Egal . . . but there's always been trust between the citizens of each side."

He's right. I trusted Chandler, and I trusted Peter, even to a fault.

I sigh and point to a few half-filled mason jars scattered on the ground. "So what's with the jam jars? Do they have something to do with letting the zomtree live?"

"We're hoping there's a way to save the tree being overtaken by the zomtree."

"There's no way to save a human bitten by a zombie. Why would you think trees are any different?"

"I don't," Jasper says, meeting my eyes. "For what it's worth, I don't think Chandler took Eagan and Garrett for their scholarly backgrounds."

"What's that supposed to mean?" I ask.

Jasper sits on the yellow grass and pats the ground next to him. "Here, sit."

I cross my arms. "Is this where you tell me something *else* that's going to change my entire belief system?"

Jasper quirks an eyebrow. "Have I done that?"

"Perhaps."

"Then probably, yeah," he says, playing with a piece of grass. I sigh and pop a squat next to him. Jasper says, "Stick a finger into the ground. Just—come on, Kota, entertain me for a second. Thanks. Feel the damp soil? That's water—the one thing that connects us all. The animals, the plants, *us*. Greeley seems to think that water is the key to curing the virus."

I narrow my eyes. "Why would anyone trust what Greeley has to say, of all people?"

"She was a scientist."

"Right. She screamed that loud enough for my dead parents to hear in their graves."

"Kota."

"Coping. Sorry."

"You don't have to apologize," Jasper says sternly. He looks like he means it, too. "You've been through a lot."

"Yeah, well, so have you."

And I don't see you *deflecting like your life depends on it.*

I clear my throat. "Back to Greeley. You were saying?"

Jasper raises his eyebrows, but drops the subject. He clasps his hands together. "Before Z Day, Greeley ran a chemistry research program at Furman University."

I gasp. "But she's so young."

Jasper nods. "Thirty-two."

"And she's so . . . *Greeley.*"

"Greeley's the smartest person I know," Jasper says without hesitation. "When Greeley came to Macoby, she wanted to keep researching. Eagan and Garrett volunteered to be her assistants—if for no other reason than to have a purpose."

"I understand." And I do. Bunny and Grandma are my purpose. My life means nothing without them.

I wonder what Jasper's purpose is.

Jasper speaks before I can give the thought attention. "The three of them took routine trips up Paris Mountain to collect water from waterfalls and small lakes untouched by the virus-tinged bombs. That's when Chandler snatched Garrett and Eagan—just to piss Greeley off, I think." Jasper falls quiet and yanks a wad of grass out of the earth. I inhale and the fresh smell of soil fills my nose.

"You don't think Chandler took them to conduct her own research?"

Jasper laughs, but the sound is hollow, broken. "Oh, I think she's using them for research."

"What do you mean?" I prod. He won't look at me. I grip his arm. "What aren't you saying, Jasper?"

"I believe Chandler is experimenting on them," Jasper says, finally meeting my gaze.

My heart plummets. *No.*

No is what I want to believe. *No* is what I want to say. But the word dies on my tongue. Could Chandler be so cruel? I go down the list: Chandler rations the insulin of a diabetic child. Chandler forces an arthritic old woman to cook all day long. Chandler refuses to take back a loyal citizen, treating me like trash. Chandler refuses to take care of her own people. So why would she take care of her enemies?

Uniformity fosters unity.

Chandler has a purpose. There's nothing she wouldn't do to succeed.

Jasper's touch is warm as he pries my hand off his arm and pulls it into his. "Come on," he says, his voice soft. "Chief's expecting us."

CHAPTER
TWENTY-EIGHT

WE CANNOT RETALIATE WITH VIOLENCE, GREELEY," CHIEF SAYS, his black brows furrowed.

The four of us—me, Greeley, Jasper, and Chief—huddle around a round, glossy table in his den. In another life, maybe Chief would be here playing poker with the boys. The walls, floor, and ceiling are made of wood, and hazy light filters in through a small skylight, a hole cut out in the hill the house hides in.

"We are smarter than that. I will not risk the survival of the Split."

Though I elbowed myself into this conversation, I'm surprised Chief speaks so openly in front of me, let alone invites me into his home. Is he so confident I won't sabotage his plans? Maybe he thinks I can't. Or maybe he believes my loyalties have shifted to Macoby. Can he see that my loyalties are, in fact, shifting?

Greeley rolls her eyes and flops back into her chair, crossing her arms over her chest. She exudes the attitude of a teenager whose mother just told her she can't go out to the movies because *the movie starts at 9:30, young lady, and your curfew is at 11:00! You won't be home until after midnight!*

"Trust me," Chief says, "I want to hurt them. I do." For a leader, he seems friendly, genuine—a strong man with a beating heart.

But the look in his murky gray-brown eyes is frightening. "Casualties are not an option."

Because casualties mean zombies. An outbreak would destroy the Split.

"I want Chandler out of power," Chief continues. "And I want our men back. I intend to accomplish both of those things—but without violence. Don't look at me like that, Greeley. They'll get what they deserve, but only if we act with tact."

"But—"

"No buts."

"I don't get any input? What is this, some kind of dictatorship? You've always told us that we *all* have power. That if we want something, we fight for it. Well, you know what I want? *I want her dead.* And I'm willing to fight you for it."

I bite my tongue because I'm scared of Greeley, but I plan to ask Jasper what went down between her and Chandler.

I had one boyfriend, sophomore year. Austin dumped me to focus on his promising basketball career. He was five foot six. A week later, I found him in the school parking lot macking on Macey, the cheerleader who left a dizzying trail of Bath & Body Works Sweet Pea Fine Fragrance Mist wherever she walked.

I was devastated, but even so, I couldn't imagine wanting to *kill* Austin. Maybe pop his favorite basketball—signed by Shaq— but not *kill* him.

So, what did Chandler do to Greeley?

Chief says, "Killing the leader of Egal would result in anarchy. Are you willing to give up everything you've fought for? Are you willing to give up *your* life?"

Greeley stomps her feet on the floor. Chief ignores her adult temper tantrum, and Greeley slumps back in her chair.

"Besides," I mutter, "Peter's second in line. He can't be in charge. He's worse than her."

"No chance," Greeley says, meeting my eyes. For the first time, I notice dark circles under her eyes. Today's events have even drained her of energy.

I say, "Bet you a hot meal he is."

"Bet you meatballs he's not," Greeley retorts.

"Meatballs, huh? My grandma used to make those. You've got ground meat, eggs, and breadcrumbs lying around?"

Greeley extends her hand. "Shake on it."

She's full of shit, but I shake her hand anyway. Her grip is stronger than any man's I've had the absolute pleasure of shaking. Which isn't many. Men don't shake hands with young women. Dad's friends would shake West's hand and then offer me a feeble wave. It was like they didn't deem me worthy of their firm touch, of their respect. Pricks.

"Back to the matter at hand," Chief says. "You may be wondering why I'm letting you sit in on all of this discussion, Kota." Chief turns to me, and I nod. Yeah. There's a lot I'm wondering about. "You're a key—a key to this puzzle. I need your help."

"My help?" I lean forward in my seat. "Why do you think I'd be willing to help you?"

"Today's events haven't been enough to shift your loyalty?"

"I'm only loyal to one thing," I say. "And that's my family."

Greeley pushes up in her chair. The legs scrape the wood floor, and the sound grates in my ears. "Let me at her. I'll convince her."

"Not necessary," Chief says. Greeley groans and sinks back down into her seat. "We're at a standstill, then, Kota. Because the plan cannot proceed without you."

The silence that follows is thick, weighing down my shoulders. Chief may not have my loyalty, but he's piqued my interest. Because what if I can use this game to my advantage? They have demands of me, but I have demands, too.

I square my shoulders. Chief may want me to be his pawn, but if I'm the key to the puzzle, I *can* be an active player.

"What do you want from me?"

"I'll tell her," Jasper says, his face stony. "I'll tell her everything."

"Excellent," Chief says. "Then we'll regroup tomorrow."

CHAPTER TWENTY-NINE

JASPER AND I RIDE HIS BIKE BACK TO THE HOUSE IN SILENCE, OUR surroundings anything but. Cicadas are alive in the rustling trees, the distinct smell of *cold* fills my nose, and the high sun leaves violent streaks of orange on the dirt roads. Bird songs are dulled by the roaring wind that sends the bike leaning left every few seconds.

I tighten my grip on Jasper's backpack, my fingernails aching with the effort and the cold. Jasper pedals fast toward our destination, fueled by some emotion I can't quite put a finger on.

As for me, my thoughts are jumbled like a basket of unmade laundry in my head. Socks, underwear, tops, jeans, all haphazardly thrown in a pile, crinkled, and a clusterfuck to sift through.

The socks: Chandler doesn't want me.

The underwear: I've got no supplies. If I stay in Macoby, how will I eat? Drink? I have nothing left to trade, and I don't have allies. Jasper, maybe.

The tops: Chief wants me to betray the place that gave me shelter for the past two years. But was it ever home? All the nights I spent crammed into a tiny apartment with my grandma and Bunny. When my back ached after another uncomfortable sleep because it wouldn't have been right to make an old woman, or a young girl, sleep on a ratty couch. And then, the countless times I overslept because of a restless night of discomfort, and then missed the breakfast bell—which meant I didn't eat for another ten hours until dinner.

All those times I drove the boys to get supplies, only for us to come home with diddly squat. Or with what we thought was a ton of food, only for it to be an insubstantial amount for each person, because it had to be divided equally between us. Or rushed to the lackluster infirmary with wounds from collapsing structures.

Was it ever home, really?

In Macoby there are beautiful trees, homes, and a *bed*, all for me to experience. And I can have anything I want, as long as I find it. As long as I take it. This place isn't home, but if I brought Grandma and Bunny here, would it be?

They would get to form relationships with *good* people, just like I have: Jasper, Chief, Bama, Sling, Clara . . . Even Greeley, who buries her feelings beneath biting words. I can see now that her anger is a defense mechanism, like sarcasm is mine. The two of us bear similar shields. One day, maybe, we could find solace in each other.

Crazier things have happened.

By the time Jasper's sprawling lot comes into view, the moon has crawled into the sky, casting pearly shadows on the driveway. I inhale sharply through my nose, the crisp air refreshing. Falling leaves crunch like Cheetos under my shoes. Soon, my footsteps will be silent; there will be no more leaves.

Jasper holds the front door open for me.

"So," I say, my stomach doing a somersault. "Shit hit the fan, didn't it?"

Jasper spins around to face me. "How about a glass of wine?"

"I don't have anything to trade—"

"It's on the house," he says, brown curls spilling over his brow. I wish I had a camera. Or, I wish I had a working camera and a charger and also electricity so I could take a picture of his smile. I settle for a mental screenshot to store away with the others. "Come with me."

"You're not one of those cult leaders who thinks he's Jesus, are you?"

Now it's his turn to ask, "First of all, you're one to talk. Second of all, what?"

"I'm not in a cult," I say.

Or maybe I was. *Cult* might not be the right word, but something similar. I mean, the whole no-gun thing, for one. Chandler's argument for not allowing guns was convincing—because yes, the sound of a gunshot draws zombies, and yes, we'll eventually run out of bullets—but why wouldn't we find some damn silencers? Why wouldn't we learn how to make bullets? There's gotta be a book about it somewhere in the damn South. Gas will spoil, but we still drive around. Canned food will run out, but we still eat it. Candles will burn away, but we still use them to see at night. Why have I never questioned Chandler's logic before? Why have I been content with being defenseless?

Jasper clears his throat. "And why would I think I'm Jesus?"

I blink. "You know, turning water into wine and all that."

"If I had that power, I'd turn water into moonshine. Much stronger. And has a much higher trade value around here."

I nearly gag, remembering the pungent, corny taste of the stuff. "Only time I've had moonshine was when . . ." I trail off. It was my birthday, a year before Dad left, and he forgot.

You'll be the first among your friends, he said. *How cool they'll think you are.*

Jasper takes my hand, and I flinch. His skin is soft and cool, and his fingers weave between mine like a plait. For a second, I never want him to let my hand go.

"Come with me?" he asks.

"Okay," I whisper, thankful for the distraction.

Jasper leads me down the hall and pushes open a door. A long stairwell leads downward, stone stairs disappearing into a black basement.

"How serial killer of you." I bite my lip, stifling a smile.

"Yeah. This is where I stash the bodies." I know he's not serious, and in this moment I trust him completely, but for a second I wonder *what if?* What if there's a flesh-eating zombie waiting for us in the dark? "Come on, Kota, I'm kidding."

"I know, it's just . . ." Milo. The theoretical zombie in the basement could have been him. It *was* him, to someone else. The zombie *was* once a living, breathing soul, once a person who was loved.

Jasper's breath tickles my ear. "I've only killed one person."

I swat his chest with our intertwined hands. "*Jesus!*"

"Yes?"

"Was that supposed to be comforting? If so, mission not accomplished." My shoulders slump as I catch my breath. I ask, despite myself, "Who was it?"

"I'll tell you when—"

"Let me guess: a conversation for another time."

"No," he answers. The trace of a smile plays on his lips. "I'll tell you when we crack open a bottle of wine."

And maybe *I'm* the serial killer—because although we're talking about killing, when Jasper winks at me, my heart flutters with delight.

I decide not to push the feeling away. I let it expand in my chest.

CHAPTER THIRTY

THE BASEMENT IN JASPER'S HOME IS DAMP AND SMELLS OF CORK. It's pitch-black and as creepy as I anticipated. I'm 99 percent certain he didn't bring me down here to murder me, but I can't know for sure. I shouldn't trust him as much as I do. I trusted Peter to keep me safe, and look where that got me.

It's too quiet. I'm used to the lack of electricity buzz, but the basement's insulation is like a thick snow blanketing the ground, dousing out the hum of the environment. I rub the goose bumps out of my arms as Jasper's feet shuffle on the dusty floor. I freeze when he pauses mere inches from me—I think. I can't see shit.

"Care to do the honors?" He hands me the kind of lighter Mom used to buy at the gas station for two bucks.

It'll give you lung cancer, Mary.

Then let it. Nothing in the world makes me feel this good.

I flick the BIC lighter and look at Jasper through the little orange flame. "What am I supposed to do with this? Stare into your big brown eyes?"

The corners of those big brown eyes crinkle. He points to the wall behind me. "There are sconces along the wall."

"Oh?"

Goes with the whole dungeon theme, I suppose. The sconces aren't unlike those in the church back in Egal. Though the space was always packed, I often felt more alone there than I do here. Even with Grandma and Bunny to keep me company. I couldn't be open with them, not really. Not when I was their strength. With Jasper, I can be weak. He's already seen me at my most vulnerable. I have nothing to lose.

I light the first sconce and gasp as a golden glow fills the small space. Hundreds of wine bottles line the stone walls, fungus growing between the cracks. This basement used to be beautiful. Maybe it still is.

The room now lit, I trace a finger along the dusty bottles. "How'd you end up in this house anyway?"

"Just like anyone ends up with anything on this side. I took it."

"By force, or by trade?" I hand the lighter back to Jasper, who drops it into his pocket and then pulls out a banged-up Swiss Army knife, the silver cross fading into the red. He's silent, and I'm impatient. "Who'd you take it from?"

And still, he doesn't answer. Instead, he grabs an unlabeled bottle of burgundy wine off the wall. "You like cabernet?"

I shrug. "I don't know." Jasper raises an eyebrow. "I was eighteen when the bombs dropped, remember? I couldn't drink."

"Most eighteen-year-olds drink, Kota."

"Most eighteen-year-olds didn't have an alcoholic dad with a taste for abandonment."

Jasper uncorks the bottle, and the *pop* echoes throughout the room. He takes a slug of wine and sits on the dusty floor. "Want to talk about it?"

"Not really." I sink down next to him and hug my knees into my chest. "My mom died of lung cancer, and my dad left twenty minutes before her funeral. Dropped us on the stoop of Grandma's house."

Jasper sets the bottle on the ground opposite me. He drags his gaze to me, eyebrows drawn together. "I'm so sorry," he whispers, reaching for me.

I stretch over his lap and grab the bottle. Take a swig. The wine is acidic in my throat and burns a hole in my stomach, right below my belly button. "Good Lord, this is disgusting. How often do you drink this stuff?"

"I don't," Jasper says, snatching the bottle away. "It's lonely, drinking without a friend."

A friend. Is that what we are?

Silence lingers in the air like a sopping-wet shirt hanging out to dry. I scan the room, desperate to find something to break it. "Was this cellar full when you found—er, took—the house?"

He shakes his head no. "Whoever owned the home before they flooded Jocassee cleared the place out. In my first few days here, I raided every wine store in Greenville I could find. Went nuts in Total Wine. I figured wine would be a hot trading commodity, and the cellar gave me a place to store, and hide, the bottles."

"I see," I say. Jasper hands the bottle back to me. I take another long swig. Oh, my belly. It's so warm, like a big, roaring fire. And my tongue—so heavy. My thoughts dissolve like salt in water. "I always wondered what happened to him," I say. "After Z Day, I mean. My dad never made any attempt to contact us. He could've moved to Nebraska for all I know."

"Why would anyone willingly move to Nebraska?"

I shrug. "I don't know. But there was a lot about my dad I didn't know. Why he left, for one." Dust falls into my eyelashes as I lean my head against the wall. "And I've spent too long wondering what happened to him after Z Day. Wasted too much energy on a man who didn't spend any on his family."

He doesn't deserve my brain space. He doesn't deserve to be alive, if he is. And yet, I want him to exist. I want him to be out there, somewhere.

I turn to Jasper. "Where were you when the bombs dropped? Was your family with you?"

Jasper wipes his mouth with his sleeve, and a splotch of red stains the gray fabric. He bites his lip, now maroon. "It's a dark story. You sure you want to hear it?"

"You don't think I can handle it. Is that what you mean?" Jasper opens his mouth to speak, but I hold a finger up to his lips. "No, please. Let's talk about the *dark* series of events I've been through the past two days."

I count the events on my fingers, one by one. "First, I watched my friend get killed. I watched you *almost* get killed—by a wild boar, no less. I found out that Chandler, my leader, the person I lived to serve for two years, thinks I'm worthless."

I stop counting fingers and grab the bottle back from Jasper. "Oh! And I ate rabbit, and now I'm sick in the head because it was the most delicious thing I've ever tasted, and every chew, every swallow, felt like eating a piece of my sister."

I chug. Keep talking. "Even though I've been through all of that, even though being in Macoby for only *two days* made me realize I've been a sheep for *two years*. Even though I want—*need*—to be with my grandma and sister again, I don't want to go back. I can't. But look at me, Jasper, look at me. I'm *fine*." My last words come out in a slur, and my heart drums in my ears. "I can handle whatever 'dark' story you're about to tell me."

Jasper extends a palm toward me, and for a second, I think he's going to lay a hand on my cheek, but he doesn't. He takes my hand.

"You don't think you're worthless, do you?"

"Is that all you got from that monologue?" I rip my hand away. "I wasn't asking for your pity."

"I wasn't pitying you." Jasper shakes his head. "You're not worthless. I just wanted to make sure you knew that."

"Whatever," I say. "Your turn—tell me your story."

Jasper twiddles his fingers, then exhales, and his breath stinks like fermented fruit. "You know how, the few days before the bombs dropped, the air was so thick and heavy, you could taste the doom?"

I nod. Of course I remember. Even lunch conversations and Instagram and dread in my friends' eyes pointed toward doom. A war was coming.

Jasper continues, "The day the bombs dropped, my dad said we should board up the windows with plywood. We had a couple sheets in the garage—my mom was a big DIYer—but not enough for all the windows. My brother stayed back to help my dad while my sister and I went out to get more. We were gone for maybe an hour. Of course, Home Depot was fresh out of plywood 'cause it seemed like everyone had the same idea as us. Anyway, when we got home, our front door was wide open."

He clenches his jaw. "When my sister and I went inside . . . my dad, my mom, and my brother were all dead. They'd been shot. Multiple times, each of them." Jasper's chest heaves as he takes a shaky breath.

I can tell from his sallow face that the words hurt coming out. "My best friend was standing in the living room, shaking, staring at their bodies. Holding a rifle." He bites his quivering lower lip before clearing his throat.

" 'Why?' I asked Jamie. He said, 'I had to. My parents are dead, and I never had any brothers and sisters like you. The world's ending, and I'm going to be alone. But *you*—you had everything. A family. A home. And if I have to do this alone, so do you.' "

Jasper pauses. "What Jamie didn't understand was that he was my family, too. But it was too late. His eyes were wild. He was looking at me but he wasn't seeing me. Every inch of his body vibrated. I don't know if he was overcome with anger, or loss, or if he had a psychotic break, or what. But he killed them. He killed three of the four people I loved most in this world."

I don't say a word. I have none.

"If they'd died differently, would it hurt less?"

I blow out a breath. "I've lost three family members in three different ways. I don't know if the *how* matters so much as them being gone."

He takes a swig of the wine. "It matters," he says. "There's more I haven't told you yet."

"Keep going," I say. Am I the first person he's ever told this to? I must be. I lay a hand on his back. His breaths are short, scattered. "I'm here."

"I shot Jamie before he could kill my sister, too. His gun wasn't cocked, but I couldn't take the risk. I just shot him, right through the heart. I feel no remorse. But then . . . they all came back. All of them, all at once."

"As zombies?"

He nods. "I had no idea what was happening. I couldn't pull the trigger. I never believed in God, but at that moment, I hoped."

"Oh, Jasper . . ."

"My sister's never been an optimist. She may not have had the language for what they were yet, but she knew they were gone. So she went into the kitchen, grabbed my mom's favorite butcher knife, and killed my family—again. I don't know how many times she had to stab them until she realized the brain was the only way to strike them down. And the next words she said to me, I will never forget: *Strike without mercy.*" He wipes his hand down his face.

"Oh my god. I'm so sorry."

"I don't want your pity."

I'm quiet for a moment. "Do you know where your sister went? If she's still alive?"

Jasper gulps down the rest of the wine bottle and stares at its empty contents. "Alive and well, on the other side of the Split." He throws the bottle against the stone wall, and it smashes into a million shards.

"Sorry—what?"

Jasper stands, wobbles, and pulls a bottle of white wine off the wall. "Care to try something sweet?"

"Um . . ."

No. I don't give a shit about the wine. I want to know more. I want to know you. I want to comfort you and hold you and tell you that I'm here for you, that it will all be okay. That I'm alone, and you are, too, but at least now we can lean on each other. And I want to play a game of twenty questions because who is your sister, and what if I know her?

Jasper pops the cork and studies me with those brown eyes. Almond-shaped eyes with thick, dark lashes. Eyes that—

The puzzle pieces. They snap into place. Suddenly, everything makes sense.

It's a small world, after all.

Just this morning, Chandler blew up Greeley's Jeep.

"It's her," I say. "Your sister. Chandler is your sister."

Jasper nods.

"That's why you and Greeley are so close. They were together . . . ?"

"Engaged. They'd been together for eight years, since college. Chandler didn't just leave me behind—she left Greeley, too."

"What do you mean, she left?"

"Chief and his son, Macoby, were our next-door neighbors. Greeley, Chandler, Chief, and I found the Split together. We were only there for a couple weeks before others started to find the Split. The community operated as we do now: on trades. But naturally, some people had more than others, and that pissed off a vocal minority. Chief is a natural leader, but the first few months the Split was formed were rocky. There were raids. Chandler took advantage of that; she banded together a group and promised pure equality—and no guns." Jasper falls silent. *Uniformity fosters unity*. After a beat, he says, "But I think Chandler just wanted control. It took a couple months, but soon we slapped together the wall and formed the Split. A way for two ideologies to exist within one community."

Jasper downs half the new bottle in a single gulp. I beckon to him with my hand. "Give me that, please." The wine is saccharine, like a floral perfume, as it slides down my throat.

Jasper's version of the events that created the Split isn't what is taught in Egal. There, it's widely believed that the violent Macs were forcefully separated from the peaceful Egals. I should have questioned the sentiment; I should have known there is never just one side to the story.

For a while, Jasper and I stare at one another, each of us processing. I don't know what to say, if I should even say anything at all. The wine showers through my veins like a rainstorm, drenching any coherent thoughts I have and washing them away into the gutters of my mind.

From me, two bottles later: "Chandler's a major bitch."

From Jasper: "Hey, that's my sister you're talking about."

I elbow him in the ribs. "Seriously?"

"No."

I wipe my mouth on my sleeve. "But she also saved you, right?" And me. Chandler saved me. The room spins around me. Or maybe I spin around the room. Either way. "So . . . I can't really hate her. I hate what she's done, and I hate the choices she's making, but I don't hate her."

"Neither do I," he says, letting out a deep sigh. One that I think he's been holding since Z Day.

"Jasper?"

"Yeah?"

I open my mouth. I want to tell him that, despite the circumstances, I'm glad we found each other, and even when I go home, he'll have me on his side. I want to tell him that I forgive him and that I no longer feel like a prisoner here, but the words won't come out. Instead, I settle for this: "You're a good person. I'd like us to be friends, if that's all right with you."

"That's more than all right with me."

CHAPTER THIRTY-ONE

EVER BEEN SPELUNKING?"

"I . . ." A response dies on my tongue. I'm not sure what spelunking is, and quite frankly, I don't care. My head throbs, red and hot behind my brows, and being alone with Greeley adds another layer of strain. She is downright terrifying. Even when she's not snarling at me.

Especially when she's not snarling at me.

She nudges me in the ribs. "C'mon, try saying it five times fast. *Spelunkingspelunkingspelunking—*"

"Can we move on?" I rub the heel of my palm against my eyes. As I pull away my hand, Greeley thumps me on the forehead. Her thumb is a mallet.

The two of us stand before a dark, dusty hole carved into the side of Macoby. According to my body's clock, usually accurate, it's six in the morning. But like the moon, trust in my own judgment is waning.

Greeley snuck into Jasper's home before dawn and dragged me out of bed. And I . . . apparently let her? The memory is hazy, and I must have been half-asleep, because why else would I *not* run screaming from Greeley?

The wine.

Oh, god, I drank so much wine.

I don't remember much of what happened last night, but I *do* know Jasper drank more than me. Is that how she snuck past him, too?

The clay is soft under my feet, and I sink deeper into the ground as I turn to Greeley. The cold air has turned the tip of her nose red, visible even in the dusk. I'm tempted to whack her right between the nostrils, but I doubt that will end well for me.

I opt for a simple question instead. "Any chance you're going to tell me what we'll be doing in there? In a place that's better suited for stashing corpses?"

Not mine, hopefully.

Greeley chuckles. Her warm breath turns the air white as she whispers, "What *you'll* be doing in there."

"Come again?"

"I prefer the fresh air."

"And I don't?"

Greeley steps closer and shoves me toward the tunnel's black mouth. The entrance is wide enough for maybe three people to fit into, but the darkness that stretches beyond looks much smaller. The tunnel itself quickly fades into darkness, and my heart hammers in my chest as I consider how cramped the space may become.

I stumble backward, and my head spins. I'm never drinking wine again.

Greeley gives my back another nudge. "In you go, Blondie."

I whirl around. "Hands off, Greeley." I ignore her glare. "Why should I do what you say?" If Greeley wants me to do her bidding, I need something in return.

Greeley jabs a finger in my face. "Because if you don't, I'll fucking skin you like a—"

"I'm not scared of you."

"Is that so?" She steps toward me and bares her teeth. I was lying through mine, but I can't let her know that. "Whatcha gonna do without Big Brawny Jasper?"

Where the hell *is* Jasper? "How'd you get inside his house without him noticing?"

She pulls a mini flashlight out of her pocket and hands it to me. "Can't spill all my secrets."

"You've spilled a grand total of one secret since I've known you."

Chandler and Greeley, sitting in a tree. K-I-S-S-I-N-G.

She narrows her eyes. "Seems like you and Jas got a little wine drunk, huh? Counted about three empty bottles on the ground when I snatched you this morning." *Wish I grabbed one to smash against your head.* "Anything else the two of you did I should know about? You know, sleeping with your superiors is a conflict of in—"

"Tell me the plan," I say, hoping she can't see the blush I feel spreading to my ears. We didn't sleep together. I'd remember if we did. Right?

Greeley sniggers, delighting in my ignorance. "Get in the tunnel. She'll explain everything."

"She'll? Who is *she*?"

Greeley balls her fists as she steps toward me. "Last time I'll say it: The answers await you inside. You did this to yourself. Made it too easy for me to haul your ass out of bed." She pulls out a pocketknife, and I flinch as she snaps it open. The blade is sharp enough to slice through glass. So is her gaze. "Now get in the goddamn tunnel. I *will* cut you."

I believe her. Not only *will* she cut me, but she *wants* to. The manic smirk on her face says it all.

"What's in it for me?"

She lowers the knife and flings it at the cave wall behind me. It plunges into the clay with a clean *thwack*. "I'll take you hunting." I raise my eyebrows. "What? You need food, don't you? Stuff to trade? You're in Macoby now, and that means you've got to provide for yourself. Last time I checked, you don't have the means to do that."

"And you do?"

Greeley flinches, no doubt catching my meaning. Her precious Jeep is dead and gone. She recovers quickly, a wicked smirk spreading across her face. "I've got this knife here, two more at home, plus a few guns. I don't need Nancy to protect me."

"Well, *I* need protection from you. I'm not stupid enough to go hunting alone with you and your stockpile of weapons!"

"So you admit you're stupid."

"Greeley."

"Fine! Jasper can come."

I huff. She's got me there. Jasper won't let Greeley murder me. And at the end of the day, she's right: I need to learn how to fend for myself.

"Fine," I repeat. I flick on the flashlight and shine the bright light right between her eyes. "I'll go in the tunnel."

CHAPTER THIRTY-TWO

ODAY, AS I TRUDGE INTO A TUNNEL THAT TIGHTENS AROUND ME like a whole-body blood pressure cuff, I learn I am claustrophobic.

My knees wobble, the walls narrow, the ceiling shortens, and a bone-chilling voice in my head screams and screams and screams. *Go back*, it says. *Abandon ship. These walls will suffocate you like Mom's lungs did to her.*

Dust drifts above my footsteps and swirls with the dim light of this shitty flashlight. The billowing dirt forms shapes, so I focus on what I can see rather than what I can't. Dragons and hippos and cars and fingers. The shapes are real, and my paranoia is not. No, I will not work for Greeley. I will do this for myself. I will conquer this newfound fear; maybe then I can stand against those who have taken advantage of it: Peter, Chandler, Greeley. The memory of my father.

You left, but I am not scared. You betrayed me, but I am loved.

The walls threaten to cave in on me, but I burst through them like dynamite, my fists proudly bloodied and bruised. Figuratively, that is.

A glowing yellow ball emerges in the distance. Quietly, I pad toward the light, and it grows larger with every step.

Eventually, a woman and a man come into view. They kneel in single file, each wearing a hand lamp. They turn their heads and lower their shovels, full of red clay, when they see me. My head hits the ceiling, and since I'm already crouched, I lower to my knees. Wet hair is plastered to the man's and woman's foreheads, their dirty clothes drenched in sweat. I can't stop staring at the woman. There's a familiarity to the black brows and sharp cheekbones that etch her face, though I can't put my finger on why.

"You made it," she says with a slight Indian accent. Her chest heaves with labored breath. "My name is Anika."

Oh my god, it's Anika. Anika of the Fig Newtons. Anika from my childhood. Anika, who is very much not dead.

Guilt washes over me. I feel nothing toward the woman kneeling before me. She is a stranger.

"Hi," I say. "I'm Kota."

"I know who you are."

It's apparent Anika's as surprised to see me here as I am her. She quickly glances me over, as if realizing I am no longer the kid she knew, her eyes pausing on the scrunchie at my wrist before flicking away, aloof. She doesn't remember loaning it to me. I almost laugh, realizing I'm more attached to the scrunchie itself than I am to any memories with her.

"What are you two doing?" I ask. "Why am I here?"

The man behind her offers a lopsided smile. "Digging through to the other side, of course." His words come out like his mouth is full of marbles. "We've been workin' like mad folk. I reckon we'll do eight feet today."

"That's Sawyer," Anika says.

When Sawyer smiles, his tongue sticks out through his missing two front teeth. He pulls a protein bar out of his pocket, downs it in two bites, and throws the wrapper on the ground.

"I can introduce myself, Ani," he says. "Sawyer. Pleasure to meet you, Kota. Puttin' a face to our infiltrator sure does make this whole thing seem more real. Reminds me there's light at the end of the tunnel."

Oh?

Sawyer licks his chapped lips. Chocolate and clay. "Fair warning, though, Miss Kota. If we're to keep up with Chief's timeline, the rest of this tunnel ain't gon' be luxurious like this. We still got quite a ways to go. It's a good thang you're small."

Quite a ways to go.

No. This isn't happening. This can't be happening.

"Got about two weeks left, I'd say," Sawyer continues, peeling back the wrapper of another protein bar. With a mouthful of nuts and chocolate, he says, "Shoot, but if our commander keeps bringing us goodies, Ani and I here could finish up sooner."

My heart pounds in my chest. "So I'm supposed to go through this tunnel—which goes under the Split—into Egal? And do what, exactly?"

Anika clears her throat. "We need you to find Garrett and Eagan and bring them back. And"—Anika pauses—"report back on Chandler. We need her plans."

"Two questions: Why me? And what plans?"

"You know the layout of Egal better than anyone in Macoby. And if you're caught, you can say you escaped us brutal Macs." Anika's voice is laced with sarcasm. "If we were to send another Mac, your people wouldn't be so kind. For obvious reasons, we cannot lose another one of our people. Finally, we need someone small enough to fit through the tunnel. You fit the bill."

I ignore the sinking feeling in my stomach. "And the plans?"

"Chandler is up to something, but we don't know what. Attaining some documentation of her plans is critical. She has the upper hand, and we must change that, especially if she plans to take us to war."

My voice shakes as I say, "You think Chandler wants war?"

"Only one way to find out."

Fuck. This is much bigger than a rift between Chief and Chandler. "Last question—why did I have to come all the way down here for you to tell me this?"

"Had to see if you could do it, of course." Anika smiles. "Can't put our faith in someone afraid of the dark."

"Oh, I'm afraid," I say, gripping the dimming flashlight. "But I'm here, aren't I?"

Sawyer hoots and pulls out a third bar. *This guy.* "Atta girl!"

"What's Chief giving you in return for digging?" Digging is an incredibly laborious task, and I can't imagine they volunteered, even if the two men Chandler took meant something to them. "Protein bars?"

"Twenty grams per bar!" Sawyer says, tossing the wrapper aside. " 'Course, that ain't all. He's givin' me six cases of full metal jacket ammo. What's he givin' you again, Ani?"

"Insulin. For my mother." My flashlight gives out. Anika steps toward me. "Do you understand now?"

My stomach drops. I remember: Anika's mom had a hot pink pump.

"Yes." I gulp. "I understand."

"Good," she says. "Now find your way out."

CHAPTER THIRTY-THREE

THE DAY BREAKS WHEN I FINALLY FIND MY WAY OUT OF THE TUNNEL. In my half-delusional state, I hadn't realized how close we are to the sloping outer edges of Macoby. The hill leading to the outside world looms to the left, and on top of it, Macoby's own set of gates. Humanity and nature collide in a monstrous yet beautiful sight. Late autumn grass blankets the hill surrounding the valley town, mustard yellow and corn silk. How many ants, worms, and critters speckle the earth? How many are alive, and how many have been turned?

And with Earth having so little time in its lifespan, why haven't I made this world all that I can for myself?

The sweet, musty fragrance of my grandma's rose perfume drifts through the air; Bunny's childlike scent of Cheerios softens my skin. She hasn't had Cheerios in years, but I cannot detach my younger sister from the association. Soon, she will be a teenager. Soon, she will see this terrible world as it is. I will be by her side when that happens.

I eye the sniper guarding the Macoby gate. The guards in Egal use crossbows. While I felt safe when I lived there, a veil hung over my eyes. What would happen if a drove of zombies attacked like they did in Costco? You can't crossbow a hundred zombies. Is Chandler as ignorant as I was? Is she blinded by what Jamie did to her family? Or does she simply not care to protect her community?

I'm starting to think she never cared. That all she ever wanted was power. In that case, Bunny and Grandma aren't safe. One's disabled, and the other's old. Chandler will use the physically strong citizens to do her bidding: the doughboys, the medboys, the builders. But she doesn't need my family. I do.

At this point, I'm not confident that Chandler wouldn't use Grandma and Bunny as lab rats. And even a tinge of uncertainty is enough for me. I've got to get them out of Egal.

"When are Anika and Sawyer set to complete the dig?" Greeley asks.

"What?" I ask, distracted by my tumbling thoughts.

"I'm sorry—let me rephrase that. How soon can we kick you back over to Egal for your imminent death?"

"Two weeks," I say, my stomach curdling at the thought of going back into that tunnel . . . and picturing how narrow it may become. I'll be a human sardine, but I'll suck it up for my family's sake. I'd squish myself into a can of King Oscar if I had to.

"Dear god." Greeley gags. "We have to deal with you for another *fourteen days*?"

"You can count that high?"

Greeley lunges for me. "I ought to wring your neck right now." I spin on my heel, but she grabs my arm. "Come *on*, you lug, we're going fishing."

"I thought you said we were going hunting?"

"Same difference."

Not really? Also . . . "With Jasper."

"Ugh, we're losing daylight!"

"Greeley . . . the sun literally just came up."

"You're unbearable."

"I'll say." I yank my arm away. Her eyes glitter with spite. I walk toward the general direction of Jasper's house, toward the center of Macoby. I think. "I'm going to Jasper's house. You don't have to come."

Greeley stomps by me. "Like you have any idea where you're going, Blondie. I'll lead the way."

INO LONGER HAVE A HOME IN EGAL, BUT I CAN'T CALL JASPER'S COTTAGE HOME either, so when we reach the front door, I knock. Greeley stands next to me with her arms crossed, impatiently tapping her foot against the stone patio.

Tap tap tap tap.

No answer.

I rap a knuckle on the door again.

No answer.

I lift my hand to knock again, but Greeley bulldozes past me. "Oh, for fuck's sake." She plows inside, screaming, "Ho, ho, ho, it's me, Santa Claus!" I shut the door behind me as Greeley plops onto the couch. She cups her mouth and shouts, "Leaving the door unlocked now, Jas? Your shit's *mine* now, tool!"

Jasper emerges from his room, his hair mussed. "Sorry, I didn't hear you. I was sleeping." He drags his gaze to me, sending a lightning bolt through my belly button. He waves as he moves to sit on the couch next to Greeley. "Hey," he says, sinking into the worn cushions.

"Hey," I whisper back.

"Well, isn't this sweet?" Greeley leans back, stretching her arms across the back of the sofa. "A budding romance."

I focus my eyes on the floor, heat rising to my ears. I realize I'm still standing by the door, twiddling my thumbs. Hands—what do I do with my hands again?

Jasper clears his throat. "Remind me why you're here, Greeley?"

"To thorn myself into your side, of course." She kicks off one shoe, then the other, and I'm shocked to find her socks are frog-patterned. They dance as she wiggles her toes. "Now, while you've been disturbed with naked dreams of this one"— she nods at me—"we've been scouting out Miss Kota here's suicide mission."

"I've been thinking about that." Jasper runs a hand through his hair. His eyes explore mine, and I drown in their brown, melting void. Then he says, "I don't think it's a good idea."

Greeley claps her hands together. "Oh shit—you actually *do* like her."

"No," he says. My shoulders deflate, but I pull them back up before they can notice. "Kota's not capable of doing what we need. I've seen her out there, in the wild, and she's not ready. I don't think she'll ever be."

Greeley rubs her hands together, smirking like a goblin. "I knew drama would go down today. But I didn't expect this. C'mon, give me specifics."

Jasper stands up and steps toward me. "I saw you, Kota. I saw you walk into Walgreens two years ago. For what it's worth, I thought you saw me, too."

I gasp. The shock that sweeps through my core is obscured by an onslaught of memories. The day replays in my head like it only just happened. Sweat dripped down Bunny's pale face as I carried her trembling body into the store. Her big eyes glazed over as she stared up at me.

Kotie, I don't want to die.

"I didn't see anything but my sick sister. Did you know the store was riddled with zombies? Did you hear our screams?"

I clench my fists, remembering the monstrous sound of that first zombie. Grandma, Bunny, and I scrambled behind the pharmacy counter as its roar ripped through Walgreens. I laid my sister down on the grimy vinyl floor while Grandma searched the shelves for insulin. My hand quivered as it gripped my balisong. I'd never killed a zombie before. My head told me I couldn't, but my heart told me I must. I squared my shoulders, ready to lunge toward the encroaching zombie.

And then another one sprang up from the candy aisle. Another, from the hair dye aisle. *Another. Another.*

I stood frozen in terror. Grandma jabbed insulin into Bunny's side. My feet were stuck in tar. I dropped my knife.

I couldn't move.

Zombies stretched their decaying bodies over the pharmacy counter, brainless but motivated. It was only a matter of time.

I peered down at my family. Grandma looked resigned as she held her granddaughter. At least Bunny no longer appeared to be in pain. At least she would be held in her final moments. I told them both I was sorry for failing them.

The front door burst open. Peter strode inside, spotting us immediately. In the blink of an eye, it seemed, he killed every zombie in Walgreens.

Anger boils in my chest. "Where were you?" I ask Jasper. "You say you were there, but you let *him* save us. Why?"

Greeley asks, "Who?"

"Peter." I grit my teeth.

Jasper recoils. "I entered through the back door, just a moment before Peter. He sprung into action, and I thought . . ." Jasper pauses. "I thought you'd have a better chance in Egal. I didn't think you'd survive in Macoby."

"Well," I spit out. "I'm surviving now, aren't I?"

My ears burn and my chest fills with fury so big I may burst. Jasper was the *one* person who believed in me. The one person who made me feel strong, capable. Now I can see that was a lie. He thinks I'm weak, just like everybody else. He didn't think I could survive in Macoby, and he doesn't think I can complete the mission.

"You don't think I'll be able to find Garrett and Eagan? That I'm not smart enough—or strong enough?"

Jasper doesn't answer. His face is stone.

"You're wrong," I tell Jasper. "I can—and I *will*—complete the mission."

I curl my hands into fists and storm out of the house. I slam the door behind me and sink to my knees on Jasper's front porch. My nose tingles but I refuse to let tears fall. Grandma would tell me crying is a sign of strength, not weakness, but if I let just one tear fall, I'll end up drowning the whole city. So I pucker my lips, scrunch my nose, and—

Achoo!

Sniffling, I close my eyes and let the dewy smells and the trickling sounds of Jasper's creek engulf me. The door creaks open behind me.

"Hey." Jasper's soft voice makes me clench my teeth, draws angry red steam out of my ears. His shoes scrape the concrete as he sits down. "Probably a bad time to offer you this . . ."

He pulls a Fig Newton out of his pocket. Where in god's name did he get such a thing, and *is it strawberry*?

I snatch the bar out of his hands, rip it open, and shove the entire cookie down my throat.

"How'd you know?" I ask, mouth full of jammy deliciousness.

"Know what?"

"Strawberry's my favorite."

"I didn't." He smirks. "But I'll file that away in case I come across a variety pack."

I lick the corners of my mouth, catching stray crumbs. "Thanks."

"You're welcome," Jasper says, something like relief spreading across his face. He clears his throat. "Are we okay, you and me?"

I turn away from him, unable to hold his searching gaze. Instead, I look down at my hands, noticing new calluses on my palms. I pick the dry skin away and fling it on the porch.

We're not okay. The anger boiling in my chest has lowered to a simmer, but it's been replaced by a wave of embarrassment and hurt. I feel Jasper's eyes on me, as though he is waiting for me to say something. I focus on the lines of my palms, little maps etched on my skin. Eventually, I'm ready to speak. "I see what you see. I'm a pitiful excuse for a survivor. I let myself get captured, and I need constant help to stay alive. I understand why you think I'm weak. I just hoped . . ." I trail off, unable to get the words out. "But my family's lives are at stake. I couldn't save them in Walgreens, but I *can* save them now." I turn to Jasper. "You have to know I'm willing to do anything to protect them. I'm going to bring them here—and I'm going to be the person they need."

Jasper's eyes light up. "You want to bring them here? To live?"

"Yes," I say. "They deserve a better life."

Jasper releases a deep breath. "So do you."

I shake my head and gaze at the winding pathway beyond Jasper's house. A single bird bounds off a curling tree branch and flies away. "Then why can't you let me do this?"

"Because, Kota," Jasper says, "I don't want you to die."

I don't want you to die?

These words.

These words make me seethe.

"I don't believe you," I spit out. "You want me to stay weak; that's really what you mean. So you can *protect* me. You want someone to hold power over. You want a plaything. Just like Peter." I push myself up and stare down at him, fists clenched. "You know that I care about two things: Grandma and Bunny. If you truly cared about me, Jasper, you would want me to do this; you would support me in getting them back."

"Dammit, Kota!" Now Jasper's standing. Staring down at *me*. "I just want you to be safe."

"My life means nothing without them!"

The front door flings open. Greeley raises her eyebrows. "Hate to break up this lovers' quarrel, but we gotta go. Get your stuff, Jas." She thumbs behind her. "We don't have all day."

If she notices the tears about to erupt from my eyes, she doesn't make it known—not with her words, and not with her body language. Is she showing compassion, or am I imagining things?

I'm probably imagining things.

"He's not coming," I say.

I don't need him.

"Whatever," Greeley says, jumping off the patio. She gestures for me to join her. "Time to get a move on, Dakota."

"Wait—don't leave yet." Jasper stands and hurries back inside the house.

"Bossy, isn't he?" Greeley jokes.

I grit my teeth.

She rolls her eyes and kicks a rock.

Greeley is desperate for someone to banter with, isn't she? We're all lonely. All in search of someone to give us comfort—and that means something different to each of us.

Jasper bursts back outside and places a gun in my hand. "Take this."

I cringe when his warm hand curls around mine. I pull away and shove the gun into the waistband of my pants.

Am I angry at Jasper? Yes. But am I stubborn enough to refuse a gun? Hell no.

"*Aw*," Greeley says, drawing the word out. "The damsel in distress found her knight in shining armor."

My ears and cheeks burn despite myself. I spin away from Jasper and join Greeley on the dying lawn. "I'm going to kill you, Greeley."

"Not if I kill you first! Tag." She slaps me on the shoulder. "You're it! Now, grab a backpack and follow me. We're going fishing."

CHAPTER THIRTY-FOUR

I FEEL LIKE A BLACKENED CHICKEN WING. MY MUSCLES ARE TAUT, BONES brittle, palms callused, and lips chapped. My thighs ache from days of hard exertion. At the risk of sounding like a big, fat, whiny baby, I'm also tired. Greeley, on the other hand, places one boot in front of the other and begins the long ascent up the hill leading outside the Split.

She turns around, craning her neck to give me the stink eye. "Are you coming or what?"

I sigh and begin the trek behind Greeley. It's not worth bickering with her. It will get me nowhere. And speaking of going nowhere . . . Today, we're leaving the Split *on foot*. Without the protection of a vehicle. I've got a gun, but I'm not confident I can use it.

At the top of the hill looms the barbed gate separating the Split from the outer world. While Egal and Macoby share the outer wall for protection, each has their own set of gates. Two men stand in the wooden watchtower with their backs turned to us, guarding this side of the Split from the outside world. They turn in unison as we approach, massive snipers slung across their backs.

Wind whistles in my ears, drowning the racing beat of my heart. My braid comes undone, and caramel-colored strands whip my face like lashes. As a child, my hair was a silky, icy halo around my head. Mom would tuck smooth strands behind my ears and call me her Snow Princess. Now I've got frizzy ropes that hang like boneless snakes around my face.

I redo my braid, using the opportunity to covertly peer at the men through my moving mop of hair. They're supposedly here only to prevent Egals and zombies from coming *inside*, but their eyes narrow as we approach. Their grips on their guns tighten.

A few feet away, Greeley comes to a standstill, and though it takes everything in me not to cower, I stand beside her. The guards leave their post, hopping off the watchtower's ledge to face us.

When he reaches us, the brawny guard with light-brown skin spits at our feet. "What's your purpose?"

"None of your business," Greeley answers.

The man's fingers inch closer to the trigger. Next to him, the guard with a shaggy mullet and pornstache curls his lips over his teeth. "Where's your Jeep, Greeley?"

"Again, none of your business. Can you open the gates?"

"Manners," says the second man.

"Fuck you."

"Please," I interject, stepping in front of Greeley. We're not even outside the Split, and she's already causing problems. What am I getting myself into? "Please let us through."

The mustached guard looks me up and down. "Who the hell are you?"

Greeley pushes me aside. "Doesn't matter who she is. Let us through, or I'll rip that ferret off your upper lip."

The guard lowers his gun and uses his peace fingers to brush his stache. "It'll cost you."

Greeley doesn't think for a second before pulling a pistol out of her back pocket. "You wanna play? Fine, let's play." She turns to me. "Kota, get out your gun." *No, thank you.* "Now."

I do as she says, though I'd rather run in the opposite direction. Or, I don't know, jump off a cliff. Except the guards look nervous when I cock the gun. They don't know I'm a total gun newb.

I say, "From the looks on your faces, you already know Greeley's aim is impeccable. Well, she's also trained me. Just my two cents, but I'd let us through."

The brawny man sighs. "Fine. Go through. But this doesn't end here."

"You're right," Greeley says. "It doesn't." She pulls a knife out of her back pocket, snaps it open, and flicks it right through his foot. Brawny buckles over, howling. His knees give out as he falls to the earth.

Pornstache bends down to check out the blood gushing from his partner's foot. He looks up to Greeley. "Why the fuck did you do that?"

"Trade guns with me," she says. "Give me your sniper."

"No!"

"Kota, take this." She hands me her gun. She swings her backpack around and throws a thing of gauze, a tube of Neosporin, and a small bottle of hydrogen peroxide on the ground. "Trade me."

Stache pulls the sniper off his back and holds it up to Greeley. "You're a bitch."

"Takes one to know one." Greeley straps the gun on her back and turns to me. "Kota, you ready?"

Well, no. I'm woozy. I'm tired. I'm scared.

But Greeley can't know that.

"Yeah," I say, a gun in each of my hands. "I'm ready."

CHAPTER THIRTY-FIVE

THE SUN IS HIGH IN THE SKY, SHOOTING DOWN RAYS OF LAVA AS WE trudge down the well-beaten path toward some destination unbeknownst to me. For November, the air is boiling. Shit, for *June*, the air is boiling. Throughout my life, there's always been spikes of heat in the winter, flashes of cold in the summer. More hurricanes and fires than meteorologists could have ever predicted.

Greenville's far enough inland that we're protected from the worst of it, but with every season, the weather gets more erratic. The environmental effects of the bombs certainly didn't help, with virus-tinged water seeping back up into the atmosphere.

Above, wispy clouds form the shape of a hand, claw-like fingers reaching toward me, desperate to consume. We're decidedly fucked.

Zombies aside, there's a high probability humanity won't make it past a few years, so might as well make the best of it while we're here. Which means getting my family to Macoby. And learning how to survive outside the Split on my own, with no man to protect me.

As we walk along the outer perimeter of the Split, the Egal watchtower comes into view. It's not much—a small ledge built on wood legs. Just like Macoby's. Only . . .

"Greeley, are those children?"

"What're you on about?" she says, gazing lovingly at her new toy. "This thing's 308 cal. You ever shoot a sniper?"

"No, I haven't," I say. Greeley shakes her head in disappointment and swings the gun around her back. When I'm certain she won't accidentally (or intentionally) shoot me in the foot, I nudge her with my elbow. "Up there. Look."

She twists her head around. "*Damn!* Those are kids. C'mon, let's go give 'em shit."

"I don't think that's a good idea—"

But it's too late. Greeley's already jogging over to the watchtower, and I'd be lying if I said I wasn't curious what the hell was going on. In my two years living in Egal, I've only ever known two guards: Terrance and Dale. While children *are* assigned to ludicrous jobs—the Sick Room, sorting and stitching clothes, sterilizing water—they've never been assigned to guard the perimeter. I could never have imagined this.

By the time I catch up to Greeley, sweat drips down my face, and my chest heaves from exertion. I search the two kids' faces—about ten years old, I guess—but I don't recognize them. And based on how they're pointing their crossbows at me, they don't recognize me, either.

The taller boy scrunches his nose. "Who are you?"

The other boy whispers in his ear, "They're not Egals—they only come and go in the truck. They must be *Macs*." Their eyes bug out, and their fingers hover too close to the trigger for my liking.

I clear my throat and raise my hands. "We're not—I mean, yes, we are, but—where's Terrance?"

The taller boy says, "How do *you* know Terrance?"

Before I consider how much I should tell these boys about who I am, the shorter boy says, "He'll be back from lunch in five. So I'd get out of here before he's back, if I was you."

Oh, to be threatened by a ten-year-old.

Greeley says, "And what're two young gentlemen like your-selves doing on guard duty?"

The shorter boy seems more keen to reveal information. Maybe he's younger, or maybe he doesn't realize he should keep his mouth shut. "We've all got mandatory shifts now to protect our land from *Macs* like you."

"Yeah! We're protecting Egal! And we're not afraid to shoot, so get on outta here!"

They don't know it, but they both look utterly terrified. From the way their hands wobble holding the too-heavy weapons, they won't shoot. They have neither the skill nor the gumption.

And they shouldn't. They're children.

Greeley giggles. "Okay, boys. We'll get going, then."

With crossbows aimed at our backs, Greeley and I walk away from the Split. When we're out of eyesight, she leans over to me. "Can you believe that?"

"No," I say. "I can't. Chandler's spouting propaganda, isn't she? About Macoby?"

Greeley nods. "Are you seeing it now? She's a dictator. Chandler doesn't want what's best for her community. She wants power."

"And what do you want, Greeley?" This is a question that's been ruminating in my mind: Who is Greeley fighting for?

"I want to find a cure. Sure, it'd be nice to keep myself and my friends alive."

"Friends?"

Greeley counts on one hand. "Jasper. Sling, Bama, Clara. And myself, of course. Gotta be your own best friend."

"Right." I get that she hates me, but why did I hope to hear my own name on that list?

"Saving them's all a bonus, though. I didn't spend years of my life getting a fucking PhD for nothing. I didn't spend *years* watch-ing Native Americans get shit on by a wacked-out president for nothing. Didn't spend years watching my father turn into a shell of a person because of that. No, I'm going to find a cure. And if it turns out that President Fuckwad and his cronies are hiding out somewhere, I'll make them all pay." Greeley cracks her neck and her knuckles. Then, she flashes a smile so bright it contends with the sun. "And that, Blondie, is why we're going fishing. Because I've got a hunch that the cure has something to do with water." She laughs. "That, and I'm hungry. Now let's get a move on."

CHAPTER THIRTY-SIX

THOUGH MY THIGHS BURN AND KNEES ACHE, I KEEP UP WITH GREELEY'S determined stride throughout our hour-long journey. I don't dare to ask her to slow down. I need her on my side. I've learned she's like a cat: She'll come when she's ready, and not one second sooner. And if you go looking for her, she'll run.

My black clothes stick against my sweaty skin, and I wish I could peel them off. Out here, though, I need the extra protection. Even a thin layer of fabric may make the difference between a zombie bite puncturing the skin or not.

I reach into my backpack and grab the flask. Jasper keeps a jug of boiled creek water in his kitchen, so before Greeley and I headed out, I filled up. He didn't seem to mind. He may not think me capable, but it's clear he wants me to stay alive. For what reason, I don't know. I thought he cared about me, but it's clear now that he just cares about what I can do for Macoby. Which, in his eyes, is nothing.

I lift the flask to my lips. *Gulp.* Guzzle so greedily the water sweetens to honey, and I'm a deprived bee.

Greeley turns to me. "You're sure you want to down that thing?"

"Um . . . no?" I wipe dribbles from my mouth.

"We've got an awful long way to go, so you might want to conserve it." She peers up at the sun as if staring directly in the center *doesn't* blind her.

"Just one more sip," I whisper to myself. *One more sip . . .*

"Your funeral," she says. Pauses mid-step. Turns to me. "Know who I'd like to see dead, sans funeral?" *Um, please don't say me.* "Peter." *Phew.* "He's more fucked in the head than I am, which is saying something. What'd you see in him? He good in bed or something?" I spit out my water onto the back of her neck. "Ah, refreshing."

"I don't want to talk about Peter."

"We've got nothing else to do for the next hour, Blondie. Might as well entertain me."

"Believe it or not, I don't exist to entertain you."

"Today, you do," Greeley says, patting the sniper on her back. "I'm your security blanket, am I not?"

"How do I know your plan isn't to feed me to the wolves?"

"I need you alive, don't I?"

"To find out what Chandler's up to." She nods. "Are your intentions as pure as Chief's?"

"No one's intentions are as pure as Chief's," Greeley says. I'm unsure if it's sarcasm in her tone I've detected. "He wants to 'save the world' because he believes 'all humans deserve a chance at life.' "

Ah, so not sarcasm, then. "Even Chandler?"

Greeley grunts.

I prod. "Do you want Chandler dead?"

Greeley swipes sweat off her forehead. "Do I want the woman I was engaged to dead? The woman who left me to start her own cult in the guise of creating a 'community of equality'? Yeah, I do. Even if she's not experimenting on Garrett and Eagan, a person like her in power is a recipe for disaster. She'll end up destroying what's left of the world. Which isn't much." She picks up a rock and skips it along the barren, cracked street, watching as it skitters into the brush on the left-hand side of the road.

The street is lined by miles and miles of destruction, all decimated by the flood.

"Don't know how I couldn't see who Chandler really was, or Chief, for that matter. Guess I was blinded by love, and Chief by the goodness of his own heart."

"I'm sorry," I say, surprised to find I mean it.

"Shut the hell up. Your turn to entertain me. Tell me about dream boy."

Greeley's not giving up. "What do you want to know?"

"You and Peter. You were an item. Why? He's a douchebag, and you're . . . a delicate little flower."

"Thanks for the compliment."

"That wasn't—"

"I know," I say.

I walk step in step with Greeley. I close my eyes and feel the sun on my skin. Hope the light will give me the answers I seek. The sun, so cruel and kind. The sun, so warm, but if you get too close, it burns. A friend or foe? Can one be both?

I exhale, the breath long and smooth. "He was kind to me. At first. He found us. That first year after Z Day, my grandma, sister, and I stayed in our home, boarded up like hermits. My brother, West, was alive back then. He went on supply runs for us, refused to let any of us go with him. Sometimes he'd be gone for an entire day, and we'd keep ourselves busy with Scrabble. And Bananagrams."

"Bananawha?"

"Never mind. When my dad left, West was away at college. Z Day gave him the opportunity to act as the man of the house, I guess. I think protecting us gave him purpose. Only, if he'd brought me with him on runs, maybe we wouldn't have ended up so defenseless . . ."

I trail off, unsure why I'm opening up to Greeley of all people. Granted, she *did* open up to me. Maybe one day I'll make her friend list.

Greeley launches past me toward the side of the road. A zombie lies flat on the ground, its skull embedded in the dirt like a stone. "Kinda like this?" She yanks a knife out of her back pocket and drives it through its skull.

"Just like that, Greeley."

She smiles, satisfaction plastered all over her face, then brushes imaginary dirt off her shoulder. "Please, continue with your monologue."

I tell Greeley the rest of our story: how Grandma, Bunny, and I were trapped behind the pharmacy counter in Walgreens. How Peter showed up. How he saved us.

And I'm reminded that it could have been Jasper.

Greeley pulls a compass out of her pocket, checks it, shoves it back in. "How heroic."

"He was," I say. "That day, he was heroic."

"A man does one good thing, and you overlook the rest of his bullshit."

I pause. Think about it. *Really* contemplate why I put up with his bullshit for so long. At first, I overlooked his actions, but eventually, I accepted them as part of the deal. "He was good to me, and then he wasn't. It was always like that. He'd do something horrible, then apologize. He'd secretly bring home medicine for Bunny and Grandma, or sneak me packs of mini M&Ms . . ."

"So he bought your love."

"He—yeah. He did." And then I'd give him what *he* wanted—sex—and the cycle would repeat. "But I was using him, too. I figured out what he wanted, and I pretended to be his doll. It was the only way to get medicine for my family."

"So you were a hustler, huh? Good for you," Greeley says. "No, really. Congratulations, Kota—you've just earned a fraction of my respect."

"A fraction, gee, how'd I get so lucky?"

Greeley winks, but then her eyes flick past my shoulder, lighting up as the screech of a turning tire fills our otherwise soundless setting. She throws me to the side of the road and screams, *"Shit!"*

A white pickup truck with oversized tires speeds down the road. I watch in awe as Greeley stands, unfazed, in the center of the road.

"I knew it." Greeley looks at me and smiles. "This fucker's so predictable." Sniper slung securely over her back, she pulls her pistol out of her back pocket, and then motions at me. "Give me your pistol."

"You literally have a sniper. *And* a pistol. Don't you think you're being a little—"

"Slide it over!"

I swipe dried leaves off my bruised ass and stand up, both because I'm not dumb enough to toss a loaded gun, but also because she has a loaded sniper. *She has a loaded sniper.* Why does she want my pistol again?

I scramble over to Greeley and smack the gun in her left hand. "Thanks," she says. "Didn't want to waste this beauty's bullets."

Greeley double-fists the pistols and sets her eyes on the rapidly advancing target.

"Why can't we just let them pass?" I call.

"Because I want the truck, Dakota, and I'm going to get it." Greeley's voice oozes with confidence, but I'm skeptical. As the rumbling engine crescendos, the feeling blooms into full-blown panic.

What if the truck driver's armed? What if the driver shoots Greeley before she gets a chance? I'd be stranded outside the Split. Hungry, hot, and alone.

Big, fat splotches of gray cloud my vision. Is it my heart that's rumbling the ground, or is it the truck? I stumble back over to the side of the road—to get the hell out of Greeley's fire—and slink into the bushes. Crunchy, dying leaves turn to dust beneath my feet. Critters weave through blades of grass.

And then it begins.

I've never played *Grand Theft Auto*, but I imagine it goes something like this.

Greeley cocks both guns, raises them. She narrows her eyes and fires the gun on the right, then the one on the left.

Both shots hit their target.

And both shots are loud.

Zombies will be here soon.

As bullets blow through the windshield, the truck veers to the right and comes to a skittering, *screeching* halt on the side of the road. The windshield wounds are clean. No spidery veins extend off either bullet hole. If uninjured, the driver could start the truck back up and be on his merry way.

Instead, the driver—a large, floppy man—slides out of the car and lands on all fours with a *thud*.

"The *fuck* was that?" he slurs, the words coming out like his cheeks are full of molasses. "Damn near blow off my ear, now did ya?" His hand cups his ear, which is indeed bloody.

"Flesh wound," Greeley says, popping her gun back into her pocket. She holds out the other one to me. "Kota, here's this back."

I stand up, snatch the gun out of Greeley's hand, and jog over to the chubby man lying in a pathetic heap on the ground. I'll be damned if I don't do the bare minimum and see that he's all right.

"He could be armed," Greeley says, her voice close behind me.

I do a quick scan of the man. He wears nothing but a muscle tee and baby blue swim trunks. Harmless. "We're good," I say to Greeley. Then, to the man, "Going swimming, sir?" He rolls onto his hip, asphalt puncturing his skin, and pushes up to a slouchy seat.

"Nah, I just like the way the trunks feel 'round my jimmies. No compression—lots of breeze. It's the little things in life, y'know?"

"Sure . . . Can I take a look at your ear?" Blood seeps down to his chin as he removes his hand from his ear for me. The bullet has barely gone through the cartilage; it's not worse than when I got my ears pierced as a kid. "You're going to be fine," I say. I pull my knife out of my pocket. The man screams, Greeley tells him to shut the fuck up, and I cut off a bit of fabric from my shirt. I ask with my eyes: *May I?* He nods, and I bandage his ear. "There. Good as new. What's your name?"

As the man opens his mouth, Greeley grunts. "His name is Andrew. Don't pity him. He's been sneaking into my yard and stealing my wood for years—"

"I didn't think you cared!"

"Of course I care, you asshole. You took what's mine, and now I can take your truck and not feel a lick of guilt about it."

"Not Telulah," he says, his eyes gazing longingly at his white truck. "Please."

"And I'm gonna rename her."

"No!"

"I'm thinking Tony?"

"*No!*"

"And I'm gonna leave your ass here. On this crumbling road."

I step in. "Greeley—"

"Come on, Kota. Let's go."

I look down at the blubbering baby on the ground beneath me, eyes spilling over with tears, fat lips quivering. My stomach sinks. "We're not leaving him here."

"Yes." Greeley strides up to me and grabs my arm. Her fingernails pierce into my skin, leaving little welts that sting like a BB gun pellet. "We are."

"No." I pull out of her grip. "It's cruel. Do you really want to turn into her?"

Greeley narrows her eyes and whispers, "Martyr," before putzing over to Andrew's truck. She flings open the driver's door. "Sweet! Another knife!"

"Please," Andrew begs. "I won't make it back alive without it. These roads ain't safe."

"We made it here on foot," Greeley says, sifting through the center console. She tosses a few quarters on the ground beside Andrew. Useless litter. "Get yourself something pretty." She hops out of the car and throws her hands on her hips. "You ready, Kota?"

I hold out my hand. "Give me the knife. You don't need it."

She rolls her eyes.

"Give me the fucking knife, Greeley."

"Fine! You want the knife? Take it. And you—stop whining. Shouldn't have stolen my wood, asshat."

Andrew throws himself face-first onto the broken asphalt with the dramatism of a stage actor. His sweaty shoulders shake with sobs as Greeley tosses the dagger to the ground beside him. I squat next to him. My knees crack like snapping pretzels on the way down. Snot drips down Andrew's lips as I unzip my backpack and lay my flask out for him.

Once, after a birthday party, I was given a goodie bag. Pink-and-white polka dot paper bags brimming with bubblegum-flavored lip gloss, stickers, friendship bracelets. Andrew's goodies come sans bag, but it's all I can offer him.

"You drove here," I tell him. "You know how to get home. It's a straight shot—one hour walking distance. Drink the water, keep your knife in your hand, and get back to the Split before sundown." I look at Greeley, whose smile I'd like to slap off her face. Partly because I also want to hug her—now we have a car. This is what it takes to survive, isn't it? "And think again before stealing Greeley's shit. I can say with 99 percent certainty—"

"100 percent certainty," Greeley adds.

"That the consequences will be much worse next time."

Andrew nods without lifting his head.

"You'll be fine," I say. I walk to the truck's passenger's side. "Let's go, Greeley."

"Goodbye, Telulah," Andrew mutters.

As I shut the door, pebbles stack up in the depths of my belly. So does power.

CHAPTER
THIRTY-SEVEN

GREELEY SHIFTS THE GEAR INTO PARK. MANUAL DRIVE. DAD NEVER had a chance to teach me. Grandma barely knew how to drive an automatic.

Greeley drives Telulah—er, Tony—up a mountain, through dense woods, and parks us in front of a small lake. An oasis.

The water is blue-green, the color of a turtle's shell. While the lake is small, it's long enough that swimming the entire distance would wear me out. Maybe not when I was an athlete in high school, but certainly now.

Out of practice, out of shape, deficient in nutrients.

Warm, humid air hits me like a slap in the face as I step out of the truck. I breathe in swampy air. Exhale.

Trees, both alive and zombie, surround the water like eyelashes. Crinkled and crushed leaves form a crown around the bank, some dipping into the water like a feather in ink. Under other circumstances, the setting would be beautiful. But as it stands, it's terrifying. It's peaceful, but peace in this world isn't a sure thing, so I can't trust it.

Every sound puts me on edge: the wind, the leaves, the creaking of our new vehicle. Every bubble of water sends shards of lightning through my core.

"When did you find this place?" I ask Greeley. The two of us stand at the edge of the bank. The water's surface wrinkles like a velvet blanket.

"We can go anywhere we damn please. Whenever we damn please. Remember?"

"There's a reason we weren't allowed to go to forests in Egal," I say. "Do you not remember the boar?"

"Can't recall . . . I was busy slaying a deer."

"You didn't answer my question."

"I've had lots of time to explore," she says, bending down to pick up a pebble. She flings it, and it skips along the surface. Ah. So her earlier skipping was practice.

"Are we safe here?" I look around for wild animals. Close my eyes and listen. I hear no creatures. *Peace.*

Greeley huffs out a laugh and smears an evil smirk across her face. "Nowhere is safe." I crack my knuckles and then squeeze my toes in my shoes, and am graced with a litany of crunches. "What are you, a Cracker Jack?"

"I think I'm dehydrated."

"Boohoo." She juts out her lower hip. "There's a big lake just over there. Why don't you jump in?"

I look at the lake, a shiver crawling down my spine as I wonder what's hiding underneath the glimmering surface. There could be zombie moccasins under there, for all I know. "What are we doing here?"

"To fish, of course," she answers matter-of-factly. She pulls bait and a bullet out of her pocket. "You first."

"You don't need to swim to fish, Greeley."

"I didn't bring a net; also, I need to get water from the center." She points out to the middle of the lake. When I make a funny face at her, she says, "Thermal stratification. Less algae and muck the deeper you go—and I need the cleanest sample I can get."

"For the cure?"

"No, for making snow cones." *God, what I wouldn't do for an ice-cold Cherry Coke snow cone right now.* "Yes, Blondie, for the cure. Besides . . ." Greeley pauses, licking her lips. "The big fish swim in the deep. And I, for one, have a hankering for pan-fried bass."

"Go fish, then. Collect your own water samples. I'm not doing your dirty work for you."

The humor drains from Greeley's face. She narrows her eyes. "You say you want to keep your family safe. How do you plan on doing that? You can't defend them, you can't *fight* for them, and you can't feed them. What can you do?"

"I won't take your bait."

"No." She shoves a rubbery worm in my hand. "*There's* your bait. Jasper won't be around to feed you, and you have nothing to trade with other Macs. We hunt to survive. What's your choice? What are you made of?"

I don't know what I'm made of.

"Fuck you," I say. "I will survive."

Greeley claps me on the shoulder and smiles. "Let's test that newfound strength, then, huh?"

Shit. Okay. Let's test it.

CHAPTER THIRTY-EIGHT

I AM BARE. EXPOSED. VULNERABLE. STRIPPED DOWN TO MY UNDERPANTS.

Greeley needs a sample from the center of the lake, and I need dinner. There's certainly a better way to accomplish our goals, but we don't have a net, a rod, or a boat. We have Greeley, and we have me. And only one of us has something to prove.

That's why I'm here, at the edge of the bank in my panties. I'm about to dive into cold, hidden waters to prove something. To prove something to myself, to Greeley, to everyone who's ever used me, not believing me capable of doing or thinking or acting on my own. Which, admittedly, is a lot of people.

I'm doing this because Greeley is right—they *all* are. I need to learn how to survive. And I will.

But why is the only solution to dive headfirst into death's grim arms?

The sky churns and rumbles. Cold air blows a loose strand of hair behind my ear. I twist it into my ponytail as Greeley elbows me in the ribs. "Better be quick," she says, handing me a small capped tube. "I reckon we've got about fifteen minutes before that storm rolls in."

"Weather's been unpredictable lately," I say. A shadow blankets the lake, turning the water a deep emerald.

"Excellent observation, Captain Obvious," Greeley huffs. She leans in close to me and points to the lake. "Look for striped bass."

"Let me get this straight. Not only do you think I'll be able to find—and catch—a single fish in this murky-ass water, but a specific species? Are you out of your mind?"

"Yes," she says matter-of-factly, "I am. And so are you, Crocodile Dundee."

"Wait. There are—"

"No crocodiles. Do you know anything about geography?"

"Well, there are zombees and zomboar and maybe *zombass*, so I don't know. I thought it was a logical fucking question, Greeley."

"You thought wrong." She bends down and picks up another rock. One, two, three, four skips. "Any further questions?"

"What if—what if there's a body in there? One that's turned?"

"You and all your questions. Relax. I've swum in this lake a dozen times and have never encountered anything other than a flailing zombie fish. All you've gotta do is take that tube, fill up a clean sample for me, and take this spear—" Greeley bends to unzip her bag where it rests at her feet. She pulls out goggles and a short, four-pronged spear, then waves them both around. "—and stab a fish. In the brain, of course, so it doesn't turn when it dies. Nothing to be scared of. Here. My gifts to you."

I accept the goggles and spear, but my hand shakes so hard I drop the weapon, and its prongs stab the sandy shore. "Screw this. I'm not going into the water."

"Oh, for fuck's sake," Greeley says, peeling off her shirt. Without a backward glance, she plunges into the water.

I hold my breath. *One, two, three* seconds she's beneath the surface. During those three seconds, fears race through my brain. If Greeley drowns, I can't drive home. I don't know how to drive a stick. If she dies, Macoby's best chance at a cure dies, too. And, if Greeley is *bit* underneath the surface and comes back up as a zombie, she'll kill me. I can't defend myself against a zomGree.

She bobs back up and swims to the shore. When she's out, she jimmies her wet pant leg like she's shaking out a turd. A small fish hits the earth and flails around. "See how easy that was? This little guy swam right in. Hand that back. Thanks." Greeley bends down and stabs the fish in the head.

Thunder claps overhead.

Prove yourself, Kota. You're a good swimmer. You have a weapon. You're strong, you're strong, you're strong.

"Jesus, fine, I'm going."

I pick the spear off the ground, square my shoulders, and take a slight step forward. As the cold water's edge kisses my toes, I curl them into the rocky sand. I imagine the lake looked a lot like this before Z Day. Quiet, blue, calm. But I've never felt more unlike myself. Ignorant, weak, reckless. I've made questionable decisions before—like shoving a dozen Quaker bars in my hoodie—but they were always made to keep me and my family safe. That's what this is, too, though, isn't it? I'm planning for the future. Maybe next time I go fishing, I can take Bunny and Grandma. They'd like the lake. And then we could trade the fish we catch for cups of lemonade.

I slide the tube into the side of my bra and shove the spear between my thighs, squeezing while I slide the goggles over my eyes. The trees turn fuzzy, blurry, like looking at Jasper through a wine-drunk haze. Distinctly beautiful, but soft around the edges.

I suck in a breath, clutch the spear in my hand, take a big step forward. The cold water hits my shins, sending needles into my skin. I've got to bite the bullet, just like Coach always said.

This one's for you, Coach Wang.

I plunge into the lake. Cool water streams through my hair, and water gurgles as it fills my ears. The world goes quiet. A mossy green blanket covers my eyes.

I don't think; I only kick. My feet join together into a make-shift tail, and I pretend I'm a mermaid. The water shifts to a bitter cold as I dolphin-kick myself toward the center of the lake. I look left and right, left and right, my feet wading ferociously to keep me from sinking to the muddy ground.

No fish.

Where are the fucking fish?

I gasp as I break the surface, my lungs filling with sweet, damp air. I've made it maybe a pool length's way toward the center of the lake. And still, no fish.

Please don't let this be how I die.

No. I will not give up. I will find a fucking fish. I will kill it and feast on its flesh and share it with *nobody*.

I am Poseidon gripping his trident, threatening all fish who beseech me to live.

I swim further toward the center.

Kick, kick, kick.

Don't quit.

Chandler's chiding voice echoes in my ears: *I'd never trade two men for one woman—especially one so dispensable. Bring me something I want, and we can talk about a trade. In the meantime . . . keep her. She's yours to babysit.*

My thoughts spiral with words she's said before. Then, words she hasn't.

Your sister does not need you. Bunny has not a mother or father, and get this, she doesn't even have a functioning endocrine system, yet she's still fine without you, Kota. Peter gave her the insulin. Peter. Not you.

Nobody needs you. Nobody wants you. You're a drain on our resources, and we're all better off without you.

I kick harder.

The water turns icy cold, and I remember I've got to get Greeley's sample. I take a quick breath of air, then plunge below, wading while I pull the tube from out of my bra. Careful not to drop the spear, I fill the tube with water and pop the lid on. Mission accomplished. And now? Now it's my turn.

Screw Poseidon. I'm a goddamn mermaid with a golden tail and pearly-white hair and gills, and I'm going to survive.

I spot a fish.

Am I hallucinating? No, there are its fins. And it's not a zombie fish—in-tact scales, breathing gills, black eyes, and a closed jaw.

I move as little as possible, lightly wading just to stay afloat. Like cats and like Greeley, should you wait for fish to come to you?

Bunny ran off the infamous neighborhood cat we used to feed on the front porch growing up. The moment her stubby little talons latched on to its swirling black tail, it never came back. No matter how many times we ran up and down the cul-de-sac, chanting, *"Black Jack, come back! Black Jack, come back!"*

My gut tells me Black Jack's still prowling a blown-up neighborhood somewhere. My gut *also* tells me that this fish, who from here forward will go by Bass Jack, will come to me if I can keep myself still enough.

Sure enough, the fish drifts closer to me. Spear clutched in my right hand, I extend my left hand out—slowly, methodically—and then I snatch. Bass Jack puts up a fight, his fins slicing into my palm. But I don't let go. I wrench myself into the fresh air, breaking the surface. I kick my feet wildly and stab the fish in the head. It goes limp. The blood drips down my wrist, finding its way into the water and turning it a muddy shade of brown.

I drop the spear, but I don't care. I've won. I pound my fist proudly in the air, but something grabs my ankle. And sinks its jagged nails into my flesh.

A warped, bloated zombie claws toward the surface. Spongy skin droops down its cheeks, eyes bulging out of their sockets. The zombie can't swim, but it can't drown, either. Unlike me. Water gurgles in my throat as I cry out for help. The zombie's own underwater shrieks ring in my ears as its nails sink deeper into my calf, hitting tendon. I ignore the searing pain coursing through my leg and *kick*. My foot connects with the zombie's shoulder, but it doesn't release its grip.

Try harder, Kota.

I kick again. Finally, the zombie's arm breaks off like a soft pretzel. My calf throbs with the release of its sharp nails. Bass Jack in hand, I freestyle back toward the shore as the one-armed zombie struggles to tread water. Its gnarly screams echo across the lake's surface. Blood gushes from my calf as I swim like my life depends on it. Because it does.

Coach Wang would be proud.

The water turns to blurs, like drunken paint strokes. My chest aches for sweet, fresh air. I've never wanted anything more. Blobs of black and purple and gray cloud my vision.

My calf throbs even more than my oxygen-depleted heart. As pain pulses up my entire leg, the water turns warm. Then, I can stand. As soon as I make it to shore, I drop Bass Jack and collapse onto the rocky sand. I sputter out water, every part of my body aching, and cough until my lungs are dry.

Blood pools on the sand by my ankle.

Dread courses down my core. I wasn't bitten, was I? No. These are puncture marks—five of them, from the thing's nasty fingernails.

I briefly scan the rest of my body, running my hands up and down my neck, torso, and legs, and exhale a sigh of relief so big that my breath could fill up a hot air balloon.

I'm okay.

I got away.

"Striped bass," Greeley's voice says from above. Her head blocks the sun, her blond-black hair swinging over her chin as she peers down at me. "Didn't think you had it in you."

"I thought you said there weren't any fucking bodies in here?" I crane my head back toward the lake, the rippling surface turning glassy once more.

"I wasn't lying—I've never seen anything in there before. Never swam as far out as you, though."

"I almost *died*—"

"Hold that thought. Unless we get that wound to stop bleeding, you very well will die." She makes a face. "Damn, that's a lot of blood. I give you a sixty-forty chance."

Sixty to live, or forty? I can't concentrate enough to care. My calf flutters with its own heartbeat as Greeley rips off a sleeve of her shirt. As she wraps the fabric around the bleeding claw marks on my ankle, I ask, "You don't think there are more zombies in there, do you?"

"Maybe," Greeley says. I try not to flinch as she tugs the fabric so it's taut against my leg. "No reason to be afraid of waterlogged fuckers, though."

"Agree to disagree."

"There," Greeley says, knotting the makeshift tourniquet. "You'll be fine. Probably."

"Why are you being nice to me?"

Greeley rolls her eyes, and I wonder how many times she does that a day. Does she ever get sick of giving attitude? "I'm not being nice to you. I'm *fixing* you. Chief needs your ass alive, and Jasper *wants* you alive for some reason—and those are the only two people I'd like to not piss off."

Greeley stares at Bass Jack for a moment, then rips off her other sleeve. She wraps leftover fabric around it, then shoves the wrapped-up fish into her backpack.

I press up onto my elbows. "You don't think that fish is yours, do you?"

"I just saved you, didn't I? Consider it payment."

"I wouldn't have gone swimming with a zombie if not for you, Greeley."

"You made your own choice. And now you have to live with it."

Though I want to tell her to shove it where the sun don't shine, Greeley is right. I'd finally been given the space to make a choice, and I made mine. A stupid, stupid choice that could very well result in an infection and maybe even death. But . . .

"Bass Jack is mine," I say. "I caught it."

Greeley crosses her arms. "We'll split it."

"No, we will not."

"Yes, we will."

Splash. I whip my head away from Greeley. A raisin-like, bloated hand scratches the shore. An arm and shoulder follow as the water-warped zombie crawls out of the lake. A gurgling groan breaks the silence, and water bubbles from its mouth.

A sudden spike of jealousy toward the zombie tears through me. This monstrous creature knows only hunger. It feels no remorse for its actions, whereas I am hindered by empathy and ego and fear. I suck in air through my teeth. The zombie does not love.

What an uncomplicated life that must be.

I grab my knife and limp-run to the water's edge. The thing's rotting torso emerges from the water. My hand shakes, but I do not hesitate a moment longer. I stab it in the skull. With a final shriek, the zombie stills.

244

My pulse jumps as realization dawns on me. "That was my first kill."

"Good work." Greeley slaps me on the back. "How's it feel?"

I stare at the yellow bones protruding from the zombie's shoulder, bloody flaps of skin caressing the lake's shore. "Sad," I answer, surprising myself. I expected to feel powerful or strong or satisfied, but I feel . . . sad. I realize I've never *wanted* to kill anything before—and maybe that's what's been holding me back. Not competence, but compassion. A piece of my humanity died with this zombie. And if I want to survive, I have to be willing to lose more. I have to let go of the Kota who froze in Walgreens. I have to be *more* like this zombie. For Bunny's and Grandma's sakes, *I have to*.

I'm done overlooking threats. No longer will I leave my life to chance.

I will do what it takes to survive.

The trees behind us rustle, and I'm ready to strike. I clutch my knife tighter, and Greeley reaches for hers. The stirring sounds intensify, and my heart creeps into my chest.

And then—

It's a deer.

A hearty deer with two delicate antlers, pure black eyes, and a large belly.

Greeley looks at me, and I at her.

I shake my head.

The deer is mine.

I slowly creep toward the creature, careful not to spook it. It doesn't move; perhaps it's just happy to see another living being.

I wish I had better news for you, deer.

Red-hot pain zings through my leg as I launch myself toward the beautiful creature. As it springs away, I tackle it.

I hear a rib crunch as the deer and I hit the earth—not sure *whose* rib crunched, but it's unimportant. I gaze into the deer's sweet eyes and wish so badly it didn't have to die. But oh, all this meat. I could feed myself—I could feed Bunny and Grandma— for months.

Mere days ago, I couldn't kill a bunny.

Today, I'm stronger.

As I pull my arm back to shove the knife into its brain, Greeley yells from behind, "Oh no, you don't."

Our knives hit the deer's temple at the same time. Metal clangs on metal, and the deer goes limp.

Greeley yanks her knife out of the deer's head, and blood spills, drenching its face in red. I pull my blood-soaked knife out and point it at Greeley's face, ignoring the rapid heartbeat in my chest. And the one in my leg, too.

"Changed my mind," Greeley says. "You can have the fish. I'll take the deer."

I step toward her. "That's not how this is going to work."

She returns my movement with a step of her own. "My knife went in first. Don't be a sore loser."

Rage like an active volcano erupts through me. My veins boil with molten lava, red splotches invading the edges of my vision. My ears ring. I clench my jaw so hard my teeth might shatter.

How *dare* she.

"I'm going to kill you."

"Try me," Greeley says, and she means it. I'm injured, and even if I wasn't, she could beat me in a physical match. I know she's egging me on, but I want so badly to give in.

Not a chance.

WWTNKD?

What would the new Kota do?

She'd say this: "You want the deer so bad? Fight me for it."

"Finally," Greeley says.

She lunges toward me, and I fumble over the massive belly of the deer. I land on my ass with a *thud*. She looms over me with a triumphant grin.

No. I'm going to take her down with me.

Ignoring the sharp pain slicing through my injured leg, I press into my hands and hurl toward her, circling my arms around her calves. She topples to the ground, a surprised breath escaping through her teeth as her shoulder catches the fall. I hitch myself over her torso and pin her down with my hips. Her brows furrow as I bring my fist up and slam it into her face.

Her nose. Her cheek. Other cheek. Nose again, because fuck you, Greeley, *fuck you.*

She squirms to escape, but she doesn't have any leverage. My knuckles burn as they make contact with her face again, again. Her head lolls side to side with every blow, each harder than the last. She may be losing steam, but I'm gaining it.

Enough, I tell myself. *Stop.*

But I can't.

I don't want to.

Three more. I get three more.

One for the fish. Another for the deer. A third and final punch for the goddamn Quaker bars she stole outside Pepsi Co.

My pulse pounds in my ears. I close my eyes to let the red dissipate—it glows orange, then yellow, then white, as I get my breathing under control. I sag backward onto my heels.

Lilac bruises bloom underneath Greeley's long lashes. There's no blood on her face, but I think she passed out. I reach down and grab her limp hand to confirm. Yep. I knocked out Greeley. And the power feels . . . good.

Only, as I pull my hand away, she snatches it and squeezes. "That all you got?"

"Let go of me."

To my surprise, she does. She sits up and wipes a bead of sweat off her swollen face. "Proud of you, Blondie. Those were some good swings. You feel better now, don't you?"

Yes, I want to tell her. But I don't.

I let my head droop in my hands. I whisper, "Half."

"What was that?"

"You can have half of the deer."

Uniformity fosters unity.

No. We both worked hard for this deer, so we'll share its meat.

"Deal," Greeley says.

I add, "But none of the fish."

"Never been a seafood girl anyway."

I offer Greeley my hand, and she takes it. Maybe this isn't the beginning of a beautiful friendship, but it's something. And that's enough for me.

CHAPTER THIRTY-NINE

"WE'LL TAKE THE DEER TO SLING TOMORROW," GREELEY SAYS. We jet down the highway, and the setting sun plunges below the horizon. "He loves skinning."

"How *did* Sling get his name?" I ask, wondering if his apparent love of skinning has anything to do with it.

"Apparently, as a kid, he had an obsession with slinging rocks at squirrels. When his dad found out, he wasn't disturbed like you might imagine. He was impressed. From that point on, his family exclusively ate game. Butchered all their own winnings. And Sling earned his title."

"That's why he's so good at cooking," I muse.

Greeley nods.

The familiar green I-25 sign tells me we're close to where we left Andrew. I don't feel terrible about taking his truck, though maybe I should.

I peer out the window, but I'm not sure what I'm hoping to find. If he had any smarts and skill, he'd be home by now.

Three exits from the Split, a zombie slogs down the road. Not just any zombie . . . a zombie wearing swim shorts. He—it—turns around as Greeley's headlights shine on his pudgy frame.

"Look what the cat dragged in," she says, slowing the truck to a crawl. Her solemn tone doesn't match her insensitive words, and disappointment pulls down her shoulders—a small chip in the callous front she wears; she was hoping he'd make it, too.

"Can you stop?"

"The idioms? No."

"The car. Please stop the car."

The car rolls to a stop, and a zombified Andrew stares directly into the headlights and meanders toward the truck. Unlike most zombies, especially newborns, he—*it*, dammit—doesn't have a lot of pep in his step. His slow pace and clumsy limbs will make this an easy takedown.

Physically, at least.

Milo's face flashes through my mind's eye.

My choices led to this, just like they led to Milo's. *My* fault. What good am I at making choices for myself if all I do is cause death?

Yet . . . I wouldn't have a truck, a fish, and a deer if I hadn't made those choices. I wouldn't have discovered strength—the strength I need to provide for myself and my family. I had to choose what served me, even if it put another in harm's way.

And right now, I choose mercy. *Rest in peace, Andrew.*

Knife in hand, I step out of the truck and limp toward him. A smell of unwashed armpits and rotten apples overwhelms me. I grab the greasy hair on the top of Andrew's chomping head, pull it toward me, and strike. He tumbles straight to the ground with a loud *thump*.

I gasp, startled at how easy it was to kill. I took down two zombies in one day. I'm proud of myself for that, but I'm horrified that I've become the kind of person who could leave another behind.

With weak knees, I bend down and fish around in his pocket for the knife and flask I gave him. Shit—he was speaking the truth before. He isn't wearing underpants. And his pocket has holes.

Zombie penis: something I never thought I'd have the distinct displeasure of coming into contact with.

Greeley drums her hands on the steering wheel as I slide in and slam the passenger door.

I take a swig from the flask. Andrew left a mouthful. Or maybe it's his backwash. I'm full of all kinds of Andrew fluid today.

I swipe the back of my hand along my mouth. "I feel like shit."

"Told you it wouldn't always be easy."

Yeah, but . . . this was our fault.

Greeley reaches over the console, and I think she's going to slap me or punch me or both. Only, she squeezes my shoulder. "Congratulations," she says. A puffy green bruise is forming under her left eye. "You've officially won my approval."

I smile, but it feels like sucking on a lemon. I've never met someone so calculating, so *loathsome*. And yet earning her respect has made this entire fucked-up day worth it.

What does that say about me?

As soon as I buckle up and slouch back in my seat, my ankle throbs. Had that waterlogged zombie bitten me—had it been its gnarly teeth that pierced my flesh instead of its fingernails—I would be like Andrew right now.

Instead, I fought it off. I swam away. Against it all, I survived.

When he hears about this, I hope Jasper will be proud.

Dammit, Kota. No. You do not *need his approval.*

I squeeze my eyes shut, images swarming behind my lids: Jasper's warm smile, his pleading eyes, the shape of his lips when he said those infuriating words . . .

I don't want you to die.

Jasper's voice echoes in my head. I want him to have meant those words, more than I care to admit. Honestly, I don't want to die, either. Because then I'd never get to see him again.

CHAPTER FORTY

JASPER IS THE SPITTING IMAGE OF GRANDMA, SWAYING IN A WOODEN rocking chair with a glass in his hand—except he's drinking wine, not sweet tea. Moths swarm to a lantern set on the ground next to his feet. All that's missing is an edition of *Playboy* hidden inside a *Better Homes* magazine. Grandma's favorite pastime.

Jasper's eyes peel open as I approach, a relieved smile forming on his wine-tinged lips.

He's happy I made it back.

I pause at the bottom of the steps, trying not to think about how those lips would taste pressed against mine. I shake the thought away. "Waiting up for me?"

He smirks. "What would you say if I was?"

Thank god it's dark outside, else he'd see the blush spreading to my ears.

Why must I blush so easily? And aren't I supposed to be mad at him?

I mosey up the steps and add an aloof edge to my voice as I ask, "Has this rocking chair always been here?"

"Nope."

"Who'd you take it from?" I ask. His face shows no signs that he's picking up on my tone.

"Someone less deserving than me," he answers, the chair creaking as he sways.

"Figures."

Before yesterday, I would have put myself on a moral high horse for hearing him say this. Today, I wish he'd stolen two.

After a long silence, Jasper says, "Listen, about earlier, I'm sorry—oh *shit*." He swipes dribbles of wine off his bloodred lips and hastily sets down his glass. The alcohol-induced haze clears from his eyes. He jumps off the porch and kneels down before me. "Kota, your ankle."

"Oh, that?" I wave a hand. "It's just a scratch."

Except it's not. It is throbbing. Like a mofo.

"What happened?"

"Did you know zombies can swim? Me neither."

Jasper stands and grabs my hand. "Come with me. We need to get some antibiotics on that or—"

"As far as I know, nobody's turned into a zombie from claw marks," I say, more to comfort myself than him. And also, "You haven't seen that happen before either . . . right?"

Jasper shakes his head and pulls me inside. "No. But if this gets infected, you *will* die. And you *will* turn into a zombie."

My chest collapses. "Comforting words, as always."

"Kota, I'm not here to comfort you."

His words are stern, but his eyes are muddled. For once, his eyes and his words don't seem to match.

"I think you are, though."

Jasper sucks in a breath but says nothing. We stand there, looking at each other, in complete silence, for quite a while. The air grows heavy. My tongue rests heavy in my mouth.

Finally, Jasper says, "Let's just clean this wound before you get infected."

"Zombie infected or *infected* infected?"

"I think it's spreading."

"What!"

"To your head."

"Oh my god." I lightly smack the side of his head, and a low, velvety laugh escapes from his lips. "Do I spot dimples under there?" I poke his prickly beard, and the divots beside the corners of his mouth deepen.

Instead of swatting my finger away like I expect, he catches it and then wraps his hand around mine. A thousand sparks race up my arm.

"You should laugh more," I say. "It suits you."

I try not to limp as he guides me down the short hallway toward his room. The cottage is dark and moody—*dare I say sexy?* Our feet are quiet on the stone floor, and I wonder if he can hear the loud thumping of my heart, too. That same damn heart plummets into the recesses of my belly when he pushes open the door.

"I thought you hid your bodies in the basement, but are they all actually in your *room*?"

Jasper ignores me, releasing my hand.

I already miss his touch.

He lights a half-melted candle resting on his dresser. Soft candlelight flickers as wind flutters in from the wide-open window on the opposite side of the room. A gentle breeze wafts inside. Crickets chirp, singing a song for the glistening moon above. The room smells of lavender soap and musk and wood.

"I've come so far," I whisper. "Please don't ax murder me."

"I don't have an ax."

"And if you did?"

"Best not to speculate."

Jasper winks and eases the closet door open. He pulls out a red first aid kit—very school nurse of him. Inside, there's rubbing alcohol, gauze, Band-Aids, and—

"I don't need stitches, do I?"

"Sit down," Jasper says. I take a seat on the hardwood, but he shakes his head. "The bed is much more comfortable."

"I—um . . ."

Jasper raises an eyebrow.

He's not here to seduce you, Kota. He's here to fix you.

"Okay," I say. "Thanks."

The cream bedding is soft and clean. No yellow spots, no dirt, nothing. Not only does this impress me greatly, but it also turns me on.

Pull it together, Kota!

I rest my head against the headboard and extend my left leg out toward Jasper. He roots around in the first aid kit and pulls out my childhood enemy: a needle. The bed sags as Jasper sits near my feet. He gently turns over my leg, inspecting the gaping, still-bloody lacerations. His fingers linger on my skin too long. No, not nearly long enough.

I want those damn fingers to graze my calf, my inner thighs, my ass, my—

"Just a few stitches, I think."

"No," I rebut, shaking my head and staring at the evil, pointy needle clutched in Jasper's fingers. "Please. No stitches."

"Kota, you just went to bat with a zombie. And you're scared of a little needle?"

"Yes," I answer matter-of-factly. "Yes, I am."

I was also scared of the zombie, thank you very much.

Jasper rolls his eyes but reaches into the first aid kit and pulls out a teeny-tiny little bottle. "This will help."

I twist open the cap and sniff. A spicy, bitter smell skips my nostrils and directly hits my brain. "Vodka?"

"My favorite," he says, opening the bottle of rubbing alcohol. "Drink it. This will hurt."

I nod and slam down the mini bottle of vodka. The warmth from the alcohol slithers down my throat, to my chest, and finally settles in the pit of my belly.

I take a deep, full breath and stare into Jasper's eyes. "Do it."

This is gonna hurt.

I guess I expect some sort of countdown, but Jasper makes his own rules. As he douses the open wounds with rubbing alcohol, bright, white, searing pain flashes through my leg. I bite my tongue so I don't scream. Coppery blood swims on my tongue.

"You all right?"

I try to keep quiet, I really do, but my mouth has other plans. "*Jesusfuckingchristthathurtsofuckingbad.*"

"I'm sorry—come again?"

"Are you done?" I ask, my chest heaving, and my body filling with heat.

Jasper wiggles a needle in my face. "Time to stitch. Focus on something else."

As he slides the needle into my flesh, I squeeze my eyes shut, but that only makes the pain worse. I'm suddenly in the lake again, the zombie's fingernails digging into me. My eyes snap open, and I involuntarily yank my leg away. The sharp sting intensifies as the needle plunges deeper.

"Kota," Jasper scolds, gently guiding my leg back in place.

I grit my teeth. "Sorry."

Heart racing, I force my focus somewhere else. *Anywhere* else. I look around the candlelit room. My eyes land on a framed dragon-shaped collage on the top of his bedside table. The art is small, and the paper used is colorful. When I make out a few words, *nodes of cherry*, it dawns on me.

"Is that dragon made out of wine bottle labels, too?"

"What'd you mean, *too*?"

"As in, *also*."

"You're cute." Before my cheeks have a chance to turn rosy, Jasper sews two pieces of flesh together. The pain is searing hot, and it takes everything in me not to slap his hand away.

Why do things have to get worse before they get better?

"You made that art piece in my room." I wince. "The framed collage. *Gah*. Made out of wine labels. *Fuck*. Right?" Jasper ignores my eyes. He couldn't possibly be embarrassed. But the look on his face . . . Through gritted teeth, I say, "It's beautiful."

Jasper wipes the needle off with rubbing alcohol. "There. You'll be healed up in no time."

The stitches are clean, the skin red and puffy. While my leg may not be a work of art, it sure as hell looks twenty times better than it did ten minutes ago.

As Jasper packs up the first aid kit, I say, "So. You can clearly clean a wound. Can you clean a fish?"

✳ ─ ✳ ─ ✳ ─ ✳ ─ ✳ ─ ✳

HEAR ME OUT: I'VE NEVER BEEN TO A JOINT FANCIER THAN OLIVE GARDEN. But I swear to God, this fish could be plated in a Michelin-Star restaurant, and critics would be none the wiser.

Could be the Old Bay seasoning. Could be that it tastes better tipsy. I've got a hunch, though, that the exquisite flavor has nothing to do with the fish and everything to do with me. I fought tooth and nail for this food. I won.

Bass Jack is the best thing I've ever eaten. And he washes down good with wine.

Jasper and I eat it simply: with our fingers on a rock next to the creek in his yard. He started a small fire for us to roast it, and I found a stick. The flames crackle, sending billows of smoke floating above us. I lick my greasy fingers clean and wipe them on my jeans. We sit in silence, staring at the rippling water and listening to the sounds of nature.

As my head starts to nod forward, I yank it up and slap myself in the cheek.

"What the hell was that for?" Jasper asks.

"Sleepy," I say. "Old trick West taught me—my brother." I turn to Jasper and force a smile. "And I can't fall asleep before I tell you something."

Jasper tilts his head to the side. "Hmm?"

"I—I'm leaving."

Silence lingers as Jasper soaks up my stuttered words. There's a flash of confusion in his brown eyes, but it's gone as soon as it comes. I twiddle my fingers, staring absently at a loose thread on my rolled-up pants.

Jasper's quiet voice shakes me out of my thoughts. "Where are you going?"

"We ran into someone outside the Split. No, not just someone—Andrew. Greeley's backdoor neighbor."

"He still rocking swim trunks?"

For once, I don't smile at Jasper's coy remark. "He was. He . . . didn't make it."

And it was my fault.

Jasper asks, "Did Gree have something to do with that?"

I nod. "So did I." I search Jasper's eyes, but I don't see the judgment I expect to find. I see pity. Pity, perhaps, because I've finally bent to the new world. I'm no longer the same meek Kota who was kidnapped and brought to Macoby. "And so his place is empty. Greeley's keeping watch tonight, since it's vacant, and I'm here. But tomorrow, I plan to make Andrew's house my home."

"You don't want to live here," he says. Not a question.

"I want to live in Macoby."

"But not here."

"I've overstayed my welcome," I add, unsure what he wants me to say. My mouth is a fountain, and I keep going. "You took me in as a favor to Chief. You fought for this place—and I've just barged in like it's mine. But it's never been mine."

You've *never been mine.*

"What if I . . ." Jasper trails off. The rhythmic chirps of crickets have never been so loud in my ears.

What if I what? *What if I wanted you to stay?*

I stay silent, yearning for him to open his mouth. To say what I desperately want to hear. But he just shakes his head, his brown curls tumbling over his forehead.

Finally, he clears his throat. "Okay. When are you leaving?"

That's it? That's all I get? Fine.

"In the morning."

I can't bring myself to turn down one last night with Jasper—even if he won't admit he wants me to stay. I crack my knuckles then yank on my thumb, all but pulling it out of its socket.

Jasper breaks the tension. He says, "I'll help you pack," and we both laugh.

Quickly, my smile falters. "I only have two things, but they're on the other side of the Split."

Bunny and Grandma.

"We'll get them back." Jasper lands a gentle hand on my knee.

I gape at both his touch and his words.

"Are you—are you comforting me?"

"I guess I am."

Jasper and I sit together, his hand on my leg, staring at the moon shimmering behind the tall trees, until I finally nod off.

At some point in the night, I wake up in bed. Much as I'd like to stay awake, to soak up the stone surroundings and memorize the collage on the wall, my eyes can't stay open. I blow out the flickering candle on my bedside table and fall asleep in Jasper's house, for the last time.

CHAPTER FORTY-ONE

THE HOUSE IS MUCH LIKE ANDREW: IN SHAMBLES. THE GUTTERS hang on by an invisible thread, the front patio is covered in a thick layer of red dirt, and sharp tree limbs threaten to pierce through a side window. The sun slowly rises before the house, shining on the peeling butter-yellow siding. A violent mixture of ivy and kudzu fight for real estate up the side of the house, crawling and twisting and reaching for the light.

I grip the strap of my backpack, tugging it higher onto my shoulder. This backpack and everything inside—a couple sticks of Jack Links, a stale bag of Goldfish, a filled-up flask, and Neosporin—was all given to me by Jasper.

This house, a one-story, disintegrating bungalow, is my home. I finally have something that's mine. I have something that I fought for, that I *took*. Well, with the help of Greeley, who was all too excited to guard the home against raiders last night. Am I surprised she wants me as her backdoor neighbor? Kind of. But she admitted herself I earned her approval. I've proved that I belong here, in Macoby. So why does it feel like I'm running away?

I wonder how Andrew spent his time on this patchy front lawn. And did he sway on this rotted porch, listening to the cicadas? Did he watch zombie spiders weave this feathery web beneath the wall sconce?

Would he be mad that I now claimed his house as my own?

I'm mad at myself.

I twist the doorknob—unlocked. Either Andrew was too trusting of his fellow Macs, or Greeley did me a solid. Both options seem impossible.

I open the door, and I'm not sure what I expected, but it's not this. The house is full of light, a little piece of heaven shining through the open windows. Tattered curtains billow in the breeze. The tile floor fits the space nicely. A worn recliner, with a saggy middle and torn armrests, sits before a mantel. On it, a flaking oil painting of a colorful field of flowers.

And then there are pictures. Everywhere.

Faded photos of Andrew and a dolled-up woman wearing a bright shade of pink lipstick in every single image: playing cards together, laughing in the middle of a dance floor, smiling with hot dogs at a baseball game . . .

My breath hitches. Tears get stuck in my throat like a fat wad of gum. I press my middle fingers into my palms to center myself.

Breathe.

But breathing feels like the hardest, most unnatural thing in the world right now as the memories held within Andrew's pictures swarm my vision.

Andrew wipes the corner of her mouth with his thumb, fixing her smeared pink lipstick, but careful not to show her his hand of cards.

Right foot, let's stomp. Left foot, let's stomp. Cha cha now, y'all! Andrew grabs her by the waist and pulls her across the dance floor.

Hot dogs! Get your hot dogs for the seventh inning stretch! Andrew makes sure to get two hot dogs, one with mustard and relish, just the way she likes it.

I choke on an inhale.

I'm the last person who will ever see these photos. Andrew and his lover's memories end with me.

How long will this churning storm of guilt plague me?

I left Andrew. *I* fed him to the wolves. And now, he's gone. Really, truly, gone.

The warm sun breaks through the window, beams of light reflecting off the glass of the picture frames, distorting the images.

Rage and guilt build in my chest, and when I can't take it any longer, I scream. I scream so hard that my throat gets rugburn. I scream until my brain throbs. My eyes bulge and my ears ring. I scream with my fists curled so tight my broken nails dig into my flesh and make me bleed. I take all of Andrew's memories—every single framed photograph—and I break them. I hurl the glass onto the hard floor and let the shattered bits cut my ankles. I pull the treasured photos from the debris, and I rip them apart, then I open the front door and scatter them in the wind.

When I walk back inside, the ground crunches under my feet, shards digging into the soles of my shoes. I slam my backpack and all my stupid shit onto the ground. And then, finally, I sit, curl my knees into my chest, and weep.

CHAPTER FORTY-TWO

THE DAY PASSES IN A HAZY BLUR. I SIT IN THE LIVING ROOM, ALONE. I walk to the front porch and pick up the pieces of the swing, alone. I rip down Andrew's curtains and bundle up the broken glass in them, tempted to use the lump as a pillow.

The sun sets, and darkness creeps into the house. There are two bedrooms. One is empty, unused. I close the door. In the second bedroom, there's an unmade bed and a mirror.

I look like shit.

Frizzy strands of hair hang in straggles around my face, yellow tinges my deep eye bags, and my chapped lips are crusty with blood. I collapse backward onto the bed.

I hate it here.

A knock jolts me out of a dreamless sleep. Begrudgingly, I head to the front door, but Greeley flings it open before I have the chance.

"Greeley." I step forward and, shocking both of us, hug her. "It's nice to see you."

Her body is as stiff as a scarecrow. "The fuck is this?"

"Please hug me."

Greeley frees an arm and whacks me with a wooden plank. "Get a grip, Dakota."

I choke up. "I—I'm just—I really—" I suck on a lemon, and the juice forms a thick bubble in the center of my throat. The lemon bursts, and I crumple to the ground and cry.

"Enough of this." She takes the corroded wooden plank and slams it against her knee. Rotted pieces fling through the air and hit the ground, scattering with the glass. I flinch, ready for Greeley to hit me with the jagged wood, but instead, she says, "I came to invite you for dinner. To Sling and Bama's."

Then the tears come. Again. Enough to fill Jocassee.

"I'm more than happy to un-invite you. Seriously—that trash you threw in my yard? I ought to beat your ass for that."

"I'm sorry," I whisper.

"It's . . . fine," Greeley stammers. "Now pull it together, or else I'm taking back my half of the deer."

My stomach roars. "No, no, I'm fine." I wipe the tears off my face. I pull in a big breath, force air down my lungs.

"Move it or lose it."

I follow Greeley outside. The dimming day is cold, and I pull my hoodie closer around me. "Hey," I say. "You don't happen to know where to find a broom, do you?"

"Ha! There's a lady who trades cleaning supplies exclusively. I'll introduce you. But it'll cost you."

"Everything does."

"Now you're getting it," she says, slapping me on the back. "C'mon, let me show you this beast of a deer."

CHAPTER FORTY-THREE

DO NOT VOMIT, DO NOT VOMIT, DO NOT VOMIT.

The deer hangs by its hooves in Sling and Bama's outhouse, the marbled meat bloody and drying. White layers of fat streak the flesh, swirling like a secret and grotesque pattern.

"How much are Sling and Bama taking?" I ask, plugging my nose.

"They like the glutes," Greeley answers.

"Are you serious?"

"I'm always serious."

"That's hardly true."

Greeley walks up to the deer and pats its face. The deer's black eyes stare blankly at the floor. "Rest in peace, Lilah."

She named it? Of course she named it. The woman knows no bounds. Me, on the other hand? My stomach curdles like milk past its expiration date.

I curl my toes in my shoes, trying to stop my rancid gut from bubbling into my throat.

Greeley turns back to me and adds, "We're eating the shoulder tonight. Slow-cooked over fire."

The door opens behind us, and Clara pops her head in. Her black hair is pulled into a waterfall atop her head, and her coral overalls remind me of a sunset. She holds a tapered candle in two hands, creamy wax melting onto palms. She doesn't seem to notice. Instead, she feasts her eyes on the hanging deer.

"Exceptional kill." She leans against the doorframe like a cowboy. "How'd you take her down?"

Greeley makes a stabbing motion. "Kota's and my blades struck Miss Lilah here in the noggin at the exact same moment."

Clara's eyes light up. "*Whoa*. Will you teach me how to hunt sometime?"

"*Hell fucking yeah* I will, little one." Greeley walks to Clara and high-fives her.

"I'll help, too," I chime in. Greeley raises an eyebrow. "My brother, West, was a Boy Scout. He taught me a lot of knife tricks. I can show you some of them, if you want."

Smiling, Clara says, "That'd be totally sweet. My teacher—"

"Dinner, my dears!" Bama calls from the house. "Dinner is served!"

Clara groans. "Mom always interrupts me." She stomps her foot. "I was just getting to the good part!"

"Come on," I say gently, remembering Bunny's temper tantrums. I walk toward Clara and rub her shoulder. She juts out her lower lip, pouting, but softens at my touch. "You can tell us all about it over dinner."

THE TABLE IS SET, TEA LIGHTS ARE AFLAME, AND PLATES ARE STACKED HIGH with hefty portions of deer meat.

"As I was *saying*," Clara starts. She grips her fork in her fist and pierces a hunk of meat. "My teacher taught us how to open pocketknives. She was going to show us how to use them this week, but she died."

Clara's voice is matter-of-fact, and her eyes are devoid of emotion. I nearly choke on my mashed potatoes. What do I say to that? I look to Greeley for help, but she just shrugs. Clara rips off a hunk of meat with her teeth and smacks as she chews.

"Close your mouth, honey," Bama chides. "It's not ladylike; nobody wants to see the pulverized deer on your tongue."

Clara sticks out her tongue in response. The sight of half-chewed deer meat is enough to make my stomach churn. I set down my fork.

Sling picks up where Clara left off. "Shame we lost your teacher, Clara. She was a good one."

"What happened?" I ask.

"Apparently," Sling says, "she went out on a run to get school supplies—never came back. Rumor around town is that a zombie got her. I don't believe it."

"Neither do I," Bama adds. "They found her car in the Office Depot parking lot, full of pens. But I tell you what, that woman always took precautions. Always had an extra layer of security." She bites into a slice of meat. Her face lights up. "Delicious! My, this is *delicious*!"

"Besides"—Sling shifts his gaze from his meal to Greeley—"you haven't seen too many zombies around the outskirts for a while now, have you? Seems like both sides of the Split have cleared out the area pretty well."

"Kota killed one just a few miles out yesterday," Greeley says.

My cheeks redden.

If Bama feels awkward about our last dinner together, she doesn't let on. She beams at me and says, "Did you now? Good on you, dear!"

I shove more deer into my mouth. This go-around, I don't have visions of eating Bunny.

Sling smiles and points his fork at his daughter. "In any case, I think the Egals are starting to play dirty. I think they're taking our people. Hunting them, maybe. And for what? Just because we operate different than them? That's the entire reason the Split was formed! So that we could all live happily without bugging one another." Bits of meat fling out of Sling's mouth and onto the tablecloth.

With the butt of her fork, Greeley hits her plate with a *cling*. Sling and Bama turn to each other, eyebrows raised. "Damn right, Sling! *Damn right!* I say we kill them all. I say we—"

I interject before she turns the fork on one of us. Me, specifically. "What are the kids going to do now, then?" I ask. "Now that they don't have school."

Please don't put them to work like in Egal. I want Bunny to have a better life. I need her to.

Bama looks at her daughter with loving eyes. "I was thinking I'd take on the job! We could bring all the kiddos to our place to—"

"I don't want them coming over here, stealing my guns!"

Plural?

"Sharing is caring—"

"Now I'm calling bullshit on that," Greeley says. "Sharing is what landed us in this situation in the first place. I stand by Clara. Don't let those little fuckers steal your shit."

"Language, dear," Bama says.

But now Greeley's riled up. Her entire face is bright red. She pushes herself up from the table, and even though she's only got a fork in her hand, she could use it to stab every one of us with her eyes closed.

There's a knock at the front door.

Thank god.

Bama shuffles up from the table and squeals when she sees who the visitor is. "Jasper! My dear!"

"Sorry I'm late," he mumbles. "I brought wine."

"Perfect! Just perfect. We saved you some deer!"

Greeley plops back down into her seat and shoves some more meat into her mouth. "Oh, *deer*," she says. "Whole gang's here."

"Come, come, take a seat, right next to Kota!"

Jasper's wary eyes land on mine. My skin flushes, and my stomach knots. As I offer him a subtle wave, my back stiffens in my seat. He pulls out the chair, the legs screeching against the wood floor. "Hey," he whispers.

"Hey," I whisper back.

"For fuck's sake, are we five?" Greeley exclaims.

Bama screeches, "*Language*!"

The rest of the night passes something like that. Banter, laughs, chiding, flinging bits of meat, wine.

Though being near Jasper feels weird, when it's time to say goodnight, I don't want to. I don't want to go home, alone, when I could stay here with this riot of people.

But when Jasper asks if he can walk me home, all I want to do is be alone with him, even if things are tense between us. Yesterday, he didn't want me enough to ask me to stay at his house—so why does he want my company now?

On the long walk back home. A crescent moon rests high in the sky, sending silvery beams across our rocky path. A burnt-tinged waft of wind floats into my nose.

Burn Day.

The acrid smell of burned humans is unmistakable. What surprises me isn't that the smell traveled over the wall; it's that bodies in Egal are burned once a month. If the burning took place more often, it would stink up the community. More than that, it's too heavy an emotional toll to bear. But the last Burn Day was right around when I met Jasper, just a couple weeks ago. Why break protocol? Are there more dead in Egal than usual?

I turn left to Jasper to see if he notices the smell, but he doesn't so much as scrunch his nose. His mind is elsewhere. I can tell he wants to say something to me—about the lingering tension between us, I'd guess—because he opens and closes his mouth a grand total of four times. I half-heartedly kick a pebble the first time Jasper does it. The second time, I send a fat rock skittering down the street. Ultimately, he keeps it shut, and neither of us utters a word the rest of the way. There's a wall between us, and it's like we're on opposite sides of the Split again. The one thing that binds us? The rancid stench of burning flesh, and he doesn't even notice it.

When we've reached Andrew's—my—front patio, Jasper asks, "How's the new place?"

"I love it so much," I quietly respond.

He picks at a peeling slat with his finger, then pulls off a leaf of overgrown ivy. "Really?"

"Really."

Jasper crumples the ivy in his hand. "Then I guess I'll leave you to enjoy it."

"Thanks," I say.

Jasper pauses and stares at me. He looks like he wants to hug me goodnight, and *I* definitely want to hug *him*, to feel him and be held by him, but he just stands before me in silence. Eventually, he offers me a captain's salute and leaves.

THAT NIGHT, I CURL INTO ANDREW'S DUSTY, SMELLY BED, AND I CRY MYSELF to sleep.

I don't want to wake up here, alone.

But I do.

CHAPTER FORTY-FOUR

RAP ON JASPER'S DOOR. ONCE, TWICE, THREE TIMES.

I wait. One, two, three seconds.

Where is he?

The yellow sun sits just above the horizon, but already cloaks the surrounding wooded landscape in scalding beams. Sweat drips down the base of my skull, and the back of my shirt sticks to my skin.

I give the door one last knock. Maybe Jasper's still asleep?

Screw it.

I allow myself to use his creek to wash up—because he owes me, right? Owes me for kidnapping me and making me want to stay here and be his friend and *kiss him*. And when he wakes up, and I do finally see him this morning, I want him to see me with clean hair.

Ten minutes later, wet blond strands drip onto my shirt. No soap, but at least the water rinses off my sweaty hair stink, plus the burn smell that tinged my skin.

I walk to the side of the house and pick up some rocks. Pelt them at his window. My aim isn't great, so I resort to using my voice. "Get up!" I shout. Nothing.

Maybe there's a spare key somewhere . . .

I walk around to the front of the house and look under the three dirt-filled flower pots, but still, no dice. For good measure,

I shove my hand inside the flower pots, dirt catching under my fingernails.

"Can I help you with something?"

I look up. I'm crouched like a crazy person, elbow-deep in dirt, while Jasper stands in his doorway, leaning against the frame, a knowing smirk plastered across his handsome face.

I mutter, "I thought you might have a spare key."

"Me. Have a spare key. In this neck of the woods? In the apocalypse?"

I pat the dirt from my hands onto my jeans. *Well, shit.* Once again, I'm covered in crud. "Stranger things have happened."

Jasper rubs the back of his neck. "Why are you attempting to break into my house, anyway?"

"I need your help."

Barely a day later, and I've come back to ask Jasper for help. Yet again. His opinion of me, though, will never matter as much as my family's safety. I need them here, with me, in my empty home, to cover Andrew's smells and broken memories.

"Say more," he says.

"Chandler took Clara's teacher like she took Eagan and Garrett. I know she did. And who knows what she's doing with them?" *Setting their bodies aflame?* Jasper raises his eyebrows. "I'm scared. For my grandmother, and for my sister. I'm ready to bring them here, to Macoby—now. But I can't do that alone."

"You won't do it alone. And they'll be here soon." Jasper steps toward me. *Closer*, I think. *I want you closer.* "They're about done digging the tunnel. Just another week or so."

I shake my head. "That's not fast enough. I'm not waiting any longer."

Jasper's shoulders sag as he releases a big breath. He knows Chandler would hurt my family. She could justify punching a butterfly. "How do you want me to help?"

"Is there any way we can break into Egal?"

"Why do you think we're creating a tunnel?"

"It's not done yet." I bite my lip, step toward Jasper, lift my chin, and meet his eyes. *Say it.* "Grandma and Bunny could be dead in a week."

He shakes his head. "I'm sorry, Kota. Breaking into Egal . . . it's a bad idea."

"Jasper, I'm scared," I admit, my voice weak. "After learning about Clara's teacher last night, I fear Chandler's on an accelerated path to destruction. What happens when there are no more Macs to take? Bunny and Grandma, they're not healthy. If she comes after her own people, they'd be top of the list. And," I add, "we still don't know *what* she's doing to the hostages."

"I understand." He's not placating me. His wide eyes are sorrowful. "Chandler is capable of terrible things." He leaves off the word that comes next. *But.*

After a moment, Jasper says, "Come with me. I have to show you something."

THE BRIGHT SUN CASTS LONG SHADOWS BEHIND ME AND JASPER, TRAILING after us like our own personal zombies. After we walk Jasper's bike toward Chief's house-in-a-hill, Jasper pulls a lock out of his backpack and ties it up to the sole zombie tree slowly overtaking the grass. His code is 2-1-2-9-9. I wonder what, if any, meaning that holds for him.

As we reach the front patio, a wet drop of blood splatters on the grass. It's mine—I've picked off the chapped skin around my fingernails and then some. I suck on my index finger to stop the blood, warm and salty on my tongue. West used to pack these little electrolyte packets for long Boy Scout trips. Now I'm sucking sodium from my own damn flesh.

I twist the bottom of my oversized shirt—thanks, Andrew—to wrap it around my finger like gauze, but Jasper finds my hand first. He pulls a crinkled Wendy's napkin out of his pocket and stops the bleeding.

"Been saving this for a special occasion," he says. I fill with warmth as he tucks the corner of the napkin under itself, wraps his hand around mine, and squeezes. "Knew the time would come to depart with Wendy. This feels like the right moment."

"Were you a chocolate or vanilla kinda guy?"

"Frosty?" he asks. I nod. "Chocolate. What do I look like, a chump?"

I use my free hand to flick him on the forehead. "Grandma's favorite flavor is vanilla, and she's not a chump."

"Wouldn't know. Never met her." I flick him again. "Hey, would you stop that?"

"You'll meet Grandma soon. And she's one of the greatest people you'll ever meet." I stick out my tongue at my captor-turned-friend-turned . . . *what?* What are we becoming?

Jasper smiles and raises his knuckle to Chief's door. Before he has a chance to knock, Chief steps out. I yank my hand free of Jasper's and jump behind his back, peering over his broad shoulders.

"What are you two doing here?" Chief asks, not unkindly.

"We need your bike," Jasper says.

I whisper into Jasper's ear, *"But we have a bike?"*

Jasper ignores me, spinning around and grabbing my shoulders. He pulls me in front of him. I'm not sure what's causing my heart to race: standing before Chief or being pressed up against Jasper.

Jasper directs his next words at Chief. "Kota needs to see it." *See what?* "At this point, we've got to give her the full picture."

Chief nods. "You may take the bike, of course, but make sure Kota knows the rules."

Jasper turns to me. "Bike's gotta return with a full tank. Premium gas."

Oh. That *kind of bike.*

"Premium?" I scoff. "You're joking." That kind of fuel will be impossible to find. We've already drained the local Exxons and Spinx. Our best shot these days is checking abandoned cars on the highway.

Jasper says, "Yeah, I'm joking."

Chief opens the door behind him and gestures wide. "Let me show you to the garage."

This man has it all, doesn't he?

CHAPTER FORTY-FIVE

'VE NEVER BEEN ON A MOTORCYCLE BEFORE, NOR HAVE I EVER HAD THE desire. Driver's ed turned me off. After retching at gruesome images of men with squashed heads, guts flung all over the asphalt, I was happy to share the Honda Accord with West. Not that *he* was happy to share it with me. God forbid I borrow it to drive to swim practice when his girlfriend needed a lift to the nail salon.

The blood-soaked Wendy's napkin, fastened around my fingernail, flies off and lands somewhere on the abandoned road behind me. Hands wrapped around Jasper's midsection, I press my cheek against his back and hold on tighter. My heart flutters, both with the closeness to Jasper and the fact that I'm riding pretty on a death mobile.

As Jasper slows to pass through the Macoby gates, I keep my face hidden in case the guards notice me; our last run-in could not have left a good impression. Last thing I want is to be hassled. Or shot.

Soon as they flag us through, Jasper hits the gas. "Dude!" I yell, squeezing his waist tighter.

Jasper shouts back, "Sorry," but doesn't slow down.

Men.

Wind whips through my hair behind me, strands waving like

a flag on a blustery day. I grip my left wrist so tight I might rip off my entire hand.

Better that than flying off this motorcycle.

We must be going seventy, but I can't see the odometer over Jasper's shoulder. Don't know that I really *want* to know.

I shift my gaze to the right, where patches of life and rubble zoom by in a blur of colors: burnt orange and mustard, smoky gray and bruised purple. Countryside and carnage.

I settle into the ride and eventually enjoy the wind racing through my hair.

Release control, Mom would say. *Let the wind carry you forward.*

After looping up a mountain, we arrive in a desecrated parking lot, the asphalt battered, bent pipes twisting out of the cracks like rusty vines. Sharp gray rocks and shards are strewn haphazardly throughout the lot, almost as if they'd rained down from the sky.

Jasper parks the motorcycle on what's left of a curb. I imagine the sunken pit to its left was once a sidewalk, but now it looks like the entrance to hell.

I hesitate before hopping off the motorcycle, because one wrong step means I tumble down the rabbit hole. Also, zombies. Gotta check for them.

The bright sun blinds me, piercing through thin wisps of clouds as if it seeks vengeance on my eyeballs.

The clouds look like snakes, Bunny would say.

I see a banana bunch, I'd respond.

You're both wrong, West would argue. *They're bunny ears.*

I cup my hands over my eyes and do a quick scan around the desecrated lot.

No zombies in sight. Just ruins. And—what's that?

My sun-blotted gaze lands on a rickety building, partially hidden by a patch of dead woods. The building looks like it's resting on stilts, the foundation jutting out for the world to see. Black zombie ivy—*zomivy?*—climbs up either side, wrapping around the walls and strangling the wood framing.

A chilling creak echoes through the lot. The wind knocks the building off-kilter, and it settles at least a foot.

Thud.

Jasper walks up beside me, his hand brushing mine as he says, "We gotta go."

"Because of the noise?"

He shakes his head. "I come up here a lot. Cleared the area of zombies a while ago. There's nothing around for a mile radius, at least."

"Okay, so, where are we going?"

He lifts a finger and points. His face is too close to mine. The building settles another foot. "Over there."

"Toward the building that's about to collapse?"

Jasper takes my hand in his. *Zing.* "So many questions."

Without another word, he pulls me forward. He notices my limp before I do. "Shit." He stops dead in his tracks, then scoops me into his arms. "Your leg."

Ah, yes. The fresh claw marks on my calf. The throbs slowly climbing up my leg. Right. *Those.* Though the adrenaline from riding on the motorcycle has numbed the wound, relief sets in as soon as my feet lift off the ground.

"Thank you," I say.

Jasper's grip tightens around me as he cradles my body in his arms.

I close my eyes and focus on the rhythmic thumps of Jasper's steps. "You've got heavy feet," I say. "When I first saw you across the lot—the day you stole our Quaker bars—you were so graceful. You moved like a ballerina."

"Thank you," he returns with a laugh. The rumble comes deep from inside his chest, a soft purr against my skin.

"But now you've got the gait of a troll," I finish. "What happened?"

"Should I set you down, then?"

"Mmm, no, I'm quite cozy up here."

"You know," Jasper says, "you were quite graceful yourself, shoving handfuls of bars into your sweatshirt."

"Shut up." I nudge his chest with my forehead. "I was docile back then. Weak."

"You were never weak," he says, setting me down on a patch of dirt. "You just didn't know what you were capable of."

Jasper's eyes hold mine for what feels like an eternity. He gazes at me like he'd fight a war to keep me safe. No, it's more than that. He looks at me like *I* could win a war with my own two hands, but he would fight for me, anyway.

I crane my head toward the building so he can't see my cherry-red cheeks. It's somehow shabbier up close: shingles fall from the sides, a majority of the roof has been blown off, and the front awning hangs at a ninety-degree slant. A small metal board, however, remains nailed into the unhinged front door, the etched lettering still visible. *Coffee and Breakfast*, it states.

Jasper crosses his arms and admires the building. "I used to come here before hikes. This place made a mean bacon and egg sandwich."

"I can't remember the last time I had eggs."

"Sling and Bama had a chicken coop in their yard for a while. Did you know that?" I shake my head no. "They thought they'd struck gold, stumbling on those two chickens—free eggs and all."

"What happened?"

"Soon enough, they had two zombie chickens on their hands. Nearly pecked Clara to death."

I slap a hand over my mouth to stop a laugh from bubbling over.

It's not funny.

"Oh my god. That's where her scar came from?"

"Yep." Jasper laughs, too. No, a child getting pecked by a zombie chicken isn't funny, but it *is* absurd. And it's that absurdity of it all that sends me into a fit of giggles. "And after Sling wrangled the chicken off Clara, it popped out a midnight black egg. When he cracked it open, a slimy black thing like an oyster slid out of the shell."

"Dead on arrival."

"The yolk's still preserved in a jar at their house, if you want a taste."

I shudder. "Thanks for the offer. How do you think that happened? How'd the zombie chicken carry the egg?"

"One of the many questions we've yet to figure out."

"Do you think we'll ever—" A gust of wind cuts off my words. The air kicks up a swirling heap of dirt and blows it into my eyes. As I blink the soot from my lids, the warped structure before us creaks.

Jasper turns to the building, wind howling through its blown-out windows. "Come around back," he says.

He takes my hand and guides us through some bushes and brambles on the side of the building. Soon enough, we stand on the edge of a cliff.

"What the *hell*?" I say, more to myself than Jasper.

The cliff slices straight down, big slabs of rock layered atop one another like books on a shelf. The building teeters over the edge, but I now realize it hasn't fallen because of its position. The building leans precariously against an old, obscenely tall tree, its spindly roots splaying down the mountain. The house won't fall until the tree does—or until it turns into a zomtree, rotting from the inside out.

More trees lie diagonal down the mountain, suspended in the air and hanging on by nothing more than slim roots. Others have plunged to their death at the bottom of the valley below.

I grab on to a sturdy-looking trunk as the wind threatens to push me over. One wrong step, one strong *gust*, and I'm toast.

"What are we doing up here, Jasper?" I ask.

My heart pounds up my chest, into my throat, and finds its final destination in my ears. The pulsating is deafening.

"You're looking the wrong way," he says, placing a gentle finger under my chin and lifting my gaze to the expansive landscape beyond. "Look *out* instead of down."

Oh. Oh my.

It's the Split. A bird's-eye view. Something I've never dreamed of seeing.

Surrounded by scrapheap gates, Jocassee Valley is a yellowing abyss. From up here, the homes and buildings are minuscule, the citizens crawling ants. In Egal, the buildings are more uniform, the scenery scarce. In Macoby, there are more homes, more vegetation, more trees, more movement. The difference is starker than I imagined.

More than ever before, I'm aware of the separation between me and the people I was allegiant to. For two years, Egal was my home, my *family*. But they've proven they never considered me family. Chandler abandoned me at the drop of a hat. Peter traded me in for Zara. And she—well, she was never my friend to begin with. But what about the boys who *were* my friends? Have they tried to get me back? Have they even asked about me?

Between Jasper, Greeley, Sling, and Bama, there are people in Macoby who care about me. I can have a future here, if I bring Grandma and Bunny. One with real friendship, real family.

I peer down at the Split, the citizens milling about, safe within the gates. They've already forgotten about the driver of the dough-boys. I wanted the people in Egal to need me, but no. Someone else can drive the damn truck—it doesn't have to be me. I'm dispensable.

But in Macoby, I have been tasked with a mission that only I can carry out.

I take a step closer toward the edge of the cliff and squint, scouting for Bunny and Grandma.

"Easy there," Jasper says. He lifts a rock and pulls binoculars out of a hole in the ground. "These will help."

I bring the scuffed lenses to my eyes and scour the land.

Sick Room, where are you?

"There's so much to see." I scan from the fields to the church. I catch sight of six-foot-something Indy and the truck outside the rectory. He's next to the truck, handing boxes to Fred. I know it's Fred because he trips and busts his chin on the lip of the truck.

"This is the best lookout spot in all of Greenville," Jasper says. "Do you see the rectory?"

"Mmm," I say, half listening.

There it is. The Sick Room. The metal roof glints in the sun, but the building itself is hidden from my view, obstructed by the block of rowhomes. I pull the binoculars away from my face and eyeball the rickety building to my right. If I could clamber up onto the ledge, I could see inside; I could see Bunny. Just to make sure she's safe. Just to see her smile.

I don't make my move yet. Jasper's intent on giving me the full bird's-eye tour. "There, behind the rectory. Do you see that tree stump?"

"I see it."

"It's a prop. There's a hatch beneath it leading to the rectory."

"Holy shit," I gasp. "How do you know that?"

"I've sat up here for hours at a time, watching Chandler go in and out. I've seen her carry unconscious people." I lower the binoculars and turn to Jasper. "I've seen Peter use the entrance, too."

"And you're just now telling me this?"

"I wish I didn't have to tell you at all. But you had to see the kind of people we're up against."

I bring the binoculars back up to my face. "What do you think they're hiding?"

"You know what they're hiding, Kota."

Experimentation. On people.

I hear Chandler in the back of my head. *It's for the common good.* And yet . . . "Even after everything I've seen, I'm having a hard time believing she could do such terrible things."

"Look at me," he says. I turn toward him, and the pores on his face are the size of craters. Zoomed in, his lips are massive, pink, and pillowy, and the lashes framing his eyes are thick and black as ink. "Kota. Put down the binoculars."

"Oops."

Jasper smiles, but his eyebrows knit together, and his expression is pained. "When I was twelve, Mom surprised me with an art set. Oil paints and brushes, a few canvases. Chandler hated art. Even at seventeen, she was fixed in her beliefs. Since art didn't improve society, artists were useless, and they had no right 'doing art for a living,' not when they could be contributing in more practical ways. 'There's no room for passion,' she said, 'in a drying-up world.'

"I painted anyway, though I always kept my canvases hidden under the bed. She found them. Slashed through them with a knife. She squeezed the paint from their tubes and graffitied my wall. *Leech.*

284

"Chandler never apologized, not when I fell to my knees and sobbed, and not when Mom yelled at her for getting paint on the carpet. She's ruthless, and she'll do anything for what she believes is right, however misguided she may be."

"Oh, god," I say, my heart breaking in half. "Did you try to stop her? When the Split was one, did you try to stop her from leaving?"

"No, but I should have. Since the beginning, Chief and I have been trying to clean up our mistake. The Egals are loyal to her, though—Chandler's a born leader. You, for one, ought to know that." *I do. She tricked me, so easily.* "And because of that, she's going to kill us all."

"We'll take her down."

I bring the binoculars back to my eyes. Fred stumbles into the rectory's yard with a black bag slung over his shoulders. A body bag. As Chandler gestures for him to bring the bag down the hatch, betrayal settles into my belly. Fred's in on this?

He trips. As he takes a nosedive, the body bag tumbles onto the ground. Dread washes over me as the body spills out.

My throat constricts.

It can't be.

I press the binoculars so hard against my forehead that it hurts, and I zoom in. I zoom in close enough to see it all: Thin lines etched on wrinkled palms. Snowy strands of hair woven throughout gray. Delicate lips, still a muted shade of rose. Closed eyelids that will never open again.

Grandma.

I scream so loud that it echoes through the valley.

Jasper places a hand over my mouth. "Kota," he says. "What's wrong?"

I double over. The ground spins, and my knees buckle, but Jasper catches me before I hit the ground. My throat is thick and aching, and there's an incessant pounding between my eyes. I can barely breathe, but I somehow whisper, "*Grandma*," before collapsing into Jasper's chest.

And then I sob.

"Oh, Kota." Jasper rubs the back of my head. I try to focus on the gentle rhythm of his hand, but I can't tame the river streaming down my face. "Shh," he croons.

We stand there for a while, Jasper holding me as I weep. I don't know how much time passes before I run out of tears, but eventually, I do. Jasper's shirt will be damp for a while, though. As my eyes dry, grief swirls into fury. The pounding in my head amplifies. My muscles tighten.

I clench the binoculars tighter and shove away from Jasper. A scream erupts from my chest. "Chandler killed her. She killed her!"

Jasper's hand smacks back over my lips. "You need to be quiet."

I shake his hand off. "No."

"You can't save your sister if a zombie attacks us."

I wipe threads of snot off my face and snap my mouth shut.

Bunny.

I need to find her. I *need* to see that she's alive.

I need a better vantage point.

I barely register Jasper saying no as I move toward the building. He doesn't stop me. The deck on the back is in okay shape, though every other wooden plank is missing. I hoist myself up onto one of the few planks that looks sturdy. The wood groans under my weight but holds.

I pull the binoculars to my eyes and hunt for Bunny. There. The Sick Room. But the windows are too grimy to see through. *God fucking dammit.*

A burst of air knocks me off balance. I teeter on my good leg, using the weight of the binoculars to keep me upright. My heart stammers. My gut wrenches. The plank beneath me yawns.

I need to get down.

I need to find Bunny.

One more try, I think. *I can do this.*

As I pull the binoculars to my eyes, the plank holding me up gives out, splitting right through the middle. My pitches straight through the teeth of the splintered wood.

I drop the binoculars, and they tumble down the cliff. I wrap my hands around my calf to pull my foot free from the grips of the wood, but it's stuck.

Jasper gracefully clambers over rocks to reach me. "Don't move, I'm coming!"

But I don't want his help.

I want to free myself.

I pull harder, mustering up all of my strength to wrench my uninjured leg out of the wood. It won't give. It'll give out *beneath* me, but it won't free my foot.

Screw you, mouse trap.

I squat down and smash my fist into the wood. Sharp pain tears through my knuckles. Stupid idea. Now I've got two mauled legs and a bloody fist.

"Stay back!" I shout at Jasper. "I don't need your help."

One more time, Kota. You can do this.

Thighs burning, I push into my legs and do my best jump squat, hoping against hope to dislodge my foot. *It worked!* I surge upward, freeing my foot and sending myself a foot above the deck.

And then, I free-fall. Belly flop down the side of the cliff.

Rocks and pebbles bite into my face as I slide down the jagged bluff, my shirt and pants scraping against my skin like a nasty rugburn.

I curl into myself to protect my head as I plummet. A rock bites into my shoulder and searing pain shoots down my arm. I yelp as another slices my spine. My hip smacks against the cliff's rough edge, and then my elbow takes the brunt. *Oof! Nothing is funny about hitting the funny bone.* Agony spreads from one spot to the next as I hit rock after rock.

Dear Lord, I pray—for the first and last time—*if Mrs. Patty was right, and you really do exist, will you save me? And will you save Bunny? Please save my sister.*

God, or gravity, answers my prayers. I land on a sandy rock with a *thud*. My body's in one piece. I'm bruised, banged up, and bleeding, but I'm alive.

Curled up into a tiny ball, knees tucked into my chest, I cry until no tears are left, until there's a puddle beneath me, until salty stains are left on my cheeks, and my throat is raw.

Chest shaking, brain throbbing, I pull my head out of the dark. The blazing sun blinds me. I peer over the edge of the sandy ledge that's saved me.

So, I didn't fall *that* far. Maybe twenty feet. What felt like years of falling was probably only a few seconds. The Split below me still looks like the model version of itself.

Red clay crumbles off the edge.

I scramble backward and look up at the rocky cliff.

How *do* I get back up?

I grip my throbbing calf, and then I grip my *other* throbbing calf. Maybe I'm stuck here forever.

"You all right down there?" Jasper's voice echoes from above, his silhouette black against the bright sky.

"Not really," I say, my voice raspy. Soot-tinged tears lodge in my throat.

He tosses something down the cliff. At first, I think it's rope, but it's too rigid—no, it's the thickest vine of kudzu I've ever seen, hanging off that massive, sturdy-looking tree. The vine wriggles like a snake with a bamboo shoot shoved down its throat.

"Can you climb?" Jasper shouts.

Doesn't matter if this vine is kudzu or zomzu. It's my only option.

Jasper tries to lower the vine to me, but it's too short. I can't reach it. I push myself to my tippy toes, ignoring the pain lacing through my entire being, trying to gauge how far I'll have to climb up the cliff to get to the zomzu. *If* I can climb.

"You can do it," Jasper yells, echoing my thoughts.

I step toward the jagged wall. I cram my foot into a little divot and clutch a jutting rock as a handhold. I push all of my strength, all of my courage, into the maneuver, and suddenly, I'm off the ground. And smooshed against the side of the cliff.

I dare to look up. The zomzu dangles a few feet above my reach. Two more upward moves, and I'm there.

My arms shake so hard I think they might fall off.

Jasper says from above, "Don't look down."

Did that asshole really just tell me not to look down?

"I hate you," I say, unsure if I'm talking to Jasper or myself. My legs are Jell-O. *I* am Jell-O.

I find another foothold and reach upward.

I am strong.

The skin on my stomach stretches as my fingers brush the monstrous vine. A rock comes loose and slices through my ring fingernail, the one I'd already bloodied myself earlier today, but I'm so hyped up on adrenaline I don't feel the pain.

I debate my next move. There are no other handholds within reaching distance. I have to jump.

Jasper swings the vine, trying to get it closer to me, but the movement will only make it harder to catch the rope if I do jump. *When* I jump. Correct. I have no other choice.

"Steady it!" I shout.

I dig my fingers and toes into the side of the cliff. Fiery pain wraps its arm around my biceps, and my vision blurs. It's now or never. If I don't jump, my body will give out—and I'll fall down the cliff again. This time, the two Gs might not be so kind.

It's time.

One, I think, squeezing my eyes shut.

Two.

I suck in a deep breath.

Three.

I blow out all the air in my lungs, open my eyes, and push myself off the wall.

While my body's midair, I reach for the zomzu and catch it. My hands slide down a foot, the rough vine scratching and splintering my palms. My feet dangle.

Mustering up strength I didn't even know I contained, I pull myself up enough to wrap my legs around the zomzu.

It's moving.

The vine spasms like it's trying to bump me off, and knuckle-like protrusions pulsate under my grip.

"Pull me up!" I scream, my voice cracking.

Jasper levers me up, fighting his own war against the zombie vine. For some reason, I look down. My entire stomach lurches into my aching throat, acidic bile coating my tongue.

Puke later, Kota. Not now.

I've always had dreams where I'd fall through the sky as a bird. I'd soar along, only for a big hand to reach through, pluck me up, clip my wings, and set me back atop clouds. I thought I'd be safe, sitting on the fluff, but the clouds were deceiving. They'd give out, made of nothing but mist, and I'd fall through the air wingless, my stomach screaming with the descent. Before I hit the ground, my eyes would burst open, and I'd be covered in sweat along with my sheets.

This time, as Jasper hoists me over the edge of the cliff, and I fall face-first onto the dirt, I don't wake up. I keep my eyes shut.

CHAPTER FORTY-SIX

WANT TO GET BUNNY."

"You can't get Bunny, Kota. You need to rest."

"But—"

"I'm not having this conversation with you again." Jasper sits on the edge of my bed and squeezes out another glob of Neosporin. "May I?"

I nod, biting back pain as he slathers more salve on my wounded calves. I stare at Andrew's old sheets strewn on the floor, because I'd rather be cold than feel dry fabric rubbing against my sticky wounds. Dust floats up from the yellowed sheets like powdered sugar. Dandruff? Skin particles? Dried eye-boogers?

I've been stuck in this room for too long. Two days too long.

I've got to get out of this bed, if not for the smell alone. *My* smell. Though the putrid tinge of infection lingers in the air, Jasper swears my puffy red wounds are healing nicely.

"Thank you for being my nurse."

"You owe me big-time after this," Jasper says, winking. He twists the Neosporin cap shut.

I slide my leg away. "On second thought . . ."

With deft hands, Jasper guides my leg back toward him and sandwiches it between his own. I try to ignore the heat building between my legs. "This is a mandatory trade, Kota. No squirming out of this one."

"I wouldn't even if I could," I admit.

Jasper looks taken aback—and he's not alone. Did those words just leave my lips?

Warmth spreads from my cheeks to my ears. I turn away, hoping he doesn't see me blush.

Peter never made me feel this way.

Peter was convenient. His apparent attraction to me was validating, and at the time, I'd needed that—to feel wanted. A tall, mysterious man chose *me*, Kota, to be his partner in the darkest of times. Chose *my* hand to hold while the world around us withered. We laughed, we kissed, we made love between supply runs and growling stomachs and grief.

It was, of course, all a lie.

Peter liked me weak. He craved it. It gave him power, made him feel strong. And I played the part because I thought I wasn't enough for myself. Peter's approval means nothing to me now, because I mean everything to me.

Jasper traded two bottles of cabernet for a half-full tube of Neosporin and a travel-sized bottle of rubbing alcohol. He didn't do that to show ownership of me. He did it because he cares. He sees my strength, and his actions only make me stronger.

And so I'll let him Neosporin the shit out of my wounds. When the time comes, I'll do the same for him.

"Thank you," I say. "And I'm sorry."

Jasper meets my eyes. "Sorry for what?"

"I'm sorry you lost your sister."

He reaches toward me, his fingers touching my chin. I soak up the foreign feeling, turning my cheek into his hand. I don't even mind his ointment-covered fingers.

"You won't lose yours," he says.

"No," I say. "I won't." Jasper drops his hand from my face as I turn away and look out the dirty window. The grime crammed into the corners, the bugs smooshed in the panes, and the dust coating the surface are nothing compared to what I'll soon experience. "When will the tunnel be ready?"

"Timeline hasn't changed."

But *I've* changed.

Jasper continues, "Five days. I know you're worried about Bunny, but she'll be okay for another five days."

"How do you know that?" I snap. "Everyone I've ever loved has died. What makes Bunny any different?"

He pauses before responding, probably pondering what words are least likely to make me detonate. "Kota, take a deep breath. Be patient."

Wrong words.

"Patient," I spit out. Any heat between us vanishes. The room tilts on its side. "I *patiently* waited for my mother to get better, and she died. I *patiently* waited for my father to come back, and he never did. I patiently waited for my brother to bring back cereal, and guess what? I only got to say goodbye to his corpse." I take a deep breath. "Patience killed my grandma, too. I will *not* let it kill my sister."

Jasper's eyes frown at the corners, like he's sorry. If he understands, then where's his resolve?

"Why won't you help me?"

"I *am* helping you—"

"No, you're not." But I'm done arguing. I won't change his mind. "You should leave."

Jasper's head ticks to the side. "What?"

"I want to be alone," I say, though it's the furthest thing from the truth.

He takes the hint and stands. "Fine," he says, his tone cold. He pauses before leaving the room and leans against the doorframe. "Promise me you won't go after your sister."

"Jasper—"

"Promise me." His eyes bore into mine. "Five days. Hold on for five more days."

I huff. "I promise," I say, my gaze fixed on my bandaged legs.

He clenches his jaw. "Good enough."

Soon as he's gone, I roll onto my side and pull a ratty pillow over my head to block out the light. Better get used to the darkness, because there will be no light when I betray his trust.

No, I'm not ready to lose him, but Greeley's voice grates in my head, shreds my brain like cheese. *Your goal is to save your sister, isn't it? Then strap on your nuts and do it.*

I think Grandma would agree.

CHAPTER FORTY-SEVEN

THE LATE-NIGHT MOON SWINGS LIKE A PENDULUM OVERHEAD. *Clang*, says the ball as it hits its neighbor. *Off to the other side you go.*

Wait—why *is* the moon swinging? Is it adrenaline twisting around in my brain? Is my leg infected? I peel back the cloth wrapped around my left leg, red skin puckering around claw marks on my calf. Nothing is yellow or oozing.

My other leg isn't faring so well. Root burns trail up from my ankle to my hip. Much nastier than the rope burn I got after tug-of-war in second grade. I wonder if Anika remembers.

Goose bumps course down my arms as a chilly wind breezes through my room's open window. I glance up at the ceiling. What I thought was the moon in my half-asleep stupor is actually a hanging glass light. The light doesn't work, of course, but moonlight reflects off its glass surface. Wonder where Andrew got it.

My roaring stomach interrupts my musings. Last time I ate was yesterday, when Jasper brought me a can of Ro-Tel before fixing up my leg. We ate the spicy diced tomatoes together, slurping straight from the can.

I miss Jasper.

Screw it—there's no time for wistful thinking.

While I scarf down a piece of deer jerky—more difficult than it sounds—I sift through Andrew's old dresser for black clothes. While I find lots of gym shorts, what I *don't* find are clothes that will fit. No underwear, either. Fuck it, I can be discreet in these smelly jeans and a stained jacket. I've got the protection of the night.

I load up my backpack with the necessities: a small, empty flask and the gun Jasper gave me. *Give, give, give*, this guy.

Slinging the backpack over my shoulder, I leave the house. It's not home, not yet.

The door shuts with a soft *click* behind me, and I don't bother locking it. If a Mac takes the damn house while I'm gone, I'll be relieved.

The air outside is cold, the sky black, but the glow of the full moon guides my way to Jasper's. Chirping crickets and rustling leaves liven the empty streets. There are a few late-night walkers, but none of them bat an eye at me. After a long trek through town, I stand in front of Jasper's long, winding driveway. The home is hidden by nighttime shadows, but a single candle flickers in the room that used to be mine.

I breathe in, squaring my shoulders as my chest fills up with fresh fall air. When I take a step forward, a twig snaps beneath my foot.

Careful, you doof.

I close my eyes and lift onto my tiptoes. I am a ballerina, a tiny dancer in a music box, full of grace like Jasper.

There are only two more twig casualties until I reach the front porch. Something rustles in the hedges, the withering leaves a pale green. As a gust of wind blows my ponytail into my face, I realize it's just that. The wind.

I need to get Jasper's bike and get the hell out of here. His bike is locked up on the side porch, hidden behind a zombie rosebush. Curled black roses twist around one another, thorns clawing at the delicate petals.

Let's think this through. I could walk onto the porch and get the bike, but the candlelight from the window shines directly on that spot. It's not likely, but there's a chance Jasper's awake, in my old room. I can't risk it. *Or* I could unlock the bike from the other side.

Shit, I have to go through the rosebush, don't I?

I squeeze my eyes shut, bracing for pain.

Thorns prick my skin as I reach my right arm into the bush, blood trickling down and splashing the ground. My shoulder aches as I reach for the bike lock. It lies just beyond my grasp. Thorns pierce my armpit, my neck, my cheek as I reach, *reach*—

I've got it. With only the moon and the dim candlelight to see, I thumb in the code. 2-1-2-9-9, twist.

I grit my teeth to keep from crying out as I wrench the bike out of the bushes. Thorns pierce every inch of skin. Even so, the stirring bushes make more noise than I'd care to admit. With hands gripped on the handlebars, I swing a leg up and over. They say riding a bike is something you never unlearn, and it's been over ten years since I last rode one. Here's hoping they're right.

I peddle forward, and the bike squeaks.

I've got to get a move on.

I pump on the pedals hard, and my legs start to burn. My sweaty palms slip off the handles, but I swivel back to center before I tip off the side. I'm almost out of the driveway when the sound of an opening door creaks in my ears. I dare turn my head around. Jasper stands in the doorway.

He cups his hands around his mouth and shouts, "Kota! Come back!"

No.

I pump harder.

As I near the street, my wheel catches on a rock. The bike jolts, and I hit the ground hard. The bike topples over me, and the wind gets knocked out of my lungs. Even through my pants, the bike gear bites into my skin. Fast-moving footsteps sound in my ears. I have to be faster.

I grip the handlebars and pull myself and the bike up. Jasper sprints toward me. My instincts tell me to stop, but my heart tells me to keep going.

I yell back at him, "You don't get it. I have to do this!"

"Kota—"

"Do you really want to hold me hostage again? Keep me here against my will? Is that what you want?" Jasper stops dead in his tracks. A bead of sweat drips down my face. Blood squelches between my knuckles. "Let me go, Jasper. You couldn't save your sister, but I can save mine."

"Kota." Jasper's voice is but a whisper. I spin around, heart twisting at the hurt plain on his face. His wide eyes are pleading, and his shoulders are slumped. He opens his mouth as if to say something else, but the words don't come out.

I turn my back to him and focus only on my destination. The handlebars sweat under my tight grip as I begin to pedal away. I leave nothing but a trail of blood in my wake.

CHAPTER FORTY-EIGHT

PROP THE BIKE ON ITS KICKSTAND JUST OUTSIDE THE GATES IN FRONT OF the other side of the Split. I made it here in one piece. Alone. Using my own smarts and willpower. I did it.

But I can't seem to move.

What the hell do I think I'm doing?

For god's sake, I couldn't even get past *one* person unseen. How am I going to get past Egal's guards? The locked gates?

Blurry colors pepper my vision—icy blue and rich orange, neon green and piss yellow. I swat them away, but it only causes more colors to flood my sight. I stumble backward, throw the bike down, and fall to my knees, covering my face with my hands.

The roar of an engine erupts in my ears, and a bright light pierces through the space between my palms. I yank my hands away from my face.

I stare straight into two headlights.

The truck. *My* truck.

It's surging straight toward me.

The smell of gasoline and metal fills my nostrils as I push myself off the ground and scramble out of the way. I force my wobbly legs into the bushes and bramble, sprinting toward a tall sweetgum tree.

Adrenaline courses through my veins as I slam my knife into the trunk. I use the hilt of the knife as a footstool and launch upward, wrapping my hands around the lowest branch. Only, I don't have the strength to pull myself up. My arms are noodles.

The truck surges forward, and I jump off just before the hood slams into the tree. Rocks and pebbles bite my skin as I roll onto the earth, using my hands to protect my head. The contents of my backpack press into my back, and I let out a wail. As I rise and fish out my gun, I glance back at the tree. The trunk is tilted, and brittle red leaves shake from the branches, but the tree won't topple over. For now, I've only got an angry flatbed to worry about.

Could be worse?

The headlights blind me as the truck reverses, tires screeching while it tears through bramble. Hands fumbling, and as the truck shifts gears, I cock the gun.

I zoom in on my target: the headlights.

The truck charges toward me.

I shoot.

Glass shatters, but the truck only picks up speed.

Shit, shit, shit, shit.

I cock the gun again. Shoot. Miss.

The truck is just feet from me now, and I close my eyes, hoping the end will be quick.

My eyes whip open at the clanging sound of metal on metal. Moving at the speed of light, a pickup truck punches right into the gut of the truck. Like it was hit by an iron fist, the long, rectangular body of a truck crumples. The truck itself teeters to the side before toppling over.

I squint through the front windows of the pickup truck and beam at two familiar figures. I push myself up and sprint toward Jasper and Greeley.

Jasper flings open the driver's-side door and shouts, "Get in!"

I jump into the car right on Jasper's lap. "Go!" I shout to Greeley. "What are you waiting for?"

"Oh, we're not going anywhere," she says, reaching behind her to the back seat.

"Yes, we are," Jasper argues.

Greeley pulls the key out of the ignition and shoves it into her pocket. She smiles as she says, "Who's ready for some chaos?"

"Jesus," Jasper says.

"No, silly," Greeley says. "I'm Greeley."

I turn to Jasper, his face mere inches from my own, and breath heaving, I say, "I'm sorry."

He shakes his head. "I should have known."

"No." I smile. "I'm not sorry about stealing your bike, and I'm not sorry for trying." Jasper's head quirks to the side in confusion. "I'm sorry for this."

I grab the sides of Jasper's head and bring my lips to his, sending all of the energy coursing through my body into the kiss. His lips are soft and powerful, and as I pull away, I say, "I didn't want to die without doing that."

"Noted," he says, his cheeks red and a curved smile on the lips I just kissed. He reaches around for the door handle. "Now let's help our hotheaded friend."

I jump off Jasper's lap, a spike of pain flashing in my marred calves as my feet land firmly onto the dirt ground. The tipped-over truck's headlights cast long, hazy shadows across the rough terrain. Greeley stands with her gun pointed at the passenger-side door. Peter pushes himself out, eyes narrowed. There's a bloody gash in his left cheekbone and a cut in his lip.

"Oy!" shouts the man in the passenger seat as Peter pushes himself over him. He leaves a bloody handprint on the doorframe and stalks forward.

"Don't shoot," I tell Greeley.

"Wasn't planning on it—quite yet. Wanna hear why this asshat was trying to kill my friend."

Friend.

My breath hitches as Peter's accomplice hauls himself out of the truck. His face is so battered and bloody, he's nearly unrecognizable, but it's him. Indy.

Indy falls to his knees, a gaping slash running from his temple to his chin. Eyes full of tears, he stares into the barrel of Greeley's gun and waves his hands frantically. "I was under his orders," he says. "Please don't shoot me."

"We get it. You don't have a spine." She rolls her eyes.

Indy whimpers. "I'm sorry, Kota. He made me!"

"Eyes over here, shithead. You don't deserve to even look at her."

Whether Indy listens to Greeley or not, I don't know, because *my* eyes are fixed on Peter. He doesn't have a weapon, does he? Otherwise, he wouldn't just stand there like a useless sack of shit.

"Peter," I breathe. "Why?" In response, Peter squeezes his fist, the snake tattoo on his bicep bulging. "You want to swing at me? Go on, let's see you try."

And no, Peter, the sleeveless T-shirt does not make you look cool.

Peter drops his fist. "I had an order to follow."

Greeley curls her lip and says, "Everyone around here's a fucking shell, is that it?" She turns to Jasper. "You mind?"

Jasper marches up to Peter and pats him down. Then, he punches him square in the face.

Peter buckles over and makes no attempt to swing back. He spits on the floor, saliva mixed with blood. "She knows," he says. "Chandler suspected your loyalties shifted."

Peter must see the confusion on my face. He thumbs at Jasper and says, "Chandler saw the way *this* one looked at you when we lit *that* one's Jeep on fire."

"My name's Greeley."

"I don't give two shits what your name is," he says, keeping his steely eyes on me. "But I swore to Chandler that you loved *me*, and not him. So we've been waiting. We've kept eyes on the perimeter, watching every time you've left the Split. Chandler wanted to be quick about killing you, seeing that you have insider information on Egal. Why did I ever think you'd make a good driver, anyway?" Peter shakes his head. "Just know that it was *me* who gave you the benefit of the doubt. It was *me* who needed hard proof that you became one of them." He steps toward me. "But it's clear as day that you've betrayed Egal. Soon enough, you'll be dead, and Macoby will be ours."

Greeley huffs. "Too bad you won't be alive to see your grand plans unfold."

"Maybe not, but I'll die knowing I'm on the winning side."

"You'll also die an asshole."

"Ask me if I care."

Greeley raises her gun. Peter flinches. "Kinda seems like you care."

Indy flops face down, arms outstretched on the earth like he's in worship. "Bloody hell, please don't kill us!"

I step toward the man I once considered my friend. "Indy, look at me. *Look at me*, Indy."

Finally, Indy unpeels himself from the ground, dirt plastered to his face. "Things are getting bad in Egal, Kota. You don't understand. My life is on the line, and . . . and we can't let them win."

"Them?" I clarify.

"*You*," Peter says, spitting again.

"Got something in your mouth, jackass?" Greeley says.

Jasper steps forward, the three of us forming a solid, straight line. "Is Egal planning to attack Macoby?"

"Like I'd share that information with you," Peter says with a scoff. His eyes flick back toward the truck. The motion's almost too small to notice. *Almost.*

His remark earns him another punch—and I hate to admit it, but the way Jasper shakes out his fist is incredibly hot. As Peter crumples to the ground and clenches his jaw, Jasper steps over him and hauls Indy up by his T-shirt. Indy's knees wobble as Jasper punches him, landing a bloody blow on his face. It hurts to watch. "When are your people attacking, Indy?"

"Two days," he coughs out. "Two days."

"Great," Jasper says, turning back around to me and Greeley. He tosses Indy aside. "I think that's all the information we need."

Greeley offers her gun to me. "Care to do the honors?" I shake my head no. *I can't take more death.* "If you're worried about the gunshot drawing zombies, we *do* have a getaway vehicle."

"*No!*" Indy cries at the same time a noise clangs inside the turned-over truck behind him.

Greeley ignores the clamor. "C'mon, Blondie. One shot between the eyes, and you're done. No? Fine." She shrugs and shoves her gun into the holster she always wears on her thigh. "Death by knife it is. I like taking it slow."

Tears trail down Indy's face, mixing with blood and brown dirt. His entire body shakes. Greeley says, "You understand why I have to do this, right, Indy?"

He nods and squeezes his eyes shut. He whispers, "Please . . . make it quick."

Greeley raises her knife and holds it to his right temple.

I'm going to watch Greeley kill a defenseless man.

I'm going to watch Greeley kill my friend.

My heart shatters into a million pieces. Indy betrayed me, but our friendship was real. That much, I'm certain of. If the tables were turned, would he show me mercy? Maybe, maybe not. But . . .

After a moment of hesitation, my feet decide they don't care what Indy would do. I spring forward, ready to shove Greeley aside—

But I'm too late.

It's over as soon as it begins.

Greeley stabs Indy. Stabs him in the soft, fleshy temple. My stomach lurches as blood streams from his head.

Greeley releases him, and he crumples to the ground. "And now for dessert."

Peter.

I don't give myself a moment to react, because I don't *have* a moment. Something inside the flipped-over truck clangs. An inhuman roar fills the air.

I gasp.

Zombies. The Egals are transporting zombies to Macoby.

"Everybody back," Jasper says, pulling a dagger out of his pocket. "We don't know how many are in there."

"And just as I thought this day couldn't get better," Greeley says, loading her gun. She kicks Peter. "Let's feed him to the shamblers."

The zombies topple out of the truck, bones crunching as they hit the ground. They snap their jaws as they shuffle toward us, fast and hungry.

Greeley doesn't waste a moment, jumping toward the truck and slicing a zombie's hand off at the wrist. It shrieks, and she brings the knife up and plunges it into its temple. The zombie falls, and another one trips over its body. Greeley doesn't miss a beat, killing the zombie as it tumbles to the ground.

Jasper grabs a third zombie by the neck and wrings it so tight its eyes bulge. He brings his knife around and drives it into the temple. Another snarling sound emerges from inside the truck. There's one more zombie inside.

I ready my knife and move toward the truck.

This one's mine.

Crawling on all fours, the zombie falls to the earth with a crunch, like its bones all broke at once. This one, I realize, doesn't have hands.

I step closer to the zombie as it crawls toward me. Peppery hair is a mess atop its head, and it wears a pink shirt stained with grease and burn marks. Its sagging face contorts into a snarl, thin lips curling around snapping teeth. The grotesque shriek that erupts from its hungry mouth is all too familiar. I hear her voice, scolding me for eating a biscuit hot out of the oven. *You'll burn your tongue, Dakota!* I see her folding laundry in the living room while *Judge Judy* plays on the television, smiling as she pairs Bunny's favorite flower-patterned socks. I feel her soft hand on my cheek as she tells me she loves me. I smell the sweet rose perfume on her neck as I hug her goodnight.

A faint wind picks up the zombie's scent. The essence of roses wafts off the zombie's skin. Only now, the roses are tainted with rot.

I search the zombie's bulging brown eyes, eyes that I never thought would open again, but they stare right past me.

I can't bear it.

Grandma.

The air around me tightens, and my breath gets stuck in my chest. The smell of her makes me nauseous, and my vision blurs at the sight of her. I wish I hadn't seen her like this. I wish I didn't have to . . .

I drop my knife, my fingers suddenly numb. I stumble backward, falling hard onto my ass, and squeeze my eyes shut.

This thing is not my grandma. This thing is not my grandma.

"Someone else!" I scream, my body convulsing. "Someone else kill her. *Now. NOW!*"

Not a second later, Jasper lunges forward and sends his knife through the zombie's skull.

My grandmother lies dead, blood dripping from every orifice on the earth.

"Grandma," I whisper. I *knew* she was dead. I knew it, and yet I was not prepared for this. Nothing could have prepared me for this.

"Well, shit," Greeley says, wiping sweat from her forehead. "Where the hell did Peter go?"

CHAPTER FORTY-NINE

GREELEY'S FIST IS SWOLLEN LIKE A RASPBERRY FROM HER RELENTLESS banging on Chief's front door. "Let us in, Chief!" she shouts.

The early morning sun rises to its designated spot in the sky. We gave ourselves until sunrise to recover from last night's events—events that *I* put into motion. Because I didn't listen to Jasper. And now images of Grandma's warped face, her hungry snarl and matted hair, her handless arms, haunt my every blink.

I didn't sleep much last night.

Bang, bang, bang.

I wonder if, when they were together, Chandler contained Greeley's inner fire so much that now it's running rampant. How much more does she have until she burns out? Who would she be without it—without all this rage?

"He's not home," Jasper says, standing a safe two feet behind her. "We'll try again later."

"Waste of our fucking time," Greeley says, kicking a rock.

I laugh. "If only we could've texted him first to ask if he was home."

"If only," Greeley mocks. "If only there were *cell phones* and *electricity* and *showers* and *same-day Amazon delivery*. Cry me a river."

"I wasn't—"

"The hell you weren't." Greeley steps in my face and narrows her eyes. "The world moved on. When will you?"

"Greeley," I say. "We're on the same side."

Greeley sticks out her tongue, but the anger drains from her face. She bangs again on the door. "*Hello!* It's your favorite squad, sir! Open the fuck up!"

"What's all the ruckus about?" Chief's voice startles me, and the three of us spin around. Chief tucks two leather gloves in his back pocket, a wide smile plastered on his face. *How does he keep his teeth so white?* "My apologies, kiddos. I was tending to some zomweeds crawling up Jamison's front door. Kota, have you met Jamison yet?"

As I start to tell him no, Greeley interjects. "Next time, tell Jamison to shove the weeds up his ass. Let us inside. We need to talk."

Chief's smile quickly fades. "Something happened."

Jasper says, "Yes, Chief. Something happened."

"So are you gonna let us in or what?" Greeley persists.

"Careful, Greeley," Chief says, pulling the house key from his pocket. "Come in, now, all of you."

I'VE EARNED MY SEAT AT THIS STRATEGY TABLE—WHICH, ADMITTEDLY, IS simply a small round dining table. Still. After just a few days here, this house feels different. Even the glass of tea and slice of bread before me. I understand Chief's offerings: a demonstration of excess. Chief has disposable things. He could dispose of us, too, since he can apparently get just about anything he wants. But he *chooses* to keep us. To trust us. To appeal to our most basic desires: food. Crusty bread, like Grandma used to make.

I will never taste her bread again.

"Southern hospitality at its finest," Greeley says, stuffing the entire slice in her mouth. She smiles, cheeks full like an acorn-glutted squirrel.

I glance at Chief, who chuckles at Greeley's lack of manners. Soon as the bread hits my tongue, saliva floods my mouth. Now I understand why Greeley went for the one-bite tactic. I follow suit.

The food lands in my stomach with a much-welcome *thud*, keeping hunger pangs and cramps at bay. If only the food could fix the wounds painted on my skin. I wash down the crumbs with the nectar from the gods: sweet tea. We never really left the South, did we?

Chief leans forward, his gaze shifting between me, Jasper, and Greeley. "Now, why don't you tell me what's going on?"

Jasper says, "Chandler's crew has been watching Kota. Last night, when Kota was outside the Split alone—"

Chief raises an eyebrow. "How did that come about?"

"Not important," I interject.

"They tried to kill her. There were two of them—Peter and Indy. We killed Indy after he admitted that Egal is planning an attack. Two days."

"What happened to the other, Peter?" Chief asks.

"He got away." Jasper turns to Greeley. "Just take it."

Greeley stops ogling at his bread only to gobble it up. She takes Jasper's comment as permission to finish his tea, too.

"And," I add, "Chandler killed my grandmother. She defiled her. Turned one of her own citizens into a zombie." An image of the handless zombie version of Grandma comes to mind. What kind of experiments was she running?

Chief barely reacts to my words. "We can't afford to lose lives. There are fewer than four hundred humans inside the Split, and not many beyond its walls. If we bring death into this valley, we bring death to us all." Chief clears his throat. "We proceed with the original plan, with one exception. Jasper, see to it that the tunnel dig is complete by sunrise."

"They won't be able to—"

"See to it."

Jasper nods. "Yes, sir."

After a long, thick silence, Chief says, "And unfortunately, we have no other choice: We must kill Chandler."

All eyes are on Jasper. His face is steely, unreadable. He doesn't so much as flinch at the mention of killing his sister. For what it's worth, neither does Greeley.

"Yes, sir," Jasper repeats.

I scooch forward on my seat, a sudden thought striking me. "Are you worried that removing their leader will cause people to revolt? Especially one as revered as Chandler. They'll want justice. Possibly even avenge her death." I'm sure many Egals were scared of Chandler; I was. But I was staunchly loyal to her. I believed in her.

"Kota, your name is known in the community, yes?"

"Maybe . . ." Being one of the doughboys did earn me some respect. "But there are new recruits who don't know me. Greeley and I ran into two boys—children—on the watchtower."

"When?" Chief asks.

"Couple days ago," Greeley answers. "When we went up Paris Mountain to gather water samples. No luck with those yet, by the way. Though Kota did catch some *juicy* fish. And claws."

"*Focus*, Greeley," Chief says. He turns back to me. "Chandler will die. And when she does, *you* can claim the title of leader."

A cold sheet of shock washes down my shoulders. I make a face that I think portrays, *Come again?*

"Fear not," Chief continues, catching my drift. "You will be but a public figure. Meanwhile, I will rule silently by your side."

My jaw nearly drops to my empty plate. "That would never work. And I don't *want* that."

In fact, I'd rather cut out the wounds on my leg with a butter knife.

Though, as I sit with Chief's train of thought, I worry it tracks. The people of Egal would trust me more than they'd trust Chief—especially considering many of them *left* Chief's rule three years ago. If I tell them I've been held captive this whole time and have come back to lead the people, would they follow me? If they called for bloodshed, and I instead ordered peace inside the Split, would they listen?

My gut tells me no.

"We have to try," Chief says, sounding desperate for the first time since I've known him.

"It won't work."

"Dakota—"

"Fine," I concede. "I'll do what you say. But I want your word that you will keep my sister safe."

"That will not be an easy task."

"I want your word."

Without further hesitation, Chief pushes up from the table and extends a hand. "You have my word." The entirety of his hand covers mine as we shake. I pull back, but Chief gives me another firm squeeze before releasing me. The small gesture gives me strength. "I believe this conversation is over. Jasper, off to the tunnels. Greeley, try not to kill anyone—"

"No promises, Chief," Greeley interrupts, elbowing Jasper with a wink.

"And Kota, get some rest. You'll need it, come morning."

I stifle a laugh. There's no way I'm getting any sleep—not with the amount of nerves jittering through my body, and certainly not with thoughts of Bunny orbiting my head.

"You got it," I say. "I'll just curl myself up on my plush Tempur-Pedic mattress."

With a toothy smile, Chief says, "That's the spirit." He doesn't catch my sarcasm. "And sweet dreams."

Ha. I haven't had a sweet dream since all of my family members were alive and well. Been a while since that was the case.

With an awkward wave, I follow Greeley and Jasper out of Chief's hobbit-like house. I'm not quite ready for another adventure, but going forward is the only thing to do.

CHAPTER FIFTY

G O HOME," JASPER TELLS ME. GREELEY'S ALREADY BOUNCED OFF TO polish her array of weapons.

The two of us stand in front of Chief's door, awkwardly staring at one another. A potted zombie fern unfurls to my left. Funny thing, zombie ferns. They look a lot like fiddlehead ferns in their infancy state, only larger: dark pink-purple, spiraling tendrils curling in on themselves. Like the roly-poly bugs Bunny used to catch.

"Home," I repeat. "Andrew's house, you mean."

"It *is* your home now," he says. *Sure doesn't feel like it.* "Get some rest."

"First of all"—I step toward him—"it won't be my home for much longer because I'll probably die tomorrow." He opens his mouth to respond, but I hold a finger up to his mouth. "Secondly, it's not even 9:00 a.m. I don't need sleep."

Jasper bends down and plucks a stem out of the pot, inspecting it. "My mom had a bunch of these around our house growing up. Sometimes, she'd fry them up in the cast iron." I make a face. "Don't knock it before you try it. They made a great after-school snack."

"What do you think would happen if we ate *these*?"

"They're rotten, just like the zombie version of everything else."

"But they're kind of beautiful, aren't they? In a jarring sort of way?" I wonder if that's why Chief keeps them potted.

"There's beauty in just about anything if you know where to look."

I glance away from him, refusing to guess at any hidden meaning in his words. Instead, I stare at my very interesting feet. Two scuffed-up black Converse. Size seven. A little Sharpie heart doodled on the rubber toe. So very interesting.

No. I force my eyes to meet his. "Jasper—I don't want to go home." His brows furrow. "Can I come with you to the tunnels?"

He shakes his head. "You'll see plenty of tunnels tonight."

"I want to come with—"

"No."

I nod, feeling utterly dejected. Why is he acting like this? Because of my Egal escapades? I assumed after last night we were fine . . .

Jasper walks to where his bike is locked up around a tree. Treading lightly, I follow close behind him.

I say, "Crazy how the bike survived, isn't it?"

"Yeah."

Give me something to work with.

I look at the whimpering rubber wheels. "If you need new tires, I'll go on a supply run to find some—after this is all over."

"Cool," he says.

I watch him punch in the lock.

"You changed your code?"

"Kota." Jasper spins around, his eyes empty. I can't read anything on his face. "I don't want to be around you right now. Please."

"But . . ." *But we kissed.* "Are you mad at me for leaving? I see now that it was reckless, but—"

"No," he says, his voice soft. "I'm not mad about that. I would have done the same thing in your shoes. It's just . . ." He runs a hand through his messy brown curls. "Chief wants *you* to crawl through the tunnel into Egal. Chief wants *you* to kill Chandler. Chief wants *you* to take her place."

"You still don't think I can do it?"

"Of course you can do it," he says. "But after all is said and done, you'll be the most powerful person in the Split. And power changes people."

"You think I'll become like her. Like Chandler."

He doesn't deny my accusation. "I can't lose you."

I reach for Jasper's hand, but he pulls away. My voice is a whisper as I say, "You won't lose me."

"Just let me be alone for a bit, Kota."

Before I can get in another word, Jasper hauls himself onto the bike and pedals away. His figure dwindles in the distance.

MY WALK HOME IS SLOW. EVERY SINGLE STEP HURTS, AND I WANT TO CURL up in the middle of the road and cry.

Soon. Soon, you can rest your head on your stinky pillow and cry yourself to sleep. You'll be home soon.

But as I push open the front door, I know full well that this house will never, ever be my home. The smell of someone else envelops me, and the sight of the sunken recliner hits me like a smack in the face. As I cross the foyer, I step on a piece of glass I missed when sweeping earlier.

I don't even make it past the bare mantel before I fall to my knees and cry. What's the point of any of this if I have no one to share it with?

CHAPTER FIFTY-ONE

THE COLD LATE-NIGHT BREEZE SWIRLS THROUGH MY HAIR AS I STAND in front of Jasper's home. The house that feels like a warm hug. The peeling red paint of the front door. The worn-down welcome mat that now reads *W-l-c-m!* The wild limbs that crawl up the awning to find their way inside.

I want to find my way inside.

Even the moon looks different here, a crescent silver slice giving voice to the white wood slats that shape the house.

I hold up a fist. Pause. Ask my hand if it *really* wants to do what it's about to do. And yes, in fact, it does. I rap three times.

I wait. I press my middle fingers into my palms. I smell the ends of my hair. I cup my palm against my mouth and sniff my breath. I repeat Jasper's words in my mind: *Just let me be alone for a bit, Kota.* It's been a bit, hasn't it?

When I've almost abandoned hope, the rusty bronze knob twists, and the front door creaks open. Jasper stands in the doorway.

The sight of him washes over me like a rainstorm on a warm summer day.

"Hey," I say.

"Hey."

A pit forms in my stomach at his words, but not the kind that clenches and twists and signals *Warning!* to my brain. It sort of shimmers and swirls around like golden sparklers on a black night. The unfamiliar sensation isn't unwelcome. In fact, I want to feel it more.

For a moment, he's silent. Then he says, "Listen, about earlier . . ."

I step toward him. "Is there room at the inn?"

"I don't know that it's a good idea."

"You know what's not a good idea? Pushing me away because you're scared. You're assuming that I'll lose myself to power when that's not what I want. I want my sister to be safe. I want a chance at *living*. And, Jasper, I want you. So," I say, taking a final step toward him, close enough to see the rise and fall of his chest. Close enough to touch his pursed lips with my own. "Is there room at the inn, or not?"

His silence sends jitters jumping down my body. Coming here, I prepared myself for rejection, but now that I'm facing it, I want to turn on my heel and run so he can't see me cry. I'm about to do just that when Jasper opens the door wider.

He says, "For you, there's always room."

I exhale a heavy breath of relief and smile. Jasper smiles back, his dimples barely visible beneath his five-o'clock shadow.

I want to poke his dimples. I want to jump into his arms. I want to wrap my legs around his torso, and I want to kiss his face.

I don't.

Instead, I place one foot in front of the other. My heart flutters in my chest like a butterfly, but I move forward in slow motion.

The door closes with a soft *click*. Jasper stands behind me, and I turn around to face him. My body is all too aware of his presence: his breath, tickling the top of my head; his gaze, on my lips; his hands, hovering by his sides.

If you don't know what to do with them, put them on me.

Jasper gestures forward. "Would you like a glass of wine?"

Would I ever.

I nod. The air caresses my skin like a languid wave as he takes my hand and walks around me toward the basement door. I keep my eyes on the flame of Jasper's lighter as we wander down. Each step creaks as it gives way to our slow, careful footsteps. I stand, arms crossed, while Jasper lights the sconces one by one.

He asks, "Red or white?"

"Red," I say, although I really couldn't care less.

As he selects a bottle, his muscled back ripples beneath his T-shirt. He reeks of BO, but I think it's *that* musky scent that taunts me. I'd rip his shirt off with my teeth if he asked.

I grit my molars so hard I think they might shatter.

Jasper turns around, the corner of his lip curling into a half-smile. "Why don't you pick?"

Breathless, I say, "Sure." I switch positions with him, but he walks up behind me—I don't hear him so much as *feel* him.

My hand stills on a bottle, but as his body presses against mine, I don't make a note of the label. He bends his head down so that his breath tickles my ears. He moves his hands to my upper arms and strokes my skin. Slow, controlled, gentle.

The space between my thighs pulsates, and I can no longer form rational thoughts. I need to feel him. Closer, closer, *more.*

Bottle in hand, I spin around . . . and then drop it as soon as my eyes find his. The bottle shatters on the floor, glass flying and red wine puddling at our feet.

Jasper's eyes narrow.

For a second, I wonder if we're on the same page. If what I want is what he wants.

But the simple lifting of the corner of his mouth erases all doubts. So I make my move. I throw my hands around his stubbled face, press myself to tippy toes, and kiss him like my life depends on it. Like *both* of our lives depend on it.

Jasper's hands grab my waist, and he lifts me, slamming my back against the wall of wine. At least six bottles slide off the shelf and shatter into a million pieces. The smell of fermentation fills the air. I wrap my legs around his waist to bring myself closer. His hands move under my butt, and he lifts me up higher. My body is on fire.

I am living.

"Jasper," I breathe. I pull my face away from his and look him in the eye. "More."

He presses his lips against mine and walks us toward the stairs, glass crunching under his feet. I'm a giggling mess, and my cheeks are aflame as he takes the full flight with my body wrapped around his like seaweed around rice.

The house is pitch black, but Jasper carries me to his room with ease. He flings the door open. I see nothing but the wide-open window on the opposite side of the room. A gentle breeze wafts inside. The room smells of soap and wood and *him*.

Jasper flops me onto the edge of the bed and kneels down in front of me. "Is this okay?"

Being with a man who respects me and understands me and values me and asks for my permission?

"Yes," I breathe, "it's okay."

He undoes my jeans, popping the buttons off one by one. "This?" he asks, meeting my eyes.

In response, I grab his head, pull it up to mine, and kiss him. I don't know how long I've wanted him, but now that he's mine, I can't ever let him go. I won't.

I've found my way home.

CHAPTER FIFTY-TWO

BROUGHT DEER JERKY."

Yellow shadows bounce across the mouth of the cave, four candles set in wall sconces emitting a glow throughout the opening. The clay walls roll like waves. Unlike my last cave adventure, I won't let the walls cave in on me—metaphorically, at least.

Sawyer stands before me, his burly body glistening with sweat.

" 'Bout time you showed up 'round here." He shares a toothless smile with me. I must make a worried face, because he says, "I know what yer thinkin'"—he points to his mouth—"and never you mind. Two missin' chompers won't stop me from eatin' that jerky."

I shrug and offer up the jerky. Hunks of meat jam themselves into the gap in his teeth. The salty, meaty, rich smell penetrates the space. "Where's Anika? I thought she'd be here."

"Doin' her final run-through. Makin' sure nothin' will cave in on you, I suppose."

"Oh. Right."

"Ha! I'm just fuckin' with ya. The tunnel's as solid as can be."

"How solid *is* can be?"

Before he has a chance to answer, Jasper turns the corner. His rugged face is dirty and unshaven, his eyes wide with worry.

I haven't seen him since I woke up tangled in his sheets this morning, which feels like eons ago. At the crack of dawn, I bolted out of bed. It felt like there was a pit of snakes wriggling around in my stomach. I couldn't bear hearing *Good luck!* or *You'll do great!* or *Go get 'em, tiger!*

From the look on his face, he's not pleased that I left without saying anything to him.

Sawyer strides forward and slaps his hand into Jasper's. "Good to see you again, man!" Sawyer's large back blocks my vision, and the walls start to close in.

Not this again.

There are too many people in this small space—not enough air.

Anika steps through the tunnel door.

Oh, god, not another body.

"Gentlemen," she says. "Might we move this conversation outside? It's a lovely day, and I'm sure Kota could use one last brush of sunlight on her skin."

One last brush.

"She'll come out on the other side." Jasper takes my hand.

Anika's gaze flicks toward us. "Interesting," she says, raising her eyebrows. "Up we go, then."

Jasper squeezes my hand as we traipse outside.

I squint as the bright day comes into view.

Anika pulls a rolled-up paper out of her back pocket and turns back to me. "Your route is self-explanatory, but we drew it up in any case. The only way out is through. The tunnel leads to the rectory basement." Anika loads me up with a gun, flashlight, digital watch, and a knife with the sharpest blade I've ever seen. "Your travel time should be half an hour. Once you reach the other side, free our men, Garrett and Eagan. Send them through the tunnel with your sister—when you find her." *No worries there.*

She'll be where she always is: in the Sick Room. "Then, you will find Chandler. And you will kill her."

"No pressure," I say. "None at all."

"This *is* a high-pressure situation, Kota." Anika narrows her eyes. "One I suggest you take seriously."

I nod. "I'm taking it seriously. I promise."

"Good," she says. She grabs my wrist and holds the watch up to her face. "It's time."

My stomach somersaults. It may be time, but I am not ready. Not ready at all.

"I'm ready."

CHAPTER FIFTY-THREE

BLACK. COLD. WET.

I'm nothing else as I crawl through the tunnel. The space is just big enough for me to squirm through like a slimy worm. The mud beneath my hands squelches as my palms dig into the earth. I pause, my heart jumping into my throat. The walls are trembling. But—no. It's the flashlight crammed in my mouth. My teeth scrape against the metal like nails on a chalkboard. I flinch away from the eerie sound, take a deep breath. Refocus. Which would be a whole lot easier if this flashlight didn't suck *so goddamn hard.* Its little glow casts long, creeping shadows along the cramped tunnel. Endless is the black that I must crawl through. Suffocating are the clay walls that kiss my shoulders.

I'm dying.

I can't breathe.

One hand in front of the other.

Drip, drip, drip.

Muddy droplets fall from the ceiling, sending chills down my spine as they wet the top of my head. The tiny bullets of water are my only friend, the only sound I can hear besides the beat of my heart.

Kota, they cry, their voices tinny like the Dinks in that movie West forced me to watch as a child. *Spaceballs.*

Puh-lease, can we watch Clifford the Big Red Dog *instead?*

He's just a big dog, Kota.

No, West, he's also red.

West thumped me on the forehead. *Too bad, so sad.*

West always won. Until Grandma killed him.

Dink, dink, dink, dink, dink, dink, dink, dink.

Fuck! A fingernail snaps off. The muddy buildup beneath my fingernails mingles with gushing blood. I've got nowhere to wipe it off, to stop the flow. *Unless . . .* I could lick it off. It's dark enough that the gory mixture looks like chocolate. Is it my imagination, It also kind of smell like a chocolate chip Quaker Oat bar.

Nope. I spit it out, opting to instead brush my left fingertips along the wall. *No, no, no*—I'm not tracing a wet clay wall. I'm touching clothes on a rack at a store. I'm caressing a cashmere blouse, a silk tank top, a cotton button-down.

And is it just me, or are the walls tighter now, constraining me?

How much longer is my journey?

I check my watch. It's been five minutes.

Drip, drip, drip.

The ceiling shakes, sending soot raining down on my head. I scream, despite myself, my voice echoing throughout the infinite chamber. A chill scurries down my spine.

It was nothing. I'm fine.

As I crawl forward, my foot gets stuck in a wet hole, and mud clings to my mottled ankle like a hand. For a second, I'm back in the lake, the zombie clutching my ankle.

And then I think: zombies.

How did I not consider there could be zombies in this tunnel?

Invisible hand wrapped around my ankle, I plunge face-forward into the mud, dropping my flashlight on the way down. The light goes out. "Shit!"

I push myself up and scramble for my flashlight. I ram the heel of my palm against the butt of it. "Come on, come on! Please!"

It's no use. The flashlight is dead.

I said it once, and I say it again: "Shit."

I must make the rest of the journey sans flashlight.

I crane my neck around, but the action is futile. I'm shrouded in nothing but darkness. My bones rattle. Colors blur my vision.

I won't let myself go down this path again.

I squeeze my eyes shut and scream. This time, to release energy. To gain power. To show this tunnel that it will be *my* bitch.

And I charge forward.

CHAPTER FIFTY-FOUR

N THE OTHER END OF THE TUNNEL, I CROUCH IN A CAVE JUST LARGER than me. A small bit of light shines down from above, displaying a patchwork hatch made of nothing but burlap. So I guess this is as far as Sawyer got. This is my grand entrance. Where's my confetti?

Nerves crawl through my body like ants scurrying from a foot-crushed hill. I clamp them down. There's no time to waste.

My arm rejoices as I extend it up toward the burlap flap, peeling open the corner. The cave exits to a storage closet in the basement of the rectory. Fingers crossed I can make it up and out of here discreetly.

Bunny, my dear sister, this is for you.

And Grandma, I'm so sorry I couldn't save you. But when I free Bunny, we'll celebrate with a cup of lemonade in your honor.

I suppress down the spring of emotions that erupts when thinking about Grandma. She wouldn't want me to be weighed down by grief; she'd want me to wield her memory as a weapon for good.

I wrap my hands around the lip of the hole and jam my feet into soft bits of the clay wall to hoist myself up. By any means, the closet isn't bright, but to my eyes, the meager light is glorious. It's like I've stepped out underneath the twelve-o'clock sun—for a moment, at least, before my eyes adjust.

I wring my wrists and stretch my arms toward the low ceiling, my muscles and bones harmonizing at the release of tension. I open the closet door and enter another room. The room is full of boxes and boxes, all stacked neatly against the walls. I was never allowed in the basement; as far as I knew, Egal's supplies were all stored on the main floor. Out of sheer curiosity, I walk over to a box and open the top.

My jaw drops. There are jars and jars of canned foods. Asparagus, beets, beans, and even—my favorite—SpaghettiOs. Where was all this food when I lived here?

I rip open another box. More non-perishable food.

Another. More.

Why isn't this being stored with all the other food upstairs? Have the boys been making extra supply runs? There's more food down here than there's ever been before.

Know what? Fuck 'em. Chandler and all the damn doughboys can get fucked!

I go back to the box where the SpaghettiOs are and rip back the pull tab. I practically swallow the entire can in one gulp, the sweet, sugary tomato sauce sliding down my throat like nectar from the gods. I chew the soft, slightly off-tasting noodles and rejoice.

A *whomp* draws my head to the opposite side of the room, where a tattered door stands. Slowly, I tiptoe toward it and pull my dagger out of my pocket. I ignore the *bang, bang, bang* of my heart in my chest, in my throat, in my head, in my ears.

The handle jangles. And then the door flings open.

A small, muscular man tumbles out of the doorframe, but jumps back when he sees me. His black hair is mussed, flecked with blood, and he wears a ratty hospital gown. His strong, muscled body glistens with sweat.

"You gotta get me outta here," he says, his voice desperate, pleading. He falls to his knees and grabs my calf.

I point my knife at his forehead.

"Off the leg," I say, my wounds rearing their ugly head. "*Now*." The man does as I say, his body trembling. "What's your name?"

"Garrett," he answers.

I lower my knife. He's one of ours.

"Where's Eagan?" I lean over his shuddering shoulder. "Is he in that room?"

"He's . . . he's . . ."

"Where is he, Garrett?" He falls forward, weeping, his hands on his face.

I walk past him and into the room where he emerged. There's a long, metal table in the center. And on top of it, a man.

He's dead.

His forehead is cut open, sliced from temple to temple, his fleshy pink brain spilling out for all to see. The smell is putrid, a mixture of rotten guts and dried, metallic blood. I plug my nose to keep from gagging, but it's no use. I puke up the SpaghettiOs—little circular pastas fly all over the concrete floor. At least the tomato sauce could pass for the blood that's already on the ground.

I spin around and shut the door behind me before crouching down to meet his level. "You need to be quiet," I say. "And you need to get the hell out of this place."

"Help *me . . . please*."

"Get in the closet."

"*Not another closet.*"

"Quiet. There's a tunnel."

"Oh, *god*."

"Garrett! Shut the hell up! If you go through the tunnel, you'll get home. I'm going to get my sister and send her through with you. Can you wait in the closet until I come back with her?"

"Who are you?"

"I'm a Mac. I came to rescue you."

His eyes widen in pure relief. He moves like he's going to hug me, but I shake my head. "I need you to wait in that closet for my sister." I can't send Garrett, or my sister, through the tunnel alone. I don't think either of them could make it. I barely did. "Oh, and Garrett? Take something to eat. Everything behind me is fair game."

"Thank you," he says.

"Don't thank me yet."

With that, I leave Garrett. The next mission has begun.

CHAPTER FIFTY-FIVE

STILTED AIR COILS AROUND THE SUPPLY ROOM LIKE A SNAKE POISED TO attack. Battered boxes soak up white noise, the cardboard stacked up to the ceiling. A thousand pops run through my knuckles as I curl them into fists. I pull the gun out of my back pocket.

When I used to unload food with the boys, this supply room ran amok—loud, full of energy, Fred always stumbling over something. Now, my soft footsteps are the only thing to break the silence.

Because half of the boys are dead.

I check my watch. Everybody will be at the church for lunch, so I should be able to make it out of the rectory without anyone seeing me. And then I'll book it back to our old apartment to wait for Bunny; hopefully she chooses to spend some of her short lunch break at home.

I shut the supply room door behind me and tread down the hallway, then peek out the small diamond-shaped window in the rectory's front door—the coast, as predicted, is clear. I pry open the door and move quietly and quickly through the grounds, urging my heart to stop beating so damn fast.

Weeks away from Egal have bled into years. It looks, smells—*feels*—different here. Cold wind blows by and bites the tip of my nose. I grab the strings of my hoodie under my chin and pull them tighter.

The streets are bare, almost as though the town has been abandoned. Logically, I know that isn't true. Everyone is taking lunch together, lest they miss it and don't get fed.

Little do they all know how much food Chandler is hiding beneath the rectory.

And bodies.

I lick my dry lips, my tongue scratchy and sour. No more time to ponder Chandler's wrongdoings. I've got to get a move on.

I squat and hunch my shoulders, the position all too familiar after my long tunnel crawl. As silently as I can, I weave through the streets, hiding behind tangled bushes and beheaded tree trunks. Every few feet, I whip my head around to check my surroundings. Every few feet, I imagine someone will spot me. My worries are in vain, because I arrive at my destination unseen.

Row house 28. Welcome home.

The apartment is empty.

It still smells like rose perfume.

A single tear escapes my eyes. I let it fall and splash onto the wood floor. Evidence of my arrival.

Everything else is the same as when I left—when I was *captured*. A ratty quilt strewn haphazardly on the worn couch, a single candle stump with a burnt wick on the floor, Bunny's drawings carved into the wood coffee table. She hasn't created anything new.

I pull down my hoodie and enter the cramped bedroom. The bed's unmade, the outline of Bunny's slight figure imprinted into the mattress. I hope she's been sleeping soundly through the nights.

I check the digital watch—12:40.

Come home soon.

Soft daylight streams through the striped sheet draped over the window, casting shadows over the bed. It looks so soft. So cozy. So . . . warm.

I take the lumpy pillow off the bed and smoosh it over my face. I breathe in the scents of my family. We weren't always happy living together in this apartment, but we had each other.

A soft, mousy voice turns my head. "Kotie."

Bunny stands in the doorway, her sweet, pudgy face all I can see. Her full lips are pulled into a smile so the sides of her mouth reach her ears. Her big brown eyes have never seemed so vibrant.

"Bunny." I reach up to caress her cheeks.

Her response isn't as gentle. My little sister jumps on top of me, embracing me in a full-body hug. "You're home! You're home, you're home, you're *home*!"

"Shhh," I say, squeezing her tight. She smells like a mixture of freshly bloomed flowers and Cheerios and sunlight. "Nobody can know I'm here."

"What? Why? The boys will be so happy!"

"Keep your voice down, Bun," I say, pushing us both up to a seat.

"The boys have been looking for you for weeks. I mean, Kota— damn! You escaped from the evil Macs! That's crazy!"

"When did you start saying damn?"

Bunny shrugs. "Grandma cursed a lot while you were gone. Before she . . ."

Grandma.

I shimmy off the bed and bend down to stand eye level with my sister, placing my hands on her shoulders. "I'm going back to Macoby, Bunny."

She quirks her head to the side. "I don't understand." I take her hands in mine, and she stares at me with her face pinched in confusion. "Tell me what's going on. I have to get back to work soon, or I'll get in trouble."

"No, Bunny, you won't. You're not going back to work. You're coming with me."

"What? No. *You're* staying *here*—with me. In Egal!"

"I promise you, Bun, it's better over there, in Macoby. There's more food—meat, even. And tons of good people." Her wide eyes well with tears. "And the best part, Bun? You don't ever have to work again."

"But . . . the Macs killed Grandma."

And then her tears well over, and my sister crumbles before me. "Oh, my love." As soon as she sags to the floor, I drop to my knees and pull her into a tight hug. We sit there for only a moment before I peel her hands away from her face. She stares at the ground, refusing to meet my eyes. "Look at me. Bunny Rebecca, pick your chin up. *Look at me.*"

She gazes at me from beneath her wet lashes and bites her wobbling lower lip.

I say, "Chandler killed Grandma." Bunny's ears twitch in surprise. "Chandler killed Grandma, and she'll kill us, too, if we don't leave."

"Wh-what?"

"Do you believe me, Bunny? Do you believe I'm telling you the truth?"

She closes her watery eyes for a second, a tear spilling from beneath her dark lashes. Her light brows pinch together as realizations dawn on her face. Everything she's been forced to see, to do, it's not right for a girl her age.

She tilts her chin up toward me. "Of course I do," she says, a layer of naivete peeled away. Bunny squeezes my hand. "You're my sister. Of course I believe you."

"Then we have to go. And we have to go *now*." I check my watch. Lunch break ends in ten minutes. Exactly how much time we need to get back to the tunnel. "I'm going to bring you to a tunnel. I went through it alone, but you won't. Garrett's waiting for you—you'll like him. He reminds me of West, but with a country accent." I take Bunny's head in my hands to direct her attention. I'm not sure she's listening to me. "Garrett will guide you through the tunnel. You don't have a flashlight, do you?"

She shakes her head no, and I feel stupid for even asking.

"It's fine," I say. "You don't need it."

BY THE TIME WE'VE MADE IT BACK TO THE RECTORY BASEMENT, BUNNY'S entire body shakes. She's an earthquake, and I fear she'll take the whole place down. But she trusted me, and deserves for me to do the same. She'll be okay. She's strong and smart, and most importantly, she's brave. I'll see her on the other side. I have to believe that.

Garrett waits behind the burlap entrance, tucked into the shadowy mouth of the tunnel where I left him. I say, "Your package has arrived," and he jumps.

"Shit! You could've made a smoother entrance."

"No time to waste." I guide Bunny into the hole, barely touching her so as to hide the trembling of my hands.

Three empty cans of SpaghettiOs lay by Garrett's feet. He looks alive again, his face full of color and his blue eyes bright.

"Garrett, this is my sister, Bunny. She'll be traveling with you today."

"Bunny," Garrett says, extending his hand toward her. She hesitates but takes it, and he gives it a proper Southern shake. "Cool name. This is gonna be—"

"What's that?" I ask, heart plummeting. A pink-red, crimped, crescent-shaped mark extends the space between his pointer finger and thumb.

"This? It's . . . it's nothin'," he says, snatching his hand away.

"I'm about to send you through a fucking tunnel alone with my sister. *Tell me what it is.*"

"Chander, she . . . It's a bite."

"What?"

He raises his arms in protest. "You don't have to worry—it's been two weeks since I was bitten. She found a way to stop it."

"And you're just telling me this now?" I spit the words out.

My mind reels. What does this mean for us, for our future? Does this justify Chandler's actions?

"I need to get out of here," he says. "Please."

He's desperate. I get it. But still.

"No." I grit my teeth. "You're not leaving with my sister." I turn to Bunny, fright building in her wide eyes. I smile and say, "You have to go alone, Bunny."

"Kotie, I can't."

"Never say those words again. You *can*."

"I'm . . . I'm so scared."

"I know you're scared. You have every right to be. But don't let it win, do you hear me? Be strong." I turn to Garrett. "And you, get the hell away from my sister."

"What am I supposed to do?" he asks, his voice trembling.

"Leave tonight," I say. "Through the tunnel. Bunny will have made it out by then. And soon as you're in Macoby, find Jasper. Tell him about the bite. This could change everything."

"But what if he—"

"Or stay here."

He practically launches himself out of the hole and slumps into a sitting position beside me. "No thanks. I'll hide until sundown."

I hand him my watch. "Wait until five o'clock. Please."

"You have my word," he says.

For a moment, I think I might let him stay here. Trust him. But too many people have proven that words are empty, that promises are fragile.

"I'm sorry." I stab him in the ankle. Before he can yelp, I slap a hand over his mouth. Bunny sucks in a shocked breath. I ignore the guilt rising in my belly. It will only hinder me. "You won't bleed out. But I need to slow you down. I can't take the risk . . ."

I trail off, but I don't need to finish. Tears well in Garrett's eyes, and he nods his head. He understands. Meanwhile, Bunny's an eight on the Richter scale. I relay my instructions to her. "Crawl through the tunnel, Bun. As fast as you can. And I'll see you on the other side."

"What if—"

"I love you." I memorize my sister's face: her gumdrop cheeks, innocent eyes, long lashes.

"I love you, too."

I shut the flap and say a silent goodbye.

CHAPTER FIFTY-SIX

FOOTSTEPS SHUFFLE ABOVE ME. VOICES CHATTER. THE FLOOR SHAKES.

My minutes are up.

The boys are back. Though I expected this—that is, after all, how time works—I'm ashamed to admit I expected a miracle. That the boys would have been drawn away by a last-minute excursion or alien abduction.

But Egal's operations are incredibly routine, and though aliens may be real, why would they zap down to this horrible, dying planet anyway?

I listen closer and make out three voices in the upstairs storeroom. Peter's low rumble, Zara's nasally tone, and a third male voice I can't put a finger on. Perhaps it's the voice of a new recruit, one to take the place of Indy or Milo. Since they're dead.

Peter mutters something that sounds like a command, the ceiling creaks from footsteps, and a door clicks shut. Only his two heavy feet remain.

My heart settles, thankful I only have one enemy to contend with: my ex-boyfriend. I hurry through the room and make it halfway up the stairs when the basement door scrapes open. Peter stands in the doorframe, looming above me like an oversized Grim Reaper.

He smiles. "Thought I saw you around."

"Peter," I say. "It's a pleasure."

"Pleasure's all mine, darlin'," he says.

His endearment makes my skin crawl.

Peter steps down. I mirror him, stepping backward, and the board groans beneath me. He tilts his head left, right, and cracks reverberate through the stairwell. He says, "Remember when you used to crack my neck for me, standing up on those little tiptoes of yours? And then I'd bend down for a kiss? Those were good days, Kota. Do you think we could go back to that?"

"Zara's kisses don't do it for you?"

"I was greedy," Peter says. "And bored. Now I have other things to satisfy me. To fill my time." *What, like murder plots and experimentation?* "The only thing missing is you."

"If you love me, you will let me through that door," I plead, trying to appeal to his ego.

He takes another step down. I do the same. "We haven't had the chance to talk for a while. I miss the sound of your voice. Tell me, how's life on the other side?"

"There's freedom," I answer honestly. "There's choice."

Peter laughs. "Tell me: How is it knowing you're fucking your enemy's brother? Someone who ordered your murder?"

"Doesn't matter," I say, and it doesn't. Family doesn't equal blood. I point my knife at him. "Let me go, Peter, and I swear I won't hurt you."

"Like you could," he huffs. This time, when he steps down, I take two up.

"I'm different now," I say.

"Bullshit."

One step down, two forward. We're now three steps apart.

His hands are empty.

"You're not armed," I say. *Again.* I reach for my gun.

"Think I'd let a five-foot bitch take me down? Yeah. Fucking. Right."

Another step down.

You know what? No. I don't need my gun for this. He's not worth the bullet.

I grip my balisong and lunge.

Peter springs forward, wraps his arms around me, and squeezes like the snake he's proven himself to be. I fight against him and try to wriggle out of his grip. His warm, sour breath tickles my ear. "You smell as sweet as I remember. Like honey."

He nips my ear with his teeth. I push against him and feel my ear rip, but get enough range to elbow him in the dick. He releases me at once and buckles forward.

In the narrow stairwell, I spin out of his way and grab him by the hair. I ram his fat, ugly head into the wall, then pull it toward mine. I lob him in the mouth with the butt of my knife. "You still smell like shit."

He spits on the ground, saliva mingled with blood. *"You still love me."*

"I never loved you." I flip the knife around and hold it to his temple. A drop of blood splashes onto the ground.

"Liar." He loses breath fighting against my grip. "You can't kill me. You wouldn't, even if you could."

"I don't want to," I say. "I don't want to kill you, Peter. But I have to."

"No!" He pulls against me.

I wrench his head back toward the knife.

"I'm sorry," I say, teasing his temple with the tip of my knife. He blinks blood out of his eyes. "You know what? No. I'm not sorry. I'm done being sorry."

"Plea—"

I plunge the knife into his temple and release him. Peter's dead body tumbles down the stairs. His large frame hits the basement floor with a *thud*.

Rest in peace, asshole.

I turn around and take the steps up two at a time, high on adrenaline and something else I can't define.

I must find Chandler. I must kill her.

The rectory is still empty. I look out the front windows—the lawn is empty, too. I push open the door and run onto the lawn.

Leaves rustle behind me. My spine curls. *It's just the wind.* I checked; there's nobody around—

Mrs. Patty springs out of a bush. *"THIS IS ALL YOUR FAULT, YOU PAGAN!"* She charges toward me, reaching for my throat. "You released it! You released the demon!"

"Mrs. . . . Patty . . . I don't know what you're talking about." I try to wriggle out of her grip, but she's strong. Stronger than Peter.

"The demons! They're here! They've made their landing! *And it is all on you. You are going to HELL! SINNER. SINNER. SINNER!"*

Stars cloud my vision as I elbow her in the ribs. I whip around, and before I have even a second to consider my actions, I send my knife into her heart. She falls to the ground, and I stab her in the temple.

My ears perk up as a slow clap starts from my right. Chandler slowly strides toward me, slow and controlled. The red hair piled on top of her head is a stark contrast against the bright blue day. "You've changed," Chandler says, drawing her applause to a close. "I'm so, so proud."

"Chandler," I spit at her feet. "Just the person I was looking for."

"Likewise."

"I've come to kill you."

"I have no doubt that you have," she says, checking her watch. "But are you so sure that's the right decision to make, after learning what I've accomplished? After learning my research and experimentation have paid off? It all makes sense now to you, doesn't it, Kota? I am working for the greater good. I am not this *evil* figure you make me out to be." Chandler points behind me. "Uh-oh, but it looks like, though I've come so far, I still have a long way to go."

My stomach lurches. My heart says *kill*; my head says *no*. "What do you—"

I turn around. A zombie lumbers atop the rectory roof. How the fuck did it get up there?

"See that? Odd how a zombie appeared right when you made your grand entrance . . ." Chandler's foxlike eyes widen in false fear. She cups her mouth and screams, *"Zombie! Zombie!"*

With a blood-curdling laugh, she pulls a walkie-talkie from her hip. "Leaders: Tell your crew to stop work and meet me in the field. We have a zombie on our hands."

I step backward. Chandler punches a different button on her walkie-talkie and lifts it back to her lips. "Fred: You have your orders."

Fred? I shouldn't be surprised—I saw him carry Grandma's body. But he even fumbled that. What order could Chandler possibly trust him to carry out?

Without even a second to think, a crowd forms around Chandler. Dozens of citizens run toward us from buildings all over town.

Soon, the rectory lawn is full. Egals form a circle around us.

Chandler screams and points a spindly finger at me. *"She* brought the zombie in! You remember her, don't you? Dakota

Ariti. One of our own, captured by Macoby—and they've brain-washed her. Look at her now! They sent her back to destroy us! *Zombies are upon us!*"

The zombie falls off the roof. Its bones crunch as it lands. The crowd roars. Children clutch their mother's legs. Men march forward to protect the circle. Some people puke.

A boy, maybe eleven years old, breaks free and sprints toward the zombie. He holds a butter knife. *"Let me at him!"*

The zombie clambers forward and latches on to his leg. The boy falls, and it bites into his shoulder.

Crunch. Scream. Slurp. Moan.

There's nothing I can do for him now. It's too late. The boy's eyes roll to the back of his head as he drops to the earth and shudders. He's turning.

The crowd turns its attention to me. *"Kill her!"* they scream. "Kill her!"

"No!" Chandler shouts. "There is a much larger enemy we must face: Macoby. Spare the girl. She is brainwashed. *The Macs are the problem.* We must claim their side for ourselves. If we don't, they will bring more zombies! They will kill us all!"

The child zombie rises, along with its creator. The two zombies surge forward into the crowd, their senses awakened and appetites raging, hundreds of warm bodies just waiting to be devoured.

A man spins around and swings at the child zombie, but misses. The thing is *fast*. It launches forward and bites the man's calf. He falls to the earth, and the zombie boy bites his heart. Another person screams and pulls him off, but then the man starts to turn.

Soon, several zombies are upon us.

And I'm stuck in the middle.

I elbow through the angry crowd, running toward the wall. On any other day, I couldn't climb it. *Nobody* could. But maybe, just maybe, with this adrenaline pumping through my veins, I can find some footholds. Jam my fingers into crevices. *Fly away.*

As I make my way toward the wall, stomps fill my ears. From my right, a group of maybe fifty men march toward me—no, they march toward the wall.

They have guns. Chandler gave them guns?

All at once, they raise rifles, pistols, shotguns—and fire. The wall separating the Split shakes.

Citizens run in every direction—toward the wall, toward the barbed-wire gates, into the rectory, back to their homes. I sprint forward, my legs pumping and chest burning with every step. I have to get to the other side. I have to find Bunny.

The wall explodes. Bricks and concrete and metal shards fly in every direction. I throw my hands over my head to protect myself from the debris. Fragments and chunks hurl into me, and a cloud of dust coats my throat. I only give myself a second to stop, because Bunny's in the tunnel.

Please don't let it collapse.

As I run toward the fallen wall, Chandler's shrill scream fills my ears. "Good luck trying to escape, Dakota!"

Thank you. I need all the luck I can get.

My first mistake? I turn around. Chandler runs toward me, a gun in hand. My second mistake—I'm too confident in my aim. I stop in my tracks and shoot in her direction, *bang, bang, bang,* but I don't make contact.

I've got one more round.

I shoot. It hits Chandler in the calf. She shrieks and falls to the ground.

I run toward her and pull my knife out of my pocket. I must finish this.

Chandler's blood spouts onto the earth and forms a red puddle around her. I think it matches her hair quite nicely. As she pushes herself up and reaches for her gun, I kick it away and snatch it for myself. She stands, limping on one leg, her eyes full of venom and fury.

"Fan of guns now, are you, Chandler?"

"You forced my hand."

I aim the gun at her face. Screams and cries echo in the distance.

"And what about the extra food in the rectory?" I ask. "Why were you hoarding it?"

Chandler's lips curl into a wicked smile. "Scarcity makes people easier to control."

"We were *starving*. Egals suffered because of you, Chandler." Both Egals and Macs clamber over the fallen wall, trying to kill each other and escape the hordes of zombies that crawl over our once-protected towns. "I thought you were trying to rebuild the world. I thought you were good. And I thought that—"

"What? You thought I cared about you? You thought there was hope?"

I don't answer.

"That's what makes you weak. That's how I know that—even if I die right here, right now—you don't stand a chance in this world. You hoped there was a way to save humanity without losing a life or two. Not only does that make you stupid, but it makes you weak."

"You're wrong," I say. "There *is* a way to stop the virus. And it won't involve lying or cheating or *torturing* innocent humans."

"It will involve all of those things, you stupid girl. And you know why? Because that's what I did. *I* figured out how to slow the process. Did you?" She laughs. "That's what I thought. Go ahead, kill me. But you need me alive. You need my help. The choice is yours, Kota."

My third mistake: I hesitate.

Chandler screams and lunges for me, knocking the gun out of my hand. We fall to the earth, wrestling and kicking and each trying to gain power. My strength wanes. Fluid oozes from unhealed cuts on my legs. Blood spews from my nose as her fists pound my face. My head and bones throb, but I will not let her win. I can't.

She swings a leg over my hips so her body is positioned over mine. Her hands find my throat. She peeks at the gun lying at my left, but if she reaches for it, she knows I can scramble out of the way. She must let me suffocate first.

She squeezes harder.

My throat closes. My vision glosses over. My chest pounds.

"Weak," Chandler says. "You're *weak*."

"She isn't weak."

Chandler's head whips to the right, and her grip loosens on me ever so slightly. I take advantage of her moment of distraction and roll out from beneath her. Jasper stands above us, pointing a gun at his sister's heart. Blood drips from her mouth as she scowls at him. Though his hand shakes, his aim doesn't waver.

"I'm sorry, sister." Jasper's eyes swell with dread. He wrinkles his nose, fighting back tears.

"Jasper," I whisper, barely able to speak through the pain in my throat. *"Don't."*

"He won't." Chandler sneers, chest heaving. "You were always too much of an optimist, little brother. You want to save me, don't you? You think you can change me to suit your misguided idea of good. *You can't.* I am what this world needs, and I will win—because you can't kill me. Hope has made you weak, just like her."

Jasper cocks his gun.

"Jasper, *no*!" I scream. I throw myself in front of the gun. Jasper's eyebrows draw together in confusion. Through aching coughs, I say, "We . . . need her . . . alive. The virus . . . She knows how to . . . slow it down."

Jasper lowers his gun. Chandler's chest bubbles with laughter as she falls backward to the ground. On feeble legs, I push to a stand and trudge toward Jasper.

"How?" His face blanches. "How did you—"

"My turn!" Greeley jumps from the broken wall and lands gently on all fours like a cat. She sprints toward us with a harpoon in her hand. "I know you hate guns, Chandler, so I brought something more to your taste."

"Greeley," I say. "Please don't."

With her free hand, she cups her ear. "Did you say please?"

"*NO—*"

Greeley ignores me. She harpoons Chandler right between the eyes. Jasper falls to his knees, staring blankly at his sister's corpse. I stand frozen in shock.

Greeley says, "God, that was delicious," but her eyes tell a different story. She looks flustered. Regretful, even, as she takes in Jasper's shuddering shoulders.

A moment later, Greeley's white truck rams through whatever's left of the wall. Through the dirt-tinged windshield, two black pigtails sprout up from the steering wheel.

Clara plows over carnage with a maniacal expression plastered on her face. An ear-splitting *crunch* sounds through the air as she zooms over a loose femur. She pulls up right beside Chandler's body. Clara's all white teeth and dimples as she rolls down the window. It's not that her scar isn't beautiful—it is—but she looks like the Joker.

"Where are your parents?" I ask, rubbing my raw throat. At least I'm able to speak now. I turn toward Greeley. "How'd she get your truck?"

Greeley ignores me, eyes stuck on Jasper. He picks up Chandler's hand and squeezes once before standing. He turns toward me, cheeks wet but expression steely. He's not ready to move on, but he must. My stomach twists. I know the feeling.

Clara's chipper voice breaks the somber mood, answering for Greeley. "Mom and Dad are packing up the meat. Didn't want to lose all the deer and bunny we'd been dehydrating." Clara cranes out of the car door toward Greeley. "To answer your second question, I promised Greeley I'd get your sister out of the Split if she let me borrow the truck."

"She—what?" Greeley traded her truck for my sister? Why would she do that—unless she cared about me? Greeley shrugs, but I barely register it, because it dawns on me. "Where is she? *Where is my sister?*" I try to yank open the passenger-side door, but it's locked. I nearly dislocate the handle from its socket while Clara just sits there, rolling her eyes.

As Clara tells me to hold my horses, she unlocks the door, and I wrench it open. Bunny sits on the ground, covered in mud, tiny knees pulled into her chest. She convulses, tears streaming down her face. Her eyes stare underneath the seat into some void.

Gunshots and screams sound in the distance. Zombies roar.

"Bunny," I breathe. "You made it through the tunnel. How?"

"I'm really fast, Kotie."

I laugh, tears pouring from my eyes. She must have been moving at two, three times my speed. It shouldn't be possible, and yet . . . here she is. Despite all odds, my sister made it. *She's alive.* I place a hand on her cheek and wipe away soot. "Clara's going to get you out of here. I know she looks young like you, but she'll take you to—where are you going?"

"Top of the hill," she says. "Breakfast shop."

The breakfast shop. That means several hills, twists, and turns.

I glance at Jasper.

He says, "She *is* a surprisingly good driver for an eight-year-old . . ."

I turn back to Bunny and cradle her face. Force her to look at me. "I'll meet you there. At the breakfast shop. There are a few things I have to finish down here." I meet Jasper's eyes, and he understands what we have to do—we have to go to the source. Find *anything* about the cure that Chandler documented. Honor the lives she took. Maybe even prevent more deaths. We have to go back to the rectory and into her office. "I love you so much, Bunny."

Her voice is a whisper as she says, "I love you, too."

I turn toward Greeley. "There's no chance you'd drive to the breakfast shop with them, is there?"

"Yeah fucking right," she says. "I'm having way too much fun down here." A sly smile slithers across her face as she thumbs at Clara and Bunny. "They'll be fine. Taught that one how to drive before she could say 'goddammit.' "

"She's eight. She *shouldn't* be saying goddammit. Or driving!"

"It is what it is," Greeley says. And with that, she runs off into Egal.

I flip to Jasper. "Ready to dive back into hell?" He smiles, but it doesn't quite reach his eyes. My shoulders slump. I open my mouth to console him about Chandler's death, but he places a finger over my lips.

"It's okay, Kota."

I shake my head, because it's not okay, but drop it. We'll talk when he's ready. I clear my throat, and Jasper lowers his finger. "So, you with me on this?"

"I'm always with you, Kota. Always."

CHAPTER FIFTY-SEVEN

'M NOT SURE WHAT'S CAUSED MORE DEATH IN THE PAST HOUR: THE humans fighting the zombies or the humans fighting the humans. The wall is torn down, and death is at every corner.

Not only are the newly born zombies more vicious than the shamblers we typically deal with, but they're people I know. Cooks, medboys, laborers. It's uncanny, knowing the human and zombie versions of someone. Smiles twisted into snarls. Bright eyes made destitute. Laughs turned to moans.

My blood boils with pure hatred for Chandler. She may have found a way to slow the virus, but *these* dying people are turning into zombies in seconds. Maybe it's not too late for damage control. Maybe we can save the Split. Maybe I, Greeley, Jasper, and anyone else with big guns can kill the proliferating zombies. Make it a game of Whac-A-Mole.

Jasper and I sprint through town, doing our best to shoot down zombies while dodging bullets aimed at our heads. Because the Egals still want me dead.

Priorities, people.

Egals run out of the rectory with armfuls of cans, bags of flour, and full boxes balanced over their shoulders. The truth settles in. This is the end of the Split.

"Nothing left for you in there, Satan-lover!" A five-foot stub of a man jumps in front of the door, arms crossed over his chest. Ah—Mrs. Patty's husband, come to defend her honor.

I'm not doing this right now.

I shove him out of the way, and he falls to his knees with a dramatic squeal.

The inside of the rectory is a flurry of movement, people elbowing one another to get whatever supplies they can get their hands on. Two zombies lie splat on the ground, their skulls crushed, probably from being stomped on. A trail of blood leads to Chandler's office, but the door is closed.

I jiggle the handle. "It's locked," I say to Jasper. He lifts a foot, and with one, two, *three* kicks, he busts the door down. "You've always wanted to do that, haven't you?"

Jasper smiles. As we burst into the office, the smell of evergreens wafts over me, mingling with coppery blood and gunpowder. I nearly keel over and vomit. "Your sister and these goddamn car fresheners. What was her deal?"

"Greeley always had one in her car, back in the day."

I grimace. "Let's search her desk. Grab anything you can find."

My eyes widen at a whimper from behind the desk. Zara's curled into a ball on the floor, mascara dripping down her cheeks, red lipstick smeared all over her chin. Her elbow is gashed. That explains the blood trail. "What're you doing here?"

"Same thing you're doing," she says through sobs. Hate and pity start a war in my chest. "Trying to survive."

"Get up," I say. "The Split's going down. You need to get out."

"I have nowhere to go."

Jesus fucking Christ.

I reach down and yank her up by the arm, then give her the knife in my pocket. "Run toward the gates, as fast as you can."

"I can't," she says. "I'll die."

I scowl into her scared, wide eyes. Eyes that I detest, but not eyes that I want dead. Because I see myself in them. I see who I was a few weeks ago. Unable to take care of myself. Lost. Living just to *survive*. "Did Chandler ever tell you anything about the experiments?"

"Experiments?" she asks. "What experiments?"

So Chandler didn't trust Zara with this information. Who did she trust it with—just the doughboys? Peter, Indy, Fred . . . *Where is Fred?* "Forget it," I say. "Time for you to go."

Zara yells, "I'm not going anywhere, Kota. Get that through your thick skull!"

"Cool it," Jasper says, stepping between us. "She's saving your life."

"Bullshit. She's trying to get back at me for stealing her boyfriend."

I laugh. "If anything, you did me a favor. That said, I don't have time to argue. You want to stick around and hide in the rectory? Let the zombies finish you off? Fine by me."

Jasper and I wrench open desk drawers. A *boom* echoes through the building, and the ground shakes. Screams erupt from outside the office. Dust shimmies from the ceiling. We exchange a look and stuff our arms with papers, then roll them up and shove them into our pants. No time for sifting through. We've got to take everything and get the hell out of here. After we've loaded ourselves up with all our bodies can hold, we make a run for it.

"Wait!" Zara says. "Don't leave me!"

Her eyes are frantic, flicking throughout the room.

"Your choice," I say, sensing her inner turmoil. "Come or stay. Decide."

Zara doesn't move.

Another *boom.*

The ceiling collapses. Zara lets out a final shriek as tiles fall directly onto her, smashing in her skull.

I scream, horrified. She made her choice, but still . . . she was so young.

At least it was quick.

Jasper shoves papers under his armpit and grabs my hand. "Bombs," he says. "We've got to go."

"Roger that."

The next several minutes are a soot-coated flurry of carnage, rubble, and bullets. My heart races as Jasper and I sprint toward the gates.

We'll make it out.

I repeat it like a mantra.

Somewhere in the back of my mind, I register that my legs are in excruciating pain, but the thoughts are fleeting, easy to ignore.

Sparks erupt in the sky as we run through the center of town. Not bombs—fireworks. To our left, I see him. Fred. The goon is setting off fireworks. Chandler knew what she was doing. Fred will kill us all.

Behind us, a motorcycle rumbles. "Jasper, Kota—hop on!" Sweat glistens like a halo on Chief's bald head. He halts the bike, and we hop on. Jasper squishes me against Chief's back. I'm a Chief-and-Jasper sandwich. Chief twists his head around and shouts, "Hold on tight. It's gonna be a bumpy ride!"

Sparkling gold fireworks erupt and shimmer like fluorescent sprinkles, and it all hits me at once. My mind erupts with gruesome images of death: Peter. Chandler. Zara. Hundreds of people died, and I played a part. I squeeze my eyes shut and bite my tongue to keep from puking. Metallic blood fills my mouth. Who have I become?

I press my forehead into Chief's back and grip his shirt so tight my fingers go numb.

You did what you had to do to survive.

"Hey," says Jasper. "Kota, I'm here. You don't have to hold on. I've got you."

As my vision slowly fades to black, I know that I'm safe. Jasper's got me.

It's over. It's done.

CHAPTER FIFTY-EIGHT

I WAKE UP ON SPIDER-VEINED ASPHALT. THE WORLD AROUND ME IS silent. Hushed.

Pebbles bite into my head as I flutter my eyes open. I gasp. There she is, standing like a cherub, glowing against the bright sky. Disheveled blond hair sprouting out of her ponytail in a thousand directions. Crinkled denim overalls, still two sizes too big. Dirt-coated dimples, smiling as big as the sun.

"You're alive," I whisper. I almost don't believe it. "You're alive."

My sister throws herself on top of me, knocking the air out of my lungs. She plants a fat kiss on my cheek, and I pull her into a tight hug. I don't care how much it hurts.

"Oh, Kotie . . . You smell like you rolled around in its shit."

"Language, Bun!"

"What? Clara says it all the time."

So this is going to be a problem.

"Hey," Jasper says, walking toward us. He kneels down and offers a hand. "Welcome back, Sleeping Beauty."

"Where are we?"

"Breakfast shop on the mountain. Promise you won't fall off it this time?"

"Haha," I say. Jasper pulls me to a stand. Defying all odds, the shop is *also* still standing. In the parking lot, a few feet from us,

Clara, Chief, Greeley, and Anika lean on stumps and concrete blocks and stacked bricks, making the most of the wreckage. "Are we safe?"

"No," Jasper says. "But better up here than back in the Split. Come on, I'll show you."

Hand in hand, we walk toward the overlook. Unlike last time, we stay several feet away from the edge. I don't need to be any closer to see that the Split is gone. The wall is torn down. Zombies crawl like ants over the grounds. There are hundreds of them.

The space between my eyebrows pulses.

Was any of it worth it?

I say, "We can't stay here. They'll smell us. They'll be up here in no time."

"Like we don't know that, Captain Obvious," Greeley scoffs, walking up behind us. As I turn around, I catch her rolling her eyes. "Jasper made us wait for your stupid ass to wake up. As if you're too heavy to lug over my shoulder." She swings her arm around. "Though I *am* fucking sore."

I turn back to Jasper. "Where do we go from here?"

Jasper thumbs behind him. "Chief's looking through Chandler's papers. Hasn't found anything documenting how to slow the virus, though."

"I bet she kept the information locked in the basement with Garrett..."

Jasper sighs. "Maybe. *But* we did find her journal."

Greeley rolls her eyes again. This time, so hard I think they'll get stuck. "He's right—between the pages lined with *anguish* over losing me, we did find something useful."

Jasper and I exchange a look. "Whatever helps you sleep at night, Gree." He shakes his head back and forth, and I hold in a laugh. "There's someone in Maine, Chandler thinks, with a cure—a real one. One that doesn't just slow down the virus but *reverses* it."

No shit? But . . . "Did you say *Maine*?"

Jasper nods. "Kennebunkport. Ever heard of Camp Bush?" I shake my head no. "Sling always said there was a hideout in California, but we believe he was fed false information. The safe haven's up north."

Greeley pumps her fist in the air. "Road trip, road trip, road trip!"

"Change of scenery could be nice," I say, blinking ash out of my eyes. Though my gut sinks as I consider the implications. Traveling north through the country with a large group feels like a recipe for disaster. "Would all of us go? All the survivors?"

"Blondie," Greeley says. "There's only a handful of us left."

"We don't know that," Chief calls. He saunters over to us, papers gripped in his hands. "There could be more survivors. There have to be." His shoulders slump—a sight I never thought I'd witness.

Oh, Chief. He lost more than any of us. His entire purpose was to save the Split, and now his home and his people are gone.

"Let's go to Maine," I say. "Find this person with a cure. We can bring it back here, to South Carolina. Administer it to the remaining survivors."

My chest fills with something like hope.

As the shrill caw of a zomcrow echoes in the distance, Jasper takes my hand and squeezes it. Our community is gone, but we've survived. We have no belongings, but we have each other. And so, together, we will head north. Toward hope. Because when all else is lost, we can count on that to carry us forward.

ACKNOWLEDGMENTS

Gosh, writing acknowledgments is certainly not for the faint of heart! I've rewritten "thank you" just about twenty times, in about twenty different ways, but I think those two little words are the perfect place to start. So, here we go: Thank you. Thank you for reading this weird piece of fiction that sprouted from the recesses of my brain. I've always had an affinity for zombies, and I hope now you do, too. Thank you for taking a zombie-filled journey through the Deep South with Kota, a character whom I have grown to love deeply. Thank you for reading my words.

To the Writing Gal Pals: I literally (*literally*) could not have done this without you. Thank you for being my cheerleaders, my accountability partners, my best friends. Michelle Campbell: You're one kick-ass woman, and your book kicks ass, too (go buy *Another Life Lesson* if you haven't already!). Casey Lewis: Your macarons are delicious, and so is your steadfast support. Lilly Frederick: I love the color pink a lot, but I love you more.

To my husband: Andre! My world took shape when I met you. Thank you for believing in me. Thank you for encouraging me to follow my dreams.

To Mom, Dad, and Wyatt: Fambeaux for life! Y'all have always encouraged me to write, and for that, I owe you everything. Thank you for not forcing me into dental school. Thank you for allowing me to be myself. To read and write and imagine is all I have ever wanted to do, and you never tried to sway me in another direction. You let me dream. I cannot thank you enough.

To Dina: The first time I told you the plot of *The Split*, your face lit up. Thank you for being genuinely excited about my story, and for cheering me on. And to the rest of you Kruks, thank you for welcoming me into your family. This may not be the place to say that, but it feels right. So, thank you and I love you.

To Writeshare: You reignited my flame.

To everyone else who has supported me in any capacity: Thank you. I simply cannot put into words how much that support means to me. Also, I'm not crying, you are.

GIGI NALLY lives in Greenville, South Carolina, with her husband, two dogs, and three cats. When she isn't writing, she's baking vegan banana bread, teaching a yoga class, writing with her gal pals (see also: gabbing), or reading in her yellow swing. Gigi graduated with a BA in Communication Studies from Furman University. For more information, visit:

WWW.GIGINALLY.COM

Instagram: @gabrielleglenn

YouTube: @gigiglenn

9 798994 092019